PRAISE FOR *THE DEVIL WEARS BLACK*

"Sparkles with wit and chemistry . . . This is a treat."

—*Publishers Weekly*

"An expert at the dark and sexy antihero, Shen brings her seductive prose to an irresistible 'second-chance romance.'"

—OprahDaily.com

"Fake-fiancé tropes for the win!"

—*Marie Claire*, selected as one of the best new romance novels of 2021 (so far)

"A deliciously seductive second-chance romance novel."

—*PopSugar*, selected as one of the ten best new romance books of March 2021

"Shen has created believable character arcs for her captivating protagonists, and the plot provides a terrifically smart twist on the fake-fiancé trope. Fans of Jennifer Weiner may enjoy this sexy contemporary romance."

—*Booklist*

RUTHLESS
Rival

OTHER TITLES BY L.J. SHEN

Sinners of Saint Series

Vicious
Defy
Ruckus
Scandalous
Bane

All Saints High Series

Pretty Reckless
Broken Knight
Angry God

Boston Belles Series

The Hunter
The Villain
The Monster
The Rake

Stand-Alones

The Devil Wears Black
Playing with Fire
In the Unlikely Event
Dirty Headlines
Midnight Blue
Blood to Dust
Sparrow
Tyed

RUTHLESS Rival

L.J. SHEN

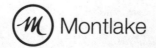

Montlake

Published by Montlake, Seattle

www.apub.com

Amazon, the Amazon logo, and Montlake are trademarks of Amazon.com, Inc., or its affiliates.

ISBN-13: 9781542036306
ISBN-10: 1542036305

Cover design by Caroline Teagle Johnson

Printed in the United States of America

For Ivy Wild, my lawyer friend, who taught me that staying on the right side of the law is not only the moral thing to do—but also the cheapest.

A person is, among all else, a material thing, easily torn and not easily mended.

—Ian McEwan, *Atonement*

PROLOGUE

CHRISTIAN

Do. Not. Touch. Anything.

That was the only rule my mother had ever enforced, but it was one I'd known better than to break as a kid, unless I was in the mood for some belt thrashing and grits with weevils for the month.

It was the summer break after I'd turned fourteen that lit the match that'd later burn everything down. The orange spark would catch and spread, devouring my life, leaving phosphate and ashes in its wake.

Mom dragged me into her workplace. She made some solid arguments why I couldn't stay home and screw around—the chief one being she didn't want me to end up like other kids my age: smoking weed, breaking padlocks, and delivering suspicious-looking packages for local drug dealers.

Hunts Point was where dreams went to die, and even though you couldn't accuse my mother of ever being a dreamer, she viewed me as a liability. Bailing me out was not in her plans.

Plus, staying back home and being reminded of my reality wasn't something I was keen on either.

I got to join her every day on her trip to Park Avenue, under one condition—I was not to put my dirty hands on anything in the Roth family's penthouse. Not the overpriced Henredon furniture, not the bay windows, not the Dutch-imported plants, and definitely—most certainly—*not* the girl.

"This one's special. Not to be tarnished. Mr. Roth loves her more than his eyesight," Mom, an immigrant from Belarus, reminded me in her thickly accented English on our bus ride there, stuffed like blue-collared sardines with other cleaners, landscapers, and doormen.

Arya Roth had been the bane of my existence before I'd even met her. The untouchable fine jewel, precious compared to my worthless existence. In the years before I met her, she was an unpleasant idea. An avatar with shiny pigtails, spoiled and whiny. I had zero desire to meet her. In fact, I'd often lain in my cot at night wondering what kind of exciting, costly, age-appropriate adventures she was up to and wishing her all kinds of bad things. Freak car accidents, falling off a cliff, plane crashes, scurvy. Anything went, and in my mind, privileged Arya Roth was put through an array of terrors while I lounged back with popcorn and laughed.

Everything I knew about Arya through my mother's awestruck tales, I disliked. To add insult to injury, she was exactly my age, which made comparing our lives both inevitable and infuriating.

She was the princess in the Upper East Side ivory tower, living in a penthouse stretched across five thousand square feet, the kind of space I couldn't even fathom, let alone envision. I, on the other hand, was stuck in a prewar studio apartment in Hunts Point, the loud arguments between the sex workers and their clients under my window and Mrs. Van berating her husband downstairs the soundtrack of my adolescence.

Arya's life smelled of flowers, boutiques, and fruity candles—the faint scent of it clung to my mother's clothes when she came back home—while the stench of the fish market near my apartment was so persistent it permanently soaked into our walls.

Arya was pretty—my mother kept banging on about her emerald eyes—while I was wiry and awkward. All knees and ears poking out of a haphazardly drawn stick figure. Mom said I would grow into my features eventually, but with my lack of nutrition, I had my doubts. Apparently, my father had been like that too. Gangly growing up but handsome once ripe. Since I'd never met the bastard, I had no way of confirming that claim. Ruslana Ivanova's baby daddy was married to another woman and lived in Minsk with his three children and two ugly dogs. The one-way plane ticket to New York had been his parting gift to my mother when she'd told him she was knocked up with me, along with a request she never contact him again.

Since my mother didn't have a family—her single mother had died years earlier—that seemed like a perfectly sensible solution to everyone involved. Other than me, of course.

That left us alone in the Big Apple, treating life like it was after our throats. Or maybe it had already clutched our necks, cutting off our air supply. It always felt like we were gasping for something—air, food, electricity, or the right to exist.

Which brings me to the final and most damning sin of all committed by Arya Roth and the main reason why I had never wanted to meet her—Arya had a family.

A mother. A father. Uncles and aunts aplenty. She had a grandmother in North Carolina, whom she visited every Easter, and cousins in Colorado she went snowboarding with each Christmas. Her life had context, a direction, a narrative. It was framed, fully plotted, all the individual pieces colored neatly, while mine seemed bare and disjointed.

There was Mom, but she and I seemed like we were thrown together accidentally. There were the neighbors Mom never bothered getting to know, the sex workers who propositioned me for my school lunch, and the NYPD, who came rolling twice a week onto my block, sliding yellow tape across shattered front windows. Happiness was something that belonged to other people. People we didn't know, who lived on different streets and led different lives.

I'd always felt like a guest in the world—a voyeur. But if I was going to watch someone else's life, might as well watch the Roths, who led perfect, picturesque lives.

And so, to escape from the hellhole I had been born into, all I had to do was follow the instructions.

Do. Not. Touch. Anything.

In the end, I didn't just touch something.

I touched the most precious thing in the Roth household.

The girl.

CHAPTER ONE

Arya

Present

He was going to come.

I knew it, even if he was late. Which he never was, until today.

We had a date every first Saturday of each month.

He'd show up armed with a shrewd grin, two biryani bowls, and the latest outrageous office gossip, which was better than any reality TV out there.

I stretched under a cloister overlooking a gothic garden, wiggling my toes in my Prada pumps, my soles kissing a medieval column.

No matter how old I was or how well I mastered the art of being a ruthless businesswoman, during our monthly visits to the Cloisters, I always felt like a fifteen-year-old, pimply and impressionable and thankful for the crumbs of intimacy and affection thrown my way.

"Move over, sweetheart. The takeout's dripping."

See? He came.

I tucked my legs under my butt, allowing Dad space to settle. He produced two oily containers out of a plastic bag and handed me one.

"You look horrible," I observed, cracking open my container. The scent of nutmeg and saffron crawled into my nose, making my mouth water. My father was flushed and shadow eyed, his face stamped with a grimace.

"Well, you look fantastic, as per usual." He kissed my cheek, settling against the column in front of me so we were face to face.

I nudged the food with my plastic fork. Soft pieces of chicken fell apart over a pillow of rice. I scooped a bite into my mouth, closing my eyes. "I could eat this three times a day, every day."

"I could believe that, seeing as you spent fourth grade living solely on mac-'n'-cheese balls." He chuckled. "How's world domination going?"

"Slowly but surely." I opened my eyes. He poked his food around. First, he'd been late, and now, I noticed he looked barely recognizable. It wasn't his form or his slightly wrinkly attire or the lack of fresh haircut that gave it away. It was his expression, which I hadn't seen before in the almost thirty-two years I'd known him.

"How are you, anyway?" I sucked on the tines of my fork.

His phone, which was tucked into the front pocket of his slacks, buzzed. The green flash shone through the fabric. He ignored it. "Good. Busy. We're being audited, so the office is upside down. Everyone's running around like a headless chicken."

"Not again." I reached into his bowl, fishing for a golden potato hiding under a mountain of rice and slipping it between my lips. "But that explains things."

"Explains what?" He looked alert.

"I thought you looked a little off."

"It's a pain in the neck, but I've danced this dance before. How's business?"

"Actually, I'd like your opinion about a client." I'd begun launching into a topic when his phone vibrated in his pocket again. I squinted at the fountain in the center of the garden, wordlessly indicating that it was okay for him to take the call.

Dad pulled a paper napkin from the take-out bag instead, patting it along his forehead. Cloud-shaped paper stuck to his sweat. The temperature was below thirty-five degrees. What business did this man have sweating buckets?

"And how's Jillian?" He raised his voice an octave. A sense of calamity, like a faint, barely visible crack in a wall, crawled over my skin. "I thought you said her grandma had hip surgery last week. I asked my secretary to send her flowers."

Of course he had. Dad was a constant I could trust. While my mom was a day-late-and-dollar-short kind of parent—always the last to figure out what I was going through, oblivious to my feelings, MIA during pivotal moments in my life—Dad remembered the birthdays, the graduation dates, and what I'd worn for my friends' bat mitzvahs. He'd been there during the breakups, the girl drama, and the incorporation of my company, going over the fine print with me. He was a mother, a father, a sibling, and a comrade. An anchor in the troubled sea of life.

"Grams Joy is fine." I handed him my paper napkins, eyeing him curiously. "Already bossing Jillian's mom around. Listen, are you—"

His phone buzzed for the third time in a minute.

"You should take that."

"No, no." He glanced around us, looking as white as a sheet.

"Whoever is trying to call you is not going to go away."

"Really, Ari, I'd rather hear about your week."

"It was good, eventful, and it passed. Now answer." I pointed to what I assumed was the cause of his strange behavior.

With a heavy sigh and a healthy dose of resignation, Dad finally pulled his phone out and pressed it to his ear so tightly the shell whitened to ivory.

"Conrad Roth speaking. Yes. Yes." He paused, his eyes dancing manically. His biryani bowl slipped from between his fingers, collapsing over the ancient stone. I tried to catch it in vain. "Yes. I know. Thank you. I do have representation. No, I won't be making a comment."

Representation? A comment? For an audit?

People floated along the bows. Tourists crouched to take pictures of the garden. A swarm of children spun around the columns, their laughter like church bells. I stood up and began cleaning up the mess Dad had made on the ground.

It's fine, I told myself. *No company wants to be audited. Let alone a hedge fund.*

But even as I fed myself this excuse, I couldn't fully swallow it. This wasn't about business. Dad didn't lose sleep—or his wits—over work.

He hung up. Our eyes met.

Before he even spoke, I knew. Knew that in a few minutes, I'd be falling, falling, falling. That nothing could stop me. That this was bigger than me. Than him, even.

"Ari, there's something you should know . . ."

I closed my eyes, taking a sharp, before-you-jump-into-the-water breath.

Knowing nothing would ever be the same again.

CHAPTER TWO

CHRISTIAN

Present

Principles. I had very few of them.

Only a handful, really, and I wouldn't call them principles, per se. More like preferences. Strong partialities? Yeah, that sounds about right.

It was my *preference* not to deal with property and contract disputes as a litigator, for instance. Not because I had a moral or ethical issue representing either side of the aisle, but simply because I found the subject morbidly boring and entirely unworthy of my precious time. Tort and equitable claims were where I thrived. I liked messy, emotional, and destructive. Throw salacious into the mix, and I was in litigation heaven.

It was my *preference* to drink myself into a mini coma with my best friends, Arsène and Riggs, at the Brewtherhood down the street, as opposed to smiling, nodding, and listening to another mind-numbing story about my client's kid's T-ball game.

It was also my preference—*not* principle—to not wine and dine Mr. Shady McShadeson here, also known as Myles Emerson. But Myles Emerson was about to sign on a hefty retainer with my law firm,

Cromwell & Traurig. And so here I was, on a Friday night, a shit-eating grin smeared across my face, tucking the company credit card into the black leather check holder as I treated Mr. Emerson to foie gras tarts, tagliolini with shaved black truffles, and a bottle of wine with a price tag that could put his kid through four years of an Ivy League education.

"Gotta say, I'm feeling real good about this, fellas." Mr. Emerson let out a burp, patting his third-trimester-size belly. He held an uncanny physical resemblance to a bloated Jeff Daniels. I was glad he was feeling dandy, because I sure as hell was in good spirits about charging him a monthly fee starting next month. Emerson owned a large janitorial company that mainly catered to big corporations and recently had had four lawsuits filed against him, all for breach of contract and damages. He needed not only legal aid but also duct tape to shut his trap. He'd been bleeding so much money over the past few months I'd offered to put him on a retainer. The irony wasn't lost on me. This man, who offered people cleaning services, had hired me to clean up after *him*. Unlike his employees, though, I charged an astronomical hourly rate and wasn't prone to getting screwed out of my paycheck.

It did not occur to me to refuse to defend him in his multiple and deplorable cases. The obvious parallel involving the poor cleaners who went after him, some of them making below minimum wage and working with forged legal documentation, went right over my head.

"We're here to make things easier for you." I stood up, reaching to shake Myles Emerson's hand while buttoning my blazer. He nodded to Ryan and Deacon, the partners at my law firm, and made his way out of the restaurant, ogling the rears of two of the waitresses.

My plate was going to be full with this tool bag. Luckily, I had a healthy appetite when it came to moving up the corporate ladder.

I sat back down, leaning in my seat.

"And now for the real reason we've all gathered here"—I looked between them—"my impending partnership at the firm."

"I beg your pardon?" Deacon Cromwell, an Oxford-educated expat who'd started the firm forty years ago and was more ancient than the Bible, furrowed his bushy brows.

"Christian believes he earned a corner office and his last name on the door after putting in the time and the effort," Ryan Traurig, head of the litigation department and the partner who actually showed his face between the office's walls every now and then, explained to the old man.

"Don't you think this was something we should've discussed?" Cromwell turned to Traurig.

"We're discussing it now." Traurig smiled good-naturedly.

"Privately," Cromwell spit out.

"Privacy is overrated." I took a sip of my wine, wishing it were scotch. "Wake up and smell the roses, Deacon. I've been a senior associate for three years. I charge partner rates. My annual reviews are flawless, and I reel in the big fish. You've been jerking me around for too long. I'd like to know where I stand. Honesty is the best policy."

"That's a bit rich coming from a lawyer." Cromwell shot me a side-eyed glance. "Also, in the spirit of open conversation, may I remind you you've graduated seven years ago, with a two-year stint at the DA's office upon graduation? It's not exactly like we're robbing you of an opportunity. Our firm has a nine-year partner track. Timeline-wise, you haven't paid your dues."

"Timeline-wise, you've been making three hundred percent more in this firm since I joined," I countered. "Fuck the track. Make me equity—and *name* partner."

"Cutthroat to the bone." He tried to look unaffected, but his brow became clammy. "How do you sleep at night?"

I swirled the wine in my glass the way an award-winning sommelier had taught me a decade earlier. I also golfed, used the firm's time-share in Miami, and suffered through talking politics in gentlemen's clubs.

"Usually with a leggy blonde by my side." False, but I knew a pig like him would appreciate it.

He chuckled, the predictable simpleton that he was. "Wiseass. You're too ambitious for your own good."

Cromwell's view of ambition varied, depending on the person who possessed it. On junior associates who clocked sixty billable hours a week, it was terrific. On me, it was a nuisance.

"No such thing, sir. Now I'd like an answer."

"Christian." Traurig shot me a smile that begged me to shut up. "Give us five minutes. I'll meet you outside."

I didn't like being tossed to the street while they discussed me. Deep down, I was still Nicky from Hunts Point. But that boy had to be curbed in polite society. Gently bred men didn't shout and flip tables. I had to speak their language. Soft words, sharp knives.

After pushing my chair back, I slipped into my Givenchy coat. "Fine. It'll give me time to try out that new Davidoff cigar."

Traurig's eyes lit up. "Winston Churchill?"

"Limited edition." I winked. Bastard rode my ass for everything cigar and liquor related like he didn't earn six times my wage.

"My, my. Got a spare?"

"You know it."

"See you in a few."

"Not if I see you first."

On the curb, I puffed on my cigar and watched yellow traffic lights turning red and green vainly, as jaywalkers glided in thick streams, like schools of fish. The trees on the street were naked, save for the pale string lights that had yet to be stripped after Christmas.

My phone pinged in my pocket. I pulled it out.

Arsène: You coming? Riggs is leaving tomorrow morning and he is getting grabby with someone who needs her diaper changed.

That could mean either she was too young or she had ass implants. Most likely, it meant both. I tucked the cigar into the corner of my mouth, my fingers floating over the touch screen.

Me: Tell him to keep it in his pants. I'm on my way.
Arsène: Being jerked around by Daddy and Daddy?
Me: Not all of us were born with a two hundred mil trust
fund, baby.

I slipped my phone back into my pocket.

A friendly pat landed on my shoulder. When I turned around, Traurig and Cromwell were there. Cromwell looked like he was the not-so-proud owner of every hemorrhoid in New York City, clutching his walking cane with a pained expression. Traurig's thin, cunning sneer revealed little.

"Sheila's been nagging me about getting more exercise. I think I'll walk my way home. Gentlemen." Cromwell nodded curtly. "Christian, congratulations on bringing Emerson. I will see you at our weekly meeting next Friday." And then he was off, disappearing in the throng of bundled-up people and white steam curling from manholes.

I passed Traurig a cigar. He gave it a few puffs, patting his pockets, like he was looking for something. Maybe his long-lost dignity.

"Deacon thinks you're not ready yet."

"That's bull crap." My teeth pressed into my cigar. "My track record is impeccable. I work eighty-hour weeks. I oversee every big case in litigation, even though it is technically your job, and I'm teamed with a junior associate for all my cases, just like a partner. If I walk away right now, I am taking with me a portfolio you cannot afford to lose, and we both know that."

Becoming name partner and having my name on the front door would be the pinnacle of my existence. I knew it was a large leap, but I'd earned it. Deserved it. Other associates didn't clock in the same hours, bring in the same clientele, or deliver the same results. Plus, as a newly minted millionaire, I was chasing my next thrill. There was something terribly numbing about seeing the hefty paycheck rolling in each month and knowing that anything I wanted was within reach.

Partnership wasn't only a challenge; it was a middle finger to the city that had purged itself of me when I was fourteen.

"Now, now, no need to get lippy." Traurig chuckled. "Look, kiddo, Cromwell is open to the idea."

Kiddo. Traurig liked to pretend I was still on the cusp of adolescence, waiting for my balls to drop.

"Open?" I said, snorting. "He should be begging me to stay and offering me half his kingdom."

"And here's the crux of it." Traurig gestured with his hand, making a show like I was an exhibit he was referring to. "Cromwell thinks you've gotten too comfortable, too quickly. You're only thirty-two, Christian, and you haven't seen the inside of a courtroom in a couple years now. You serve your clients well, your name precedes you, but you don't sweat it anymore. Ninety-six percent of your cases settle out of court because no one wants to face you. Cromwell wants to see you hungry. He wants to see your fight. He misses that same fire in your eyes that made him pluck you from the DA's when you got in hot water with the governor."

My second year at the DA's office, a huge case had landed on my desk. It was the same year Theodore Montgomery, the then Manhattan district attorney, got slammed for letting the statute of limitations run out on a few cases due to overwhelming workload. Montgomery tossed the case on my desk and told me to give it my best shot. He didn't want another outrage on his hands but also didn't have any staff to work on it.

That case turned out to be the one all Manhattan talked about that year. While my superiors were chasing white-collar tax crooks and banking fraudsters, I went after a drug lord who'd run over a three-year-old boy, killing him instantly, to make it to his daughter's glitzy sweet-sixteen birthday. A classic hit-and-run. The drug lord in question, Denny Romano, was armed with a line of top-notch lawyers, while I arrived in court in my Salvation Army suit with a leather bag that was falling apart. Everyone rooted for the kid from the DA's office to nail the big, bad, macho man. In the end, I managed to get Romano convicted of vehicular manslaughter and sentenced to four years in prison. It was a small win for the poor boy's family and a huge win for me.

Deacon Cromwell had cornered me at a barbershop when I'd been fresh out of Harvard Law School. I'd had a plan, and it had included making a name for myself at the DA's office, but he'd told me to look him up if I ever wanted to see how the other half lived. After the Romano case, I hadn't had to do anything—he'd come back to me.

"He wants to see me back in court?" I practically spit out the words. My appetite for winning cases was healthy, but I had a reputation for coming in real hard at the negotiation table and walking away with more than I promised my clients. When I did show up in court, I made a spectacle of the other side. No one wanted to deal with me. Not the top litigators who charged a cool two grand an hour only to lose a case to me, and not my ex-colleagues from the DA's office, who didn't have the resources to compete.

"He wants to see you sweat it." Traurig rolled the lit cigar between his fingers thoughtfully. "Win me a high-profile case, one that you cannot tie together in a sweetheart deal in a fully air-conditioned office. Show yourself in court, and the old man will put your name on the door, no questions asked."

"I'm doing a two-person job," I reminded him. This was true. I worked unholy hours.

Traurig shrugged. "Take it or leave it, kiddo. We got you where we want you."

Leaving the firm at this stage, when I was a breath away from becoming a partner, could set my career years back, and the bastard knew it. I was going to either suck it up or get a partnership at a much smaller, less prestigious firm.

It wasn't the way I'd wanted tonight to go, but it was better than nothing. Besides, I knew my capabilities. Depending on court schedules and the case I'd pick, I could be made partner in a few short weeks.

"Consider it done."

Traurig let out a laugh. "I pity the unlucky counsel you are going to go against to prove your point."

I turned around and made my way to the bar across the street, to meet Arsène (pronounced *aar-sn*, like the *Lupin* character) and Riggs.

I didn't have principles.

And when it came down to what I wanted from life, I didn't have any limits either.

The Brewtherhood was our go-to place in SoHo. The bar was a stone's throw from Arsène's penthouse, where Riggs could be found whenever he was in town and wasn't crashing at my place. We liked the Brewtherhood for its variety of foreign lagers, lack of fancy cocktails, and ability to repulse tourists with its straight-shooting charm. Mostly, though, the Brewtherhood had an underdog appeal—small, stuffy, tucked in a basement. It reminded us of our *Flowers in the Attic* adolescence.

I spotted Arsène straightaway. He stood out like a dark shadow in a carnival. He was perched over a barstool, nursing a bottle of Asahi. Arsène liked his beer to match his personality—extra dry, with a foreign air—and was always dressed in Savile Row's finest silks, even though he did not technically have an office job. Come to think of it, he did not technically have a job, period. He was an entrepreneur who liked to stick his fingers in many lucrative pies. Currently he was in bed with a few hedge fund companies that waived their two-and-twenty performance fees just for the pleasure of working with Arsène Corbin. Merger arbitrage and convertible arbitrage were his playgrounds.

I shouldered past a drunk group of women dancing and singing "Cotton-Eyed Joe," getting all the words wrong, and leaned against the bar.

"You're late," Arsène drawled, reading a soft paperback on the sticky bar counter and not even bothering to take a look at me.

"You're a pain in the ass."

"Thanks for the psychological assessment. But you're still late, on top of being rude." He dragged a pint of Peroni my way. I clicked it against his beer bottle and took a sip.

"Where's Riggs?" I shouted into his ear over the music. Arsène jerked his chin to his left. My eyes followed the direction. Riggs was there, one hand leaning against the wooden, taxidermy-decorated wall, probably knuckle deep between the blonde's thighs through her skirt, his lips dragging across her neck.

Yup. Arsène definitely meant her ass implants. She looked like she could float on those things all the way to Ireland.

Unlike Arsène and me, who prided ourselves on looking the part of the 1 percent club, Riggs loved sporting the billionaire-bum look. He was a con artist, a crook, and a delinquent. A man with so little sincerity I was surprised he didn't practice law. He had the clichéd appeal of the wrong-side-of-the-tracks bad boy. The floppy flax-gold hair, deep tan, unshaven goatee, and dirt under the fingernails. His smile was lopsided, his eyes depthless and bottomless at the same time, and he had the annoying ability to talk in his bedroom voice about everything, including his bowel movements.

Riggs was the richest of us three. On the outside, however, he looked like he was cruising through life, unable to commit to anything, including a cellular network.

"Had a good meeting?" Arsène popped his paperback shut next to me. I glanced at the cover.

The Ghost in the Atom: A Discussion of the Mysteries of Quantum Physics.

Can someone say *party animal?*

Arsène's problem was that he was a genius. And geniuses, as we all know, have an extra hard time dealing with idiots. And idiots, as we also know, make up 99 percent of civilized society.

Like Riggs, I'd met Arsène at the Andrew Dexter Academy for Boys. We'd connected instantly. But whereas Riggs and I had reinvented ourselves to survive, Arsène seemed to be consistently himself. Jaded, cruel, and dispassionate.

"It was fine," I lied.

"Am I looking at Cromwell and Traurig's newest partner?" Arsène eyed me skeptically.

"Soon." I dropped onto a stool beside him, flagging down Elise, the bartender. When she moved over toward us, I slid her a crisp hundred-dollar bill across the wooden bar.

She quirked an eyebrow. "That's one hell of a tip, Miller."

Elise had a soft French accent, and a soft everything to go with it.

"Well, you're about to have one hell of a task. I want you to walk over to Riggs and splash a drink on his face à la every corny eighties movie you've seen, acting like you're his date and he just ditched you for Blondie there. There's another Benjamin waiting for you if you can produce some serious tears. Think you can do that?"

Elise rolled up the note and tucked it into the back pocket of her snug jeans. "Being a bartender in New York is synonymous with being an actress. I have three off-off-Broadway shows and two tampon commercials under my belt. *Of course* I can do that."

A minute later, Riggs's face smelled of vodka and watermelon, and Elise was two hundred bucks richer. Riggs dutifully got called out for leaving his date waiting. Blondie stalked off with an angry huff back to her friends, and Riggs made his way to the bar, half-amused, half-pissed.

"Jerk." Riggs grabbed the hem of my blazer and used it to wipe off his face.

"Tell me something I don't know."

"Penicillin was first called mold juice. I bet you didn't know that. I didn't, either, until last month, when I sat on a flight to Zimbabwe next to a very nice bacteriologist named Mary." Riggs grabbed my beer, downing the whole thing and then clucking his tongue. "Spoiler alert: Mary was no virgin between the sheets."

"You mean in the lavatory." Arsène made a disgusted face.

Riggs let out a roar of a laugh. "Need some pearls to clutch, Corbin?"

That was the other thing about Riggs. He was a nomad, drinking other people's drinks, crashing on their couches, flying economy like a heathen. He had no roots, no home, no responsibilities outside of his job. At twenty-two, it had been tolerable. At thirty-two, it was skirting the edge of pitiful.

"Which reminds me: Where are you off to tomorrow?" I snatched the empty beer before he could start licking the damn thing.

"Karakoram, Pakistan."

"Ran out of places to visit in America?"

"About seven years ago." He grinned good-naturedly.

Riggs was a contributing photographer for the *National Geographic* and a few other political and nature magazines. He'd won a bunch of awards and visited most countries in the world. Anything to run away from what was—or *wasn't*—waiting for him at home.

"How long will you be gracing us with your lack of presence?" Arsène asked.

Riggs kicked back his stool, balancing it on two legs. "A month? Maybe two? I'm hoping to get another assignment and fly straight from there. Nepal. Maybe Iceland. Who knows?"

Not you, that's for damn sure, you industrial-refrigerator-size baby.

"Christian asked Daddy and Daddy for a promotion today and got denied." Arsène filled Riggs in, his voice monotone. I picked up his Japanese beer and downed it.

"Yeah?" Riggs clapped my shoulder. "Maybe it's a sign."

"That I suck at my job?" I asked pleasantly.

"That it's time to slow down and realize there's more to life than just work. You've made it. You're in no real danger of becoming poor again. Let it go."

Easier said than done. Poor Nicky was always going to live inside of me, eating two-day-old kasha, reminding me Hunts Point was just a handful of bus stops and mistakes away.

I elbowed Riggs's ribs. His stool snapped back into place. He laughed. "And it's not that I didn't get it," I said, setting the record straight. "They want me to give them a show-off case. A big win."

Arsène tossed me a cruel smirk. "And here I thought things like that only happened in movies with Jennifer Lopez."

"Cromwell just pulled it out of his rectum to buy time. Jumping through one more hoop won't make a difference. The partnership is mine."

Cromwell & Traurig wasn't more than a pile of bricks and legal-size papers on Madison Avenue without me. But it still had that shine as Manhattan's best white-shoe firm, and leaving it for a partnership, even one in the second-biggest firm in the city, would raise questions, as well as eyebrows.

"I'm so happy the wrong-side-of-the-tracks syndrome isn't contagious." Riggs flagged down Elise again, ordering another round. "It must be exhausting to be you. You're determined to conquer the world, even if you have to burn it down in the process."

"No one'll get burned if I get what I want," I said.

They both shook their heads in unison. Riggs looked at me with visible pity.

"This is what you're designed to do, Christian. Let your demons run free and wild and see where they take you. This is why we're friends." Riggs patted my back. "Just remember, to become king, you must dethrone someone first."

I sat back in my stool.

Heads would roll, all right. But none of them were going to be mine.

CHAPTER THREE

CHRISTIAN

Present

My opportunity to prove I was partnerworthy presented itself the following Monday, wrapped in a red satin bow, just waiting for me to unwrap it.

It was godsent. If I were a believing man, which I had absolutely no reason to be, I would have given up something for Lent to show my appreciation to the big man above. Not anything critical, like sex or meat, but maybe my wine-club subscription. I was more of a scotch man, anyway.

"There's someone here to see you," Claire, a junior associate, announced. I could see her in my periphery, tapping my office door, a thick manila file pressed to her chest.

"Do I look like I accept walk-ins?" I asked, not lifting my gaze from the papers I was inspecting.

"No, which was why I sent her on her way, but then she told me what made her come here, and well, now I feel like you should definitely swallow your pride and hear her out."

I was still scribbling on the margins of the document I was working on, not looking up.

"Sell it to me," I barked.

Claire gave me the elevator pitch. The bare bones of the case, as they were.

"Sexual harassment lawsuit against a former employer?" I asked, tossing a red Sharpie that had run out of ink into the trash can and uncapping a new one with my teeth. "Sounds standard."

"Not just any employer."

"Is it the president?"

"No."

"SCOTUS justice?"

"Um . . . no."

"The pope?"

"Christian." She flicked her wrist flirtatiously, her giggle husky.

"Then it's not a big enough case for me."

"He's a power player. Known around all the right circles in New York. Ran for mayor a few years ago. Friend of every museum in Manhattan. We're talking real big fish here." I glanced up. Claire ran the heel of her stiletto around her shapely calf, scratching it. Her voice wrapped around the words with a quiver. She was trying to tamp down her excitement. I couldn't blame her. Nothing gave me a semi like knowing I was about to land a juicy case with hundreds of billable hours and win it. There was only one thing more exciting to a natural-born killer than the scent of blood—the scent of *blue* blood.

Swinging my gaze from my notes, I dropped my Sharpie and leaned back in my chair. "Did you say he ran for mayor?"

Claire nodded.

"How far'd he get?"

"Far-*ish*. Got endorsed by the former White House press secretary, some senators and local officials. Mysteriously dropped out of the race due to family issues four months before elections. Had a very pretty, very young, very not-his-wife campaign manager who now lives in another state."

Getting warmer . . .

"Do we believe the family-issue excuse?" I stroked my chin.

"Do we believe Santa slides down chimneys and still manages to be jolly all night?" Claire tilted her head, pouting.

Picking up my Sharpie again, I tapped it against my desk, mulling this over. My instincts told me it was who I thought it was, and my instincts were never wrong. Which technically meant I shouldn't touch this case with a ten-foot pole. I was familiar with the key players *and* held a grudge against the defendant.

But *should* and *could* were two different creatures, and they didn't always get on well.

Claire launched into all the reasons why I should accept this walk-in like I was some C-grade ambulance chaser until I held up a hand to stop her.

"Tell me about the plaintiff."

Funny, how admirable my impulse control was in every other area in life—women, diet, exercise, ego—until it came down to one family. Riggs was wrong. Not about the demons part. I had plenty of them. But I knew exactly where they'd lead me—to this man's doorstep.

Claire's blush deepened as she relished my eyes on her. I made a mental note to screw her senseless tonight for that sultry look.

"Reliable, trustworthy, and forthcoming. I did get the sense that she is lawyer shopping. It's going to be a big case."

"Give me five minutes."

Claire headed for the door, then stopped. "Hey, there's a new Burmese restaurant opening in SoHo tonight . . ."

She left the sentence hanging. I shook my head. "Remember, Claire. No outside relationship." That was our agreement.

She tossed her hair with a huff. "What can I say? I tried."

Ten minutes later, I was sitting in front of Amanda Gispen, CPA.

Claire was right. Ms. Gispen was the perfect victim. If this case went to trial, the jury would likely be taken with her. She was educated without coming off as condescending, middle aged, soft spoken, attractive without being sexy, clad head to toe in St. John. Her carefully highlighted hair was pinned back, her brown eyes intelligent but not shrewd.

When I entered the conference room Claire had made her wait in, she rose from her seat like I was a judge, offering me a respectful bow.

"Mr. Miller, thank you for making the time. I'm sorry for showing up unannounced."

No, she wasn't. She could've tried to book an appointment. The fact that she hadn't, that she'd honestly believed I'd see her, made me curious.

I sat opposite to her, sprawling over a Wegner swivel chair, my latest Christmas splurge. Obscene luxuries were a constant in my life. I had no family to shop for. The swivel chair was supposed to stay in my office, but Claire, who very much enjoyed taking liberties and straddling invisible scarlet lines, sometimes wheeled it into conference rooms and used it as a sign of our friendship and intimacy. Everyone else knew they could never get away with such a thing.

"Why me, Ms. Gispen?" I cut straight to the chase.

"Please, call me Amanda. They say you're the best in the business."

"Define *they*."

"Every employment attorney I've visited the past couple weeks."

"Word to the wise, Amanda—don't believe lawyers, myself included. Who'd you end up hiring?"

When dealing with a sexual harassment lawsuit, I always advised my clients to get an employment attorney before making a move. I cared who I was going to work alongside with. Lawyers in New York were a dime a dozen, and most were about as reliable as the E subway line when it snowed.

"Tiffany D'Oralio." She smoothed away invisible wrinkles from her dress.

Not bad. Not cheap either. Amanda Gispen clearly meant business.

"I know the man who wronged me is going to be armed with a convoy of the best lawyers in town, and you are known as the most ruthless litigator in your field. You were my first call."

"Technically, I was your first drop-in. Now that we've officially met, I assume you think I won't be able to represent your former boss."

She smiled hesitantly. "If you knew that, why did you agree to meet me?"

Because I would rather endure a long, meticulous death being thrashed by a million plastic spoons than represent the piece of flaming crap you are going after.

Running my gaze along the planes of her face, I decided I respected Amanda Gispen. Pushy was my love language, *assertiveness* my favorite word. Plus, if my hunch was right, we indeed had a mutual enemy to take down, which made us both allies and fast friends.

"I gather your former boss knows you are seeking legal action." I picked up a stress ball I kept in the conference room, rolling it in my fist.

"Correct."

Shame. The element of surprise was half the fun.

"Elaborate."

"The incident that brought me here occurred two weeks ago, but there were telltale signs before it."

"What happened?"

"I threw my drink in his face after he'd invited me to play strip poker in his private jet on our way back from a meeting in Fairbanks. He grabbed me by the arms and kissed me against my will. I stumbled and hit my back. When I saw he was advancing toward me again, I raised my hand to slap him, but then the flight attendant barged in with refreshments. She'd asked if we needed anything really loudly. I think she knew. The minute we landed, he fired me. Said I wasn't a team player. Accused me of giving him mixed signals. That's after twenty-five years of employment. I told him I'd sue him. That would be a dead giveaway, I'm afraid."

"I'm sorry you had to go through that." I genuinely was. "Now tell me about the telltales you were referring to."

She drew a ragged breath. "I heard from someone that he sent her a picture of his . . . his . . . *thing*." She shuddered. "And I don't think she was the only one. Understand, there was a whole vibe to this company I worked for. Men would get away with just about anything, and women had to sit there and take it."

My jaw flexed. Her attacker was probably already lawyered up through the nose. In fact, I wouldn't be surprised if he was working on a motion to be filed for the case to be dismissed on technical or procedural grounds. However, from my experience, hedge fund princes were fond of settling out of court. Their victims, too, weren't too hot on lamenting their most sensitive and shameful moments in a room full of strangers only to get ripped apart by lawyers afterward. Problem was, I didn't *want* to settle out of court. If he was who I thought he was, I wanted to put him on the chopping block and make meatballs out of him for everyone to see.

And I wanted to make him my means to an end. My prized win, when I finally got the partnership.

"Have you thought this through?" I rolled the stress ball along my palm.

She nodded. "I've seen him get away with too much. He's wronged so many women along the way. Women who, unlike me, weren't in a position to complain. They went through things much harsher than what I had to deal with. I'm ready to put an end to this."

"What are you looking to get out of this? Money or justice?" I asked. Usually, I'd butter my client up to go for the former. Not only because justice was an elusive, subjective goal, but also because, unlike money, it wasn't guaranteed.

She shifted in her seat. "Both, maybe?"

"The two are not always mutually exclusive. If you settle, he walks away unscathed and continues abusing women."

Let the record show that this wasn't just the out-for-blood monster sitting in the pit of my stomach that was speaking, *or* fourteen-year-old Nicky, but also a man who'd met enough sexual harassment victims to know a predator's pattern when he recognized one.

"And if I go to court?" She blinked fast, trying to absorb it all.

"You might get your payday, but then . . . you might not. But even if we lose, which—no promises—I don't think we would, he'd hopefully become more wary and potentially have a harder time getting away with this sort of behavior."

"And if I choose to settle?" Her teeth sank into her lower lip.

"Then I cannot, in good conscience, take the case."

This was Nicky speaking. I couldn't see myself sitting with this man in an air-conditioned room, running numbers and meaningless clauses, while knowing he'd get away with another atrocity against humanity. I leaned forward.

"So let me ask you again, Ms. Gispen—money or justice?"

She closed her eyes. When she opened them again, there was thunder in them.

"Justice."

My fingers squeezed the ball more firmly, adrenaline pumping through my bloodstream.

"It's going to be hard. It'll force you to step out of your comfort zone. And I mean leave its zip code completely. Assuming we can get past their inevitable motion to dismiss, we'll move into the discovery phase. During discovery, his lawyers are going to serve interrogatories and requests for production with the sole objective to dig up dirt and drag your name through the mud a hundred different ways. There'll be depositions and evidentiary hearings, and even after all of that, your former boss will certainly file a summary judgment motion to try and get the case dismissed without a trial. It'll be painful, and perhaps long, and definitely mentally draining. And when you come out of this, on the other side, you will change the way you look at the human race as a whole."

I felt like an ambitious frat boy covering all his bases before getting someone into bed—was she sober enough? Willing enough? Did she have a clean health sheet? It was important to align our expectations before getting started.

"I'm aware," Amanda said, sitting a little straighter, tipping her chin up. "Trust me, this isn't a hasty reaction, nor a power trip to get back at a former employer. I want to go through with this, Mr. Miller, and I have plenty of evidence."

Three and a half billable hours and two canceled meetings later, I knew enough about Amanda Gispen's sexual harassment case to understand I had a good shot at this. She had time stamps and call logs aplenty. Witnesses in the form of the flight attendant and a receptionist who'd been let go earlier that year, and damning text messages that would make a porn star blush.

"Where do we go from here?" Amanda asked.

Straight to hell, after the amount of ethical rules I'm about to break.

"I'll send you an engagement letter. Claire will help you with gathering all the information and prepare for filing a complaint with the EEOC."

Amanda's fingers bunched the hem of her dress. "I'm nervous."

I handed her the stress ball like it was a shiny apple. "That's natural, but completely unnecessary."

Amanda took the ball. Pressed it shyly. "It's just that . . . I don't know what to expect once we file."

"This is what you have me for. Remember you can settle a sexual harassment case at any time. Before and during litigation, or even throughout the trial."

"Settling is not really something I'm considering right now. I don't care about the money. I want to see him suffer."

You and I both.

Her upper teeth caught her lower lip, biting. "You believe me, don't you?"

How peculiar, I thought, was the human condition. My clients asked me this question often. And though my real answer was that it didn't matter—I was on their side, rain or shine—this time, I could appease her and still speak my truth.

"Of course."

I wouldn't put anything past Conrad Roth. Sexual harassment seemed within his capabilities.

She handed me the ball back, drawing a breath. I shook my head. "Keep it."

"Thank you, Mr. Miller. I don't know what I'd have done without you."

I stood, buttoning up my blazer. "We'll discuss your expectations, and I will relay my recommendations based on the evidence."

Amanda Gispen stood up, one hand clutching the pearls around her neck, the other reaching for another handshake.

"I want this man to rot in hell for what he did to me. He could've raped me. I'm sure he would have, if it wasn't for the flight attendant. I want him to know he'll never be able to do that to anyone else."

"Trust me, Ms. Gispen. I'll do everything in my power to ruin Conrad Roth."

CHAPTER FOUR

CHRISTIAN

Past

Like all things born to die, our relationship started at the cemetery.

That was the first time I met Arya Roth. On the fifth or maybe sixth time Mom dragged me along to Park Avenue over summer break. Administration for Children's Services had been raiding apartments in Hunts Point the previous winter, removing neglected kids from their households, after Keith Olsen, a boy down my street, had died of hypothermia in his sleep. Everyone had known Keith's father traded the family's food stamps for cigarettes and women, but no one had known just how bad the Olsens were doing.

Mom knew ACS was a bitch to handle. She wanted to keep me, but not enough to ask Conrad and Beatrice Roth to let me stay in their apartment while she worked. This resulted in Mom leaving me outside their building six days a week to fend for myself from eight to five while she cleaned, cooked, did their laundry, and walked their dog.

Mom and I developed a routine. We took the bus together every morning. I drank in the city through the window, half-asleep, while she knitted sweaters she would later sell for pennies at the Rescued Treasure thrift shop. Then I would walk with her to the arched, white-brick entrance of the building—so tall I had to crane my neck to see the full height of it. Mom, clad in her uniform of yellow, short-sleeved polo shirt with the logo of the company she worked for and blue apron and khaki pants, would lean down moments before the jaws of the grand entrance swallowed her to squeeze my shoulder and hand me a wrinkled five-dollar bill. She would hold the note for dear life as she warned: *This is for breakfast, lunch, and snacks. Money doesn't grow on trees, Nicholai. Spend it wisely.*

Truth was, I never spent it at *all*. Instead, I'd swipe stuff from the local bodega. After a few times, the cashier caught me and said I was welcome to the expired stash in his storeroom, as long as I didn't tell anyone.

The meat and dairy stuff were nonstarters, but the stale chips were okay.

The rest of my schedule was wide open. At first, I loitered in parks, burning time people watching. Then I realized it made me really angry seeing other kids and their siblings, nannies, and sometimes even *parents* spending time together on the lush park lawns, swinging from monkey bars, eating their prepacked lunches with their star-shaped sandwiches, smiling toothlessly at cameras, collecting happy memories and stuffing them into their pockets. My already profound sense of injustice expanded in my chest like a balloon. My poverty was tangible and palpable in the way I walked, talked, and dressed. I knew I looked shit poor and didn't need a reminder by seeing the way people eyed me. With detached concern usually reserved for stray dogs. I was an eyesore in their pristine existence. A ketchup stain on their designer outfit. A reminder that a few blocks away, there was another world, full of kids who didn't know what speech therapy, time-shared vacation houses, or gluten-free brunches were. A world where the fridge was mostly empty and getting spanked every now and again filled you with a sense of pride, because it meant your parents gave half a shit.

The first few days were soul crushing. I counted down the seconds until Mom got off work, ogling my cheap wristwatch like it was purposefully slow, just to see me sweat. Even the gummy hot dog Mom bought me from a street food vendor once we got back to our neighborhood, out of guilt and exhaustion from a day of fawning over another family, didn't soften the blow.

On the third day of summer break, I found a small private cemetery, nestled between the edge of Central Park and a bus-tour booth. It was hidden from view, was empty most hours of the day, and offered a vantage point of the Roths' building entrance. It was, ironically, heaven on earth. I barely ventured out of the cemetery in the days that followed. Only briefly, when I needed to find a tree to pee behind, looked for cigarette butts to smoke, or raided the expired stash at the bodega, padding my pockets with more than I could eat so I could sell the remaining food for half price in Hunts Point. I would take the food and hurry back to the cemetery, where I would lean against the gravestone of a man named Harry Frasier and stuff my face.

It wasn't a morbid place, Mount Hebron Memorial. To me, it looked like everything else in the neighborhood. Neat and impeccable, with roses that always bloomed, carefully trimmed bushes, and paved pathways. Even the gravestones shone like the leather on a brand-new pair of Jordans. The few cars that were parked by the office cabin were Lexuses and Porsches.

The cemetery was like an invisibility cloak. Sometimes I'd pretend I was dead and no one could see me. No one *did* see me. That knowledge comforted me. Only stupid people wanted to be seen and heard. To survive in my world, you had to slip off the grid.

It was all going smoothly until the fourth day. Let the record show I was minding my own business, taking a nap using Harry Frasier's tombstone as my pillow. It was hot and humid, the temperature engulfing me from all directions. The heat rose from the ground, and the sun sliced through the trees. I woke up with a jerk, a thick layer of sweat coating my brow, light headed with thirst. I needed to find a garden hose. When my eyes popped open, I saw a girl my age maybe six graves down, under a giant weeping willow. She wore short jeans and a strappy shirt. She was sitting on one of the graves, staring at me with eyes the color of a grimy swamp. Her brown hair was out of control. Curling everywhere, like Medusa's snakes.

Homeless? Maybe. I was going to punch her if she tried to steal from me.

"The hell you looking at?" I crowed, sticking my hand in my front pocket, pulling out a cigarette butt, and placing it in the corner of my mouth. My jeans were about three inches too short, exposing my twiglike shins, but loose around the waist. I knew I didn't look twelve. Ten, on a good day.

"I'm looking at a kid sleeping in a cemetery."

"Funny, Sherlock. Where's Mr. Watson?"

"I don't know who Mr. Watson is." She was still staring. "What are you doing sleeping here?"

I shrugged. "Tired. Why else?"

"You're creepy."

"And you're not minding your own *business*." I started talking in italics to scare her off. Mom always said the best defense was an attack. "What are *you* doing here, anyway?"

"I sneak out here to see if my mom figures out I'm not home."

"Does she?" I asked.

She shook her head. "Never."

"Why here?" I scowled. "Why not anywhere else?"

"I'm also visiting my twin brother." She gestured to the grave she was standing above.

Her twin brother was dead. Even at twelve I had a firm concept of what death was. Mom's parents were dead, and so was Keith Olsen, and Sergey from the deli down the block, and Tammy, the sex worker who had lived in a tent in Riverside Park. Been to a funeral before too. But this girl losing her brother . . . it weirded me out. Kids our age didn't just *die*. Even Keith Olsen's story had made waves in Hunts Point, and we were a pretty tough crowd.

"How'd it happen?" I rearranged my limbs on Harry Frasier's tombstone, narrowing my eyes at her so she would know she was not off the hook just because she was sad or whatever. She drummed her bare knee, which had a nasty gash. She must've flung herself over the gate to get inside like I had. This was a private cemetery, and you couldn't pick the front lock; you had to call the office to get in. My bad impression of her shifted to reluctant respect. Even the girls in my neighborhood, who weren't very girly at all, wouldn't jump that gate. It had wrought iron spikes and was at least eight feet high.

"He died in his sleep when we were babies."

"That really sucks."

"Yeah." She toed the ground with her Chuck, frowning. "Ever wondered why we do that?"

"Die? Not sure it's intentional."

"No. Bury the dead?"

"I don't really think about stuff like that." My voice hardened.

"At first I thought it's like planting seeds, so that maybe hope could bloom."

"And now?" I wiped sweat from my brow. She sounded smart. Most kids my age had the intelligence of a houseplant.

"Now I think we bury them because we don't want to share the world with them. It hurts too much."

I continued frowning, contemplating what to say.

I was getting pretty thirsty, but I didn't want to move. It felt like a test. Or a competition, maybe. This was my territory. My cemetery for the summer. I didn't want her to think she could walk in here and steal my spot, dead brother or not. But there was also something else. I didn't know what. Maybe it didn't feel so bad after all, not to be alone.

"Well? Are you just gonna stand there and stare at me? Do what you came here to do." I sucked on the cigarette butt, trying to relight it unsuccessfully with a lighter Mr. Van had dropped in the communal hallway the other day.

"Yeah. Fine. Just don't interrupt, you . . . you *freak*." She flung her arm impatiently toward me.

I rolled my eyes. She was weird. Her brother was a baby when she'd lost him, right? It's not like they were close or whatever. Still. What did I know about siblings? One thing, really: that I wasn't going to have any. Because, as my mother pointed out every time a toddler threw a tantrum at the Dollar Tree or Kmart, *Children are ungrateful and costly. An expensive liability.*

Gee. Thanks, Mom.

The girl turned her back to me, toward the grave. She caressed the tombstone, which I now noticed was smaller than the rest. Actually, all the graves on that row were small. A chill rolled down my back.

"Hey, Ar. It's me, the other Ar. I just wanted to check in on you. We miss you every day. Mom has been having some pretty bad days again. She's ignoring Dad and me hard core. The other day I spoke to her, and she looked right through me, like I was a ghost. She's doing that on purpose. Punishing me. I thought maybe you could visit her a little less in the next few weeks? I know she sees you all the time. In your room, the couch where we used to nap, the window . . ."

She talked for about five minutes. I tried not to listen, but it was like trying to nail Jell-O to a wall. She was *right* freaking there. I thought she was going to cry, but in the end, she held herself together. Finally, the girl picked a small rock from the ground and pressed it against the marbled grave before standing up.

She was moving back toward the gate, walking away.

"What'd you do that for?" I blurted out.

She turned to look at me in surprise, like she'd forgotten I was there. "Do what?"

"That stone thing."

"In Jewish tradition, you place a small stone on the grave to show the person that someone came to visit. That they are not forgotten."

"You Jewish?"

"My au pair was."

"So you're a rich kid, then."

"Because I had an au pair?" She looked at me like I was an idiot.

"Because you know what the word means in the first place."

"So do you." She folded her arms across her chest, refusing to let me win an argument, no matter how small and insignificant. "You don't look rich to me, though."

"I'm not an example for anything." I collected dirt, enjoying the texture of the grains against my finger pads. I consumed the world in larger quantities than the average kid. Read, listened to, and watched things every second of the day. I treated life with the same practicality I did my wristwatch. I wanted to turn it over, unscrew the pins, and see how it worked, what made it tick. I'd already promised myself I wasn't going to be like Mom. I wasn't going to be eaten by the rich. I was going to eat them, if need be.

"Guess I'm rich, then." She picked up another small stone, rubbing her thumb over its smooth surface. "You're not?"

"Would I sleep in the cemetery if I was rich?"

"I don't know." She ran a hand through her uncombed hair. It was full of dead leaves and debris and knots. "I guess I don't think everything is about money."

"That's because you have it. But you don't look it. Rich, I mean."

"How come?" she asked.

"You're not pretty," I said smartly.

That was her cue to leave. I'd successfully insulted her. Given her a verbal middle finger. But instead, she spun in my direction. "Hey, do you want some lemonade and stuffed cabbage?"

"Didn't you just hear me? I called you ugly."

"So what?" She shrugged. "People lie all the time. I know I'm pretty."

Christ. And she was still standing there, waiting.

"No, I don't want lemonade and stuffed cabbage."

"You sure? It's pretty good. My maid makes them with rice and minced beef. It's, like, a Russian thing."

Alarm bells reverberated in my head, all the exit signs flashing in red neon lights. Stuffed cabbage leaves were Mom's specialty, when we could afford minced beef, which wasn't very often. And if this girl offered to bring food here, that meant she lived nearby.

"What's your name?" I asked, my voice deadly calm.

"Arya." There was a pause. "But my friends call me Ari."

She knew who I was.

She knew, and she wanted to make sure I remembered where I stood in the food chain. *My maid,* she'd said. I was just an extension of my mother.

"You know who I am?" My voice sounded rusty, thick.

She flipped her endless hair. "I got a hunch."

"And you don't care?"

"No."

"Were you looking for me?" Did she just want to taunt the boy who waited downstairs for his mother to finish catering to her?

She rolled her eyes. "As if. So. Lemonade and stuffed cabbage?"

Saying no would have been silly. I was a hustler, first and foremost. Emotions weren't a part of the game. And she was offering me food and drink. Whatever I thought about her didn't matter. It wasn't like we were going to become best friends. One meal wasn't going to douse a six-year-old flame of hatred.

"Sure, Ari."

Famous last words.

This was the beginning of everything.

CHAPTER FIVE

CHRISTIAN

Present

"You gotta be shitting me." Arsène stabbed at a piece of ahi tuna with his chopsticks at the poke bar later that evening. I'd been too eager to tell someone about my day, so Claire had had to settle for a quickie in a nearby hotel during lunch and hadn't even gotten a nice takeout out of it. "You can't represent this woman. You *know* Conrad Roth. You feel *strongly* about Conrad Roth. Conrad Roth is the man who ate your lunch."

I pushed the seaweed in my bowl from one corner to another, letting his reasons—all valid, logical reasons—roll off my back. Vengeance did not have any rhyme or rhythm. It was karma's unrelenting, sexier sister.

The days might have been long, but the years were short. Conrad Roth had shaped and molded me to be the man I was today, and the man I was today wasn't someone he wanted to cross. There was no way I could turn down the opportunity to see him again. To show him that I was back in his home field of the Upper East Side, wearing his brands, dining at his restaurants, fucking the same gently bred women his precious daughter had gone to school with and called friends. The scum of the earth had risen from the filth and dirtied up his pristine world, and he was about to take a closer look at the monster he'd created.

I was no longer Nicholai Ivanov, the bastard son of Ruslana Ivanova.

I was brand new, shiny and reborn. Clad in Tom Ford suits, a cunning smile, and well-practiced trust fund–baby mannerisms. People like Ruslana Ivanova would never chart in the world of Christian Miller. They were invisible. Props. Not even a short paragraph in my story. Not a sentence, even. Something between brackets—only if they accidentally broke one of the pricey vases in my living room.

"He won't recognize me," I clipped out, noticing the two young women who'd served us were whispering among themselves animatedly, writing their phone numbers down on pieces of paper.

Arsène's face contorted in abhorrence. "You're as discreet as the pyramids, Christian. A six-foot-two giant with distinct turquoise eyes and a crooked nose."

From Conrad's open-handed hook almost two decades ago, no less.

"Exactly. What he remembers is a scrawny kid he saw a few times during summer break before I needed a damn shave." I pointed my chopsticks at him.

I was lying. I didn't think Conrad Roth remembered me at *all*. Which made taking the case all the easier.

"You're playing with fire," Arsène warned.

"Doesn't matter what I play, as long as it's always to win."

"Fine. I'll humor you for a second. Let's say he really doesn't recognize your miserable face and has no idea who you are—why go through the trouble? Where's the satisfaction?"

"Ah." I clucked my tongue. "Because anyone else in my position would take a settlement and call it a day. I want to drag him through the mud. Make him suffer. Bonus points: He'd help me become partner. Seal the deal."

Arsène stared at me like I was insane. Which, admittedly, wasn't a stretch. I was making very little sense. "Fifty grand says he recognizes you."

I snorted out a laugh. "Hundred says he doesn't. I'll pick up my check Monday."

There was no way in hell Conrad Roth would know who I was. I'd slipped off his radar shortly after graduating from the Andrew Dexter Academy and changed my legal name, address, and phone number. Nicholai Ivanov had gone MIA weeks after graduation and was presumed dead by the handful of people who gave two shits about him. The irony wasn't lost on me. Roth had paid for my education up until college—though this was hardly a charitable act—and I'd used the knowledge I'd gathered as weapons against him afterward.

After all, he hadn't been shy about haunting me even when I'd lived a state away.

"Look, Conrad Roth *will* recognize you. There are no ifs about it." Arsène flashed his wolflike white teeth. He hated illogical things. Revenge was one of the least rational things in the world. Ninety-nine percent of the time, it only made things worse.

"And?" I quirked an eyebrow. "Who cares?"

"Your career," Arsène deadpanned. "Your career cares. I see your deductive reasoning has gone out the window. You could be disbarred if he files a complaint. Is this pissing match worth losing your career over?"

"First of all, it's not that easy to get someone disbarred. I didn't get my JD from Costco." I tossed a piece of edamame into my mouth. "Second, even if he recognizes me—which he won't—he wouldn't dare. I have too much leverage on him. No one knows what he did to me."

"Even if all of those things are true"—Arsène drew a circle with his chopsticks in the air—"you still won't be able to handle this case with clarity, focus, or an ounce of the sanity you are obviously losing in quantities each passing minute. You lack all three where the Roths are concerned."

"It's time they pay for what they did," I hissed.

One of the women who'd served us swaggered over to us, hips dangling like a pendulum, and slid the two phone numbers across the bar, along with complimentary beers. "Take your pick, boys." She winked.

"*They?*" Arsène lifted a dark, thick eyebrow. "We're talking plural now?"

He stuffed one of the phone numbers in his pocket, even though I knew he wouldn't call. Between the three of us, Riggs was the one most likely to tumble into bed with someone outside his tax bracket, followed by me, with Arsène lagging far behind. He was a connoisseur of upper-crust, ultrasuccessful women and was very particular about everything: how they tasted, how they smelled, what they wore. If I had to put my money on who was a psychopath between us three, I would place my bet on him.

"You're grasping." I walked over to the trash can and disposed of my half-eaten poke.

"And you're in denial." Arsène followed behind me. "You're holding a grudge against a fourteen-year-old girl, Christian. Not your best look."

"She is not fourteen anymore." I slammed my palms against the glass door and marched into the dead winter night, sleek sheets of rain coming down on me from the sky. The roar of the city reminded me that I was under the same piece of sky as her and probably only a few streets away.

So close and yet so far.

She might have forgotten me, but she was about to be introduced to a new version of the boy she'd liked to toy with.

Arya Roth was all grown up now, and she was about to pay for what she'd done.

CHAPTER SIX

CHRISTIAN

Past

She came back again, and again, and a-mother-freaking-gain.

We spent most of that summer break in Mount Hebron Memorial, jumping between gravestones like they were puddles.

The day after our first encounter, she brought a book downstairs called *The Secret Garden*, and we read it, sweaty temples stuck together as we each held one side of the book. We each read a page on our turn, and I could tell we were trying to impress each other.

The next day, I brought Sherlock Holmes from the local library, and we read it in intervals, when I wasn't yelling at her to stop with the doggy ears because I was paranoid about paying the library fee.

We sat on Harry Frasier's grave and read. Sometimes we talked to her brother, Aaron, like he was there with us. We even gave him a personality and everything. He was the party pooper who trailed behind and never wanted to do anything. The cemetery became our own secret garden, with treasures and mysteries to unravel. Every nook and corner was explored, and we knew its residents' names by heart.

One time, the groundskeeper found us playing hide-and-seek. We both ran like our asses were on fire. He gave us a good chase, spewing profanity and waving his fist in the air. When we got to the wrought iron gate, I gave Arya a leg up so she could escape before hopping over myself. The groundskeeper almost caught me, but Arya grabbed my hand and fled before he snatched my shirt through the rails of the gate. That was the last time we went there.

We spent the leftovers of summer break exploring hidden alcoves in Central Park and hiding in bushes, scaring runners. Arya brought down food and drinks and sometimes even board games. When she started coming downstairs with double everything—chocolate milk, granola bars, bottled water—I knew Mom was onto us and looked the other way.

Sure enough, one evening when Mom and I had made our way back to Hunts Point, she grabbed my ear and squeezed until white noise filled it. "Just remember Mr. Roth would kill you if you touched her."

Touch her? I barely wanted to *look* at her. But what other choices did I have? Arya made the time move faster, and she brought me snacks and Gatorade.

By the time summer was over, Arya and I were inseparable. Once the school year started, that was when the friendship ended. Talking on the phone was lame—and also kind of stilted; we tried—and neither of our families was going to agree to a playdate, a concept Arya tried to explain to me several times.

I sometimes wrote to her, but I never sent the letters.

The last thing I needed was Arya thinking I liked her.

Plus, it wasn't even true.

Another summer break rolled in. I was four inches taller. My mother, yet again, brought me over with her to work. This time, I was allowed inside the penthouse. Not because Mom worried *for* me, but because she was worried *because* of me. Earlier that year, I'd started hustling at school, selling counterfeit Jordans for a 500 percent profit margin after the commission Little Ritchie, who gave them to me, charged. The principal warned Mom I was headed straight to juvie if I didn't cut it out.

The first time I set foot in the Roth penthouse, I was light headed. Everything was stealable. I'd knock down the walls and stuff them in my pockets if I could.

Onyx marble gleamed like a panther's coat. The furniture appeared to be floating, hanging on invisible wires, and large, imposing paintings were everywhere. The wine fridge alone was bigger than our bathroom. There were dripping chandeliers, marble statues, and plush rugs everywhere. If this was how rich people lived, it was a wonder they ever left the house.

But the real gem was the view of Central Park. The silhouette of the skyscrapers gave the impression of a thorny crown. And the person wearing that crown was Arya, who sat at a winged, stark-white piano, her back ramrod straight, the view her backdrop, wearing a Sunday dress and a solemn expression.

My breath caught in my throat. It was then that I noticed she was pretty. I mean, I knew she wasn't ugly. I had eyes, after all. But I'd never considered she was the *opposite* of ugly. Last summer, Arya had just been . . . Arya. My partner in crime. The kid who wasn't afraid to jump over gates and ambush people in bushes. The girl who'd helped me find cigarette butts I could suck on.

Arya's head snapped up, her eyes flaring as she took me in. For the first time in my life, I felt self-conscious. Up until then, I hadn't cared about my big nose and Dumbo ears or that I had a good six or seven pounds to gain to fill into my frame.

Her parents were standing behind her, watching her play the piece. Her dad had one hand pressed against her shoulder, like he expected her to evaporate into air any moment now. I knew she couldn't talk to me, so I ignored her, smearing the bubble gum I had stepped in across their floor. Mom and I stood like unattended grocery bags at the entrance, Mom kneading her blue apron nervously as she waited for Arya to finish the piece.

When Arya was done, Mom stepped forward. Her smile looked painful. I wanted to scrub it off her face with one of her bleach-fumed cleaning cloths.

"Mr. Roth, Mrs. Roth, this is my son, Nicholai."

Beatrice and Conrad Roth stirred toward me like evil twins in a horror flick. Conrad had the dead, beady eyes of a shark, trimmed silver hair, and a suit that reeked of money. Beatrice was a model trophy wife, with a blown-out blonde mane, enough makeup to sculpt a three-tier wedding cake, and that vacant gaze of a woman who'd married herself into a corner. I saw the same look on mobsters' wives in Hunts Point. The ones who realized money had a price.

"How darling you are," Beatrice said crisply, but when I reached for a handshake, she patted my wrist down. "Lovely boy you have, Ruslana. Tall and blue eyed. Why, I would never."

Conrad glanced at me for a fraction of a second before turning to face Mom. He looked ready to burst with anger. Like my existence was an inconvenience. "Remember what we discussed, Ruslana. Keep him away from Ari."

A boulder the size of New Jersey settled in my stomach. I was *right* freaking there.

"Absolutely." Mom nodded obediently, and I hated her in that moment. More than I hated Conrad, I think. "Nicholai will not leave my sight, sir."

Behind them, Arya rolled her eyes and pantomimed aiming a gun at her temple. When she fake-shot herself, her head jerked violently. Any concern I had of her forgetting about our alliance evaporated immediately.

I bit down a grin.

Hope was a drug, I realized.

And Arya had just given me my first, free-sample hit.

◆ ◆ ◆

Mom didn't enforce the stay-the-heck-away-from-Arya rule. She had too much on her plate to give a crap. Instead, she warned me that if I ever touched Arya, I would be dead to her.

"If you think I'll let you ruin this for me, you're wrong. One strike and you're out, Nicholai."

Despite that, the summer Arya and I were thirteen was by far the best of my life.

Conrad was a hotshot Wall Street wolf who ran a hedge fund company. Arya tried to explain to me what a hedge fund was. It sounded dangerously close to gambling, so of course I made a mental note to check it out when I grew up. Conrad worked crazy hours. We rarely saw him. And between her weekend-long shopping sprees in Europe and country-club luncheons, Beatrice seemed more like a flighty older sister than her mother. Quickly, Arya and I settled into a routine. We went to the building's indoor pool every morning and raced laps (I won), then lay on Arya's balcony to dry off, faces tilted up to the sky, the chlorine and sun bleaching the tips of our hair, competing over who'd get more freckled (she won).

We also read. A *lot*.

Hours spent every day tucked under the big oak desk in her family's library, sucking on boba slushies, toe fighting with our legs stretched across the Persian carpet.

That summer, we read *The Wonderful Wizard of Oz*, *Treasure Island*, *The Outsiders*, and all the Goosebumps books. We devoured thick spy novels, trudged through history volumes, and even blushed over a couple of kissing books that made us declare in unison that touching someone else that way was super gross.

Though to be honest, the more time passed, the more the idea of touching Arya like that didn't seem gross at all. Maybe even the opposite of gross. But of course, I wasn't dumb enough to let myself think about it.

Our friendship didn't go completely unnoticed. Conrad did walk in on us a few times while we were reading or watching a movie. But I think what was obvious to me from the beginning trickled into his conscious too. That Arya was way out of my league. That her beauty, strength, and sophistication terrified me, and that I could barely look at her straight on. She was in no danger of being corrupted.

"He wouldn't know what to do with an opportunity even if your daughter would present him with one," I once heard Arya's mother say, letting out an impatient huff, when she thought Mom and I had already left for the day. It was one of the rare times she was at home. I found it interesting Beatrice knew what Arya would and wouldn't offer me, seeing as she hadn't exchanged one word with her daughter all summer.

I was tucked in the shadows of their walk-in closet. My mother asked me to steal something small from there each week so she could sell it. This time, Arya's parents had walked in before I could complete my mission. I squeezed the Gucci belt in my fist, sweating buckets as I retreated behind the layers of gowns hung on one side of the wall.

"People outgrow innocence. He is not one of us, Bea."

A metallic laugh filled the air of their en suite bathroom. "Oh, Conrad. It's a bit late for you to become a prude, don't you think? Such hypocrisy. Is it a wonder I can barely look at your face?"

"Darling, you're the prude between us, and you're also too damn naive. All you care about is Aaron, shopping, and your plastic friends, half of which I fuck behind your back."

"Who?" she demanded, turning toward him sharply. Her entire face changed. She looked . . . weird. Older. In a span of seconds.

It was Conrad's turn to chuckle. "Oh, wouldn't you like to know."

"Stop playing games with me, Conrad."

"Games are the only thing I have left with you, Bea."

My fingers dug so deep into the belt that the buckle bit into my skin and popped it open, blood filling my fist.

Mr. Roth had no idea his paper tiger of a wife was right. That the only time Arya and I had touched in a way that wasn't innocent that entire summer was when Arya herself had initiated it.

Two weeks ago, we'd broken into Mr. Roth's study, where he kept his Cuban cigars. I wanted to steal one and share it with my Hunts Point friends, and Arya was always up for mischief. It was a lazy afternoon, and the penthouse was empty. We found the engraved leather box just when my mom got back from the supermarket. The surprise click of the door made Arya drop the cigar case with a loud thud. Footsteps reverberated across the hallway, the sound ricocheting in my stomach like a bullet as my mother approached to investigate.

Arya grabbed my wrist and dragged us both to the space between the filing cabinets and the floor, where we were smooshed together under the belly of the console, limbs tangled, hidden from view. We were chest to chest, our hot breaths mixing together, fruity bubble gum, slushies, and a kiss that could never happen permeating the air, and suddenly, all the times I'd been told not to touch Arya made sense.

Because the need to touch her shot from my spine to my fingertips, making the pit of my stomach feel empty and achy.

Mom walked into the room. We saw her worn-out sneakers from our spot on the floor as she turned 360 degrees, surveying the area.

"Miss Arya? Nicholai?" Her voice was shrill.

No answer. She cursed softly in Russian, stomping one foot over the marbled floor. Adrenaline made my veins tingle.

"Your father will be very mad if he finds out you've been in here." Mom tried and failed to lace her tone with authority. My eyes held Arya's gaze. Her whole body shook with a giggle. I pressed my palm against her mouth to stop her from laughing. She poked her tongue out and licked between my fingers. The shot of pleasure that bolted through my spine made me dizzy. I let go of her immediately, gasping a little.

After a few minutes, Mom finally gave up and walked away. We stayed completely still. Arya took my hand and flattened my palm over her chest, her smile so big it threatened to split her face in two.

"*Whoa.* Feel how fast my heart is beating?"

Actually, all I could feel was the need to put my lips on hers. The way my own heart flipped and twisted in my chest, trying to break free from its arteries and veins, and the way I didn't feel so brave anymore next to her.

"Yeah." I swallowed hard. "You okay?"

"Yeah. You?"

I jerked my head yes. "Thanks for saving my ass."

"Yeah, well, I still owe you from that time we were being chased." Her smile was big and genuine and told me I was definitely, *definitely* on the brink of catastrophe.

"Arya?"

"Hmm?" Her hand was still on mine.

Let go of me.

But I couldn't say it.

I couldn't deny her anything. Even what could have been my goddamn destruction.

Instead, I kept my hand on her chest until the coast was clear and she slipped away on her own.

That was my first mistake of many.

The day with the cigar box changed everything.

We were skidding on the brink of disaster, always dangerously close to the edge. Not because I wanted to kiss her that bad—I could probably go for eternity not touching her, even if I didn't like that idea all that much. But because my ability to refuse her was nonexistent, which meant sooner or later, she was going to get me in trouble.

Funny how her parents were so worried I'd corrupt her, when she could probably convince me to kill a man with no more than a toss of her crazy Medusa hair.

A few days before summer vacation came to an end, I eavesdropped on the Roths again. This time, it was no accident. I was worried they wouldn't let me spend next summer with Arya. I wanted to know where the wind was blowing. At this point, Arya was the closest thing to happiness I'd ever achieved, and I was willing to do some screwed-up things to keep our arrangement going.

I hid in Mrs. Roth's closet while she was getting dressed for an event. Through the sliver of space beside the sliding door, I watched Mr. Roth tying his tie in front of the mirror.

"Did you know I caught him packing the leftovers Ruslana usually throws out and taking them home without asking?" He flipped the tie's tail and tugged the knot upward. I followed his every movement, taking notes. I'd decided earlier that summer I was going to have a job that required you to wear more than sweatpants. "Course, I didn't say anything. Can you imagine the headline if it ever got out? *Hedge fund tycoon denies the poor help's boy his scraps*? Pfft."

"Deary me." Mrs. Roth was on the other side of the walk-in space, so I couldn't see her. She didn't sound interested. She was never interested in her husband. Conrad continued anyway.

"You know what Ruslana told me? She said over the weekends, he shines shoes on the corner outside of Nordstrom. Puts them out of business by charging half the price. And last year, well, he got his hands on a few Nike knockoffs and sold them around his school. That, she didn't volunteer. I found out all by myself."

"You looked into him?" Mrs. Roth said, snorting. She liked to show she hated her husband. "Darling, you have too much free time on your hands. Maybe find another lover to keep you occupied? Oh, and your obsession with your daughter is quite off putting. I'm here too, you know."

This was not good. Not good at all. My next summer with Arya was in jeopardy. I was going to have to ignore Arya in the next few days, even if it hurt her. Even if it hurt *me*.

"That kid has the kind of ambition that will land him either on *Forbes*'s richest list or in prison." The scowl on Conrad Roth's face indicated exactly where he preferred future me—and it wasn't brushing shoulders with Bill Gates and Michael Dell.

Mrs. Roth came into view through the crack of her walk-in closet. She caught the tip of his tie and tugged hard, choking him a little. His lips came smashing down toward hers, but she dodged him at the last minute, laughing cruelly. He groaned in frustration.

"Wherever he ends up, it will not be with your daughter."

"*Our* daughter," he corrected.

"Is she? Ours, I mean?" Beatrice wondered aloud. "You seem to be under the impression she is all yours."

She kissed him hard on the lips. Closemouthed. He cupped her butt. I looked away.

I liked Arya a lot, but I hated her parents.

CHAPTER SEVEN

ARYA

Present

The satisfying clinks of my Louboutins snapping over the rich marble floor reverberated through the walls of the Van Der Hout building on Madison Avenue. A cold smile touched my lips when I reached the receptionist.

"Cromwell and Traurig?" My fingernail, the same scarlet shade as the bottom of my heels, tapped over her desk impatiently after I handed her my ID. I couldn't believe I was wasting my time on this.

The receptionist handed me a visitor badge and my ID back, and I slipped both into my purse.

"That'd be floor thirty-three, ma'am, which requires access control. Please hold while I get someone to escort you."

"No need to call someone down, Sand. I'm on my way up." A baritone so low and deep it slithered into my veins boomed behind my back.

"Hey, boss," the receptionist squeaked, her professional demeanor melting like ice cream on hot asphalt. "New suit? Gray is definitely your color."

Curious and a little put off by the flirt-fest, I turned around and came face to face with one of the most attractive men to grace planet Earth—past, present, and future. A carved Greek god in an Armani suit. Dimpled chin and eyes the color of a kingfisher. A walking, talking bottle of premium DNA, and if that wasn't enough, he oozed enough testosterone to drown a baseball field. I didn't even know if he was classically beautiful. It looked like his nose had been moved back into place unprofessionally after being broken, and his jawline was a little too square. But he reeked of confidence and money, two forms of kryptonite in Manhattan's over-saturated dating pool. Despite myself, I felt my cheeks flushing. When was the last time I'd blushed? Probably when I was a preteen.

"Ready to see the Van Der Hout from the inside?" His tone light, his face impassive.

"I could go a lifetime without seeing the inside of this building, but fate brought me here."

"Did it bring you to a specific floor?" His good mood was unwavering.

"Cromwell and Traurig," I clipped out.

"With pleasure." He flashed me a row of pearly whites. He was a good ol' rich boy. I recognized them from miles away. The cigars. The golf. The Daddy-will-get-me-out-of-everything smirk.

As we waited for the elevator to arrive, I ran a hand over my dress, chastising myself for checking if this random stranger had a wedding band (he did not). I had bigger fish to fry. Mainly, the fact I was going into Dad's first—and hopefully last—mediation meeting regarding his sexual harassment case.

Sexual harassment! What a joke. Dad was hot tempered, but he would never hurt a woman. He was merciless at his job, no doubt about it, but he wasn't a sleazy Harvey Weinstein type. The kind of man to slip a hand under a woman's skirt or ogle her cleavage. I'd been around the corporate block and could recognize predators before they opened their mouths to take a bite. Dad didn't tick any of the corrupt-boss boxes. He wasn't overly nice, never tried to charm his way in and out of social circles, and kept his hands to himself. His female employees adored him openly, oftentimes praising him for his devotion to me. He was his secretary's son's godfather, for crying out loud.

Hot Stranger and I both watched the red numbers on the screen above the elevator descending. I tapped my foot.

Twenty-two . . . twenty-one . . . twenty . . .

Was this man really the receptionist's boss? That would make him the building manager, if not owner. He looked young. Early to midthirties. But seasoned too. With the flippant, tranquil air of someone who knew what he was doing. Old money opened doors to new opportunities; I was the first person to admit that. Just to be on the safe side, I decided to ask if he had anything to do with Cromwell & Traurig.

"Are you a partner at the firm?" There was no way Amanda had hired an associate.

His slightly crooked smirk widened half an inch. "No."

I let out a relieved sigh. "Good."

"Why?"

"I hate lawyers."

"Me too." His eyes flickered to his Patek Philippe watch.

Silence descended over us. He didn't *feel* like a stranger. Not exactly. Standing next to him, I could swear my body recognized his.

"Terrible weather," I commented. The rain hadn't stopped for three days straight.

"I think it was Steinbeck who said the climate in New York is a scandal. New to the city?" His tone was airy yet undistinguishable. My instincts told me to watch out. My ovaries told them to shut up.

"Hardly." I patted the chignon at the nape of my neck for stray flyaways. "You'd think I'd get used to it after so many years. You'd be wrong."

"Ever thought of moving?"

I shook my head. "My parents and business are here." And so was Aaron. I still visited him more often than I liked to admit. "What about you?"

"Lived here on and off my entire life."

"Final verdict?"

"New York is like a fickle lover. You know you deserve better. Doesn't stop you from sticking around."

"You can always leave," I pointed out.

"I could." He adjusted his maroon tie. "But I'm not a fan of quitting."

"Me either."

The elevator pinged open. He stepped aside, motioning for me to get in first. I did. He swiped an electronic key over a pad and pressed the thirty-third button. We both stared at the chrome doors, our reflection twinkling back at us.

"Here for a consultation?" he asked. I had a feeling I was getting his undivided attention, but I also knew he was not flirting with me.

"Not exactly." I examined my hot-red nails. "I'm here in the capacity of a PR consultant."

"What fire are you extinguishing today?"

"A blazing building. Sexual harassment settlement."

He tucked his phone back in his pocket, unbuttoning his peacoat. "Know what they say about big blazes."

"Takes big hoses to get them under control?" I curved an eyebrow.

His smirk widened. My thighs informed me they were sold on this man and had no qualms about running off with him to Paris. I usually chose my lovers with the same pragmatism I chose my clothes in the morning and always went for the average-looking, gallant type. The ones low on drama. But this guy? He looked like a piñata full of crazy ex-girlfriends, rich-boy fetishes, and mommy issues.

"Sharp tongue." He gave me a once-over.

"You should see my claws." I batted my eyelashes. "It's going to be swift and painless."

The man turned around and looked at me. His teal eyes turned glacial, like a frosted-over lake. There was something in them. Something I recognized in myself too. Stubbornness born from bitter disappointment with the world.

"Is that so?"

I stood a little straighter. "I'm not going to let it turn into a media circus. There's too much on the line."

There was no way Amanda Gispen truly thought she had a case. She was obviously after Dad's money. We were going to send her away with a hefty check and ironclad NDA and pretend it had never happened. It wasn't Dad's fault he'd hired someone who'd chosen to go this route when he'd fired her. Now it was all about minimizing the publicity this case was going to get. Luckily, Gispen's lawyer, this Christian Miller guy, hadn't brought any attention to the lawsuit. *Yet.* A calculated move on his part, no doubt.

"I'm sorry." His smile turned from pleasant to downright chilling. This was when I realized his teeth were pointy. That the bottom front two were overlapping. A small imperfection that highlighted his otherwise-ravishing features. "I don't believe I caught your name."

"Arya Roth." I turned to him, the pressure against my sternum becoming more prominent. My body tingled with danger. "And you?"

"Christian Miller." He took my hand in his, giving it a confident squeeze. "Lovely to make acquaintances with you, Ms. Roth."

My breath was knocked out of my lungs. I recognized a disaster when I saw one, and looking at Christian's shrewd smirk, I knew for a fact I'd been played. Only one of us was surprised by the revelation of our identities, and that someone was me. He'd already had the upper hand when he'd walked into the reception area ten minutes ago. And I'd foolishly—*unbelievably*—played into his hands. Shown him my cards.

"The receptionist called you her boss." Thankfully, my voice was still flat. Unfazed.

"Sandy's fond of nicknames. Adorable, right?"

"You said you weren't a partner," I insisted.

He shrugged, as if to say, *What can you do?*

"Did you lie?" I pushed.

"Why, that wouldn't be very sporting. I'm a senior associate."

"So you're . . ."

"Ms. Gispen's attorney, correct," Christian finished for me, removing his peacoat, his gray five-piece suit on full display.

The doors slid open, as if on cue. Christian motioned for me to get out first, his manners impeccable, his grin insufferable. It was both bizarre and amazing, how he'd turned from the potential father of my hypothetical children to the big, bad wolf in less than sixty seconds.

"Third door on the right, Ms. Roth. I'll be there in just a minute."

"Can't wait." I smiled sweetly.

I let my legs carry me to my destination, not daring to look back as I gathered my wits. I felt Christian's smoky gaze the entire time, prickling the back of my neck. Assessing, calculating, scheming.

This man, I knew, was going to take every weakness I'd show him and use it to his advantage.

One–zero to the home team.

"Thank you so much for taking the time to be here, sweetheart. I know how busy your day is, and I'm, well . . . embarrassed." Dad squeezed my hand as I took my seat next to him. We sat at the oval desk at Cromwell & Traurig's conference room. The lantern-in-the-sky ceilings, ceremonial staircases, rose-gold-veined Italian marble, and brass penholders told me Amanda Gispen was not playing around. She'd probably sold a few internal organs for the pleasure of being represented by Mr. Miller.

"Don't be ridiculous, Dad." I rubbed my thumb across his outer palm. "A couple of hours from now, all of this will be ancient history, and we can go back to our day. I hate that you have to deal with this."

"It's a part of the job," he sighed.

Terrance and Louie, Dad's lawyers, sat to his right side, already making notes in their legal pads. They talked animatedly between themselves, paying us no attention. When all this had started, they'd explained that a complaint had been filed with the Equal Employment Opportunity Commission against my father. Apparently this mediation was part of the EEOC's conciliation process.

The mediator, a stern, silver-haired woman in a black dress and white Peter Pan collar, was typing away at her laptop, already waiting for the plaintiff and her team.

A petite, attractive woman in a knitted beige dress ambled into the room clutching an iPad and a clipboard, accompanied by a PA who balanced a tray full of beverages. The fashionable blonde introduced herself as Claire Lesavoy, a junior associate. By the way she completely ignored my existence, I gathered Christian had yet to fill her in about my slip of the tongue. I wondered if he filled her with anything else and hated myself that I even cared. He was a jerk. She could have him.

"What's the holdup?" Terrance, who had the wrinkly face of an armadillo, regarded Claire like she herself was responsible for the delay. "Your client is running thirty-five minutes late."

"I believe Mr. Miller is ironing out the kinks with Ms. Gispen ahead of the meeting. Shouldn't take long now." Claire smiled brilliantly, enjoying Terrance's obvious impatience. She took a seat in front of us. Upon a closer inspection I decided Christian certainly fraternized with *this* staff. She was magazine beautiful.

Christian and Amanda Gispen walked in fifteen minutes later. By then, the meeting was running almost an hour late. I glanced at the time on my phone. Jillian and I had an appointment with a potential client in Brooklyn in less than two hours. Between the rain and traffic, there was no way I was going to make it on time.

"Apologies for the delay. Ms. Gispen and I had to go over the pre-mediation statements one more time." Christian's smirk was so dazzling, so good natured, there was absolutely zero chance the man wasn't in need of deep, lengthy psychological treatment. Who took such pleasure in dealing with a sexual harassment case? Even a bogus one? A lawyer. That was who. My father had warned me about them. Lawyers, not psychopaths—though both should be avoided, if possible. As someone who'd had to deal with plenty of lawyers in his lifetime, he had nothing but bad things to say about them. Conrad Roth was of the school that believed the fine line running between lawyers and criminals was opportunity and a scholarship. He detested lawyers with a passion. I was quickly coming to understand why.

"That's absolutely fine, Christian, my dear." The mediator patted his arm warmly. Well, crap. He already had the advantage of being well loved and respected. Amanda Gispen and Claire Lesavoy were also ogling him adoringly.

Christian sat directly in front of me. I kept my eyes on Amanda, whom I'd known my entire life. Blinking in disbelief, I tried to reconcile the person I'd grown up with and the woman in front of me. It was hard to digest that she was the lady who'd slipped cookies to my kid self when I'd hidden behind her desk on days Dad had taken me to work. She was the one who'd given me a book about the birds and the bees when I was twelve because my mother had treated my sexuality like a unicorn that would never arrive. The very same person sitting here, demanding Dad pay for something he hadn't done.

The mediator began with a short presentation of what could be expected during the process. I chanced a glance at Dad, who looked pale and a little seasick. My father had always been larger than life. Seeing him like this was shattering. When we'd first gotten the call about Amanda taking legal action, my mother's response had been odd, to say the least. I'd expected door slamming, shouts, and a theatrical production. Instead, she'd received the news with quiet resignation. She'd refused to discuss the subject again and, of course, booked a two-week retreat in the Bahamas to get away from it all. She'd never really been a partner to him or a mother to me.

Dad needed me. Now more than ever.

I slipped my hand in his under the desk and pressed.

"I got you," I whispered.

When I looked back ahead, I noticed Christian watching our exchange, his jaw twitching.

What the hell is his problem now?

The mediator finished explaining the procedure.

"Let the record show we are entirely unimpressed with your method of mind games, namely showing up an hour late." Louie scribbled something on the margin of the document in front of him, referring to Christian.

"Let the record show I don't give two shits what you think about me," Christian responded, making all the gazes in the room snap to him.

Dad's jaw slacked. Amanda turned to look at Christian, her face marred by horror. Even Claire looked a little pale. Christian seemed to miss the social cues, settling comfortably in his seat. "Now, if we may continue."

Each of the attorneys proceeded to give their statements. The mediator explained we were now going to offer a settlement and discuss it privately in different rooms. Dad had told me he wasn't going to rebut Amanda's complaint, upon his counselors' advice. Louie and Terrance thought it could make Amanda strike even harder. I wasn't happy about it, but I also knew nothing about sexual harassment cases and just wanted to get it over with. From the PR side, I knew the right thing and the correct thing weren't always the same thing. The *correct* thing would be to make this go away quietly, even if you had to swallow your pride and pay a crook like Amanda.

An hour later, it was obvious I wasn't going to make it to the meeting with Jillian. Any ballpark number Louie and Terrance came up with and handed the mediator was rejected on the spot by a solemn Christian

Miller before he even dragged his client to a private room to discuss it. Dad's back curled forward like a shrimp. He shook his head and closed his eyes in disbelief. We were getting nowhere fast.

"I don't understand any of this," Dad told me, pale as a ghost. "What is she trying to achieve? If we take it to court, everyone is going to get hurt. She must know that."

"Don't worry, Dad. She knows the truth. She won't go to court." I patted his arm, but he didn't look convinced.

Discreetly, I slipped my phone under my desk and texted Jillian that I wasn't going to make it to our Brooklyn meeting. My best friend's reply was prompt.

Don't worry about it. Best of luck to Conrad. Keep me posted. X

"Are we boring you, Ms. Roth?" Christian drawled. I nearly jumped out of my skin and bumped my knee against the desk. Internally, I screamed in pain. Outwardly, I grinned.

"Funny you ask, Mr. Miller. The answer is yes, in fact. You, specifically, do bore me."

He'd been targeting me ever since I'd walked into Van Der Hout building. I got that this was business and that he was charging Amanda Gispen a fortune he needed to justify somehow, but not on my back.

Christian popped his knuckles, his eyes never leaving mine. "My apologies. Miss Lesavoy, would you be so kind as to fetch Ms. Roth a copy of *Us Weekly*? Perhaps she's in the mood for some fine literature."

I crossed my arms over my chest, meeting his gaze head-on. "Make it the *Enquirer*, Miss Lesavoy. And could I, like, get the audio version? I'm not *super* good with words." I adopted the dumbest, airiest tone I could produce.

"Perhaps you two could engage in verbal foreplay *after* we finish the negotiations," Louie scolded me. "Counsel, I—"

"Put your phone on the desk, Ms. Roth," Christian snapped at me over Louie, his eyes boring into mine with open hatred.

What in the ever-loving hell is wrong with this man?

It was Dad's turn to spin his head and look at me. A haughty smile touched my lips. "Sorry, Mr. Miller, did I miss the memo where you're the boss of me?"

"Arya," Dad hissed, shocked. "Please."

Christian's eyes narrowed. "I suggest you listen to your daddy and put your phone down. My time costs money."

"Pissing you off is worth the invoice," I retorted. "I'll even throw in foreign currencies and some Bitcoin if it means seeing you suffer."

Christian let out a metallic chuckle. "You haven't changed."

"Excuse me?" I snapped. His smile vanished in a second.

"I said you need to change."

"That's *not* what you said. I have ears."

"You have a mouth too. And that's the organ you seem to be needing more control of."

"Who raised you?" My eyes were wide and wild, I could tell.

He tossed the documents in front of him aside. "No one, Ms. Roth. Interested in hearing my life story?"

"Only if it has a tragic and abrupt ending."

Well, well. This got off the rails real fast.

Dad put his hand on my wrist, his eyes pleading. "What's gotten into you, sweetheart?"

Finally, I put my phone down on the desk, feeling a little sick. I couldn't take my eyes off Christian. His teal irises glimmered back at me. There was something frightening about them.

The negotiation proceeded for twenty more minutes, in which I stayed (bitterly) silent. Each time we thought we were getting somewhere, we hit a roadblock. Finally, Terrance rubbed at his sweaty forehead.

"Mister, I don't understand. You got yourself a reputation of a lawyer who settles out of the courtroom, yet you've refused every single proposition we came up with."

"That's because I believe this *should* go to court." Christian lounged back, readjusting his maroon tie, which, tragically, looked lovely with his pale-gray vested suit. So it was true, then. The devil *did* wear Prada.

"Then what did you invite us here for?" Louie's lower lip trembled with rage.

"I wanted to read the room." Christian examined his perfect, square fingernails, looking like a surly, spoiled prince bored out of his mind.

"Read the room?" Terrance spluttered, at the same time that my father piped up, for the first time since the meeting had started. "You cannot seriously want to take this to court! This will become a circus—"

"I rather enjoy circuses." Christian rose to his feet, buttoning his suit (yup. Definitely Prada). Claire and Amanda followed his cue, rising on each side of him, a loyal harem. "Colorful. Full of entertainment. Sweet popcorn and cotton candy. What's not to like about a circus?"

"Neither of us need the media attention." Dad shot up. The tips of his ears were red, a film of sweat coating his entire face. I held myself back from lashing out, knowing that I needed to be cold and calculated now.

"Speak for yourself, Mr. Roth. I quite enjoy being seen."

"This could get very messy and very risky for all of our careers." It was Terrance's turn to warn.

"Au contraire, Mr. Ripp. Mine will flourish as a result. In fact, I think it'll earn me a principal spot at this very firm."

And just like that, Christian and Amanda were gone. Claire and the mediator stayed behind to talk to Dad and his lawyers. I couldn't help myself. I got up and rushed into the hallway after Christian. He escorted Amanda toward his office. When he noticed me coming, he nodded for her to wait for him inside and stayed behind, stuffing his fists into the pockets of his dress pants. He leaned against a wall. "Missed me already?"

"Why are you doing this?" I skidded to a stop in front of him. My emotions were frayed, tangled. All red wires. Hatred, annoyance, desire, and exasperation. The man threw me off balance, something not even my five-inch stilettos could do.

Christian tapped his lips, pretending to mull this over. "Let's see. Because I'm about to get a whole lot richer and even more famous in my field off your father's spineless back?" he asked. "Yeah. That must be it."

My fists balled at my sides, my whole body humming with rage. "I hate you," I whispered.

"You *bore* me."

"You're a vile man."

"Ah, but at least I *am* a man. Your father is a wuss who got grabby with his staff and now needs to suffer the consequences. Sucks when your money can't get you out of trouble, huh?"

I let out something between a bark and a snicker. "Mr. Miller, at least have the decency not to pretend *you* weren't born into good fortune and dubious scruples."

Something passed across his face. It was brief, but it was there. I'd say I'd hit a nerve, but I doubted this man had any.

"Do you have legs, Ms. Roth?"

"You know I do. You made a point of ogling them in the elevator."

"I suggest you make good use of them now and take a hike before security escorts you out. Then the only fire you'll have to quench is the one perishing your career."

"This is not over," I warned, mainly because it sounded really good in the movies.

"I wholly agree and advise you to get the hell away from it before it explodes all over *you*."

Then the bastard slammed his office door in my face.

Stunned, I marched back to the conference room. By the time I got there, Dad and his lawyers had already left.

"My apologies, Ms. Roth. There's another conference scheduled in twenty minutes in this room." Claire offered me a venomous smile as she collected her documents. "I told them they could wait for you at the lobby downstairs. You don't mind, do you?"

I smiled just as tightly. "Not at all."

I headed straight to the elevator bank, my head high, my smile intact.

Christian Miller was going to go down, if the last thing I did was drag him to the pits of hell.

◆　◆　◆

"They're in, and they love us more than the Oscars love Sally Field." Jillian slapped the signed contract on the nightstand by my bed later that evening, proceeding to do a little dance. I was buried under the duvet, still hiding from the world after the disastrous afternoon at Cromwell & Traurig. A stomach-turning vision of my father standing in a courtroom, shriveled into paper-thin pieces of himself, flashed through my mind.

My family life had always been complex. I'd lost my twin brother before I could even get to know him. My memories of my mother throughout my childhood were a revolving door of rehab visitations and missed birthdays, graduation ceremonies, and other landmark events, as well as a lot of public meltdowns. Dad had been the only constant in my life. The one person I could count on who didn't cut a nice paycheck from being there for me. To think he was going to go through something so mentally exhausting as a public trial made me want to scream.

"Yoo-hoo. Arya? Ari?" My friend rubbed my back, hovering over my figure. "Did you come down with something?"

I groaned, peeling the duvet down to my waist and turning to face her. Jillian gasped, slapping a hand over her mouth.

"Have you been crying?"

I propped my back against the headboard. My eyes were the size of tennis balls, but I think I'd run out of tears, energy, and damns about a couple of hours earlier.

"Allergies," I mumbled.

Jillian's delicate eyebrows twitched. She had the maddening skin complexion of a Kardashian *after* the Photoshop treatment, curly black hair, and eyes the color of toffee. Her dress, a lilac tweed number, was borrowed from my closet.

"What'd the clients say?" I sniffed.

Jillian and I had incorporated Brand Brigade, our public relations consultancy firm, when we were both at a crossroads. Jillian had been working for a nonprofit organization as a PR specialist and got hit on by every privileged douche in and outside her office, making her life miserable and her then boyfriend jealous, while I'd interned my way through two political campaigns that had ended in a scandal and annihilation respectively, clocked in forty-five-hour weeks, and gotten paid mainly in compliments.

Finally, we'd both decided we'd had enough and could do better on our own. That was four years ago, and we'd never looked back. Business was booming, and I was proud of my ability to provide for myself, even if my mother viewed it as an act of defiance.

Now I was doing what I did best—getting people out of the pickles they'd gotten themselves into. Because as Jillian had said, there were two things we could always count on in this world: the IRS cashing in our checks every April 15 and people's unique talent for making mistakes.

"They said that we're hired and that they loved the Real Bodies presentation you made for Swan Soaps." Jillian plonked next to me, grabbing one of my pillows and hugging it to her chest. "They want a three-month trial run, but they signed the contract and paid the advance. They'll go over the fine print tomorrow. It's a huge opportunity, Ari. Stuffed is the biggest reusable-diaper company in the world."

I cooed and gushed over Jillian nailing this client, but my heart wasn't in it. It was still bleeding all over Christian Miller's limestone office floor.

Jillian bumped her shoulder against mine. "Are you going to tell me what happened? Because we both know the allergies were just an excuse so I could talk about the deal."

There was no point keeping secrets from Jillian. She had the instincts of an FBI agent and the ability to smell bullshit from continents away.

"Dad's case is going to court."

"You're kidding me." She reared her head back, her mouth dropping into an O shape.

"I wish I was."

"Oh, honey." Jillian rolled out of my bed and returned a few minutes later with two glasses of red wine. She toed off her heels and discarded them in the hallway. "Promise me one thing—*don't* overthink this. They have nothing on your dad. You said so yourself. We'll spin PR gold around this case and make him look like the angel Daddy Conrad really is." She handed me one of the glasses, which I noticed could double as a bucket and was completely full.

I took a sip, blinking at an invisible spot on my wall.

"Should I be looking into this more?" I grumbled, mainly to myself. "I mean, if you strip away the fact that this man is my dad, the allegations against him are pretty gross."

Jillian shook her head vehemently. "Hello, I grew up with you, remember? Been to your house every day since junior high. I know Conrad. He's the guy who takes you to the Cloisters every month, who gave his secretary a yearlong paid vacation when she gave birth. Hello? Who cares what Amanda Gispen says?"

I wanted to take every word Jillian had said and ink it into my flesh.

"If Amanda lied—why would she go all the way to court?" I played devil's advocate.

"Because he turned her down? Because they had a thing and he broke things off?" Jillian offered. "There could be a hundred different reasons. People perpetuate drama all the time. Amanda can say whatever she wants."

"Under oath?" I took another sip of my wine. "She could face jail time if she gets caught."

"She could, but it's unlikely. I just don't see this thing having legs, Ari." Jillian offered me a comforting smile. "He'll be fine."

I nibbled on the side of my lip, my thoughts ping-ponging from Christian's hate-filled eyes to Dad's expression, full of pain, embarrassment, and disbelief.

"Side note—I can't stand the lawyer who represents Amanda Gispen."

"Lawyers aren't exactly known as the professional world's Labradors." Jillian gave me a pitying, you-should-know-better look.

"Yeah, but this one takes the seven-tier shit cake, Jilly."

"Who is it?" Jillian bumped her toes against mine over the duvet, the way Nicky used to do when we were kids, reading books under my library desk. A wistful smile touched my lips. *Oh, Nicky.*

I remembered the day I'd called Dad's personal PI and asked him to look Nicky up. To see if he was okay. It was the first call I made after I turned eighteen. I paid the PI with the money I'd saved over the summer selling tourist paraphernalia.

Nicholai is dead, Arya.

The revelation was followed by denial, anger, tears, and a mini breakdown. You know, to wrap it all up in a nice bow. The PI explained to me that this was the nature of the beast. That kids like Nicky often fell through the system's cracks. That he'd probably died of an overdose or in a knife fight or as a result of a DUI. But I'd known Nicholai well, and he hadn't been some punk who was up to no good. It was hard to believe he was no longer sharing the same slice of baby-blue sky I lived under.

"Just the most infuriating man on planet Earth," I groaned into my drink.

"Does the most infuriating man on planet Earth have a name?" Jillian probed.

"A generic one," I huffed. "Christian Miller. Or what I prefer to call him—Lucifer incarnate."

Jillian sprayed the red wine all over my tweed dress *and* duvet, choking on a laugh.

"Say that again?"

"I prefer to call him Luc—"

"Yeah, I got that part. What's his name?"

"Christian Miller," I repeated, annoyed. "Thanks for staining my Egyptian cotton sheets, by the way. You're a pal."

Jillian stood up and dashed out to the living room and returned clutching a glossy magazine I did not recognize, because contrary to Christian's belief, I did not read *any* gossip or fashion magazines (not that there was anything wrong with doing that).

She leafed through the pages until she found what she was looking for, then proceeded to wave it in my face in triumph. I recognized Christian through puffy eyes, looking to the camera in a dashing tux, his hair sexily disheveled, his smirk promising a good time and a bad breakup.

"What am I looking at?" I asked, as if my ability to use my vision had evaporated sometime in the last five seconds.

"Read the headline."

"'Thirty-Five under Thirty-Five: New York's Most Eligible Bachelors Revealed!'"

Great. Not only was he rich, handsome, and dead set on ruining my family; he was also widely celebrated in the city we shared. I skimmed through the details.

Name: Christian George Miller.

Age: 32.

Occupation: Litigator at Cromwell & Traurig.

Net Worth: 4 Million dollars.

Height: 6'2".

Dream Woman: Would it be politically incorrect if I said I preferred blondes? Deep brown eyes. Tall and leggy. A science-related degree a bonus. Someone serious, a must. Enjoys parties, fine wine, and taking the paths less traveled in life.

I clutched my glass of cabernet to my chest, feeling personally attacked. His dream woman happened to be the polar opposite of me. Almost like he'd designed her envisioning everything that I wasn't.

Calm your tits, Ari. He wasn't throwing shade. He didn't know you existed until six hours ago.

"I know we're supposed to hate him, but since he is going to lose this case and get a giant slice of humble pie, can you tell me if he is as gorgeous in real life as he is in the picture?" Jillian repositioned herself on my bed.

Sadly, he looked even better up close. Of course, I wasn't gracious enough to admit that.

"He's hideous. Barf worthy." I flung the stupid magazine into a trash can nearby, not surprised to find Christian's face still smirking at me from the edge of said trash can. The man was going to haunt me through this lifetime and, very likely, the next four, if reincarnation was a thing. "It's all Photoshop. He looks like a cross between an ogre and Richard Ramirez."

"Richard Ramirez has been dead for years."

"Exactly."

Jillian pursed her lips, obviously not buying this. Finally, she said, "Well, screw him, even if he looks like a demigod. If he's after your family, I consider him an enemy too."

"Thanks." I drew in another deep breath, feeling marginally better from the alliance declaration. If nothing else, I'd robbed Christian Miller of the ability to date one of the finest women in Manhattan. Jilly was a catch.

"Just to be sure—does that mean I can find his number on LinkedIn?" Jillian joked.

I swatted my best friend's shoulder. *"Traitor."*

CHAPTER EIGHT

A RYA

Past

He was here.

Finally.

I could tell by the footsteps. The way they brushed against the limestone. Steady, measured, precise. His knockoff sneakers kissed the floor. I closed my eyes, balancing against a bookshelf in the library, my breath fluttering in my chest like a butterfly.

Ten months. It's been ten long months. Come find me.

A shot of thrill rolled through my belly. I'd never done this before. Made myself unavailable to Nicholai. No matter how much I wanted to wait for him by the door, like an eager puppy, ready with all the books and stories I wanted to share with him, I didn't. I wanted to reinvent myself this summer break. To be mysterious and alluring and all the other things I read about in the books that made heroines worth fighting for.

I was in the library, clutching a black-and-white paperback of *Atonement* by Ian McEwan, wearing a mint-green satin nightgown. I'd read the book in February, after stealing it from the school's library just to feel what it was like to take what wasn't mine, and then every month since I'd waited to tell Nicky about it. Even though we lived in the same city, we might as well be living in parallel universes. Our worlds didn't touch, our lives orbiting around different schools, people, and events. It was only during summer break that we collided. That the universe burst with colors.

Several times throughout the year I'd found myself itching to send him a letter or an email or even pick up the phone and call. Each time, I'd had to talk myself off the ledge. He never sought me out between summers—why should I? Maybe to him we were nothing but a lame version of summer camp. Maybe we weren't even friends. Just two kids spending the summer in one confined space, carelessly forgotten by the adults who'd made us.

Maybe he had a girlfriend now.

Maybe, maybe, maybe.

So I waited. Stewed on the book. Marinated in the feelings it evoked within me. They always brought me back to him. Nicholai. My Nicky.

The footsteps grew louder, closer.

I tucked a flyaway behind my ear, willing my heart to beat slower. I'd been crushing on Nicholai Ivanov since that first day at the cemetery; I'd just never put a name to that feeling I had for him before. Not until this year, when everyone at school had seemed to pair up into couples. Having a boyfriend had somehow switched from a shameful thing only bad girls did to the height of one's existence overnight, and I'd fallen behind on the trend. None of these couples actually talked to each other during school hours or hung out, but they had the title, and whenever there was an outing or a birthday, the couples would whisper to each other and kiss.

Kissing, too, had become a rite of passage. Something to be checked off a list. There was not one boy at school I wanted to kiss.

The only lips I wanted to feel against mine were Nicholai's.

I flipped through the pages of *Atonement*, but the words kept slipping, as if falling from the pages. I was surprised there wasn't a pile of letters at my feet. It was hopeless. Trying to concentrate on anything that wasn't him.

And then . . . bliss. Nicholai's body filled the doorframe in my periphery. Holey shoes, jeans ripped in all the wrong places, and a faded shirt, frayed at the edges. Each year he sharpened into something more beautiful.

I pretended not to notice him.

"Sup." An unlit cigarette butt was tucked in the corner of his mouth. I pondered what the great Beatrice Roth would think about the fact I wanted to kiss a boy who shoved used cigarettes from the street into his mouth. Probably not much, to be honest. As long as I didn't bring a disease into the house, she wouldn't have minded if I sawed my own limbs off as a fashion statement.

I looked up. "Oh. Hey, Nicky."

His beauty struck me like lightning. He hadn't been so handsome two years ago. Each summer, his features were honed into something more male. His jaw became sharper, the slash between his eyebrows deeper, his lips redder. His eyes were his best feature, though. The exact, astonishing color of blue topaz. He was tall, smooth, and lithe, and above all, he had that quality that couldn't be named. The badassness of a kid who knew how to fend for himself. How to fight for his survival. It made me nauseous to think some kids had him two semesters a year. To ogle, to admire, to enjoy.

"You good?" He pushed off the doorframe, waltzing over to me. I noticed that his scrawny arms had filled out over the past year. Veins ran through the muscles. He didn't stop until our toes touched, and he plucked the book from between my fingers and flipped through it nonchalantly.

He tucked the cigarette behind his ear, his eyebrows knitting together.

"Hi," I said.

"Hello." He looked up, flashing me a grin, then returned his attention to the book. I couldn't wait to see him in swimming trunks this summer.

"Have you read it?" I wheezed out the question, my face blazing hot.

He shook his head. "Heard some of it is pretty raunchy, though."

"Yeah. But, like, that's not the point of the book."

"Making out is always the point of everything." His eyes lifted to meet mine, and he let loose a rakish smirk. He handed me back my book. "Maybe I'll give it a try one day, if Mr. Van stops giving me *Penthouse* hand-me-downs."

This was my in to tell him what I'd thought about the entire year. What I dreamed about at night.

"Congratulations, you officially became gross."

He laughed. "I missed you."

"Yeah. Me too." I twisted a piece of hair over my index finger, feeling so strange in my body, like it didn't belong to me. "I'm thinking of taking theater class, now that I'm going to high school."

I absolutely wasn't, but I needed a solid background story.

"Cool." He was already roaming the room, opening drawers, looking for new, shiny things to explore. My house was like a theme park for Nicholai. He liked to use my dad's lighters, to cross his ankles on the mahogany desks, to pretend to take important calls on the vintage Toscano office phone.

"I thought maybe we could reenact part of the book. You know, as practice, for my audition in September."

"Reenact what?"

"One of the raunchy scenes. In the book. I need to do something risqué for my audition."

"Risqué?" he murmured, pulling drawers open, sticking his hands in them.

"Yes. They're not gonna let me in if I give them something mild."

What the hell was I talking about? Even I had no clue.

"How raunchy are we talking?" He was too distracted, on his hunt for something to steal.

I grabbed the book and flipped through it before stopping at page 126 and handing it over to him. He stopped rummaging through drawers. His eyes dropped to the text. I held my breath as he read it. When he finished, he passed it back to me, and I tucked it in the library behind me.

"You're kidding, right?"

I shook my head, my pulse nearly jumping out of my skin.

Nicholai froze. His gaze flew from one of the desk's drawers to mine, disbelief touching his topaz eyes. There was knowledge in them. Irreverence and annoyance too. I wanted to recreate that scene at the library, where Robbie pins Cecilia against the shelves and kisses her like the world is ending. Because to him, it is.

Every hair on my arms stood on end. I didn't want to throw up on my own shoes. At the same time, it seemed like I was about to do just that.

"We'll just kiss," I clarified, faking a yawn. "None of that other weird stuff, obvs."

"*Just* kiss?"

"Hey, you were the one who just told me everything begins and ends with making out." I raised my hands in surrender.

His lips curled into a slight smirk. My heart free-fell to the floor.

"Have you raided your old man's liquor cabinet, Ari?" Nicky erased the little space we had between us. He trailed a finger along the shell of my ear. A shiver ran through me. "We can't kiss. Unless, of course, you want our parents to kill me."

"You mean us."

"Nah." He took the cigarette from behind his ear and chewed on its butt, keeping his hands and mouth busy. "You'll get away with just about anything under Daddy Conrad's watch. The blame always lies at the feet of the poor person with the funny-sounding name. Haven't you noticed a theme in all of the classics we read last summer?"

"I'm not gonna tell anyone." My throat felt tight. Full of pebbles. Suddenly, rejection had a taste, a scent, a body. It was a living, breathing thing, and the sting of its fist burned my cheeks. I couldn't even be mad at Nicky. I was a reluctant observer all the times my father, my mother, and Ruslana tossed threats like arrows into the air, aimed at Nicky.

Don't you dare touch her.

Take a step back, son.

Nicholai, don't you have to help your mother with the dishes?

"I know; it's not that I don't trust you," Nicky agreed. "It's that I don't trust my luck. If they find out somehow, if this place is wired or whatever . . . Ari, you know I can't."

It was gentle, but it was final. Subject closed. And while I understood him, I was also angry at him, because he was still levelheaded about us, whereas I was as logical as a truck tire where he was concerned. The bile in my throat rolled an inch forward toward my mouth. But I wasn't that kind of girl. I prided myself in being exactly what Nicky wanted me to be. I watched action flicks and played wall ball and said *dude* at least fifteen times a day.

"Hey, we going down for a swim or what?" Nicky wrapped his fingers around a small crystal ball on the shelf behind me and pocketed it. He did that a lot, and I never minded. Maybe because I knew he'd never take something that was dear to me. "I practiced at the YMCA pool all year. Prepare to be crushed, silver-spooned girl."

The sharp bite behind my eyes told me that I had three seconds, maybe five, before the tears began to fall.

"Dude." I snorted. "Who's being high now? I'm going to end you. Let me put my swimsuit on."

"Meet you at the door in five."

I turned around and walked away, closing my bedroom door behind me, then fished for my swimsuit in my drawer, nicking my thumb in the process. I was bleeding but couldn't feel a thing.

I sucked on the blood, looking in the mirror and practicing my best, brightest smile.

That was my first lesson of adolescence.

Heartbreaks were dealt with discreetly. In the back alleys of your soul. On the outside, I was strong. But inside—I cracked.

After the swimming competition—in which Nicky indeed annihilated me—I avoided him the entire first week of summer break.

I did it casually. Made plans to go to Saks with some friends one day, went to the library on another. I even went as far as joining my mother and her boring friends for brunch.

But Nicky still came every day and had the determined, stoic expression of someone who wanted to make our friendship work. And each day, I came up with something else to do. Something that didn't include him in my plans.

I knew I was punishing him for not kissing me, even if in a round-about way. Ruslana made him help her around the house to keep him busy. She allowed him a few breaks each day, which he took on the living room balcony, which adjoined my bedroom terrace. Hopping between the balconies was doable but risky. The glass barrier was too tall, so you had to go over the rails and hang on the edge of the skyscraper for three feet until you made it to the other side.

One time during that first week, when Ruslana had taken out the trash and I'd just come back from another pointless outing to avoid him, Nicky hurried to the glass window between us, pressing his hands against it. I did the same, instantly drawn to him like a magnet.

"Are you punishing me?" he asked, no hint of anger in his voice.

I laughed incredulously. "Now, why would I do that?"

"You know exactly why."

"Wow, Nicky. Inflated ego much?"

He studied me expressionlessly. I felt like the world's biggest jerk. He tried another tactic. "Are we still friends?"

I gave him a pitying look I hated. The kind of look popular girls gave me at school when I said something nerdy or uncool. "It's okay if I don't want to spend all summer with you, you know."

"Guess so." He was watching me so closely I felt like he was undressing me of my lies, one item at a time. "But it looks like you don't want to spend one minute with me."

"I do. I'll swim with you tomorrow. Oh, wait." I snapped my fingers. "I promised Dad I would go to his office and help his secretaries to do some filing."

"I'm losing to *filing*?" His eyes flared.

"Whatever, Nicky. It's work experience. We should both be thinking about getting summer jobs next year, anyway. We're getting too old for this."

He narrowed his eyes, glancing between the railing and me. I shook my head. I didn't want him to die. I mean, okay, maybe just a little, because he'd rejected me and it hurt, but I knew I wouldn't survive if something happened to him.

"Don't cross the barrier," I warned. I had a feeling we were talking about much more than just the banisters.

He made a move, though. About to cross. I gasped.

His mother called him to come back. He smiled.

"For you, Arya, I just might."

◆ ◆ ◆

And he did.

After nine excruciating days, punctuated by a weekend full of scream-ing into my pillow. I was lacing my sneakers, getting ready for an after-noon of wandering around Manhattan aimlessly to avoid him. Ruslana was out, getting groceries, and my parents were at work and at a tennis lesson respectively. The house was quiet save for Fifi, a shih tzu, who was barking up a storm at a new statue Beatrice had won in an auction over the weekend. That dog had infinite amounts of cuteness and stupidity.

In my periphery, I noticed movement on my terrace, and when I turned my head to get a better look, I saw Nicky hanging between life and death.

I shot up from my bed and ran to the balcony.

"You jerk!" I cried, my heart beating five thousand times a minute.

But Nicky was lithe and athletic, and he jumped to safety and was dusting his hands off before I unlocked the balcony door.

"You could've died!" I pushed him into my room, railing.

"No such luck, silver-spooned princess."

I loathed and enjoyed this nickname in equal measures. The dig was annoying, but he *did* call me a princess.

"Well, I could've been naked!"

"I could've been lucky," he responded smoothly, closing the door behind us and sloping against a credenza, his ankles crossed. His face looked soft yet intense. Like an oil painting. I wanted to cry. It wasn't fair that he wasn't mine. And it wasn't fair that even if he could be, we'd always have to keep it a secret. "We need to talk, *pal*."

The way he said the word *pal* told me he did not consider me one anymore.

"Be quick about it. I'm seeing friends in half an hour."

"No, you're not."

Crossing my arms over my chest, I was already on the defensive. I felt foolish. Up until now, Nicky and I had been kindred spirits. Tangled together by an invisible bond. Two forgotten kids in a big city.

Even though we came from different backgrounds, we had so much in common. Now, it all felt wrong. He had the upper hand. He knew I liked him like *that*. The balance had shifted.

"Look." He rubbed the back of his obsidian hair. "I freaked out, okay? It's not that I didn't want to kiss you. It's just that I would really like my balls to be intact by the time I go to high school, and . . . well . . ."

"You cannot guarantee that'd happen if my dad catches us together," I finished for him.

He smiled, a smile that told me he didn't give a rat's ass about what my dad thought about him, only about the consequences that might follow if he crossed him. "In a nutshell, yeah."

I took a step forward, letting my arms fall at my sides. "I know my dad is overprotective of me. It's an Aaron thing—"

"No," Nicky said flatly. "It's a rich-man-poor-boy thing."

"Dad's not like that," I protested.

"He's exactly like that, and a half. Honestly? If you were my daughter, I wouldn't want you anywhere near me either."

His conviction told me there was little point in trying to convince him otherwise.

"Anyway, I never would have offered if I thought we'd get caught. I'm sorry. I was being stupid. And reckless. And—"

"Arya?"

"Yeah?"

"I'm not done talking."

"Oh." An invisible ribbon tightened around my neck. "Sorry. Um, continue."

"As I said, if you were my daughter, I wouldn't want you anywhere near me." He paused. "But since you're *not* my daughter, I decided your theater-class thingy is worth the risk. *Not* because I want to kiss you"—he lifted a finger in warning—"but because I wouldn't want to deprive the world of the next Meryl Streep."

Everything in my body shuddered. "Hey, I don't want to kiss you either. But I want to become an actress."

I should've felt worse than I did about the lie. After all, my desire to become an actress was akin to my desire to become a circus clown. As in, not quite. Or not at all. But somehow, I told myself the end justified the means.

"I expect two tickets to whatever film you star in when you grow up. And a limo waiting outside my house to take me there." Nicky was still wagging his finger.

"Limos are a little outdated."

"My balls, my rules."

"What else?"

"It better not be a bad movie. If you pull a Demi Moore in *Nothing but Trouble*, I swear to God, Ari, I'm washing my hands of you forever."

A canned laugh escaped me. "Fine." I pushed stray locks of hair from my face. "I'll send a limo and make you proud if you promise to bring a girl no prettier than I am as a date."

"First of all, this is not a negotiation. I'm the one taking all the risk here. Second, easy peasy." He rocked on the balls of his feet, a little embarrassed. "I don't really know anyone as pretty as you."

The silence between us felt heavy all of a sudden. Full of things we were too afraid to say. He cleared his throat.

"Also, if you don't give me some company, my mother is going to make me scrub your ceiling clean. So you better haul ass outside this room, or this whole deal is off."

Breathless hysteria took over my body. It was happening. Nicholai Ivanov was going to kiss me.

"Wait for me in the library," I instructed.

"'Kay, ballbuster." He turned to leave.

"Oh, and Nicky?"

He stopped but didn't turn around.

"If you skip over the rails again, you don't have to worry about falling. I will kill you myself."

◆ ◆ ◆

His back was to me when I entered the library.

Something compelled me to stop on the threshold and soak in the view of this boy that I loved, watching New York sprawled in front of him, hands clasped behind his back, stance straight, looking no less powerful than the city that devoured dreams and hopes on a daily basis.

It was suddenly terrifyingly clear to me that Nicholai was going to go places, and wherever they were, he wasn't going to take me with him. He couldn't afford baggage. His last stop wasn't Hunts Point.

"Is your dad here yet?" Nicky asked, his back still to me.

I stepped inside, clicking the door shut softly. "He has a fundraising event tonight. Said he won't be back until after dinnertime. Coast's clear."

My knees felt like jelly. I'd checked the time before I'd gotten here. It was four in the afternoon. My mother was on another yoga retreat, an ocean away. Ruslana might come back from grocery shopping, but she always made herself known whenever she knew we were together. Banging pans, vacuuming the hallway, talking on the phone loudly. She didn't want to catch us in case we were doing something wrong. Knowledge came with liability.

Nicky spun on his heel, his face both grave and determined, like he was about to walk death row. I knew he was doing this for me. A part of him—most of him, I assumed—dreaded kissing me. I could call the whole thing off. Spare him the discomfort.

But I wasn't good enough.

Virtuous enough.

Dad said scruples were a beggar's jewels. That I shouldn't bother myself with morals. "We pay too much tax to be good," he'd once laughed out.

I glided toward one of the floor-to-ceiling shelves, pressing my back against it and closing my eyes. I felt like I was acting, so at least that part wasn't a lie. Not in that moment. The sound of his footsteps echoed behind my rib cage. The heat of his body told me he was near. When he stopped right in front of me, my eyes opened. He was so close I couldn't take his entire face in. Just those turquoise eyes that twinkled like an excavated part of the ocean. I wondered if I looked as lost as he was. He looked so scared. So . . . *not* sexy.

"It's my first kiss." My voice came out syrupy and apologetic. Foreign to my ears.

"Mine too." He gnawed at his lower lip. The pink hue on his cheeks made everything more precious. I wanted to devour this moment like it was a juicy peach. To feel the sweet, sticky juices of it on my chin.

"Oh, good. I'm pretty sure I'm going to suck at this." I giggled.

"Impossible," he said gravely, and for some reason, I believed him.

He leaned over to kiss me and missed. Our foreheads bumped clumsily. We drew away and chuckled. He tried again, this time palming the sides of my neck and guiding his mouth to mine. His lips were hot and soft and tasted of tobacco and ice cubes and boy. We both kept our eyes open.

"This all right with you?" he murmured into my mouth. There was a thin line of hair above his upper lip, wetted by saliva. He still hadn't had his first shave. My heart drummed in my chest. I hoped he would always remember this. The girl who'd kissed him before everyone else.

I nodded, catching his lips in mine. "Mm-hmm."

"Good," he whispered. "Shit, you're pretty."

"You said I was ugly. Years ago." We were kissing. Talking. Holding each other.

"Lies." He shook his head, his lips still exploring mine. "You are and always will be beautiful."

My heart soared. He kissed me again, lacing his fingers through mine from both sides. It was still awkward, but I shoved the feeling of self-consciousness aside. The euphoria of being kissed nearly made me nauseous. It wasn't the sensation that I liked but the fact I was experiencing it with *him*. The knowledge of how much he was risking for me set my soul aflame. There was an ache in my chest that unfurled like a small piece of paper. Expanding and expanding with each second that passed.

"Get your dirty hands off my daughter!"

The next few things happened fast. One second, Nicky's body was pressed against mine, and the next, he was on the floor, huddled in a nest of thick, hardcover books, my father's figure crouching above him, fisting the collar of his shirt.

There was a thwack—the sound of skin slapping skin. My vision blurred around the edges.

"I should've known . . . you little shi—"

I didn't let Dad finish the sentence. I launched myself at him, yanking him away from Nicky by the arm. "Daddy! Please!"

"—will ruin your life." Dad dragged him upright from the floor now by his collar, smashing Nicholai's back against the shelves. More books rained on both of them, but neither of them paid attention. Dad's face was red, almost purple, while Nicky looked defiant, his expression passive. He didn't try to deny or explain what had happened. Didn't chicken out. He was going to see this one through, the way he had everything else in his life.

Another jab sent Nicky's face flying, and this time, by the crack, I knew my father had broken his nose.

Ruslana blasted through the library door holding a broomstick. I tried jumping between Dad and Nicky, prying Dad's fingers from his throat. I was confused, upset, and sick to my stomach. I'd never seen my father being violent. He'd always been gentle and loving with me, making up for all the things my mother wasn't.

"What's happening here?" Ruslana shrieked. When she saw her son's purple face staring back at my dad, she jumped between them, poking Dad away with the broom in her hands.

"Off! Get off him!" she roared. "You'll kill him, and then I'll be the one who needs to answer the authorities."

This was what she cared about right now? Really?

"Your filthy, stupid son touched my Arya. I got back home early to grab a new tie before the fundraiser and . . ."

"Mercy!" Ruslana cried, turning to her son, who was nothing but a heap of jumbled limbs, blood, and swollen flesh in that moment. "Is this true? I *told* you not to touch her!"

Nicky jerked his chin up boldly.

"Say something!" she demanded.

Nicky turned to my father, smiling. His gums were bleeding. "She tasted good, sir."

My father slapped him with the back of his hand, using his fraternity ring to draw more blood. Nicky's face flew to the other side. His cheek banged against the shelf. This was all on me. My fault. I wanted to do so many things.

To tell him I was sorry.

To say I hadn't known Dad would come.

To help him out.

To explain everything to Dad, to Ruslana. I needed to salvage this. To protect him.

But the words got stuck in my throat. Like a ball of puke, blocking my air pipes. My mouth fell open, but nothing came out.

It's not his fault.

"Go to your room, Arya," my father snarled, marching to the open door and tilting his head in the hallway's direction. I didn't move at first. "Go, God dammit!"

And then I thought about how my life would change if Dad decided to be like Mom. To neglect me, look the other way, treat me like I was another piece of furniture.

Shockingly—disgracefully—I moved, my legs heavy as lead.

I could still feel Nicholai's eyes on my back. The heat of the betrayal. The burn of knowing I would never be forgiven.

That things would never be the same again.

That I'd lost my best friend.

CHAPTER NINE

CHRISTIAN

Present

I'd recognized her instantly.

The swanlike neck. The ethereal Ava Gardner gaze and feline green eyes. Arya wore every passing year with grace and elegance. At thirteen, she'd been pretty. At thirty-one—a real knockout. Even her innocent halo, the sense of something wholesome and unreachable, was cracked but still intact. She glowed from miles away, and I wanted to douse her magnificence. Dim her light and drag her to the shadows with me.

When I spotted her at the building's reception, I couldn't believe my luck. She'd decided to tag along and get a front seat to her father's downfall. I had no idea what she was doing there. My immediate response was to talk to her. To see if she, too, recognized me. If I'd ever mattered. Or if I'd just been the help, who'd stolen her first kiss and paid for it with interest.

She had no idea who I was. No surprises there. I'd always been a blip in her world. An unimportant anecdote. The need to punish her, to show her this new version of me could not be overlooked or tucked away in an establishment no one could see or reach, slammed into me. I hadn't been able to stop myself.

Not from dropping profanity in the middle of a mediation meeting like a D-grade rapper.

Not from rejecting any defrayal offered, including a mouthwatering eight-figure deal.

Not from drinking in her face thirstily. Like I was still the same fourteen-year-old boy with a stiffie, vying for crumbs of her attention, consuming her in any shape or form she'd throw my way.

I took a swig of my whiskey, watching the Manhattan skyline from my Park Avenue apartment. It was a one-bedroom, but it was all mine, fully paid. I'd always preferred quality over quantity.

"Are you coming to bed?" Claire asked behind me. I could see her reflection in the glass of my floor-to-ceiling window, leaning against the doorframe of my bedroom, wearing nothing but my white dress shirt, her bare legs on full display.

"In a minute."

"I'm here if you need to talk," she suggested. But there was no point in talking to Claire. She wouldn't understand me. She never did.

I hate you, Arya had told me this afternoon in my office, and by the way her lower lip had trembled like it had all those years ago when she'd talked about Aaron, I knew she'd meant it.

The good news was that I hated her, too, and was all too pleased to show her just how much.

You're a vile man.

With that, I had to agree. Especially after I'd taken this case.

With a low growl, I tossed the tumbler of whiskey onto the double-glazed window, watching the golden liquid slosh along the glass and crawl to the floor, where twinkling shards of crystal waited to be picked up by whoever cleaned up this place.

This was the person I'd become.

A man who didn't even *know* the names of the people who worked at his apartment.

So detached from the reality I'd grown up in that sometimes I wondered if my early childhood had been real after all.

Then I remembered the only thing separating me from Nicholai was money.

Arya Roth was going to pay in the currency that was the dearest to her.

Her *father*.

◆ ◆ ◆

Days later, it was everywhere. The filing of Amanda Gispen's complaint in the US District Court for the Southern District of New York. As soon as the EEOC had given us our notice of right to sue, I'd had the complaint hand delivered to the clerk's office. The national newspapers were all over it. News channels broke the story, making it the first headline. I had to take an Uber home and slip through the garage to avoid the press. Claire and I had been paired together for the case. Claire's parents sent a huge bouquet of flowers to the office to celebrate, as if she'd gotten engaged.

"They really want to meet you when Dad visits from DC." Claire dropped the bomb when I complimented her on the flowers. "That's next week. I know you have depositions on Wednesday and Thursday . . ."

"Sorry, Claire. Not gonna happen."

Amanda was under strict warning not to talk to anyone about this. She went off the grid, moving to her sister's place. I didn't want Conrad Roth or his toxic daughter to pull any strings. That night, for the first time in almost twenty years, I slept like a baby.

CHAPTER TEN

CHRISTIAN

Past

There was a lot of hot anger afterward.

Hot, impotent, what-the-fuck-do-I-do-with-it anger.

At Arya, who'd probably set me up so her dad would catch us and pretty much ruined my life as a result.

And at Conrad Roth, the obnoxious, abusive, piece-of-shit billionaire who thought (no, scratch that, *knew*) he could get away with what he did to me, just like he got away with everything else.

And to an extent, even at Mom, whom I'd stopped expecting much of but who somehow managed to surprise me with each betrayal, no matter how big or small.

But there was nothing to do with this anger. It was like a big, fat black cloud hovering above my head. Unreachable but still real. I couldn't get back at Arya—she had Conrad. And I couldn't get back at Conrad—he had Manhattan.

After Conrad delivered his final punch, I managed my hasty, bloodied escape from the Roths. I bled all over the bus's floor and attracted uncomfortable looks, even from New Yorkers, who were used to pretty much *everything*. I stumbled back into my apartment building, only to find out when I got there that I didn't have a key. It had stayed with Mom back at the Roths, probably burning a hole in her handbag while she cleaned her son's blood off the shiny marble floors.

So I found a temporary solution for my rage.

I punched the wooden door.

Once, twice, three times before my knuckles started bleeding.

Again and again and again, until I created a hole in the wood and fractures in my bones.

And then some more, until the hole became big enough for me to slip my blood-soaked hand into it and unlock the door from the inside. My fingers were twice their original size and wonky. *Wrong.*

This was the thing about broken stuff, I thought.

They were more exposed, easy to tamper with.

I vowed to fix myself up real fast and put my feelings for Conrad and Arya Roth in my pockets.

I would revisit them, later.

◆ ◆ ◆

I couldn't stay in New York after that. That was what Mom said.

Granted, she didn't say that to *me*. I was just a useless kid, after all. Rather, she shared this piece of information with her friend Sveta over a loud, heated phone call. Her screechy voice carried through the small building, rattling the roof shingles.

I only heard shards of the conversation from downstairs, where I was flung over the Vans' plastic-covered couch, pressing a bag of frozen peas to my jaw.

". . . will kill him . . . said I made him a promise, I did . . . thinking about, what you call? Juvenile institution? . . . told him not to touch the girl . . . maybe a school somewhere else . . . never have kids, Sveta. Never have kids."

Jacq, Mrs. Van's daughter, who was seventeen, stroked my hair. I was lucky Mr. Van had been there, delivering me his hand-me-down *Penthouse*, when Mom had kicked me out, or I wouldn't have anywhere to sleep tonight.

"Your nose's broken." Jacq's long fingernails raked over my skull, making frissons run through my back.

"I know."

"Shame. Now you won't be pretty anymore."

I tried to smile but couldn't. Everything was too puffy. "Crap, I was counting on this moneymaker."

She laughed.

"What do you think is going to happen to me now?" I asked, not because I thought she'd know but because she was the only person in the world who was speaking to me.

Jacq mused, "I don't know. But honestly, Ruslana seems like a bit of a shit mom. She'll probably get rid of you."

"Yeah. You're probably right."

"Should've kept your lips to yourself, lover boy. Hey, anyone ever told you you have pretty eyelashes?"

"Are you hitting on me?" I would arch an eyebrow, but that would make a wound open again.

"Maybe."

I groaned in response. I'd sworn off girls for life after today.

"Has your mom ever cut your eyelashes to make them grow thicker?"

I shook my head. "My mom never gave enough crap to change my diaper, probably."

That was my last night in New York City for several years.

The next day, Mom knocked on the Vans' door and threw my meager possessions into the back of a taxi.

She didn't even say goodbye. Just told me to stay out of trouble.

I was shipped off to the Andrew Dexter Academy for Boys on the outskirts of New Haven, Connecticut.

All because of one stupid kiss.

CHAPTER ELEVEN

CHRISTIAN

Past

She was going to come. She had to.

I didn't dare dream anymore. Not often, anyway. But I did today.

Maybe because it was Christmas, and there was a part of me—small as it might be—that still believed in the holiday-miracles mumbo jumbo they spoon-fed us as kids. I wasn't a good Christian by any stretch of the imagination, but word on the street was God showed mercy to all his children, even the screwed-up ones.

Well, I was a child, and I sure as hell needed a break. This was his time to make good on his promise. To show he existed.

I hadn't seen Mom in six months. The days came and went in a flurry of homework and swim team. For my fifteenth birthday, I'd bought myself a prepackaged cupcake from a gas station and made a wish to make it to my next birthday alive. I hadn't even gotten a half-assed by-the-way-are-you-alive phone call since I'd been shipped off from Manhattan. Just one crumpled letter two months ago, stained with rain and fingerprints and an unidentified sauce, in which she'd written to me in her signature italic handwriting.

Nicholai,

We will spend Christmas in my apartment. I will rent a car and pick you up. Wait for me at the entrance at four o'clock on December 22nd. Do not be late or I will leave without you.

—Ruslana

It was impersonal, cold; you could find more enthusiasm at a funeral, but I was still stoked that she remembered my existence.

Tapping my holey loafer against the concrete stairway at Andrew Dexter's double-doored entrance, I glanced at my watch. My backpack was flung between my legs, all my worldly possessions inside it. Waiting for time to slog forward reminded me of all the times I'd waited for Mom in the cemetery outside Arya's building. Only now I didn't have a pretty girl to pass the time with. *That* specific pretty girl had turned out to be nothing but a bag of snakes. I hoped wherever Arya Roth was these days, karma fucked her long and hard, without a condom.

A kick to my back snapped me out of my mental fog. Richard Rodgers—Dickie to anyone who knew him—peppered the gesture by flicking the back of my head as he typhooned down the stairs to the waiting black Porsche pulling in front of the boarding school's entryway.

"Mom!"

"Darling!" His socialite mother got out of the passenger door with open arms, wearing enough real fur to cover three polar bears. My classmate threw himself into her embrace. His father waited behind the wheel, smiling glumly, like a child during Sunday service. It was hard to believe Richard, whose claim to fame was farting the alphabet with his armpit, was worthy of this hot woman's love. Dickie's mother pulled away to take a better look at him, bracketing his face with her manicured hands. My heart lurched and jerked like a caught worm. It hurt to breathe.

Where the hell are you, Mom?

"You look so good, my love. I made you your favorite crumble pie," Dickie's mother cooed.

My stomach growled. They needed to get the hell out of here and stop blocking the driveway. Richard hopped into the car and screwed off.

She'd come. She said she would. She must.

Another hour passed. The wind picked up, the sky turning from gray to black. Mom was still nowhere in sight, and my already shaky confidence was crumbling like the stale pie the janitor had slipped into my room the day after Thanksgiving because he knew I was the only kid who stayed on school grounds.

Four hours and sixteen smacks on the back and "see ya next years" later, it was pitch black and freezing, the snow falling from the sky thick and fluffy, like cotton balls.

The chill didn't register. Neither did the fact my holey loafers were soaking wet, or that the two tears that had slipped from my right eye had frozen midroll. The only thing that sank in was the fact that Mom had stood me up on Christmas and that—as per usual—I was alone.

Something soft and fuzzy landed on my head. Before I could turn around to see what it was, this boy I knew from the swim team, Riggs, plopped down on the stair next to me, mimicking my pathetic hunch.

"Sup, Ivanov?"

"None of your business," I hissed, ripping the red velvet hat from my head and dumping it on the ground.

"That's a big-ass attitude for someone who weighs forty pounds." The good-looking bastard whistled, giving me a once-over.

I twisted his way, punching his arm hard.

"Aw. Shithead. What'd you do that for?"

"So you shut the hell up," I growled. "Why else?"

What was he doing here, anyway?

"Die in hell," Riggs Bates replied cheerfully, finding the situation infinitely amusing.

"Already am," I replied. "I'm here, aren't I?"

The Andrew Dexter Academy was a Catholic, all-boys institution right in the middle of rural Connecticut. It had been built in 1891 by a railroad financier. It was supposed to become the number one luxury hotel on the East Coast, but due to financial failures, the construction was boarded up for a few years, before a bunch of rich newcomers flocking from post–World War I Europe threw money at it, shoving a few priests, teachers, and their problematic offspring into the place. One of those priests was Andrew Dexter, and this was how the number one all-boys boarding school in the States had come to be.

There was no way of sugarcoating it—the Andrew Dexter Academy was a shithole. To get to the closest 7-Eleven, we had to walk ten miles each way. We were isolated from the world, and for good reason. This place housed some of the most notorious teenage douches in the country. Silver lining: in case of zombie apocalypse, we would have some buffer before the brain eaters came for us.

It was obvious my mother wasn't coming. Even more so that I was going to spend this Christmas on my own, just like I had the previous one. Last time, the only person keeping me company had been the groundskeeper, who'd mostly checked in to see I didn't off myself. I hadn't. Instead, I'd read and printed out good college-application examples. The goal was to become a millionaire. If all the idiots around me and their parents were—why couldn't I?

"What the hell are you doing here, anyway?" I wrapped my arms around my knees, glaring at Riggs.

He hitched one shoulder up. "Don't have a family, remember?"

"Actually, I don't remember." I arched a brow. "Keeping tabs on your ass is not my favorite hobby."

I barely ever spoke to Riggs, or anyone else at the school. Speaking to people led to being attached to them, and no part of me wanted to get attached. Humans were flaky.

"Yeah. My grandfather, who raised me, kicked the oxygen habit last Christmas."

"Shit." I wiggled my toes inside my loafers to try and get rid of the numbness. I was starting to feel the cold. "Well, I'm sure you can buy a new grandpa or something," I volunteered. Word was that Riggs was swimming in it.

"Nah." Riggs seemed cool about my dig, even though I deserved to be thrashed for it. "The original was irreplaceable."

"That sucks."

Riggs puffed on condensation coming from his mouth from the cold, trying to make smoke rings. "Christmas is the worst holiday in the world. We should defund it. If I ever open a charity, it'd be called Kill Santa."

"Don't expect fat donations."

"You'd be surprised, Ivanov. I can be pretty persuasive, and rich people like to throw their money on dumb stuff. Grandpa had a toilet seat made of solid gold. I used to take royal craps." He tsked, looking faraway now. Nostalgic.

"So you don't go home during holidays?" I asked, slowly letting go of the hope Mom was coming and digesting what Riggs had said. "Wait a minute. You weren't here during Thanksgiving break."

Riggs cackled. "Was too. Arsène and I went camping in the woods when no one was looking. We made a fire and s'mores and, fine, caused a small, mostly accidental fire."

"That was you?" My eyes bulged out of their sockets. There'd been a whole health-and-safety day after that, and we'd all gotten collectively grounded for a weekend.

Riggs beamed proudly, puffing his chest. "A gentleman doesn't burn and tell."

"You just did."

"Yeah. We totally started that fire. But the s'mores were worth it, dude. Fluffy and sweet." He gave his fingers a kiss.

"So where's Arsène now?" I looked around, as if he were going to materialize from behind the pine trees. I didn't really know Arsène

Corbin, but I'd heard he was crazy smart and that his family owned a shitload of fancy-ass neighborhoods in Manhattan.

"Upstairs, making mac 'n' cheese with bacon bits and some ramen in the kitchenette. He sent me to fetch this." Riggs reached into the gap between his zipped jacket and neck, pulling out a flask. "From Headmaster Plath's office. Then I saw your sorry ass on the stairway and figured I'd let you know we're here."

"Arsène doesn't have a family either?" A knot of hope settled in my throat. It felt good, knowing I wasn't the only one. And bad, too, because apparently grown-ups were just trash.

"Oh, he has a family. He just hates them. Got some major beef with his stepsister or something."

"Cool."

"Not for him."

"He could always ignore her and kick back in his room."

"Eh, I don't think it's that simple." Riggs tilted the flask in my direction, offering me a sip. My eyes traveled from the silver vessel to his face.

"Plath'll kill us," I said pithily. I knew Conrad Roth threw a lot of money at this institute to ensure I'd never get kicked out of the haunted redbrick mansion. This was where all the kids who hit their teachers, gambled away their families' estates, or got into drugs were sent. Now we were all Headmaster Plath's problem, not that of the people who'd sent us here.

"Not if we kill ourselves first. Which, for the record, I think we might, between Arsène's cooking, the amount of alcohol I managed to get my hands on, and the fires we start. Are you coming or what?" Riggs stood up, his floppy golden hair falling across his eyes.

It was the first time I saw Riggs Bates as the awesome human being he saw himself as and not as some rich prick who thought he was better than everyone else.

I threw another hesitant look at the empty road.

"*Don't*, Ivanov. People are overrated. Parents, especially."

"She said she'd come."

"And I said I didn't eat Dickie's homemade lasagna last week. Yet there I was, shitting pasta sheets and eggplant in the communal bathroom two hours later."

I palmed my knees and pushed myself up, following Riggs's example.

"C'mon." He clapped my back. "There's something liberating about realizing you don't need them. The people who made you."

Maybe it had snowed and she'd gotten stuck somewhere without reception.

Maybe the preholiday traffic had made her late.

Maybe she was involved in a horrific car crash.

Whatever it was, one thing was for sure.

She didn't come.

◆ ◆ ◆

Arsène's mac 'n' cheese was atrocious. Lumpy and unevenly cooked, with balls of orange powder everywhere. His ramen made you wish you were drinking bleach instead, and I hadn't even known screwing up ramen was possible. Yet here we were, eating stale instant ramen swimming in what looked suspiciously like piss from Styrofoam cups. Riggs mixed whatever was in the flask with Tropicana, which gave it the diluted yet sharp taste of dish soap. This had to be the lowlight of my life. If God did exist, I was going to sue.

The three of us were sitting on Arsène's bed. It was a bunk. We sat on the bottom part, using his roommate Simon's top mattress to prop our legs.

"Love what you did with the place." Riggs motioned with his wooden chopsticks around the room. Arsène had an entire wall on which he'd graffitied a thousand times in neat, black, and bold handwriting:

I hate Gracelynn Langston. I hate Gracelynn Langston. I hate Gracelynn Langston. I hate Gracelynn Langston. I hate Gracelynn Langston. I hate Gracelynn Langston.

"Who's Gracelynn Langston?" I swallowed a lump of mac 'n' cheese without tasting it.

"Arsène's evil stepsister," Riggs supplied, slurping a noodle into his mouth. I was still trying to work the chopsticks. There were a ton of things rich kids knew how to do and I didn't. Using chopsticks was one of them.

Arsène flashed me a deadly look, his brown eyes scanning me head to toe. I could tell he wasn't sold on me. Riggs was a go-with-the-flow type of guy, but Arsène didn't seem hot on extending his social circle, which currently only included Riggs.

"You sure about this, dude?" Arsène asked Riggs. "We don't know anything about him."

"That's not true. We know he's dirt poor and is a good swimmer." Riggs laughed, but somehow, I couldn't be offended by anything this guy said. There was no malice in him, something I couldn't say about Arsène.

"What if he tells about the flask?" Arsène spoke directly to Riggs, ignoring my existence.

"Look at him. Does he look like he can hurt anyone? I wouldn't trust him to kill a cockroach. He won't tell about the flask." Riggs waved him off. "So. Arsène. How do you feel about Gracelynn Langston? And please don't hold back." Riggs chuckled into his Styrofoam cup of MSG and sewer water.

"I'd murder her if she was worth wasting a bullet on," Arsène ground out, his eyes hard on his food. "She's the reason I'm spending Christmas with you dickheads."

"Not this again." Riggs yawned. "Either fess up to what happened with her, or stop bitching about her."

"*You* were the one who asked." Arsène kicked Riggs in the shins. "Hey, can this guy even talk or what?"

"I can talk," I clipped out, stirring the noodles in my cup. I just didn't want to. There was nothing much to say, really.

"I'll amend—can you say anything interesting?" Arsène pinned me with a look.

"Cut him some slack. His mother stood him up," Riggs explained.

"Bummer." Arsène sucked his teeth. "So what's your story, morning glory?"

"How do you mean?" I scowled.

"How'd you end up in this prison for teenagers? No one came here willingly."

Forcing myself to look up from my food, I met his gaze. "Got caught copping a feel of a billionaire's daughter. This is my punishment. Haven't seen my mom in over a year. Don't know if I ever will again."

It was only when I said these words that I realized I genuinely didn't know if I'd ever see her. Arsène stroked his chin, considering this. He looked like he could murder someone for real. Whereas Riggs had that scruffy, cute look girls really liked.

"Whose fault was it?" Arsène asked. "The getting-caught part." He put his Styrofoam cup on the floor, grabbed mine, and did the same. He opened his nightstand drawer and took out vinegar chips and some popcorn. He popped both bags open, and I let out a relieved breath.

"Does it matter?" I asked.

"Does life matter?" Arsène deadpanned. "Of course it matters. Vengeance keeps a person going. If there's someone to blame, there's payback."

I thought about it.

"It was her fault, then." I helped myself to a handful of popcorn. "The more I think about it, the more it feels like a setup. Her dad walked in a second after I put my lips on hers."

"Definitely a setup." Riggs nodded, chewing his chips loudly, cross-legged. "Was she at least hot?"

"Um." I rubbed my chin, willing Arya to materialize in my imagination. I didn't need more than to think her name before I had a clear vision of her. Her swamp eyes and full mouth. "Yeah, I guess."

"Your guess is not good enough. Show us," Riggs demanded.

"How?"

"She must have social media."

"Bet she does, but I don't have a computer," I said. It was half the truth. I did have a computer, but the ancient type. One that I could barely use Word on. Even that was because Andrew Dexter Academy demanded we have computers.

Arsène took out a brand-new laptop from his leather backpack and handed it to me. "Here. Use my MyFriends. Just type in her name."

"You have a MyFriends?" I eyed him skeptically. All I knew about Arsène Corbin was that he was an evil genius who barely attended any classes and yet somehow ended up passing each year with honors. While Riggs spent his time trying to get himself killed by climbing trees, skipping between rooftops, and getting into brawls, Arsène was more the type to build DIY bombs and sell them online. Come to think about it, they were an odd pairing. They were probably so close only because they were forced together by loneliness.

"For research purposes."

"You mean stalking."

Arsène kicked my side with his socked foot. "I tolerated you better when you kept your mouth shut."

I typed Arya's name in the search bar, feeling my fingertips going clammy. I didn't even know why. I had thought about Arya often—mainly bad things—but it wasn't like I liked her anymore or anything.

Arya's smiling face popped into the feed, and I clicked on it.

"I can't believe her account is not private." Arsène's head almost knocked mine when he peeked into the screen. "Her parents must be dumb as bricks."

"Her mom is kind of MIA. She's always on some shopping trip. I think she hated Arya for not dying instead of her twin brother. And her dad is clueless about this shit." I began to scroll through her pictures.

As suspected, Arya was having a ball while I was away. In the last couple of months alone, she'd posted pictures of herself attending the winter ball at her school, ice-skating in Rockefeller, having a girls' night in with a friend called Jillian, and licking ice cream in the Bahamas. But the image my eyes kept getting stuck on was the last picture, posted only four hours ago. The location showed as Aspen, Colorado. Arya was standing on a mountain of snow, in full snowboarding gear, smiling to the camera, next to her father. The lava-hot anger that stirred in my stomach wasn't from the sight of both these assholes having the time of their lives while I was stuck here in an asylum for troubled kids. I was used to getting screwed over by now. It was the person behind them who made my pulse skyrocket. The woman who stood behind them. She was holding their ski poles, looking like she was about to topple over, catering to their every need, as always.

Mom.

"Nicholai?" Riggs waved a hand in front of my face. "How's that mental breakdown going?"

"It's her." I meant Mom, but they both blinked at the picture of Arya, their attention fully on the younger girl.

"No shit it's her. We have eyes. She's kind of hot, but not enough to get thrown into Andrew Dexter for." Riggs scrubbed his stubble with the back of his hand.

"Hotter than Gracelynn," Arsène spit out, like his stepsister was right here with us and could take offense. I got why he was mad. All these fuckers were off living their best lives, while the three of us were left behind, forgotten.

"No. I mean my mother. She went with the Roths on their Aspen vacation and didn't even tell me she changed her plans. There she is." I zoomed in on her.

It was a stupid thing to get mad about, everything considered, and still—what the fuck? Couldn't she call? Text? Write another stupid letter? She was not stuck in the snow or in traffic or suffering from a horrible accident. She was right there, in the flesh, choosing these people over me, time and time again.

It drove me nuts. How little I mattered to this woman.

I wondered if I'd ever stood a chance in the first place. If maybe she'd given up on me because I'd always reminded her of my no-show father. Or if I'd messed it up myself.

Arsène clapped my back. It was the first time he'd touched me. That anyone had touched me, really, since Conrad had beaten the daylights out of me. "Sounds like she's a piece of work. You don't need her. You don't need anyone."

"Everyone needs someone," Riggs pointed out. "Or so I read in the self-help books I steal from the library."

"Why do you steal them?" I asked.

Riggs threw his head back and laughed. "What else am I supposed to use to roll up my DIY joints?"

"I need people," I heard myself say. "I can't get through this alone."

This school. This life. This bitterness that cut through my skin every time I thought about Conrad and Arya.

"*Fine.* Then we'll be each other's someone." Arsène perked up, letting the popcorn bag he was holding fall to the mattress. "Fuck them. Fuck our families. Our parents. The people who have wronged us. Fuck Christmas dinners and decorated pine trees and scented candles and neatly wrapped gifts. We'll be each other's family from now on. The three of us. Every Christmas. Every Easter. Every Thanksgiving. We'll stick together, and we'll fucking win."

Riggs fist-bumped Arsène. Arsène raised his fist and offered it to me. I stared at it, feeling like I was on the cusp of something big. Monumental. Both Arsène and Riggs were glaring at me expectantly. I thought about that thing Arya had said all those years ago, in Mount Hebron Memorial, about how money wasn't everything in the world. Maybe she was right after all. These kids were rich, and they didn't seem happier than I was.

I raised my arm, my fist touching Arsène's.

"Attaboy." Riggs laughed. "Told you Nicholai was one of us."

And from that moment on, I was.

CHAPTER TWELVE

CHRISTIAN

Present

"Arya Roth must be good in bed, because she sure knows how to screw with a narrative." Claire ricocheted a newspaper onto my office desk Monday morning.

I was neck deep in going through the documents Amanda Gispen had sent me over the weekend. The discovery stage was crucial for an iron-clad case. I knew Conrad's lawyers were going to file a motion in limine to keep the EEOC's determination letter out of the case. I'd been so wrapped up in the material over the weekend that Claire and I had gone through the evidence instead of engaging in a screw-fest like we'd planned. The only thing I was in the mood for screwing was the Roth family, and hard.

I glanced at the newspaper's headline, frowning, while Claire parked a hip against my desk, hovering over me. In the photo in front of me, Conrad Roth was seen hugging kids at a hospital. Apparently, he'd gifted each of them a brand-new gaming console, from the variety most mortals couldn't get their hands on.

. . . Roth has donated 1,500 GameDrop consoles to the Don Hawkins Children's Hospital, along with a generous $2 million donation . . .

"This is bullshit." I rolled up the newspaper and slam-dunked it into the trash next to me. Claire pulled out her phone and swiped her finger across the screen.

"There are three more positive items about Conrad Roth running on various news sites today. The hashtag #NoRothDoing is trending on Twitter. Ex-colleagues are coming forward and talking about how nice and professional he is. Women of power. Arya Roth is working extra hard on Daddy's image."

Arya's name alone made me break out in hives. The woman didn't just manage to get under my skin; she dug her way into my gut and lit a bonfire there.

"#NoRothDoing is the stupidest hashtag I've ever heard, and unfortunately, I've heard many."

"I happen to agree, but it's working." Claire sighed. "What are we going to do?"

"Nothing." I shrugged. "I'll do my talking in the courtroom, in front of a jury that actually makes a difference. Internet trolls are not my target audience."

"Should we be more tactical about this? Maybe scare her a little?" Claire perched her ass on the edge of my desk, folding her arms. I rolled my executive chair back, putting some space between us. Claire was a gorgeous, ambitious, well-off twenty-seven-year-old. But she was starting to become a liability, wanting things like weekends away and for me to meet her parents. I'd laid out the rules when we'd started sleeping together, explaining I was so deep in the playboy zone I couldn't find my way out of it into a healthy relationship with a map, a flashlight, and GPS. She'd said she understood, and maybe she had, once upon a time, but things were getting complicated, which meant I was days away from breaking things off.

"You want me to start talking to B-grade journalists? Because prejudicing the defendant is third-grade tactics."

"I'm saying Arya Roth is undermining our case."

"No. She is sweating, and it smells. I'm not worried about her."

But Claire wasn't completely wrong. As I skimmed through one of the articles on her phone, I realized I should've taken into consideration that Arya was still cunning, resourceful, and—most maddening of all— talented at what she did. By the time the news about Conrad Roth's sexual harassment case had broken, Arya had found a hundred different ways to spin it. She used all the dirty tricks too. Amanda Gispen was recently divorced. Her ex-husband had been cheating on her, it was claimed. Arya had portrayed Amanda as a man-hater. Bitter about her divorce, her ex-husband, and the opposite sex in general. Amanda had recently fallen behind on her mortgage—obviously due to the divorce. Now tabloids were speculating she was going after her ex-employer to try to make a quick buck. Which couldn't be further from the truth, as Conrad had offered her more than enough to cover seven hundred mortgages to not take the case to court.

Arya was thorough and persistent, and she worked twenty-four seven.

Unfortunately for her, so did I.

"Claire's right." Traurig's low tenor came from the door. Claire stood up promptly, smoothing her pencil skirt. Traurig pushed off my doorframe, pretending like he didn't see her channeling her inner Sharon Stone in *Basic Instinct*. "Ms. Roth may pose an issue. You should keep an eye on her. Media coverage is everything. You should know that, kiddo. You won that case at the DA's office because you were the tabloid's darling."

My jaw ticced. More than Arya was undermining my case, Traurig was undermining my prestige by calling me *kiddo*. He wouldn't subject Claire to the same nickname, no. That would be viewed as sexist. But I was another alpha male whom he wanted to put in his place.

"It's under control."

"All I'm saying is you cannot afford to lose this case. There's a lot on the line." Traurig took on the role of Captain Obvious. He meant my chance of making partner.

"The line is mine to conquer. Sit back and enjoy a cocktail."

"That's what I like to hear, kiddo."

"And cut the *kiddo* crap."

He laughed, elbowing Claire on his way out. "Touchy. You take care of that one, will you?"

Traurig left my office. Claire loitered behind, playing with the wisps of her silky hair.

I arched a sardonic eyebrow. "Anything else?"

"Look." Claire cleared her throat. "This may be out of line . . ."

From experience, sentences that started like this *always* preceded something out of line. Already, my patience was thin, snappable, like crème brûlée.

"But I couldn't help but pick up on a weird vibe between you and Arya Roth. Now, obviously, knowing you, I'm aware you would never jeopardize a case or take it on if there is any . . ."

She trailed off, hoping I'd volunteer some information. I flashed her a lethal stare, daring her to finish the sentence. She squirmed. "*Funny business.* I'm just wondering if you'd like me to take on more responsibility in the case where she is concerned. If she makes you feel uncomfortable in any way, maybe I could liaise with her directly so you don't have to deal with her personally, or . . ."

"That won't be necessary."

"Oh." She faltered. "May I ask why not?"

Because I'm rabid with revenge and want a front-row seat when Arya finally gets what she deserves.

"Because I can handle a community-college-degreed aging teeny-bopper who has a few contacts at some local newspapers just fine."

The way I'd managed to reduce Arya to nothing more than a glorified Bratz doll surprised even me. Although I doubted I was on point about most of those things. Her issue had never been a lack of IQ points but lack of a soul.

"Point made." Claire nodded with dignity. "You know, you look different this morning. More . . . *alive*."

I swallowed but didn't reply. What could I say? That seeing Arya again gave me a hard-on from hell?

Claire swaggered her way to the door, then stopped on the threshold and knocked on the doorframe. "Just let me know if you need anything, Christian."

How about Arya, spread eagle on my desk, panting my name—the old and the new one—begging me for mercy?

Well, now. I really needed to break things off with Claire if I'd started answering her that way. Even if it was just in my head.

"Absolutely."

The minute Claire left my office, I plucked the newspaper back from the trash and began highlighting potential holes in Arya's carefully constructed narrative.

She was about to find out I did not take any prisoners when I went to war.

"This is the worst thing that's ever happened to me, and I just got back from a war zone." Riggs took a pull of his beer, his hooded eyes scanning the room like a hawk.

"It's trivia night, not the plague." Arsène knocked back his beer. We were at the Brewtherhood. I propped my elbows against the bar, watching groups of people huddling together around tables, getting ready for the main event. A stool was placed on the small podium usually reserved for college girls who danced half-naked. The host of the trivia night was some New Jersey–based reality star who was apparently semifamous for having sex with one of his fellow contestants in a public pool. This was the reason why I'd sworn off TV and the people on it.

The line between culture and a steaming bag of shit blurred when it came to twenty-first-century entertainment.

"Bars were invented to get drunk and laid, not educated." Riggs tilted his empty beer in Elise's direction, motioning for her to get us another round. "I need a vacation."

"You *live* to vacation," I amended. "Settle the fuck down for a minute."

"Never," Riggs vowed. I believed him. The nomad turned to me, frowning. "Speaking of holiday destinations, how does Alice like her new Florida condo?"

Alice was the most important woman in my life. In all our lives, to be honest. But I was considered to be the "good" kid. The one who gave a shit and sent flowers for birthdays and Christmas cards whenever I wasn't able to make it.

"She's crazy about it. Between all the senior field trips and tai chi classes, she's zen as shit," I confirmed. "I talked to her a couple days ago."

"We should visit her," Riggs said.

"If anyone is able to drag me out of New York City, it's her," Arsène agreed.

"I'll talk dates with her." I nodded curtly, though I knew there was no way in hell I was leaving before winning the Conrad Roth case.

"Hey, we should do the trivia bullshit." Arsène turned his back to a woman who was gingerly approaching him on high heels. God forbid he had a conversation with someone who wasn't in the MacArthur Fellowship Program. "My head is full of useless pieces of information, and I enjoy winning."

"Even if what you win is a two-night vacation in a three-star hotel in Tacoma?" I took a swig of my whiskey. "Because that's the shit you'll be winning here."

"*Especially.*" Arsène accepted his fresh beer from Elise, slipping her a tip without making eye contact. The man hated women with such a passion I suspected he'd be one of those people who died alone and left all their millions to the neighbor's dog or someone random on the other side of the world. "Helps me see how the other half lives."

"You don't give a crap how the other half lives."

Arsène clinked his beer bottle with mine. "Said other half doesn't need to know that."

"I take everything I said about trivia night back. Apparently, it has its merits." Riggs's gaze cut to the entrance. I followed his line of sight, biting down on my tongue until the metallic taste of blood spread in my mouth.

You have to be kidding me. What are the goddamn odds?

It had been three weeks since I'd met Arya in my office. Three whole weeks in which I'd regrouped, gotten myself together, and managed to forget about her annoying mouth and delectable body. Now here she was, waltzing into my home field, wearing a little black number with a pearl choker and killer red Balenciaga heels. There were three more women with her, all wearing beauty-pageant-type sashes that said *The Sherlock Holmesgirls*. Apparently, she wasn't only cold and mean; she was also lame.

"Pick your jaw off the floor, buddy, before someone steps on it." Riggs clapped my shoulder in my periphery, chuckling. "All right, I see you're eyeing little Audrey Hepburn over there. Luckily for you, I'm not picky. I'll take Blondie."

"How about you take a hike." I brushed his touch away. "I'm out of here."

"Long day at the office?" Riggs flashed a grin full of dimples and stubble. No wonder he melted panties and hearts solely by existing. "Let me guess, oatmeal and a Dan Brown book for dinner?"

Maturity-wise, my best friend was no older than the carton of milk in my fridge, and not half as sophisticated.

"This woman is the daughter of a defendant in a case I'm working on, dum-dum."

"So?" Arsène furrowed his brows. "It's trivia night, not a public orgy."

"Can't put it past Riggs not to make it one." I slid into my peacoat. The last thing I needed was to ogle Arya Roth. Impulse control was my favorite form of art. I always reined in my needs. I hadn't googled or checked on her since I was fifteen. Ignored her existence thoroughly since freshman year. To me, she was as good as dead. Seeing her all pretty and happy and *alive* wasn't on my agenda. Not if I could help it. "Stay out of trouble, and make sure this guy puts a rubber on it." I clapped Arsène's back, about to head out.

"Thanks, Dad. Oh, and by the way." Riggs blocked my way with his body. He glanced at something behind my back. "Audrey Hepburn is coming our way, and unlike you, she seems mighty happy to see you."

"Of course." Arsène's eyes flickered behind me curiously, a grin spreading across his face. *"Arya Roth."*

I stuffed my pocket with my wallet and phone, my jaw hardening. "She's a bombshell." Riggs whistled.

"She sure detonated my life," I ground out. "I'm out of here."

I turned around, colliding with someone small. That someone, of course, was Arya. I almost knocked her down on her ass. She stumbled a few steps back, and one of her friends, presumably the one Riggs wanted to make the latest notch on his belt, caught her.

"Fancy bumping into you. *Literally.*" Arya recovered, her sharp smile intact. Was she following me? Because that was illegal, on top of being unethical. I eyed her with open disdain.

Impulse control. You're Christian, not Little Nicky. She can't hurt you. "Ms. Roth."

"Leaving already?"

"I see nothing escapes you," I drawled flatly.

"Apparently, *you* escape me. Is trivia not your strong suit, Mr. Miller?"

Smirking, I tilted my head down to whisper in her ear. *"Everything* is my strong suit, Ms. Roth. You'd be wise to remember that."

Straightening, I noticed there was a flicker of something in her face. Recognition? Confusion? Did she remember me? Whatever it was, it vanished, replaced by a frosty smile.

"Actually, your media management could use a few tweaks. I happen to be here with my business partner, Jillian, and our dream team, Hailey and Whitley. Give us a call after our case is over. We'll give you some pointers." Arya produced a black business card with rose-gold cursive lettering, shoving it into my hand. I caught the words *Brand Brigade*. Well, well. She had her own company. Then again, she also had a daddy who'd buy her a spaceship if she wanted to play astronaut.

"Thank you, Ms. Roth, but I'd rather get advice from the street person on the corner of Broadway and Canal, who shouts into a megaphone that aliens kidnapped him and he is now immortal." I flicked her card straight to the trash can behind the bar.

"Good idea, Mr. Miller. He still understands more than you do about media management."

Her smile didn't waver, but I could tell by the glint in her eyes she wasn't used to men looking at her like she was less than solid gold.

"You're still here," I sighed, when she made no move to stop blocking my way. "Please enlighten me as to why."

"Did you see they assigned Judge Lopez to the lawsuit?" Arya's eyelashes fluttered.

"I'm not discussing the case with you."

I sidestepped her. At the last minute, she slipped her hand out to touch my bicep. The touch shot an arrow of heat straight to my groin. My body always had a way of betraying me where she was concerned.

"*Stay,*" she demanded, just as the reality TV dropout announced into the microphone that all groups needed to be registered and take a seat before the game began. "Let's see what you're worth."

I stuffed my fists into my front pockets. "Whatever I'm worth, you can't afford it."

"Good. Show me what I'm missing."

"I doubt you'll be graceful in defeat."

"I'm a pretty honorable person," she argued.

I snorted. "Sweetheart, you and the word *honor* shouldn't even be in the same zip code, let alone sentence."

Arya turned around and walked away, her minions wobbling behind on stiletto heels.

"Riggs, sign us up, we're staying," I barked out. My eyes were still on Arya. Riggs moved toward the stage. I was sure whatever name he chose for our team was both offensive and at least a little sexually demeaning to women.

Reality TV Douche, who identified himself as Dr. Italian Stud (credentials unconfirmed), announced there were eight teams, including the S Team D, as Riggs had dubbed us.

Leave it to Riggs to associate me with genital herpes in front of someone I was supposed to see in court next week.

"I'd call you an idiot, but then idiots all over the world would take offense." I turned to Riggs, resisting the urge to bash his head against the colonial table. I tried not to look at Arya, but it was hard. She was right there. Beautiful, shiny, and destructive. Like a human red button.

By the time the first few rounds were up, only four teams were left. There were Team Quizzitch, a group of tech bros in round reading glasses and trendy haircuts; Girl Squad, a bunch of college girls; the Sherlock Holmesgirls—that was Arya's team—and Arsène, Riggs, and I.

The warm-up questions for the second round required the IQ of a beer sleeve. From naming the capital of the US to how many points a snowflake traditionally had. Despite the questions barely requiring two functioning brain cells, Girl Squad got kicked out next for not knowing which country *The Sound of Music* took place in, confusing Austria with Australia.

"Reminds me of that time you told a chick you had a BA in astronomy and she told you she was a Taurus and asked if it's really true that they're perfectionists," Riggs ribbed Arsène, cackling.

Begrudgingly, and only to myself, I had to admit the Sherlock Holmesgirls were good. Arya and Jillian especially. Unfortunately for them, between Arsène and myself, they stood no chance. During holidays, when Arya had been working on her tan in Maui or skiing in Saint Moritz, Arsène would drag Riggs and me to the library at the academy, and we would read entire encyclopedias to burn time.

Forty minutes after the evening had begun, Team Quizzitch fell apart for getting the month Russians celebrated the October Revolution wrong (the answer was November), leaving us and the Sherlock Holmesgirls to go head-to-head.

"Things are heating up over here." Dr. Italian Stud rubbed his palms together excitedly, speaking too close to the microphone onstage. He had enough hair wax to sculpt a life-size statue of LeBron James and teeth as big and white as piano keys. It didn't help that he had the whole ripped-jeans-and-tacky-branded-designer-shirt look going on, his top clinging to a body that had seen more steroids than an ICU unit. I was still surprised he was literate enough to read the questions. "Holmesgirls, who do you think is going to win?" He turned to Arya, who sat all the way across the room.

She tucked flyaways of her chestnut hair behind her ears, and again, I found myself ogling. "We'll win, no question about it."

"What about you guys?" Dr. Stud forced himself to rip his gaze from Arya. Arsène shot him a pitying look.

"I'm not even going to grace that with an answer."

By the look on Dr. Italian Stud's face, I could tell his heart was firmly with the Holmesgirls, and so were other parts.

"All right, someone here is competitive. We're entering the final round. Remember—one strike and you're out. This is the money time. Or to be exact, the Denny's voucher time! One hundred bucks, y'all!"

"I can hardly contain my excitement." Arsène took a pull of his beer, his voice paper dry.

"What's Joe Biden's middle name? Holmesgirls, this goes to you and will pass to the STDs if you can't answer the question."

The women huddled with their heads touching, whispering, before Arya straightened her spine and said, "Robinette. Final answer."

"You're correct. *Huh*. Didn't know that." Dr. Italian Stud scratched his stiff hair. I doubted he knew what continent he was on, so that didn't surprise me. He turned to us. The room was still crowded, brimming with people who wanted to see which group was going to hit the jackpot.

"Next question goes to the STDs—how fast does the earth spin?"

"One thousand miles per hour." Arsène yawned.

"Holmesgirls—what did the Romans use as mouthwash?"

"Urine!" Jillian called out, practically leaping from her seat, the cocktails on her table sloshing over. "They used urine. Which is super kinky, but who are we to judge?"

"Correct! STDs, what was the ice cream cone invented for?"

"Holding flowers," I said without missing a beat.

Dr. Stud whistled. "Dang, I'm finding out all kinds of interesting things tonight! It almost makes me want to open a book." He turned toward our rival team. "Okay, Holmesgirls—what can't a cheetah do that a tiger and a puma can?"

Arya opened her mouth instinctively to answer, but the words didn't come out. She frowned, taken aback by the idea of not knowing something.

"Cat got your tongue?" I arched a brow, scanning her in amusement.

She turned to Jillian. They whispered back and forth. I sat back, folding my arms over my chest. Arya Roth out of sorts was my favorite view in the world. More than the sunrise, probably.

"I'm guessing you'll want to take that one when they pass it to us." Arsène was selling stock on an app on his phone as he spoke.

"Hey!" Dr. Italian Stud shrieked. "You're not supposed to use your phone! You're cheating."

"You're not supposed to be hosting a knowledge-based game. You're a dumbass," Arsène retorted, not taking his eyes off his screen. "Yet here we are."

But Riggs snatched the phone from our friend, tilting it toward Dr. Italian Stud so he knew Arsène was selling stock, not googling anything.

Arya scratched her cheek, and my dick twitched in my slacks. I would never touch her again with a ten-foot pole—I'd learned from my first and last mistake with her—but it was tempting to make her scream my new name and deny her an orgasm or two.

"Holmesgirls?" Dr. Italian Stud probed, checking the time on his phone. "The clock's ticking. Ten more seconds before I pass it to STDs."

"One moment," Arya snapped, turning her gaze back to Jillian and the other women. For a second, I saw the old Arya. The scraped-kneed girl who would growl in protest when we did laps in her pool and I'd start a nanosecond before her. She would splash me, then proceed to talk me into a dozen more competitions—who could hold their breath underwater the longest, who could cannonball farther into the pool— until she won *something*. We were both fiercely stubborn. That hadn't changed. What had changed was my willingness to pacify her. To give up something just for the pleasure of seeing her smile.

Arya's ears turned a nice shade of scarlet. Our eyes met. Something passed between us. A faint recognition.

"Four . . . three . . . two . . ." Dr. Italian Stud counted back the seconds.

"Swim!" Arya cried out. The word stabbed me in the gut. I'd *just* been thinking about our pool time together. "Maybe a cheetah can't swim? And a tiger and a puma can?"

"Your answer is incorrect." Dr. Stud made an exaggerated sad face, shifting toward us in his seat. "I'm passing this to the STDs. If you get this answer right, you win."

I turned to look at Arya, staring at her dead in the eye, her humiliation radiating from her body in waves. "Retract their claws."

"Excuse me?" Her eyes narrowed.

"The one thing cheetahs can't do that pumas and tigers can is retract their claws. Not all felines were born equal."

"Correct!" Dr. Italian Stud cried out. "S Team D, you are the winners!"

"No!" Arya stood up, stomping her foot. It was ridiculous, bratty, and—underneath all of this—stupid adorable.

Because it proved she was still the same spoiled little princess I loved to hate.

There was a flurry of excitement. Dr. Stud even shot a confetti gun and called us up to the stage to receive our prize and an unnecessary bro hug. Arsène threw a wad of cash at Elise and retreated into the night without as much as a goodbye, done with the human race for one evening. Riggs moved to a corner of the bar, being pawed by the Girl Squad chicks, who cooed over him. Arya thundered into the restroom, her cheeks flushed, probably to cry into the sink.

A wiser man wouldn't follow her. Yet here I was, making my way to the unisex restroom. Since going inside with her was deranged, I opted for loitering around and answering emails on my phone until she got out. Still creepy, but not restraining-order worthy. When she stepped out, her face was wet, her shoulders slumped. She stopped midstep when she saw me.

"Are you following me?" she demanded.

"Funny, I was about to ask you the very same thing. This is my hangout spot. There are over twenty-five thousand nightlife establishments citywide. What are the odds of you showing up here for the first time in my life right after news of the trial broke?"

"Pretty good, considering we probably live in the same neighborhood, went to the same schools, and travel in the same social circles."

"Got me all figured out?" I stroked my jawline, my eyes skimming her face.

She tilted her chin up. "More or less. Although I will say, you're a hard man to track, Mr. Miller. Not a whole lot of info available about you on the net."

My lips twitched. She had bought into my high-flying-millionaire charade. Probably thought we were a part of the same yacht club.

"How far did you get in your research?" I braced an arm over her head, trapping her between me and the restroom wall. She smelled like Arya. Of peachy shampoo mixed with the sweetness of her skin. Of long, lazy summers and spontaneous pool swims and ancient books. Like my impending downfall.

Her eyes met mine. "You finished Harvard Law School. Got pulled straight into the DA's office. Traurig and Cromwell recruited you after you nailed a huge case even though you were the small fry. Lured you to the white-shoe dark side. Now you're known as the shark who gets his clients fat settlements."

"Where's the mystery, then?" I leaned forward an inch, breathing more of her. "Sounds like I'm an open book. Need my Social Security number and full medical history to complete the picture?"

"Were you born eighteen?" She cocked her head sideways.

"Fortunately for my mother, no."

"There's no information about you prior to your time in Harvard."

A bitter laugh escaped my throat. "My accomplishments before eighteen include winning beer pong games and getting lucky in the bed of my truck."

She eyed me skeptically, her delicate brows furrowing. I spoke before she could ask more questions.

"I'll give you one thing: you make that bag of trash who sired you look like a real angel in the media."

"That's an easy task. He is innocent." Her lips were inches from mine, but I was in complete control of the situation.

"That's not for you to decide. If you continue tampering with the narrative before the trial, I'll be inclined to move for a gag order on the case. The temptation of shutting your mouth up is already too much."

"Are outspoken women an inconvenience to you?" she purred, her eyes sparkling. It felt so much like our banter from a decade and a half ago that I almost laughed.

"No, but whiny little girls are."

That made her pull away. She twisted her mouth in annoyance. "Did you come here for anything other than to rub your small, insignificant win in my face?"

Would you rather I rubbed something else in it?

"Yes, actually." I pushed off the wall, giving her—and myself—some space. "First things first—the Brewtherhood is my domain. My territory. Find a girly cocktail bar that hosts trivia nights. Better yet—read a book or two before you try it next time. Your general knowledge could use a few *tweaks*." I used the word she'd used for my media-management skills.

She opened her mouth, no doubt to tell me to go shove my self-importance up my rear in five different languages, but I proceeded before she could cut into my words.

"Second—I think I deserve one piece of information in return for this." I produced the Denny's voucher Dr. Douchebag had handed me earlier tonight. Her eyes zinged with exhilaration. I knew she didn't care for the actual voucher. Only about what it represented. About going home with the prize. This was classic Arya. She would catch my foot when we did laps at the pool, playing dirty sometimes. Anything to win.

"You want a piece of information?" she asked. "You're insufferable. How's that for a fun fact? Now hand that over. My employees deserve free Denny's meals."

She reached to grab the voucher. I raised my hand higher, chuckling. "Sorry, I should've specified. *I* get to ask the question."

She tossed her arms in the air, unused to being challenged. "Shoot."

"How shall I address you—Miss or Mrs.?"

I'd made it a point not to check Arya's marital status, but that didn't mean I wasn't curious. There was no ring on her finger. Then again, she didn't strike me as the type of woman who'd flaunt a statement ring.

Her mouth curled up in a smile. "You are interested." Her eyes flared.

"You are delusional." I suppressed the urge to brush away one of her flyaway hairs with my thumb. "I like to know things. Knowledge is power."

She licked her lips, peering at the voucher I held between my fingers. Willy Wonka's golden ticket. I could see her resolve crumbling. She wanted to keep the mystery alive but wanted to win even more.

"I'm single."

"Color me surprised." I handed her the ticket. She snatched it, like I was going to change my mind any second, stuffing it into her purse.

"I'm guessing you're with the pretty associate."

"Now why would you guess that?" I was surprised. I ignored Claire completely during work hours, unless it was related to a case we were working on.

Arya shrugged. "Call it a hunch."

"I can also call it jealousy."

She smiled easily. "Tweak the narrative as you please to help your fragile ego, honey. It's a free country." She turned around, ready to leave.

"You have good instincts, silver-spooned princess."

Her head spun so fast I thought it was going to dislocate from her shoulder. "*What* did you just call me?"

Well, shit. It had just spilled out of my mouth. Like it hadn't been almost two decades. Like we were still the same kids.

"Princess," I said.

"No. You said *silver-spooned princess*." Her eyes narrowed into slits.

"Nope," I lied. "But that's not a bad nickname."

"Your gaslighting game is weak. I know what I heard."

"Well, seeing as you don't have any way to prove it, and I'm not budging, I would strongly suggest you let it drop. I called you a princess. Nothing more."

She considered it for a full minute before nodding curtly. "See you at the pretrial hearing next week." She saluted, not waiting for me to confirm or deny my relationship with Claire.

Of course. Next week. I had to wait seven days until I'd see her again.

Which is dandy. You hate her, remember?

"Can hardly wait."

She walked away, her stilettos rapping over the sticky wooden floor. Typical. She always left dents wherever she went.

"Oh, and Ms. Roth?"

She stopped and turned around, arching a brow. I ran my tongue over my teeth.

"Nice *claws*."

◆ ◆ ◆

That night, I allowed myself one slipup.

Okay, fine, two slipups.

First—I googled Arya. She was the director and founder of Brand Brigade, along with Jillian Bazin. Had gone to Columbia University cum laude, participated as a consultant in several political campaigns, and frequented charity events with Daddy dearest. Suppose they were two peas in a messed-up pod, running over everyone on their way to their next target. There were a few photos of her too. Of the stunning woman who'd made me swear off green-eyed brunettes for life.

The second slipup happened in the shower, while I pressed my forehead against the tiles, closing my eyes and letting the hot needles of water wash the day away. Looking down, I found myself hard as a stone. My cock was engorged, begging for release.

Impulse control. Remember you hate her.

But what my brain knew very well, my idiot body refused to accept. Every time I thought about Arya in that black dress and those pearls, my cock tapped against my abs to draw attention. *Excuse me, sir, but*

I'd like to be relieved. I could call Claire and have her take care of the problem, but Claire wouldn't do.

This was when I started making excuses for my cock, which was never a good place to be in.

As with everything, I presented myself with astute arguments.

1.   What is one jerk-off, in the grand scheme of life?
I still loathed Arya Roth. I was still going to take her and her father down, ruin her perfectly constructed universe. The plan hadn't changed.

2.   Better get it out of my system now than with her.
I couldn't have her. She was off limits. Caving in to temptation in the shower was far better than yielding to it in the Mandarin, going through an entire box of condoms while screwing my entire lawsuit in the process.

3.   She'd never know.
My favorite out of the three.

Arya would never guess the man she'd seen today was the kid who'd kissed her with trembling lips. Who used to count up the days each September until next summer break. Who would sneak into Duane Reade to sniff the shampoo she used when missing her had become too much.

I grabbed my dick, my palm moving up and down. I closed my eyes, squeezing it harder, imagining my fingers running up her thighs, flipping her dress up, pressing her against my office desk, flattening her back over a pile of documents and my laptop . . .

A low snarl ripped from my mouth. I didn't even get to the part where I was inside her before my hand was coated with warm, sticky release.

I staggered backward, turning off the faucet and pushing the glass door open. I wrapped a towel around my waist and walked over to the mirror, leaning against the vanity, scowling at myself.

You fool. I shook my head. *She's already dug her way deep inside your veins.*

CHAPTER THIRTEEN

ARYA

Present

There was a medical term for what I was being right now.

Pathetic.

Okay, maybe it wasn't medical, but it sure as hell was the current situation I was dealing with.

Though I didn't appear that way, sitting next to Dad at the pretrial hearing. I looked presentable in a gray wool dress and high heels, my hair pinned into a french twist. But I felt like a fool, my heart twirling in my chest, because I knew *he* would be here.

Silver-spooned princess.

I was starting to imagine things now too.

It was bad enough Christian had been at the Brewtherhood the other day. What were the chances that the place Jilly and I had wanted to try for so long was his hole-in-the-wall? Now I had to watch as he destroyed the only real family I had left.

I squeezed Dad's damp hand. He'd aged a decade in a month. Ever since news about the lawsuit had broken, he'd been hardly sleeping or eating. Last week, I'd taken him to a psychiatrist. She'd prescribed him

Ambien and another pill that was supposed to raise his serotonin levels. So far neither had helped.

"Hey. Don't worry. Terrance and Louie are the best in the business." I brushed the back of his hand. He turned to look at me, red eyed.

"The *second* best in the business. Amanda hiring Miller makes no sense. I heard he's not even accepting new clients."

"He saw a huge case and took it." I scanned the room. I'd never been in a courtroom before, so I had nothing to compare this one to, but the Daniel Patrick Moynihan Courthouse struck me as swanky. Downright theatrical, even. Red velvet curtains with gold tassels; never-ending, spiraling marble stairways; mahogany stands; and church-like pews that would be filled to the brim with journalists, photographers, and courthouse staff as soon as the actual trial began. For now, it was just the judge, the defendant, the plaintiff, and their teams.

I felt Christian Miller before I saw him. The back of my neck prickled with a hot sensation, and my whole body came alive, tingly everywhere. My hand quivered inside Dad's. Guilt washed over me.

"I haven't done anything wrong. Maybe a joke here and there—nothing sexual." Dad stared down at our entwined hands. "With Amanda. It's wrong to make an example out of me. I want this to be over, Arya."

"It will be, soon."

"Thank God I have you, sweetheart. Your mother is—"

"Useless?" I cut into his words. "I know."

Christian, Amanda, and Claire appeared in my periphery. I didn't dare look at him, but I saw the way he carried himself: sharklike, wry, and unruffled. His hair was freshly cut, his dark suit pressed, his tie a shade darker than his blue eyes. He sucked the attention out of everything else in the room.

Judge Lopez's eyes lit when he saw Christian. It was obvious they knew each other.

"Saw you on the golf course this weekend, Counselor. Did Jack Nicklaus give you private lessons?"

"Your Honor, not to be humble, but I played against Traurig. You'll see better swings at a school's playground."

I could tell Dad, Louie, and Terrance didn't like that Christian was chummy with the judge by the way they shifted in their seats, scribbled notes on their legal pads, and sweated buckets. Dad released my hand from his and massaged his temples. I swiveled to look at him. "Everything okay?"

He nodded but didn't answer.

A few minutes later, when Louie and Christian moved to talking about voir dire and juror selection, it was obvious Christian had come more prepared and ready. Claire shot him adoring looks, and a pang of jealousy sliced through me. It was perfectly obvious they were sleeping together and that she was in love with him.

It was also perfectly obvious I needed to stop drooling over the lawyer who wanted to destroy my father.

The rest of the hearing was a blur. The two parties discussed dates and how long the trial was expected to last—four to six weeks. I spent the time mainly studying Christian, wondering why on earth he seemed familiar.

"See something you like?" Dad's voice broke me out of my daydream.

I straightened in my seat, clearing my throat. "Would like to push off a cliff, more like."

It wasn't anything about his looks. I'd never met a man so beautiful. Rather, there was something about his eyes. The way he cracked his knuckles when he spoke and that boyish, bashful grin he let loose when he thought no one was looking and was writing down notes for himself.

When all was done and dealt with for the day, Christian, Amanda, and Claire dashed out first. Dad, Louie, and Terrance loitered behind. Dad's mouth was pressed in a thin line. I produced a bottle of water, handing it to him. "This means nothing. So Judge Lopez knows Miller. It was expected. He's a litigator, after all."

"Put a lid on it, Arya. This wouldn't have happened if it wasn't for you." Dad brushed my shoulder as he advanced toward the door, Louie and Terrance at his heel. I followed him, frowning. Insert record scratch.

What in the hell?

"Excuse me?"

This was the first time my father had ever been anything other than adoring to me, and the sting of his words caught me off balance.

"This whole charade is a long middle finger in our direction. A way to prove a point. To take us Roths down."

"Well, okay, but how does it have anything to do with me?" We glided through the halls of the courthouse, toward the exit. He stopped, turning to face me.

"You aggravated Mr. Miller every step of the way during mediation. You were *begging* for a reaction. And you indeed got it in the form of my having to stand trial for this."

"You blame *me?*" I stubbed my finger into my chest.

"You're obviously fascinated with him."

"Because I answered him back?" I felt my eyebrows hitting my hairline in surprise.

"Because you've always had a taste for troublemakers, and I've always been the one who needed to clean up after you."

Oh. *Oh.* This was richer than his bank account. I reared my head back to avoid the flecks of saliva flying from his mouth. I hadn't been myself that day at Christian's office, no doubt, but Christian had come in cocked and loaded to go to trial, and that had nothing to do with my behavior.

"First of all, I'm glad you rewrote history in the years when I worked my way through forgiving you for what happened. Second, I'm going to go ahead and chalk this conversation up to the fact that you haven't slept in three weeks and live solely on coffee and prescription pills." I took out a napkin from my bag and handed it to him. He grabbed it, dabbing at the saliva coating his lower lip.

We got out of the courthouse and slipped straight into his waiting Escalade.

"Where am I dropping you off, Ari?" Dad's driver, Jose, called from the driver's seat, while Louie and Terrance gave Dad the bottom line of what had happened today in hushed voices.

I gave Jose my work address and turned my attention back to Dad. "Christian Miller has a bone to pick with you. Nothing could've changed his mind."

"Why?" Dad cut both Louie and Terrance off, his eyes nailing me to the window. "Why am I his hill to die on? He sees cases far worse than mine on a daily basis. All I did was give Amanda a few pats and sniff around for an affair," he spit out.

"You gave her a few pats?" I was dizzy with anger.

He added with an eye roll, "*Allegedly.* For Chrissakes, Arya. Allegedly."

"Adding the word *allegedly* doesn't make you innocent," I pointed out. "*Are* you innocent?"

"Of course I am!" He threw his arms in the air. "Even if there were a few gray lines, a consensual affair is not akin to sexual harassment. It's not like your mother ever gave me the time of day."

"You keep contradicting yourself." Even as I said it, though, I knew I wasn't going to dig into the family's skeleton closet for fear I'd be buried in bones. "Have you or have you not had an affair with Amanda Gispen? Did you or did you not touch her inappropriately?"

"I haven't done anything wrong," Dad snapped.

"We're going in circles," I mumbled, closing my eyes.

"Feel free to get off at any time."

I tried to take his words at face value. But Dad did have a point.

Christian Miller wanted to rip my family apart, and I was beginning to worry he had a good reason to want to do it.

After Jose dropped me off at work, Jillian and I got into a meeting with a potential new client. I screwed it six ways to Sunday. Jillian very nearly kicked me out of there—through the window—and I couldn't even blame her. The CEO of Bi's Kneads, a bakery chain that was becoming a publicly traded company, left our office underwhelmed after I stuttered my way through the presentation. It was obvious we weren't getting the contract.

"I'm so sorry," I told Jillian as we got out of the conference room, standing in our open-plan, exposed-brick office. "I should've come more prepared. I went over our presentation this morning, but my brain turned to mush after the hearing."

Jillian waved her hand, tired and annoyed. "It's fine. You had a really long day. How was Mr. Prick?"

"Still a prick."

"Did you try and murder him today?"

"Only telepathically."

"Proud of you." She sighed, giving me a sympathetic look. "And your dad?"

"Acting like a teenager and making very little sense."

"He's under a lot of stress," she pointed out.

I proceeded to my desk and powered up my laptop. I laced my fingers together and stretched before typing Christian's name into the search engine. I'd done it before, when I'd first realized he would represent Amanda. But this time, I didn't get into his LinkedIn page or his professional profile at his firm. I went straight to his social media. There wasn't much there. Just one forgotten Facebook page that looked like it hadn't been updated since the Stone Age. I double-clicked on a picture of a younger version of Christian, smiling to the camera with the two men who'd been with him during trivia night.

I scrolled through his profile, but there was nothing other than people congratulating him on several promotions and tagging him in company pictures. The only person who seemed to be liking most of his pictures consistently was a woman named Alice, but she had no profile photo. An ex? An admirer? I was sure Claire wasn't happy about Alice's existence.

The last thing he'd been tagged in was a post from seven months ago by a guy named Julius Longoria. There wasn't a picture, just a check-in at a glitzy gym downtown. The post read: *Here to sweat!*

Drumming my fingers on my desk, I contemplated my next move. Going to his gym was crazy. Then again, I'd never claimed to be within the lines of sanity. He'd thought I was a stalker before, when we'd bumped into each other randomly at the Brewtherhood. This would pretty much confirm all his *Fatal Attraction* theories about me, and then some.

On the other hand, there was something about Christian Miller that didn't sit right with me. I couldn't put my finger on it, but something felt . . . *off*. It was worth looking into, seeing as he held Dad's future in his hands. Besides, what if I found Christian hitting on a cute trainer or doing something sleazy himself?

Then there was Claire. I suspected he was sleeping with her too. Wasn't there a no-fraternization policy for people who worked in the same chain of command? This was worth looking into.

Any leverage I could get on him would work in my favor at this stage, and all was fair in love and war.

"I know that look on your face." Jillian tsked across the room, typing something on her laptop. "Whatever you are up to, Ari, drop it. It's got disaster written all over it."

But the seed had been planted.

Christian Miller was going to get another surprise visit.

◆ ◆ ◆

Solstices was a three-floor gym on Columbus Avenue, fitted with a spa, indoor pool, hair salon, and wax parlor. Basically, you could walk in there looking like the cover of the *Enquirer* and come out looking like the cover of *Sports Illustrated*.

I signed up for a trial month and paid an obscene amount of money for the pleasure.

Contrary to popular belief, I'd done a lot of penny counting along the years. Came with the territory of becoming financially independent at age eighteen (excluding college tuition, which my parents had paid for). I enjoyed fancy brands and shopped for them at discounted second- and thirdhand stores, but I didn't enjoy splashing money unnecessarily.

I arrived at Solstices both in the morning and in the evening to try and catch Christian, hitting the treadmills and keeping an eye out for him. By the third day, I figured I might as well get a real workout while I was doing my detective work and brought my bikini and a swim cap.

Since swimming was the only workout I could actually tolerate, I hit the indoor pool. It brought memories from when I was younger, with Nicky.

The first two laps were excruciating. My lungs burned, and I swallowed some water. By the third lap, I got into the rhythm of things. On my tenth lap, I broke the water when I reached the edge of the pool, taking a greedy breath, letting waterdrops slip into my mouth. I was delirious with exhaustion.

"Look what the cat dragged in."

My head snapped up, and I was met with Christian Miller in the flesh. He was wearing swim trunks, his Adonis six-pack on full display. The dusting of hair on his chest glistened. That was how I knew he'd been swimming right beside me this whole time when I hadn't been paying attention.

"Am I not allowed to attend the gym either?" I propped one arm over the edge of the pool, ripping the swim cap from my head with a satisfying thwap. "Why don't you just email me a list of places I can and cannot go to in the city?"

Christian readjusted the waistband of his trunks. His V cut gave Joe Manganiello a run for his money. "That's actually not a bad idea. I'll get my secretary on that."

"Let's see how that works out for you." I braced myself on the edge, pulled out of the water, and sauntered to the bench where I'd left my towel and flip-flops. Christian followed me, sneaking a peek at my legs as I wrapped the towel around myself.

"Are you saying you haven't come here because of me?" He folded his arms over his chest.

I let out a snort, like the idea itself was preposterous. "Believe it or not, Mr. Miller, the world doesn't revolve around you."

He watched me pat myself dry. "Do you swim often?"

Huh. No verbal sparring. Maybe he'd come down with something.

"Just started again. You?"

"Every day since I was twelve."

I could tell. He had the sinewy, long, and lean body of a swimmer. His muscles were defined but not bulging.

"It's a healthy sport," I said. Great. Now I sounded like my grandmother. Next, I'd give him a granola-cookie recipe.

"Yes," he replied flatly, not letting me off the hook.

"I missed swimming." More meaningless words from yours truly.

Christian began circling me like a shark, a smirk playing on his lips. "Why are you here, Roth? Really, now. What's your game?"

"Something about you feels familiar." I secured the towel around myself, turning to look at him. "And I intend to find out what it is. Other than that, I'm just enjoying my new daily workout routine."

His blue eyes held mine in a vise grip. For the first time, I could see something that wasn't hate or disdain in them. There was curiosity, with a dash of hope thrown in. I felt like I was missing something. Like we were having two different conversations about two different things. Most of all, I thought what we were doing was wrong somehow. Forbidden.

"Are you saying we know each other, Ms. Roth?" he asked, very slowly, almost like he was clueing me in on something.

"I'm saying the pieces of the puzzle aren't adding up, and I'm not going to give up until I get the full picture."

"Tell me, Ms. Roth. What's going to happen if you lose this case?"

"I don't lose," I said quickly, too quickly. Because not wanting to lose was a better incentive than actually asking myself the million-dollar question—whether Dad was guilty or not.

There was a beat. The silence hung in the humid, hot air like a sword over a neck.

"Meet me in the wet sauna in twenty minutes." The words ripped out from his mouth, like he was fighting them. He turned and stalked away. I watched his triangle back, sensing I'd seen it before. Touched it, even. But it couldn't be. I'd remember a man like that if I'd gone to bed with him. The only other person who'd ever made me feel quite so desperate for something I could never define was long gone. Nicky had died, and even after I'd been told that he'd died, I still vainly looked for him every now and then.

But Christian was here, and Christian was different. Callous and cunning, miles away from the sweet, surly boy who'd stolen my heart.

I was going to do what I needed to do to protect the only man in my life who cared.

Even if it meant dying on the sword of my principles.

CHAPTER FOURTEEN

CHRISTIAN

Present

Something about you feels familiar.

The sentence had undone me, and here I was, twenty minutes later, sitting on the wooden bench in the wet sauna, waiting for Arya.

It didn't help that she looked good enough to eat in her red bikini. Or that I'd been hitting the Brewtherhood almost every night, hoping she'd defy me by showing up. Picking up where we'd left things off last time.

I rested my head against the wall, beads of sweat slithering down my torso into the white towel wrapped around my waist. I was hard. I was always hard when Arya Roth was around. And for some reason, she always seemed to be around. I couldn't get rid of her, now that she'd reentered my sphere.

I detested that she'd come to the pretrial hearing. Not only because it had made me deal with a constant semi while exchanging golf tips with Judge Lopez, but also because seeing her miserable didn't have the desired effect on me. As much as I hated her—and I truly did—her father was my main fish to fry.

Not to mention Claire was getting antsy. I hadn't invited her over since the hearing had begun, and it didn't help that she'd noticed I couldn't take my eyes off Arya whenever we were in the same room. I had to remind myself that Claire knew it had never been serious. That I'd stressed it to her time and time again.

The door of the sauna whined open and shut. My eyes remained closed. I waited for her to say something. She was the one who'd jumped through hoops to find me, after all.

"Christian." Her voice was raspy, full of warmth.

"Sit down," I ordered.

"Not before you look at me."

"Sit. Down," I enunciated.

"Look at me first."

"Make it worth my while." A smile tugged at my lips. That was when I heard it. The soft whoosh of her towel as it hit the wet floor. Was this crazy woman completely naked? Only one way to find out.

I popped my eyes open. Arya stood in front of me, like every single time I'd imagined her in my fantasies. Her breasts were spectacular. Her nipples small and pink, her hips silky and round. Her body was an hourglass, dripping with sweat. Her skin smooth and velvety, begging to be touched.

She's not worth the partnership, not to mention nailing her father. She is doing this to ruin you. This one-trick pony seduces for destruction.

She took a few steps toward me. We were alone, but someone could walk in any minute. The wet sauna was unisex. I could tell she was going to mount and straddle me if I didn't put a stop to it. As much as it pained me—especially one part of me—to reject her, I couldn't cave in to her advances.

She leaned toward me, bracing one of her arms behind my shoulder, her green eyes meeting mine. She put her other hand on my pecs. They flexed instinctively. My cock threatened to play peekaboo with the towel. Suddenly, we were back to being fourteen.

I laced my fingers around her wrist, pushing her hand away. "I'll pass."

"Why?"

"Never show your neck to someone who wants to chop your head off."

"It is a pretty neck, though." Arya's eyes twinkled. I wanted to laugh. She didn't move away. "Is it because of Claire?"

Claire. Her name on Arya's lips felt strange. Wrong. In my thirty-two years, there'd never been another woman who held a candle to Arya's pull, capabilities, and demolition.

"Jealous?" I swiped my tongue along my lower lip.

"Maybe." She slid her hands back over my shoulders.

My heart thudded faster. I hadn't been expecting that answer. "Don't be."

"Are you saying you're not sleeping with your associate?" she asked, and I couldn't lie, although it was tempting.

I shook my head. "I'm saying she doesn't matter."

There was always the chance Arya was fishing to find some leverage against me, and screwing my fellow associate was definitely not a great look.

"What's the problem, then? The chemistry is there." Her tone was businesslike, almost terse.

"Yes." I flashed my teeth, cool and collected. "But the willingness to fuck up my case isn't. If I touch you, I lose, and you and I both know it. Now wrap a towel around yourself and park your ass all the way across the bench. We need to talk."

She retreated, stepping back and picking up her towel. She wrapped it around herself and walked toward the farthest end of the wraparound bench, sitting in front of me, calm and collected, like she hadn't been rejected minutes ago.

"You should clean your hands of him." I ran a hand over my hair, which was slick with sweat.

"No," she said simply.

"He is guilty."

"You would say that; you are Amanda Gispen's lawyer."

"I'm saying that because I have eyes and ears. I looked through your side's discovery responses. This will cause a lot of destruction to your father. Just because shit is about to hit the fan doesn't mean you have to get dirty."

"Christian," Arya said, almost chidingly. Another memory from our thirteen-year-old selves. She'd always been bossy. "What are you doing?"

"Giving you advice."

"Are you going to charge me five hundred bucks at the end of this hour?"

"You mean two grand. And the answer is no. This advice I am giving you for free, though you should consider it priceless. Your father's attorneys—are they a part of his in-house litigation team?"

I had no idea what I was doing or why the hell I was doing it. I just knew I had to throw her a bone. I wanted to win, but not by default. Conrad Roth's case looked weak right now. A walk in the park.

"No." Arya shook her head. "They're outside counsel. He's worked with them before. They come highly recommended by his team."

"His team ain't worth a dime, and his general counsel should be fired. Any rookie would tell you that when dealing with any gender-related lawsuit, the jurors would respond more sympathetically to a female litigator. Especially someone young."

"Like Claire," Arya pointed out.

"Like Claire. But that's beside the point."

"Are you saying he needs to hire a female lawyer?" Her green eyes sparked with curiosity, and there it was, the Arya I knew and was obsessed with. Apparently she was still there, under the thick layers of designer clothes and ballbusting moves and bullshit.

"Correct."

"That's sexist."

I shrugged. "Doesn't make it any less true."

"Why are you telling me this?" Her eyes tapered. "No part of you wants my father to win this case."

Smiling at her like she was a foolish child, I deliberately mansplained. "I'll be buttoning up this puppy if you bring in Jesus Christ himself to represent your father. It'd be nice to break a little sweat while I do. I'm giving you a head start."

Arya's eyes glided over my chest. I was glad I couldn't do the same to her, now that she'd wrapped herself back up. My IQ had dropped by sixty-nine points when she was naked.

"You look pretty sweaty to me," she remarked.

"In *court*."

She extended her bronze legs, wiggling her toes. I couldn't help it. I sneaked a look. First at her shapely calves, then at those toes she used to entwine with mine when we were kids, reading under the desk at her library.

"So tell me, Christian, how do I know you?"

We were on a first-name basis now. That wasn't good. Still, it felt weird to refer to Arya as Ms. Roth.

I flexed my muscles. "You seem like a smart cookie. Figure it out."

You're playing with fire, I could hear Arsène warning in my head.

That may be, I answered. *How could I not, when the flame is so beautiful?*

◆ ◆ ◆

The next day, I called Claire into my office.

"Miss Lesavoy, please take a seat."

Claire always looked good, but she seemed to be putting in extra effort in recent days. Perhaps to remind me she had more to offer than her sharp mind.

She sat in front of me, smiling breezily. "Hey, stranger. Tried to call you last night. Your voice mail has been working extra hours."

I'd been busy jerking off to mental pictures of Arya. But I supposed she could do without this piece of information.

"Sorry." I smoothed my tie over my dress shirt. "I was busy. Listen, Claire, I'm going to cut straight to the chase. You are gorgeous, intelligent, smart as a whip, and completely out of my league. I'm a washed-out, jaded asshole who cannot say no when a good thing lands in his lap, and in doing so I'm slowing you down. So this is me doing you a favor and calling things off before you begin to resent me and working together becomes tasking."

I thought it was a nice little speech. Especially considering none of these things were lies. She *was* too good to me. I *was* jaded. And things were becoming more complicated, especially now that we were handling the Roth case.

Claire scowled, not bothering to appear unwounded. I knew I should adore that about her, but I couldn't help but miss Arya's mind games. Her arrogant pride. Her obstinacy.

"Don't you think it's on me to decide whether you're good enough or not?" Claire asked.

"No," I said softly. "I fake quality quite well."

"I think you're selling yourself short." Claire leaned across the desk, capturing my hand in hers. "I like you very much, Christian."

"You have no reason to."

"Even more so, because you don't get how amazing you are."

I gave her an it's-not-going-to-work look.

"Is it Ms. Roth?" She dropped my hand.

"Don't, Claire."

"It is, then." She stood up but didn't leave. Waiting for a blanket denial. For me to change my mind.

I masked my annoyance with concern. "You deserve better."

"I obviously do." She smiled humorlessly but didn't make a move toward the door. She was waiting for something else. Something I was incapable of giving her. Humanity. Remorse. Sympathy. I wanted to kill Arya and Conrad just then. For robbing me of all the things I could have given others.

"I trust this matter is settled and behind us," I said.

And that was when I saw it. The realization sinking in. The way her eyes turned off told me everything I needed to know. She got it.

"Yes. Everything is perfectly clear. Will that be all, Mr. Miller?" Claire stuck her nose up in the air.

"Yes, Miss Lesavoy."

It was the last time Claire spoke to me that day.

CHAPTER FIFTEEN

ARYA

Present

"Are you sure you're going to eat this muffin?" Mother—or just Beatrice, since she wasn't hot on a woman in her early thirties referring to her as Mom publicly—glanced from behind her menu, twisting her mouth disapprovingly.

My father sat beside her, silently slathering a piece of toast with butter. Maintaining eye contact with Beatrice, I took a large bite of the orange-and-cranberry muffin in my hand, crumbs tumbling down on my mint-green Gucci dress. "Looks that way, Bea."

We were sitting at the Columbus Circle Inn, a charming restaurant in pastel colors with blown glass flowers, for Sunday brunch. Beatrice Roth didn't see me very often. She had committees and charities and luncheons to run, but she did once a year, when we went to Aaron's grave for the anniversary of his death. It was tradition to have brunch afterward. While every year of my twin brother's loss was punctuated with an exclamation point, I couldn't remember the last time my mother had treated my birthday as more than just a comma.

"You need to make sure you maintain your figure, Arya. You're not twenty anymore." Mom readjusted her new diamond earrings for the sole purpose of drawing attention to them.

I rarely saw my mother, even though I lived right down the block from her. And whenever I *did* see her, she always had something unkind to say. She was disgusted with my lack of desire to become a kept woman. In her opinion, I worked too hard, exercised too little, and talked politics too often. All in all, I was a dazzling failure as a socialite.

"I'll keep that in mind when I'm on the lookout for a misogynist husband who requires a no-brain and no-appetite trophy wife."

"Must you be so crass all the time?" She took a sip of her gin and diet tonic.

"Must I? No. Do I? Sure, when I'm in the mood."

"Leave her alone, Bea," my father warned tiredly.

"Don't tell me what to do." She shot him a look before returning her attention to me. "This attitude of yours is not doing this family any favors. Your father tells me you pushed Amanda Gispen's lawyer to the edge. Practically baited him to go to trial."

"Beatrice!" my father roared. He had apologized for that day at the hearing, and I'd accepted, although something had broken between us since then. A fragile trust we had restored when I was fifteen.

I choked on my muffin as she continued, with an air of irritation. "Frankly, I'm surprised you haven't put more hours and resources into trying to spin this in the media."

"Actually, I've been working nonstop on garnering positive press. Not an easy task, considering the allegations he is facing. There's only so much I can do before the trial starts. Also"—I turned to my father—"I spoke to someone whose opinion I value, and he suggested you hire a female litigator as a part of your team. Apparently the jurors will respond favorably to a woman."

Dad took a sip of his sangria. "Thank you, Arya. Your job is to make me look good, not give me legal advice."

"You said I needed to help you more," I challenged.

"Yes, in your area of expertise."

"Well, don't you think—"

Our conversation was interrupted by the waitress, who placed our quiches, Bloody Marys, and eggs Benedict on the table. We all paused until she was out of earshot. When she was gone, he began talking before I could finish my sentence.

"Look, I'm not interested in hiring any other lawyer, female or not. It's going to look like we're desperate." He began cutting into his spinach quiche furiously.

"We *are* desperate." My eyes nearly bulged out of their sockets.

"That's not something I'd like Christian Miller to see."

"Oh, *now* you care about the optics?" I cried out, knowing all of this could've been prevented if Dad had been a little less brash when he'd fired Amanda. Assuming everything else she'd said wasn't true, which was a hypothesis I found more unlikely with each passing day. Also, I honestly didn't want to care what Christian thought. If I allowed myself to dwell on it, I'd crawl into a hole and die of humiliation from his rejection at Solstices' sauna. He and Claire were probably having a good laugh about it. That was fine. It wasn't like Miller's opinion kept me up at night.

"There's no sin greater than hubris, Dad. Pride is a luxury you cannot afford right now," I said measuredly, trying another angle.

"Arya, I'm not going to make a last-minute change just because some nameless friend of yours told you I should do so." My father tossed his napkin over the table, standing up. "On that note, I think it's time you upped your game. You've been following me around like a lost puppy and doing very little so far to help me get out of this."

Get out of this? He thought I had the agency to help him get off the hook?

"My bad. Let me go look for my magic Your-Honor-he-is-innocent wand." I wasn't sure how Dad and I had gotten where we were right now. My mother looked between us like we were two strangers interrupting her brunch.

He shook his head. "I'll see you at home, Beatrice. Arya." He dipped his head, got up, and left. I sat there, speechless, while my mother took another sip of her G&T. She was hardly affected by how upset Dad was. Then again, I hadn't seen my parents act like a normal couple even once. Their relationship looked more like that of two siblings who didn't like each other very much.

"Do you think he did it?" I blurted out.

My mother's seamless demeanor didn't crack. In fact, she continued dissecting her eggs Benedict with her fork and knife and took a small bite of her food. "Arya, *please*. Your father has definitely had his fair share of affairs, but all of them were consensual. These women flung themselves at him shamelessly. I'm sure he and Amanda enjoyed each other's company at some point and she expected more compensation after he discarded her for a newer model."

"He cheated on you?" But I already knew the answer to that question.

My mother laughed throatily, tearing off a miniscule piece of sourdough bread and popping it between her scarlet lips. "Cheated, cheating, will cheat. You choose the tense. But I wouldn't use that term, exactly. *Cheating* implies I care. I haven't had an interest in fulfilling my marital obligations in a while. It was always understood that if he wanted female affection, he'd have to seek it elsewhere."

"Why didn't you get a divorce?" I spit out, anger humming beneath my skin. I was under no illusion that my parents had a happy marriage, but I'd thought they were semifunctional.

"*Because,*" she droned, "why should we go through that horrible, tacky mess when we have an understanding?"

"Where's your pride?"

"Where's *his*?" she asked, almost cheerfully. "Virtues don't age well in upper society. You think slipping in and out of strange women's beds like a thief is more honorable than my sitting at home and knowing about it?"

My reality as I knew it came tumbling down. I wouldn't say I put Dad on a pedestal, but I definitely viewed him through rose-colored glasses. Now I wondered what else my parents were keeping from me.

"How many affairs did he have?" I rearranged myself in my seat, feeling a rash coming my way.

Mom waved a hand dismissively. "Six? Seven? Serious mistresses, I mean. Oh, who knows? I wasn't aware of Amanda, but there were others. His infidelity started early on. Before you and your brother were born, in fact. But after Aaron died . . ."

My heart cracked. Not breaking all the way but enough that she was human and lovable in that moment, not just the woman who'd ignored my existence from the day she'd lost my brother.

"That's terrible."

My mother smiled delicately. "Is it? He's been a wonderful father to you all these years when I could barely look at you. You remind me too much of your brother."

Was that why she hated me? Why she ignored my existence?

"He never demanded a thing from me, even when it was clear I was no longer the woman he fell in love with. Is it terrible of him to seek love somewhere else or simply natural?"

"What he is being accused of has nothing to do with love."

Mom mulled it over. "Your father is a twisted man. Can be, anyway."

"Do you think he is capable of all the things they accuse him of?" I tried holding her gaze, but it was vacant. Empty. No one was home beyond Beatrice Roth's emerald-green eyes. "Of sexually harassing someone?"

My mother signaled for the check, not meeting my stare. "My, it's getting chilly. Let's continue this some other time, shall we?"

◆ ◆ ◆

"Ari?" Whitley, our office manager, popped her head from behind her Mac screen the following day at work. "There's someone downstairs to see you."

I double-clicked on my digital planner, frowning. "I don't have any meetings until three." Even that was in SoHo, a few blocks down from my office.

Jillian flashed me an inquisitive look from across the room, as did Hailey, our in-house graphic designer. Whitley nibbled on her cuticle, pinning the intercom phone between her shoulder and ear. "He's downstairs."

"Does *he* have a name?" I arched an eyebrow.

"I'm sure he does."

"Now's the time to ask what it is."

Whitley ducked her head down, asking the person buzzing to come up what his name was. She tilted her head so she could see me beyond her screen. "Christian Miller. He says you'll be happy to see him."

My stomach flipped nervously, and a can of butterflies cracked open, filling it with velvety, flappy wings.

"He's lying."

She relayed my reply to him, then listened to what he said and laughed.

"He says he knew you'd say that but that he has information you'd like to know."

"Tell him I'll be down in a minute."

I half-heartedly patted my hair into submission, grabbed my phone and sunglasses, and headed for the stairway. Since there was zero chance I was going to enjoy this conversation, I decided to get it over with. No doubt Christian was here to hit me with more bad news. Question was—how did he know where I worked if he'd tossed my business card the day we'd met at the Brewtherhood?

I took the stairs two at a time. Christian waited on the curb, playing with a matchbook, talking on the phone. When he saw me, he lifted his finger up, in no rush to finish his conversation. Only *after* he gave one of his associates a detailed explanation of how he wanted them to file a motion to compel something in court, he turned off his cell and tucked it back into his breast pocket, whirling to look at me like I was three-day-old moldy takeout he'd just found staring back at him from the kitchen sink.

"Ms. Roth. How are you?"

"Good, until about five minutes ago." I slid my sunglasses over my nose. "Now I'm wondering what fresh hell you've prepared especially for me."

"You wound me." He produced a cigar, speaking in a tone that very much didn't sound wounded. "I would never prepare fresh hell *especially* for you. Although you are about to be delivered a generous piece of it."

"Get it over with, Miller."

"I wanted to tell you in person before you found out through the grapevine. Those lawyers your father hired seem about as competent as a pet rock and can't even seem to slow the speed at which the trial date is moving." He lit the cigar. Tragically, even while puffing the stench straight to my face, he looked more like an *Esquire* cover model than the antihero in a mobster film.

"Four more women stepped forward and decided to join Amanda Gispen's lawsuit. One has some colorful, very intimate pictures your father had sent her. Not something you'd like to see yourself but something I'm obligated to share with others to zealously represent my clients, which means including this in the evidence, so the photos will be presented, enlarged, in the courtroom during trial."

Pressing a hand against the redbrick building of my office, I inhaled a jagged breath, trying not to appear as devastated as I was. This was getting out of control. There were now *five* women testifying against him? And there were pictures?

Did he do it? Could *he?*

Now I knew why my mother had said she didn't want to know. The answer was terrifying. One complaint was something I could rearrange in my head. Make excuses for, in the absence of context and other victims. Five were problematic. Especially as, being a woman myself, I knew how overwhelming the prospect was of sitting on a stand in front of seasoned lawyers, getting grilled and questioned about something so deeply triggering. I felt my knees go weak.

Christian studied me intently, like he was waiting for the penny to drop. "This thing is not going away, Ari."

"Ari?" I jumped, my eyes widening.

"Arya," he amended, flushing slightly. "Your life's about to implode if you don't step away from this."

"Seems like it, and you're all too eager for the fireworks part. Are you expecting me to drop my own father as a PR client?" I tossed my hair to one shoulder.

"No, I'm expecting *him* to drop *your* firm and spare you the awkward conversation. Ask Jillian to drop him if you don't feel comfortable doing it." How did he know about Jillian? Did he genuinely think I believed he was worried for me and mine? "You should do the right thing by taking a step back from this. Though come to think about it, I have no idea why you haven't done so already."

"Don't pretend like you know me," I bit out. "And don't exhale smoke on me." I grabbed the cigar from between his fingers, snapped it in two, and dumped it in a nearby trash can.

"You're crazy," he said, but his face showed amusement, not anger. He *enjoyed* riling me up. Got off on my wrath. "Which, by the way, I find oddly delightful."

"Don't flirt."

"Why not?" he asked. *Ugh.* Good question. The attraction was maddening.

"Claire?" I asked tiredly.

He shook his head. "Firmly in the past as of last week."

"Sorry to hear," I said, in monotone.

He grinned. "No, you're not."

"You're right. I'm pretty focused on the shit show called my family life right now."

"Understandable." He couldn't stop staring at me, and vice versa.

"I appreciate the heads-up, Mr. Miller."

"The trial will be fast. Judge Lopez doesn't want a spectacle. The evidence is overwhelming. This should be a quick wrap-up."

"Now would be a good time to stop talking." I swiveled toward the entrance door, ready to leave.

"Arya?"

Was he deaf?

I turned back to face him, a plastic smile on my face. "Yes, Christian?"

"Don't go to court next week. There will be things there you don't want to see. Not to mention it's career suicide for you." His voice was soft, his eyes not as cold as they had been days before, at the sauna.

"Some things are worth dying for. He's my father."

"Yes. Your father. Not *you*. As soon as the motion for joinder is granted, the media will be all over this, and no cute picture of your dad in a hospital kissing babies is going to make this go away. Investors will pull their money from his hedge fund. The board will probably make him resign. The charges have changed, and so has the punishment, the very fabric of the case. Conrad Roth is not coming back to Wall Street. If you still want a career, now's the time to distance yourself from him."

"Would you turn your back on your parent like that?" I tapered my eyes, searching his.

Christian smiled sadly, looking down. His thumb rolling over his matchbook. "I would run over my parents with a semitrailer for a luke-warm cup of tea. And I'm not even a tea person. So I'm not sure I'm the right person to be asked this question."

Something about what he said made me feel raw, naked. *Guilty.*

"Do you want to talk about it?" I asked.

He shook his head, finding my gaze. "No. You have your own family to worry about."

"Yes. And I choose to give my father the benefit of the doubt."

"There *is* no doubt. His crimes are objective reality, fully recorded and witnessed. I'm not the murderer of your father's good reputation. I'm merely the coroner. The body was already cold when I got here. Plus, there's also another matter to consider."

"And that is?"

"I can't ask you out as long as you're linked to the case."

My mouth fell open. Was I more angry or shocked? I couldn't tell, but I knew I would punch him if my family weren't already swimming in bad press. That was beyond the pale. The arrogance of him was shocking.

"You want to *date* me?" I spit out.

"I wouldn't go that far. I'd like to sleep with you and am willing to check all the civilized boxes to get from point A to B."

"Did you use that line on C—"

"No. I didn't have to."

I tipped my shades down, half smiling. "Funny, you didn't seem so eager to be with me when we were in the sauna together."

"The sauna was a badly plotted scheme. Not to mention I didn't want to be within the gray area of infidelity. Now that's out of the way . . ."

"You don't even like me." I threw my arms in the air, exasperated. I began pacing the sidewalk, ignoring the curious gazes of people around us. Christian looked more than comfortable, like he was used to pushing people into corners.

"I don't have to like you to want to bed you. I'd think you'd be familiar with the concept of hate fuck by your fairly advanced age."

"And how would you know what my *fairly advanced age* may be?" I stopped, turning to look at him. I saw it then. Just a flash of an oh-crap expression, of someone who'd said something he shouldn't have, before his face smoothed back to normal.

"I know everything about everyone concerning my cases."

"If you think I'll sleep with someone who is trying to make my father go bankrupt, you need a reality check with a side of therapy."

"So it's a yes, then."

"Don't come here again, Christian."

With that, I turned around and pushed the entrance door to my building.

I went back to the office, tripping over the stairs at least three times. My mind was jumbled. With Christian, with Dad, and with my parents' Molotov cocktail of a marriage. When I pushed the door open, I was met with Jillian's stony face. She was holding her briefcase, her lipstick freshly applied, signaling me she was on her way out.

"You forgot about our meeting with ShapeOn. They just called us saying you are thirty minutes late." Jillian tried to keep her voice down but failed, as she did often when she was upset. I guessed I had forgotten to put it in my planner. *Crap.* That was the second client I'd messed up this month.

"I . . ." I trailed off, thinking of something to say. Jillian shook her head, pushing past me as she went out the door. I stood rooted to the threshold, wondering what the hell happened.

I tried to reach my father on his cell for the rest of the day. He didn't pick up. The truth was closing in on me like an envelope, sealed around me one inch at a time.

By the time I left work for the day, I decided desperate times called for desperate measures and called my mother. She answered on the third ring, sounding frostier than usual.

"Arya. You are calling me out of nowhere, so I'm going to go ahead and assume you want to ask about your father."

Hello to you too, Mother.

"I don't remember you calling to check in on me either," I replied, because frankly, I was fed up with her attitude. "And yes. I am, in fact, calling to ask about Dad. He's not answering."

I heard her moving across her grand living room, her designer slippers gliding over the marble. Her pocket-size dog was barking in the background.

"Your father has been holed up in his study with his lawyers all day, conducting a meeting I want absolutely nothing to do with. The new evidence and plaintiffs will definitely make things more difficult. Can you imagine what I'll have to face when I go to the country-club luncheon next week? I'm thinking of canceling the entire thing. Dick pics, Arya! How absolutely tacky."

Dick pics. That was one term I'd never thought I'd hear my mother say.

Again, she made this about her, not him. I reached my apartment building's door, punched in the code, and pushed it open.

"Do you think he did it?" I repeated my question from our brunch. Only this time, I wasn't met with amusement anymore but somber silence. I never could read Mother. Not enough to know what she was thinking, anyway. If she had an obvious answer to my question, I didn't know.

"It doesn't matter, does it? We're his family. We must stick by him."

Must we? I thought. *Even if he hurt others badly? Maliciously?*

I pushed my apartment door open, then took off my heels and stared at the antique shelves on my walls. They were full of pictures of me and Dad from vacations, charity balls, and holidays. None with my mother. She never tagged along for anything. Dad had raised me all by himself.

"The financial implications are another thing to take into consideration." Mom's voice drifted from the phone I was holding. "The company will head straight to bankruptcy if Conrad doesn't step down, and even if he does, it might be too late. Not to mention they're suing him for most of his net worth. I can't believe he did this to us."

"Let me sleep on this, Mom."

"Okay. Oh . . . and Arya?" My mother sniffed on the other end. I stilled, waiting for her next words. "Don't be a stranger. You can call me, too, you know. I'm still your mother."

Hardly, I thought.

You were never my anything at all.

CHAPTER SIXTEEN

ARYA

Present

I decided to take a day off to decompress. And by *decompress* I meant totally compress. I wanted to get some answers and dig into the claims against my father. Before yesterday, I'd cautiously assumed Dad was speaking the truth when he gave me a blanket denial. Now, I wasn't sure. Last night, I'd texted Louie, who'd confirmed they'd received additional discovery requests. Other women were joining the lawsuit, and the sum on the recently filed statement of damages was astronomical; it would strip my father of most of his assets if he lost.

I thought about Christian the whole subway journey from my apartment to my parents' Park Avenue penthouse. I absolutely loathed that he was right about me taking a step back.

When I got to my parents' apartment, my mother waited at the door.

"Thank you for coming. I was thinking maybe we could order sushi for lunch or something?" A hopeful smile tugged at her lips.

"Hmm, what?" I wanted to make sure this wasn't a prank. She'd never offered to do anything with me. And upon getting rejected a few times during my preteen years, I'd stopped trying.

"Sushi. You. Me. I can help you dig through Dad's stuff."

Going all *Brady Bunch* with my mom wasn't in my plans right now, but I acknowledged that she did make an effort. I patted her arm, brushing past her toward the master bedroom. "Sorry. I work best when I'm alone."

I reached the master bedroom's door, using the secret knock only Dad and I had. *One rap, beat, five raps, beat, two raps.*

"Dad?"

There was no answer. Mom appeared beside me, twisting the hem of her dress. "You know, he's been moody all day. He wouldn't even take his lawyers' calls."

"Dad!" I knocked again, ditching the secret knock. "Open the door. I can't help you if you don't talk to me. I need to understand what happened."

I couldn't sleep a wink during the night. To think that my father could be capable of such things made me want to hurl myself into the Hudson River.

Mom huddled nearby, serving as a curious audience.

"Go away," Dad called out through the door.

"Dad, I want to help."

"You do? Because you haven't been too helpful so far."

"I have questions," I bit out. My growing suspicions and his attitude were a bad combination.

"If you don't believe me, maybe you shouldn't come to court."

"No one said I don't believe you." Although admittedly, my confidence in his innocence was *very* wobbly. "I just want—"

"I'm not going to answer any of your questions. Leave!" he roared.

I took a step back instinctively, feeling my cheeks go hot, like he'd slapped me. My father hadn't once yelled at me before. That didn't mean I hadn't witnessed him being aggressive to others. If I was honest with myself—which I wasn't, most of the time, when it came to him—he'd had anger-management issues for as long as I could remember. But of course, anger was cancer. It touched everything in your life. The way you behaved inside the office always bled into your homelife. Your love life. Your life-life.

I turned to my mother. "Do you have the key to his file cabinets? I would like to go through his employment contracts."

Dad was an old-school businessman. He believed everything needed to be printed out and stored for safekeeping. Any correspondence he'd had with an employee would be filed in his study. He was too cautious to keep these things at work.

My mother wrung her hands. "Do you think it can help?"

"Worth a shot." Even if it wouldn't help his case, it was going to help me understand if there was merit to any of the allegations.

Ten minutes later, I sat on the lush carpet of my father's study, thirty years' worth of documentation in front of me. Everything was there. From service agreements to personal emails and termination letters. I wondered how much of these he'd handed over to Louie and Terrance. I wondered if he'd handed them anything at *all*. He seemed caged up where this trial was concerned. A part of me wanted to call Christian and try and gauge what exactly they had on him. But as Christian had mentioned—his chief objective was to bang me, not help me.

"Arya?" My mother knocked on Dad's study's door three hours into my research, holding a tray with lemonade and cookies. Whatever had happened to the muffin tsar? Guess I was okay to eat carbs now that it was a real possibility I'd be her only family left. I doubted she'd stay with my father if he were penniless.

"I'm just going to leave these right here," she said gingerly, tiptoeing into the room and placing the drink and snack beside me. "Let me know if you need anything."

I needed you to be exactly like this when I was young. To acknowledge my presence, instead of resenting it.

I might not have known Aaron, but I'd always felt the loss of him. It was in the air in this house, every piece of furniture, each painting, drenched with it. The vast emptiness that remained where another family member should have been.

"Thank you." I didn't look up from the mountains of files surrounding me. She lingered by the door.

I plucked another cordial email printout between Amanda and Dad, adding it to my Amanda pile. I was trying to figure out where it had gone sideways between them. "Um, Mom? I'm kind of trying to work here."

"Oh. Sure. Okay."

She closed the door with a soft click.

"Come on. Heartbroken admirers. Moneygrubbing opportunists. Show me your true faces. Tell me it's all a lie . . . ," I whispered to myself, skimming through the documents.

The universe must've heard me, because two minutes later, a black envelope fell from one of the manila files. It was padded with paper and sealed.

What the . . . ?

I looked up, scanning the empty room, listening for noises in the hallway. The coast was clear. I took an envelope opener to it and ripped the thing clean. A batch of yellowed papers rained down on the carpet. I picked one letter up, my heart ramming its way through my chest. The handwriting looked familiar yet strange. Italic, pushed together, like the person was trying to save paper.

> Dear Conrad,
> I did as you told me to do. I did not answer any of Nicholai's letters and telephone calls. I feel bad about this. He is my son after all. But you know my loyalty is with you. I miss him and would like to see him soon. Do you think I can spend Christmas with him? Of course, I would like to spend it with you, too. But only if she doesn't come along. I cannot bear the sight of her. She doesn't deserve you or Arya.
> Love,
> Ruslana

The letter fell from between my fingers. *Nicholai.*

Ruslana was talking about Nicholai. But what did she mean by doing what Dad had asked her to do? Why would Dad ask her not to answer Nicky after he'd moved? This was not the version Dad had given me all those years ago for what had gone down after that shameful day.

One thing that didn't take a detective to conclude from this was their insinuated affair. I guessed "she" was my mother, who had indeed opted out of our annual Christmas celebrations in favor of working on her tan in Sydney. It wasn't out of the ordinary for Dad and Ruslana to take me someplace during the holidays, distract me from my mother-less existence. But Ruslana always stayed in a separate room and barely spoke a word to my father. I picked up another letter.

> Dear Conrad,
> I suspect you are a liar. If you aren't, then why are you still with Beatrice?
>
> You said you would leave her for me. Yet it has been three years and look at us. Nicholai is a man now. He doesn't even talk to me. I lost my connection with my only family, thinking I would join yours. Nicholai was supposed to take care of me when I grow old. Now he won't even take my calls. There is a saying I'm sure you are familiar with. You the Yankees love it. You don't buy the cow if you can get the milk for free.
>
> I feel like cattle now, Conrad, and I do not like this feeling at all.
> Still yours,
> Ruslana

My stomach turned violently. Ruslana and Nicholai hadn't been in contact all these years? How was my father connected to all this? He'd looked rabid that day when he'd found Nicky and me in the library, reenacting *that* scene in *Atonement*. But he couldn't . . . wouldn't . . .

Poor Nicky. Was my father really capable of such atrocities?

If it smells like a pig and looks like a pig . . .

I grabbed another letter. And then another. The words blurred, fuzzing behind a sheet of unshed tears.

> Dear Conrad . . . I can't eat . . . I can't sleep . . . my love for you burns like midnight oil . . .
>
> Dear Conrad . . . I'm considering taking matters to my own hands and talking to Beatrice . . . if you don't tell her, I will. You said you'd leave her. Did you lie?
>
> Dear Conrad . . . I'm desperate. When will you call me back?
>
> Dear Conrad . . . please don't fire me. I will be good. I promise. I will not overstep your boundaries. I'm sorry I did. I was . . . confused. I can't afford to lose this job. I've already lost too much.

The last letter was the one that shattered the rest of my hope on the floor.

> Dear Conrad,
> You are leaving me no choice. I am telling Beatrice myself.
>
> Buy my silence, or pay for what you did.
> —Ruslana

Ruslana hadn't quit; she'd been let go.

Fired. Tucked away where my mother couldn't see her. Banished from Dad's kingdom, just like Nicholai.

I still remembered what Dad had said the day Ruslana had stopped coming without as much as a call or a note. College-student me had dropped in to say hello.

"I suppose she just wanted to move somewhere where there're a lot of Russians. Fox River fit the bill," he'd said. It seemed so odd to me back then that our trusted housekeeper, who moaned about the winter as early as each September, would willingly choose to move to Alaska. It also struck me as weird I couldn't get her address. Send her some flowers or a gift basket for all those years she'd helped us. She'd disappeared from the face of the earth.

Now, the pieces of the puzzle were beginning to fall into place.

Nicholai.

Ruslana.

The affairs.

Amanda.

Above all—the way my father was treating me now, when he thought I was onto him. How he locked me out of his kingdom too.

I stood up, leaving the scattered papers on the study's floor. My mother tried to stop me at the door, but I pushed past her, ran out of the apartment building, leaned into a bush, and threw up.

CHAPTER SEVENTEEN

A R Y A

Past

"Where is he?" I demanded the day after Nicholai had been sent home, standing at the edge of my father's study. It had taken me a full day to look at him without fearing I'd physically attack him.

Ruslana had continued fulfilling her duties as if nothing had happened, but each time I tried to ask her about Nicky, she either pretended not to hear me or made a show of washing the dishes and folding the laundry, as if she couldn't possibly talk and perform her tasks at the same time.

Dad glanced up from his paperwork, dropping his pen and leaning back in his seat. "Sweetheart. Where's your mother?"

"Take a wild guess." I propped a shoulder against the doorframe, my voice barely a hiss. "It's fashion week somewhere in the world. She is probably burning your money while bitching about you simultaneously." Actually, she was at a yoga retreat, but I wanted to badmouth her. This was the first time I said something mean about her to make myself feel better. Weirdly enough, it didn't work. The bitterness clogging my throat was getting sharper each day. Like a rubber ball with more bands. "Now answer my question—where's Nicky?"

Dad rolled his executive chair back, gesturing for me to take a seat in front of him. I made my way to the chair, keeping my expression stern.

"Listen, Arya, there's no easy way of saying this. But I suppose the truth is one thing even I can't protect you from." He scratched his cheek. "Let me start by saying I regret the way I reacted when I found you two. I cannot stress that enough. You are my daughter, and protecting you is my chief concern. When I saw him cornering you against the shelves, I thought . . . well, actually, I *didn't* think. That was the problem. I acted out of pure paternal instincts. I would like to assure you that I later went to see Nicholai and expressed my remorse over my behavior. I am not a primitive man. Violence is beneath me. So first, let's get this out of the way. He looked fine and well. A few scratches, but nothing more."

I looked skyward, at the cathedral-style ceiling, to prevent myself from crying. I knew I couldn't let him get away with what he'd done. More than that, I couldn't get past that even if I wanted to. What I'd seen was a violent, mean man. A man I didn't want as a father.

"You're lying," I said coldly.

"You think I'd lie to you?" He looked at me helplessly, a different man from the one I'd witnessed yesterday beating Nicky to a pulp.

"Yes," I said flatly. "You've done much worse to Nicholai."

"About that." Dad considered his next words. "Sweetheart, I just . . . I wasn't sure what I was seeing. I know you and Nicholai were close. But after I went to apologize to Nicholai in person, he made a request I couldn't deny. You have to understand, I only did what he wished for me to do because I felt so guilty. And . . . well, I couldn't exactly turn him down, in case he'd use what I'd done against me. I had our family to think of. You can't just stay here with your mom on your own."

"What did you do?" My voice was so cold shivers ran down my back.

"Arya . . ."

"Spit it out, Dad."

He closed his eyes, letting his head fall into his hands. This week was the first time I wondered if Dad wasn't all good. The idea was too much to stomach. He was, after all, my only family.

"He asked me if I could buy him a one-way ticket to his father, who lives in Belarus. I agreed."

The world around me spun, though my feet were still rooted to the ground.

Nicholai. Gone.

"He wanted to start over fresh somewhere else. Live in a place where he didn't have to be holed up all summer next to temptation. It was killing him, sweetie."

I was about to throw up. The bile hit the back of my throat, the sour taste exploding in my mouth. I swallowed it all down. The anger, the shame, the disappointment. Most of all—the humiliation.

So this was what a broken heart felt like. Being stabbed in the soul a thousand times. I was never going to date. Ever.

"He said he doesn't want to spend his summers here anymore?" I blinked rapidly, narrowly avoiding breaking down in tears. Dad covered his face with his hands, propping his elbows against his desk. He couldn't see me like this.

"I'm sorry, Arya. I'm sure he cares about you very much. He just doesn't want things to be . . . complicated. I can respect that. Although I did try and persuade him to stay. Mainly for Ruslana. He is her only son, you see."

As I digested all of this, I felt my hands shaking in my lap. The sense of betrayal robbed me of my breath. Even though Nicky and I only had the summers, those summers kept me afloat. They filled me with all the good stuff. Made it easier to face the world.

"You'll forget about him. Right now, it seems like the end of the world, but the truth is, every hello ends in goodbye. You're so young; you won't even remember him."

"I'm going to ask Ruslana for his number," I heard myself say, ignoring his words. My pride was bruised, but not speaking to Nicky ever again was worse than a tarnished ego. Dad ran a hand over his salt-and-pepper mane, blowing out air.

"She won't give it to you," he said sharply. Then, to soften the blow, he explained, "Ruslana is trying to mend the relationship with Nicholai, and right now he wants nothing to do with the Roth family. Rightly so."

"Because of what you did?" My teeth chattered with rage.

"No. Because he thinks you did this on purpose. He doesn't want to talk to you."

This felt like another blow, this time to the place where my soul was tucked. Between the breastbone and the stomach.

"Do you have his father's address? So I can at least write to him?" I asked, my voice steely, squaring my shoulders. I wasn't going to give up. Nicky had to know the truth.

"Sure. I'll write down the address for you. Take it easy when you write to him, okay? Don't be mad or anything. I feel terrible about how everything unfolded. Hopefully he'll be able to find his place there."

No. Hopefully, he'll crawl back home. To me.

I wanted Nicky to fail.

To admit defeat and come back.

That was the first time I discovered love had another side. Dark and barbed wired. Rusty nailed and full of pus. Poisonous, like me.

"Hey, Dad?"

"Yes, sweetie?"

"Don't bother talking to me. As far as I'm concerned—you're good as dead."

◆ ◆ ◆

That night, I wrote Nicky my first letter. It was four pages long and consisted of an apology and an explanation of what had happened that day. I added some pictures of us too. Taken at the pool and in the park. For some reason, I was terrified that he'd forget my face. I handed Ruslana the letter, already stamped, watching carefully for her reaction. My housekeeper's expression remained stoic as she assured me she would send it in the mail.

Two weeks later, I sent Nicky another letter. This time, I accused him of things. Of ignoring me, of betraying me, of turning his back on our friendship.

The entire time, Dad tried worming his way back into my good graces. Showered me with gifts—a new camera, tickets to *Wicked*, a handbag most grown women would find too lavish—but I didn't relent.

The following week, I sent Nicky a third letter, apologizing for letter number two.

The more time went by without a reply, the more my desperation grew. I felt homesick, panicked, swollen with guilt and indignation. If he decided to discard me so easily, maybe he deserved my pestering. My pride—already as fragile as a thorn crown—was torn into ribbons. All I wanted was to speak to Nicky. To hear his voice. To see his lopsided grin once again as he quipped at me with another sarcastic remark.

I spent the first four months of my freshman year writing to him. His answer arrived in the form of an unwelcome present the day before Christmas: all my letters, stamped with my return address, still sealed and unopened.

And so, finally, I broke.

He didn't want to talk to me. Hear from me. Be reminded of my existence.

Meanwhile, Dad was lurking in the shadows, waiting to pounce on a chance to reconcile.

"I'm so sorry," he would say. "I would do anything to make this better."

The months had passed, but my anger hadn't. I barely saw my dad that year, making plans every evening and weekend and not including him in them.

One day, when the Nicky-shaped hole in my chest felt particularly hollow, Dad walked past my room on his way to the master bedroom. I was flung over my bed, staring at nothing.

"What's so interesting about it?" he asked. "The ceiling."

"No better view in this rotten house." I sounded like a brat, and I knew it.

"Get up. I'll show you a view."

"You've already shown me plenty." We both knew I was referring to Nicky. Dude was still taking over my every thought.

"I'll make it worth your while," Dad coaxed, his voice pleading.

"Doubt it." I huffed. While my anger toward him had not diminished, I'd also come to realize that I didn't have anyone other than Jillian to lean on. My high school friends were casual, and my relatives lived far away.

"Give me a shot." He leaned a shoulder against the doorjamb. "You're either going to give it to me today or next month or next year. But I will make you forgive me. Make no mistake about that."

"Fine," I was surprised to hear myself say. "But don't think we're going to be cool with each other after or something."

He took me to the Met Cloisters, to see medieval art and architecture. We strolled shoulder to shoulder, silent the whole time.

"You know," Dad said when we got to the tomb effigies, "there are more of those in Westminster Abbey. My favorite one is of Queen Elizabeth the First. I could take you to see it, if you'd like."

"When?" I demanded haughtily. At some point during that year, being awful to him had become like eating. Just another thing on my agenda.

"Tomorrow?" He lifted his eyebrows, offering me his cunning Conrad Roth smile. "I'm free tomorrow."

"I have school tomorrow," I supplied, my voice thawing considerably.

"You'll learn plenty in London. Lots of history."

And so, after a year, I cut a corner and added Dad back into my life.

We made the Cloisters a monthly thing.

◆ ◆ ◆

London didn't change me.

Neither did the trips to Paris, Athens, and Tokyo.

I was still obsessed with everything Nicky, hungry for crumbs of information about him.

I changed tactics from constant preoccupation with him to spurts of questions and pestering. I could go weeks without speaking about him, then spend a few days asking about him nonstop.

Ruslana explained that Nicky was happy in Minsk. That if he didn't answer, it was because of his busy schedule. Dad was supportive, but every time I tried to ask him to check on Nicky through his private investigator, he refused, saying he was doing it for *me*. That *I* needed to move on. That he hated seeing me all wrapped up in my fixation.

Maybe there was something wrong with me. Could love make you sick? I supposed it could. I'd watched my mother mourning my brother my whole life and didn't want to pine for someone who'd never return.

Still, when I turned sixteen and got my second first kiss from Andrew Brawn, all I could think about was that he wasn't Nicky.

But I knew pushing Dad into doing something was impossible. Besides, I had to pick my battles. Mom was barely with us anymore. My only steady family was my father, and I didn't want to ruin it by fighting over a boy who didn't even bother writing back to me.

The years flowed like a river, drowning me in all kinds of firsts with boys who weren't Nicholai Ivanov. First seven minutes in heaven (Rob Smith). First make-out session under the bleachers (Bruce Le). First boyfriend (Piers Rockwysz) and first heartbreak (Carrie and Aidan from *Sex and the City*, because let's admit it, Piers was great but not Aidan great). Nicky always sat there on the sidelines of my conscious, making each boy I dated fall short. I wondered how many girls he'd kissed over the years. If he still thought about me when he touched other girls, his hands slipping under their shirts. It felt crazy that I couldn't ask him. But maybe lucky, too, because a big part of me didn't want to know.

And so, when I turned eighteen, the first thing I did was make a call to Dad's private investigator. David Kessler was the best in Manhattan.

David came back to me four weeks after I asked him to look for Nicky, informing me of his death.

I didn't get out of bed for three days, after which the fear of turning into my mother outweighed the misery of knowing he wasn't alive.

From that point forward, I vowed to forget Nicholai Ivanov had ever existed.

If only it were that easy . . .

CHAPTER EIGHTEEN

CHRISTIAN

Present

Arya arrived at the courtroom the first day of the trial.

Clearly, she'd decided to give my friendly advice a nice, long middle finger with a side of mind-your-own-business clapback.

At least she opted to take a seat in the public seating area and not the family bench, where she'd be visible. Conrad Roth never had hired a female litigator like I'd suggested to his daughter. Whether it was out of pride or because he knew he couldn't worm his way out of this mess was anyone's guess.

Five victims, accusing Roth of six counts of harassment each, seeking $200 million combined in compensation, $40 million each.

Unlike other sexual predators of his position and wealth, he'd done a piss-poor job at covering his tracks. I estimated it at four weeks before Judge Lopez would ask us for our closing statements.

I stood in front of Judge Lopez's bench for my opening statement, clad in my Brunello Cucinelli suit and grave expression. It took everything in me to rip my eyes from the woman in the last row of the courtroom. Arya sat with her back ramrod straight and her nose tilted up. The picture of poised elegance. She'd stopped hitting the pool, so I'd had a week to stew on our last encounter, in which she'd pretty much told me to go shove it when I'd offered to take her for dinner. Naturally, it made me want her even more.

I wasn't sure when, exactly, the line between wanting to screw her over and screw her, period, had begun to blur. But I knew I was straddling it like an eager stripper performing at a bachelor party for tips.

No matter how irrational, how illogical, how *dangerous* (and there was no denying that touching her could complicate my case, my partner prospect, and my life in general) it was, I wanted Arya.

Deserved her too. After everything she'd put me through, having her in my bed was the perfect consolation prize.

She could go her merry way after I was done with her, probably to marry beneath her pedigree, now that Daddy dearest would be banished from the hedge fund company he managed and exiled from polite society.

Unfortunately for Arya, and maybe for myself, my opening statement included a presentation showing a dick picture of her father, which he'd sent a twenty-three-year-old intern, and which was enlarged on a screen in the middle of the room, pubes and half-mast erection intact.

I tried hard not to look at Arya while I explained to the jurors that her father had sent an image of his penis to someone younger than his own daughter, feeling sick to my stomach. And then ignored her after that, too, when my client tearfully explained on the stand how scarred she was by the (quite literal) revelation that her boss was a dick.

The first day of trial proceeded smoothly. The plaintiffs were compelling. The jurors warmed up to them. I gave an Oscar-worthy performance, making a show of listening and bunching my eyebrows together in concern at all the right places.

When Judge Lopez banged his gavel and said the court stood in recess, I turned around to Arya's seat and found it empty.

I proceeded with the plaintiffs and Claire through the double doors of the courtroom, out to the foyer, breaking the day down to digestible bullet points for my clients. I descended the courthouse stairway, slipping between the grand columns. Rain clung to my suit. Across the street, a flash of rowdy chestnut hair I'd recognize anywhere disappeared behind the door of a coffee shop.

Arya.

"I'll catch you back at the office." I touched Claire's arm, just as she turned toward me, saying, "Would you like to grab some coffee on our way so we could talk?"

She stopped, swallowed hard, then nodded. "Yes. Yes. Of course."

With my eyes still glued to the coffee shop's door, I crossed the street and strolled inside. Arya was already seated, cradling a cup of coffee at a high window-facing table, staring into it. I slipped into the stool in front of her, knowing full well that I was playing with matches next to a six-gallon barrel of explosives.

"How're we feeling today?" I recognized on impact that it was the wrong thing to ask. How the heck did I think she was feeling? I'd just spent the last seven hours nailing her father's metaphorical coffin closed before dumping it in the ocean.

Arya looked up from her coffee cup, a little disoriented. The rain knocked on the window in front of us.

"Aren't lawyers supposed to be good with social cues? Take a hint," she groaned, rubbing at her eyes.

"I'm more of a straight-shooting kind of guy." I placed my briefcase between us.

She put the rim of her cup to her lips, nibbling on it. "Is that so? Here's a truth bomb for you, then—I don't want to talk to you, Christian. *Ever.*"

"Why'd you come here today?" I asked, ignoring her words. I didn't make it a habit to harass women, or even give them the time of day unless they vied for it. But I knew Arya's defense mechanism was pushing people away—we were cut from the same cloth—and wasn't completely certain she wanted to be alone right now. "He didn't even acknowledge you."

"There was a picture of his penis the size of a movie screen in the middle of the courtroom. A little hard to look your child in the eye after that."

"Exactly. You can't possibly believe he's innocent after that."

"I'm not sure he is innocent at all." She set her cup back on the table and spun it with her fingers absentmindedly. "I'm in the reasonable-doubt zone. But you are right. He has been ignoring me. He wouldn't even take any of my calls."

"That's a form of guilt admission." I grabbed the cup from between her fingers and took a sip. She took her coffee with no sugar and no milk. Just like me. "Which brings me to my original point—why are you here?"

"It's hard to let go of your only family. Even if said family is horrible. It's worse than if he'd died. Because if he died, at least I could still love him."

Being the son of two asshole parents, I could relate.

"What about your mother?" I asked.

"She's not much of a mother, to be honest. That's why I think I managed to overlook the glaring signals from Dad. You said you're not close to your parents, right?"

I smiled tersely. "Not particularly."

"Only child?"

I nodded.

"Do you ever wish you had siblings?" She propped her chin on her fist.

"No. The less people in my life, the better. What about you?"

"I had a brother," she mused, staring at the rain, which was coming down harder. "But he died a very long time ago."

"I'm sorry."

"Sometimes I think I will always be a half of something. Never a whole person."

"Don't say that."

I'd never met anyone as whole as you, imperfections and all.

Suddenly, Arya frowned, cocking her head sideways as she studied me. "Wait, are you even supposed to talk to me?"

"You're not a part of the case anymore. You no longer provide professional services to your father, and your name is not on the witness list."

Though ethically, my speaking to the defendant's daughter was unorthodox at best and a dumpster fire at worse.

She arched an eyebrow. "I don't?"

I shook my head. "He removed all mentions of your company from his websites a couple days after I visited your office. At your request, I assumed."

Arya's thickly fringed eyes flared. Obviously, my assumption had been wrong. She shot up to her feet, knocking her coffee over. Brown liquid spilled over the table and floor. She righted the cup with shaky hands. "Have a nice evening, Mr. Miller."

She slapped the door open, running off to the street. I grabbed my briefcase and followed her, recognizing how goddamn thoughtless I was. At this point, I was begging to get in trouble. Judge Lopez would have every right to dismiss me from the case if he found out what I was doing.

History repeats itself.

"Arya, stop." I shouldered past the Manhattan evening crowd. Rain came down in sheets on both of us, weighing her crazy hair down. She picked up her pace. She was running. From *me*. And I was chasing her.

My legs moved faster.

"Arya!" I barked. I didn't even know what I wanted to say to her. I just knew I wanted to get the last word in. The rain beat down on my face. She halted at an intersection, at a red light. Trapped, she turned around, her posture guarded, like she was ready to pounce. Her green eyes danced in their sockets.

"*What?* What do you want from me, Christian?"

Everything, and nothing at all.

Your tears, your apologies, your regret, and your body.

Most of all, I want you to remember. What we used to be. And what we can never be anymore.

I ran a hand over my soaked hair. "Why did you stop coming to the pool?"

She threw her head back and laughed. She was so beautiful I wanted to strangle myself for taking the case. For not letting Conrad Roth get nailed by someone else while I conducted a sordid affair with his daughter. Full of naked weekends in exotic places, champagne, and kinky sex.

She grumbled. "I wanted to get some dirt on you. Then I . . ." She trailed off, stopping herself at the last minute, not wanting to complete the sentence. "Then I realized you are not the real villain in the story," she finished quietly.

"I'm not." But the words felt funky in my mouth, because in some ways, I was. Neither of us gave a rat's ass about the rain pounding on our faces as we stood in the middle of the street. Her scent, of peaches and sugar and Arya, amplified through the rain. The light turned green behind her back. I stepped closer, my fingers twitching to cup her cheek. "Cut your losses. Turn your back on your father like he turned his back on you. Have dinner with me."

She shook her head, squeezing her eyes shut. Raindrops flew from her hair. Suddenly, we were back to being fourteen. I glued my forehead to hers, breathing her in. Shockingly, she didn't push me away. Our hair was plastered together, our noses touching. Her heart pounded against mine. I wanted to do things I had no business thinking about.

"God." She curled her fists, pressing them against my chest. "I want this to stop."

"I'm sorry. I'm so, so sorry."

I was, at least in that moment. It was a moment of pure, simple old Nicky, with his stupid weakness for this girl.

"I feel so lost." She exhaled.

"You'll find yourself, soon enough. When the trial ends. When the dust settles."

"Is fucking a Roth a longtime dream of yours?" Her lips moved so close to mine I could taste them.

"Not generally, no. But one in particular, yes. It's on my bucket list."

"And do you always achieve what's on your bucket list?" Lips against lips. Skin against skin.

"Most times," I admitted.

"Well, you're not getting me."

"You're already halfway mine."

Our bodies were flush together, our clothes soaking wet, but she didn't cower. She didn't step back. I remembered the twelve-year-old girl who wouldn't let me win one stupid argument while we hung out at the cemetery. That girl was still there.

"Wanna bet?" Drops of water hung from her eyelashes, and she'd never looked more beautiful, more destructive, more real.

"Sure." I spoke into her mouth. "Let's make it interesting. If we have sex, you are paying me for all the dinners I'm going to take you to retroactively."

Someone pushed past us, almost knocking Arya into the street on their quest to find a dry spot. I pulled her by the waist into me, back to safety. Our gazes didn't break.

"How chivalrous of you. And if I win and we don't sleep together, you are going to answer all of my questions about my father's case."

"I can't do that."

"*After* it's over," she clarified. "Which is also the timeline for this bet."

I tucked wet tresses of hair behind her ears. "Within reason, and with my attorney-client-confidentiality agreement in mind, you have a deal."

"How long will the trial last for?" she asked. I was mesmerized by her lips. How wet they were. The way they pouted around different vowels as she spoke.

"Four weeks. Five, if your father's legal team gets its head out of their asses and shows up, which frankly seems unlikely."

"Better get your game on." She offered me a vixenish wink.

I watched her go, feeling robbed somehow.

Ari and Nicky.

Nicky and Ari.

Then, I hadn't been enough.

I was going to prove to her that nowadays, I was more than she could handle.

Later that evening, Arsène and I were in a trendy SoHo bar when we met Jason Hatter, a nice enough chap who'd gone to Harvard Law School with me. He spotted us from across the bar, kissed his date's cheek, and made his way to us. He told us he'd recently made it to partner at his own firm, but he looked about as jolly as a man who had to lick armpits for a living.

"You're still not partner?" Jason asked, more surprised than cocky about it. He was a nice guy, but he sure was as tactless as a used napkin.

"Christian is still working his charms on Daddy and Daddy." Arsène patted the small of my back, like I was his date or some shit. I swatted his hand away with a glare.

"I'll be made partner this year," I told Jason.

"Well, I don't doubt it. You have made yourself quite a name. My girlfriend's asking if you're seeing anyone."

I thought about Arya, not Claire, before shaking my head. "But no offense, pal, I'm not into the whole threesome thing."

Jason laughed. "I meant she wants to set you up with a friend."

"Oh." I frowned. "Not into that either."

After Jason left, Arsène turned to look at me, a smirk full of triumph playing on his lips. "Back to your story. Just so we're on the same wavelength here, you're saying you *chased* her down the street?"

I cradled my brandy, rubbing my knuckles over my jaw. "Correct."

"And then," Arsène continued, speaking extra slowly, staring at me like I should be wearing a helmet, because I was a danger to myself and everyone around me, "you bet her you could make her sleep with you, even though you don't even have her phone number?"

"I do have her phone number," I pointed out. "She just didn't technically volunteer it to me."

"Define *technically*."

"I asked my secretary to find it."

Arsène nodded silently, letting me digest just how crazy it sounded to an outsider.

"Then you almost kissed her."

"But I didn't."

"Because . . . ?"

"That would complicate things."

This one was a lie. Truth was, I'd known she'd push me away, and I was biding my time.

"Sorry to break it to you, bud, but the train of complicated has departed. You're in dumpster-fire territory. Bottom line is, you're toast," Arsène said matter-of-factly. "You never cross the line of professionalism. With Arya, you ran over that bitch with a Formula One car, then did doughnuts on it."

"Don't make me the saint I'm not." I swirled my drink in its tumbler. And then, because apparently I now wanted to prove my lack of professionalism, "I had sex with Claire."

"Some sex it was. The woman was more vanilla than a fudge-cake ice cream. You kept her around out of sheer convenience and

178

did everything in your power to keep your affair under wraps. Plus, it didn't even last three months."

"Claire was bad press, even after I informed HR about us." I waved him off. "She works under me."

"Not in the way she'd like." Arsène tilted his glass up, downing his drink, and slammed it against the wooden bar. "Besides, it was never about the press. Arya Roth is your kryptonite. You should've never taken the case, and now you can't back down. Unless, of course, you want to see your career go up in flames."

A busty redhead slid between us just then, wrapped in a black leather skirt and what looked like a red bra missing a few parts. She shot me a feline smile, jerking her head sideways. "My friends over there bet me fifty bucks I couldn't get you to buy me a drink. What do you think?"

"I *think*"—I smiled cordially, leaning toward her, whispering in her ear—"you just became fifty bucks poorer."

The woman's smile morphed into a scowl, and she backed away, stomping back to her clones. She was exactly my type, but I needed a little more than a carbon copy of my last one-night stand. I wanted someone to challenge me, to fight me, to drive me nuts. And that someone was currently blue balling me for going after her father.

I turned back to Arsène, finding him beyond amused as he shook his head. "*So* toast."

"What now?" I hissed.

"Old Christian wouldn't say no to a night of no-strings-attached sex with Jessica Rabbit."

"Old Christian doesn't have to wake up at six tomorrow to prepare for trial."

"Sure." Arsène patted my shoulder, chuckling. "New Christian can sell himself this load of baloney if it makes him feel better."

◆ ◆ ◆

That evening, when I took an Uber back home, I asked the driver to make a pit stop at Arya's work address. I didn't care what Arsène thought. All I needed was one taste before I discarded Arya right along with her father back to my past.

I knew Arya and I had no future. Not only because she'd pretended to be a trustworthy person only to stab me in the back, but also because she literally thought I was someone else. A relationship wasn't on the table. Arya would run for the hills the minute she found out who I really was.

Besides—fourteen-year-old Arya had crushed me for nothing more than blood sport. What would thirty-one-year-old Arya do when she found out the game I was playing?

The damp streets of Manhattan blurred through the window before the driver stopped by the redbrick building where Brand Brigade was situated. It was ten thirty at night. Arya's office light was on through her window.

I watched as she floated around her office, plucking paper from the printer, while talking on the phone.

She'd grown up to be a workaholic. Just like me.

"Sir?"

"Hmm?" I asked absentmindedly, still staring at her through the window.

"It's been fifteen minutes."

It has?

"Yes," he said, clearing his throat. I hadn't even known I'd said it out loud. "We good to go?"

"Yeah." I played with my matchbook. "Home it is."

CHAPTER NINETEEN

CHRISTIAN

Past

"Faster." Headmaster Plath smacked the back of my head. He glided along the kitchen tiles, lacing his fingers behind his back. Half my body was inside an industrial pot as I scrubbed it clean. My knuckles were so dry they bled every time I washed my hands. Which was often enough, seeing as I was on dishwashing duty at least four times a week.

I sucked in a breath, rubbing the cast-iron cleaner against the tar-like crust that had settled around the edges, refusing to submit.

"Mr. Roth was right. You're so ugly you could snag lightning." Headmaster Plath cackled, stopping by a window overlooking the green grass. There were students splayed on a hill by the fountain, catching sunrays, slurping slushies, telling each other about their summer plans. Mine included trying to get some work at the nearest town and walking ten miles to and from boarding school each day, because I couldn't afford the bus tickets. I imagined Ruslana—there was no point calling her Mom at this point—was playing second violin to the Roths. Making Arya her fancy acai bowls, braiding her hair, carrying a beach bag for her across golden dunes in exotic places near the ocean.

"He is doing you a huge favor, you know," Headmaster Plath continued, staring idly at his students through the window. His eyes growing large and greedy. I always got the idea that he liked what he saw just a little too much when he looked at some of the boys. "Nothing would have become of you if you'd stayed in New York."

"It'd have been nice to have a choice in the matter," I muttered, changing the angle of my arm while scrubbing the pot. My muscles were burning with exhaustion. It was not unheard of for my arms to be numb all night after hours of kitchen duty.

"What'd you say?" His head spun so fast that for a second I thought his neck might snap.

"Nothing," I hissed. Students weren't supposed to take on kitchen or laundry duties unless they'd misbehaved. It was supposed to be a detention of sorts, but I seemed to be a part of the staff here. Arsène and Riggs always told me it was bullshit, and I agreed, but there was little I could do about it.

"No." Plath rushed toward me, eager to pick a fight. "Say it again."

I turned to face him. My face felt red and hot. I was furious with him for pulling this kind of crap, and with myself for putting up with it. And with Conrad, who kept taunting me years later, albeit from a safe distance, just because I'd dared to touch his precious, stupid, spoiled girl.

"I said it'd have been nice if he gave me a choice!" I turned around, sticking my chin up.

He took a step closer, his nose almost brushing mine. "Do you have any idea how much he pays to keep you here every year?"

"I bet I shell out most of the fee, since I work here all year round."

Plath pressed his nose against mine, towering over me, pushing my face backward, his eyes boring into mine. "You work here all year round because you're a piece of trash who cannot stay out of trouble," he jeered. "Because you're a useless little prick whose entire contribution to society is cleaning and ironing good boys' clothes."

Something inside me snapped just then. I was tired. Tired of waking up at 5:00 a.m. to do other people's laundry. Tired of doing my homework at two in the morning because I had to clean and scrub pots and pans. Tired of mowing the lawn on hot summer days without getting water breaks. Exhausted from being punished for something I hadn't even *wanted* to do. At the same time, I knew Plath was challenging me. He waited for me to talk back. To retaliate. Wanted an excuse to strike me. I wouldn't put it past him to put his hands on me. He'd been careful so far, but his mean streak overrode all his other traits.

So even though I knew I was going to regret it, I forced myself to smile. Stretching my mouth across my cheeks hurt my face, but I still did it, then uttered the words I should have told Conrad that time he'd beaten me up: *"Fuck. You."*

I spit in his face, but not before gathering a respectable amount of phlegm. I knew I was going to pay for it, but it felt good. The spit landed on Plath's right cheek and slithered down to his neck. He made no move to wipe it off. Just stared at me with an expression I was too anxious to decode.

The next few seconds were a blur. Headmaster Plath cracked his knuckles loudly. On cue, the kitchen door flung open, and three burly seniors who were on the rowing team walked in.

"Gentlemen." Plath stepped backward, my saliva still on his cheek. Crap on a cracker. They'd been waiting that entire time. This was all a plan to aggravate me. "I have to step away to clean up this mess. Please keep Mr. Ivanov company while I'm away. Care to do that for me?"

"No problem, sir."

One of the boys—the biggest, dumbest one, naturally—waved his hand like a fortune cat toward the headmaster as he stomped toward me. The door to the kitchen closed with a click. I looked between the three of them. I knew what was about to happen. Still, I wasn't sorry.

Shithead Number One cracked his knuckles, while Shithead Number Two slammed me against the wall. Shithead Number Three stood by the door, making sure no one was coming. I knew it was the end for me. That I'd probably die.

"Why, hello there, Oliver Twist. Found your way into the upper crust and thought we'd just let you walk in like you own the place, huh?" Shithead One asked. I didn't answer. He punched me square in the jaw, sending my head flying to the other side, while Shithead Two held me firmly in place.

Shithead One laughed. I was bleeding from my mouth. My jaw was numb, but I felt something hot trickling down my chin.

"And to talk back to your headmaster like that . . . where were you raised? The jungle?"

He kicked me in the gut, and when I folded in two, he kicked my face repeatedly, holding my shoulders to keep me from falling. There was a lot of thrashing after that, but I was only half-conscious at this point. My eyelids were too heavy to keep open, and the noises around me became muffled. Like I was at the bottom of the ocean. I didn't know how much time had passed. Maybe it was a few minutes. Maybe an hour. But at some point, there was screaming and punching around me—people were hitting one another, not just me—and then there were two pairs of hands dragging me away from the kitchen, their owners barking at one another. I recognized Arsène's voice first. It remained calm throughout. Chillingly so. Riggs, however, wanted to go back there and hand them their asses.

"You already broke that dude's nose," Arsène said, groaning with effort as they dragged me up the stairway to my room. I kept my eyes closed, too ashamed to open them. I didn't want to answer any questions.

"That asshole looked like a stomped possum to begin with. I want to inflict permanent damage," Riggs complained, tugging me as they got to my floor and rounded the carpeted hallway to my dorm room.

"The most permanent damage that kid will suffer is having the intelligence of a goddamn Froyo, and that has nothing to do with you. Let it go. They're chummy with Plath."

"We should strike Plath too," Riggs said, giving my door a round-house kick. They dumped me on my bed. I cracked one eye open and spotted Riggs hauling his shirt off by the collar, discarding it in my sink, and letting it soak in cold water.

Arsène plopped down beside me, forcing some water between my cracked lips. "No. This Conrad guy has him in his pocket. We'll have to keep a better eye on Nicky."

Riggs squeezed his shirt, unbuttoned my uniform, and began pressing his balled wet shirt as a compress against my hot, bruised skin. I groaned in pain, but it felt good.

"Aw, look. The princess is up," Riggs cooed. "You okay there, sweetie?"

"Eat shit, Riggs."

Riggs laughed. "He's okay. Hey, how about I get us some burgers? I can drive downtown."

I shook my head frantically. "You might get caught."

Riggs had graduated from exploding random things and causing small fires to stealing the staff's cars and sneaking into town. He didn't have a driver's license. That didn't put a damper on his big plans.

"Good." Riggs patted my knee, while Arsène wrote a list of all the things he needed to bring back. Extra-garlic fries among them, no doubt. "That way I'll get kitchen duty and you won't. Or better yet—we'll do it together. The big, fat, dysfunctional happy family that we are."

"You can't do that," I mumbled, too tired to argue.

"We can and we will." Arsène pushed me back down on the bed. "And you better fucking reciprocate when it's our turn to fuck up."

The next day, Arsène got caught buying weed he had no intention of smoking from one of the seniors, while Riggs brought an actual *mountain lion* he'd somehow managed to get a leash on and declared his new pet. Both my best friends got three weeks of kitchen and laundry duty.

After that day, Riggs and Arsène made sure I would never do a kitchen shift all by myself again.

CHAPTER TWENTY

A R Y A

Present

I decided to attend the trial during the days and catch up on my work during the evenings. It wasn't ideal. Then again, nothing about my situation was.

Christian Miller wasn't wrong. The evidence didn't leave room for much doubt. Each line of defense Louie and Terrance tried was answered with even more evidence from Christian and his clients. Louie and Terrance couldn't even deny the harassment. When it was time to present their case, they simply suggested all advances were fully consensual. One of the accusers was twenty-three, for crying out loud. Younger than me, and a devout Catholic. The idea of her flinging herself at my father was delusional. And all of them had been fired by him after refusing his sexual advances.

Still, I came to court every day. Maybe to punish myself, but more likely to punish Dad. I knew how much it killed him that I witnessed all this.

I didn't do a whole lot of sleeping these days. I mostly cried myself to exhaustion, my mind running through all the memories of Dad's interactions with his female employees in my head, like a broken record.

Then I'd wake up and drag myself to court again and again and again.

After each day in court, Christian would hand me a printed reservation he'd made for one of the most talked-about restaurants in town. Be it Benjamin Steakhouse, Luthun, Pylos, or Barnea Bistro.

"I'll wait there for an hour tonight. We'll have a private room, or at least a booth where no one can see us."

"Oh, I'm sure it'd be all your pleasure to get caught," I'd answer.

"Not at all. If we get caught, we both lose."

He never pushed, never begged, and never expressed any disappointment or anger over my absence the next day, even though I knew he was sitting by himself at restaurants every day.

Each day I ignored his invitation, my resolve would crack a little wider. A tad deeper. I would watch him in action in court, my gut filled with anger and longing, and exasperation, too, because for the first time in my life, I couldn't tell if someone was an ally or an enemy.

Most of all, I observed Christian with fear, because I suspected he'd figured out that I wasn't coming to court for Dad anymore.

I was coming to court for *him*.

One night, I was fast asleep in my bedroom, clad in a simple sweatshirt I'd stolen from Jillian some years ago in college. I was pooped from a day of attending court and working (I'd pretty much managed to get back on top of work, but it was killing me to be present in two things that took over my life). I'd drifted into sweet slumber when I felt a shadow hovering above my body, and when I looked up, Christian was there, standing at the foot of my bed, still in his sharp suit.

He smelled like the rain and pencil shavings, and I was tired of pushing him away. So tired, in fact, I didn't even ask him how he'd gotten in.

"What are you doing here?" I asked instead. My voice lacked that furious fight I used every time we were bickering.

But Christian didn't answer. He took a seat on the edge of my bed, grabbed my ankle, and perched my foot in his lap to give me a foot massage.

I groaned, throwing my head back and letting him work his magic. I was appalled with my inability to push him away.

His hands hiked up to the back of my knees, working restlessly, kneading and squeezing the soft, sore spots in my body.

"This will mean nothing," I mumbled, closing my eyes. Because I knew where it was heading, and so did he.

A low chuckle emerged from his throat. "I'll cancel our wedding invitations."

"But not the cake. Send the cake to my office. I've been craving sugar all week."

His hands went higher up, to my inner thighs, and he tugged me down so he could touch more of me, until his fingers were right there, between my thighs, in the holy triangle no man had touched in such a long time. I let out a shaky sigh when his hand pushed past the side of my panties. He dipped two fingers in, finding me soaking wet.

"That's my girl. Now, I'm only going to use my fingers tonight so that tomorrow, you'll wake up aching all over and ask me for the real thing. You understand?"

I opened my eyes, frowning at him. He had some nerve to sound so self-assured and cocky. I had no intention of seeking him out tomorrow, but if I could get an orgasm out of it *tonight*, I would put up with his grandiose ideas.

"Whatever, Napoleon. Just make it good for me." I took his hand and pushed it deeper into my underwear, and he laughed his deep male laugh that danced in the pit of my stomach.

And then he was fingering me. His fingers sliding in and out of me, curling when they were inside me and hitting me somewhere deep and sensitive. He massaged my sensitive bud as he worked me, and I begrudgingly had to admit he wasn't wrong—he *was* good at everything. Especially with his hands.

My hips bucked forward, rolling to meet more of his touch. My panting became quick and shallow at the same time as I chased that elusive feeling of being pleasured by someone else.

"Christian. I . . . I . . . I . . ."

"Can't form a coherent sentence?" he hissed into the shell of my ear, chuckling softly.

"Screw you."

"Already way ahead of you, darling."

He played with me faster and deeper. His hands were everywhere now—on my breasts, clutching the back of my neck, roaming my legs. But he didn't kiss me, and he didn't have me, just like he'd promised.

The climax washed over me in waves. Everything shuddered, and I squeezed my eyes closed, unable to look at him when he gave me such pure pleasure and joy.

When I finally opened my eyes again, Christian wasn't there.

The only thing I had left was dampness between my thighs, ruined underwear, and my fingers, which were still tangled in the elastic of my panties.

It was a fantasy.

A dream.

Christian had never been here.

"Your father is asking to see you."

My mother delivered the news with morbid dejection. I supposed it was warranted, since I'd been ghosting her for a few days now. I didn't blame her for not coming to court. I was a first-grade masochist for doing this to myself. I *did*, however, blame her for pretty much everything else, including (but not limited to) neglecting my existence up until the last few weeks, when everything with Dad had blown up. Now she wanted my company. To make amends. This was a classic case of too little, too late.

"Can he not ask me himself?" I replied, waiting in line for my cup of coffee across from court, pinning my phone between my ear and shoulder. My leg bounced impatiently, and I glanced at my wristwatch. The trial had wrapped up for the day, and I still hadn't eaten a thing today.

"With everything going on, he wasn't sure if you wanted to see him," my mother explained. I knew she wasn't to blame for any of it, and yet, I couldn't help directing some of my anger toward her. She was, after all, a participant in the breakdown of this marriage.

"So he sent you as his mouthpiece?"

"Arya, nobody accused him of being overly graceful. Are you coming or not?" she asked.

The line moved at a snail's pace. I desperately needed a coffee.

"I'll be there in thirty minutes. Twenty, if traffic is light." I turned off my phone and tucked it into my bag. My turn finally arrived. "Grande Americano, no cream, no sugar. Thank you."

I fished for my purse before feeling a hand brushing my shoulder, handing the barista a black American Express.

"She'll take the southwest veggie wrap and chocolate-covered espresso beans too."

I whipped my head around, ready with a scowl. "What do you think you're doing?"

"Padding that open tab of all those dinners you are going to pay me for." Christian's smirk felt more like a brush of his knuckles over my spine. "Right now you're about eleven hundred in the red. All those restaurants I've been enjoying by myself this week don't come cheap, and I always insist on a good bottle of wine."

"Drinking alone every night has a name." I smiled sweetly. "Alcoholism."

His eyes crinkled with a grin. "Don't worry, Ms. Roth, I donate the wine to the people sitting next to me. Very generous of you, if I may add."

I had to hand it to him—no one was immune to his charms. Not the jurors—male and female alike—not the court reporter, and not his junior associate. Which, again, made me wonder why he was pursuing me. Sure, I was good looking and successful in my field, but Christian Miller could have his pick of the crop. Why waste time with someone who dedicated every ounce of her energy to trying to hate him?

"Don't forget I don't owe you a penny if I don't sleep with you. Which reminds me." I spun to the barista in front of us with a smile. "I'll also have sweet potato chips, *all* of your shortbread cookies, and five hundred dollars' worth of gift cards."

"Your optimism is commendable." Christian ran the tip of his tongue over his upper lip.

"Your delusions are concerning," I quipped back, nodding in thanks to the barista in front of us, who took Christian's order next. A coffee. I stuck around next to him until my Americano was ready. "Where are we *not* dining together tonight?" I inquired airily, to change the subject.

"I'm glad you asked. Tonight, I'll be waiting for you at Sant Ambroeus. It's in the West Village. Italian. They say the cacio e pepe is to die for."

"Oh, is that so? A girl could hope."

He grinned down at me, making me feel like a toddler being humored by a grown-up.

"Stop smiling," I ordered. "It puts me in a bad mood."

"Can't help it. Your aversion to losing is sweet."

"I'm not sweet," I said tersely. I wasn't. I was a badass boss bitch with a high-flying career. And then some.

"You are," he said, almost regretfully. "And that wasn't in my plans."

Another barista called my name, and I walked over to accept my order.

"All I ask from you is one hour," Christian reminded me. "And this time, I'm getting the Château Lafite Rothschild 1995. That's eight hundred dollars a bottle. You don't mind, do you?"

I turned around and stomped my Jimmy Choos while simultaneously ordering an Uber on my phone.

What a jackass.

◆ ◆ ◆

"Brand Brigade is going to have to take me back as a client. Individually, not as a part of a corporation."

Dad sat back on his brown leather recliner in front of the crackling fire. His study was in disarray. Files everywhere. Including the stacks I'd sifted through the other day, which must've given away the fact that I knew about his affair with Ruslana. Not that it mattered. I doubted he was in the business of explaining himself to anyone at this point.

"Now why would we do that?" I asked coldly.

Conrad, who had lost at least ten pounds over the past weeks, blinked at me like I was an idiot. "Because I'm your father, Arya."

"A father who hasn't taken any of my calls and refused to see me for weeks," I pointed out. Mom scurried into the study with a tray of sugar cookies and tea. I'd seen more of her in the past few weeks than I had in years. She completely ignored her husband, setting the tea and cookies in front of me. I hadn't even asked her how *she* was taking all this. Guilt unfurled inside me.

"Sorry, didn't mean to interrupt. Just thought you'd appreciate a treat. Sugar cookies are your favorite, right?"

Actually, I was more of a chocolate chip kind of girl, but that was beside the point and super trivial. I smiled tightly. "Thank you, Mother."

After she closed the door behind her, I turned to look at my father again. "You were saying?"

Conrad rubbed his cheek, making a show of heaving a sigh. "Look, what was I supposed to do? You are my precious baby. No one wants to get caught with their pants down in front of their loved ones."

"So you lied," I said flatly.

"Yes and no. I've had affairs. Many affairs. I'm not proud of my infidelity. But I didn't harass anyone."

"Your dick pic tells a different story." Even if in not so many words.

He shifted uncomfortably. "This was reciprocated, and a dark time in my life. I'm not a monster."

"This is for the court to determine, not me." I crossed one leg over the other, cupping my knee with my hands. "And until I know the answer to that, I cannot, in good conscience, link my company to your name. Especially as you dropped us without even giving me the heads-up shortly before the trial started."

"I did it to protect you!" Conrad slammed his palm against the desk between us, making the whole thing rattle.

I shook my head. "You did it because you wanted to hire someone bigger, with more street cred. But no one would take you on, right? No one wanted to get their hands dirty."

He leaned over the desk between us, inching closer to me, a vein throbbing in his temple. "You think this is a game? I could lose every penny I have, Arya, robbing you of your inheritance. You could be *poor*."

The last word was uttered with complete disdain.

"I'll never be poor, because I provide for myself. But if I lose my inheritance—whose fault would that be?"

"Theirs!" My father jumped up from his seat, tossing his arms in the air in frustration. "Of course it's their fault. Why do you think it took them so long to come forward? They piggybacked on Amanda Gispen's complaint!"

"They were scared you were going to ruin their lives." I rose from my chair, too, baring my teeth. "Like you did to Ruslana and Nicky. What happened to them? Tell me."

My father stared at me with contempt. I'd never thought I'd see that look on his face. Of sheer hatred. I wondered where the man who'd kissed my boo-boos and read me good-night stories had gone. How I could bring him back. And most importantly—if he'd ever really existed.

"Do you think a settlement is still on the table?" He changed the topic.

"How should I know?"

"This Christian guy seems to be taken with you."

"He does?" I asked, buying time. My heart jackrabbited in my chest at the mention of his name.

"I see the way he chases after you like a puppy. He's doing a bad job at hiding it. Dig around for me."

It took everything in me not to hurl something against the wall. "He is not going to be swayed. He wants your ass on a silver platter."

"He wants in your bed more."

He looked at me then, his eyes asking something his mouth didn't dare utter aloud. Internally, I keeled over and threw up. All the love I had left for him. The good memories, and the bad ones too. And the sliver of loyalty running between us. Because a man who could ask something like that of his daughter was capable of doing much worse. He'd just given himself away.

"Wow. Okay. This is my cue to leave."

"If you don't help me," he hissed, shooting out a hand to stop me but pulling it back before I could smack it away, "you are dead to me, Arya. This is your chance—your *only* chance—to pay me back for giving a damn when your mother didn't. I need to know, are you in or are you out?"

We were both standing now. I didn't know when that had happened. I closed my eyes. Took a deep breath. Opened my mouth.

"Be honest with me first. Did you hurt them?" I asked. He knew what I meant. "Did you?"

There was a pause. The truth was hanging in the air between us, dangling over our heads. It had a taste and a smell and a pulse. I knew it before I heard it. Which was why he knew lying would be pointless.

"Yes."

The word rang in my ears. I opened my mouth, refusing to let the tears fall. I turned around and fled. Rushed out of the penthouse. My mother followed me. She'd been waiting outside, in the hallway, eavesdropping, I suspected.

"Arya! Arya, wait!"

But I didn't. I took two flights of stairs down before punching the elevator's button, just to make sure they weren't following me. In the elevator, I realized I'd stopped referring to him as Dad, even in my head. He was Conrad Roth now, the man who'd fallen from grace, dragging his family down with him.

When the elevator opened, my instinct was to cross the street and go to the cemetery. To visit Aaron. I needed to talk to someone. To unload.

But I didn't want to talk to Aaron.

For the first time in a long time, I wanted to talk to someone who could answer back.

"Sorry, buddy." I ran past the cemetery, then caught a yellow cab.

I checked my watch.

Maybe I could make it after all.

◆ ◆ ◆

I spotted Christian through the restaurant's window, sitting in one of the upholstered red booths. An entire meal sat in front of him, untouched. He was working on his laptop. He sat up straight, his face stoic, ignoring the curious glances of people around him. My heart beat a little faster. I wiped the tears I'd shed on my way here from my face and handed the driver my credit card.

"How do I look?" I asked the middle-aged woman behind the wheel.

She peered at me through the rearview mirror. "You want honesty?"

Generally yes, although now I'm not so sure.

"You look like a wreck. No offense."

"None taken."

"But you got good bones and a nice rack, so go knock him dead, sweetheart."

With those powerful words of encouragement, I shot out the back door of the cab.

It was five minutes to nine, but I made it. I walked into the joint and explained to the maître d' that my companion was waiting, then hurried through the maze of booths, an unexplainable rush of affection slamming into me when Christian looked up from his screen, boyish surprise coloring his face.

He closed his laptop, sitting back, enjoying the view. I stood in front of him, not taking a seat just yet. I was panting, my hair was a mess, and I was in desperate need of washing the day away.

"Should we be seen together like this in the open?" I wanted to get the important bits out of the way.

"No one knows us here. At any rate, if we see each other once or twice in public, no touching, no flirting, this could still be summed up to you working on the case, trying to convince me to talk my clients into settling. As long as we don't . . . *canoodle*."

"We won't *canoodle*," I said briskly.

"You okay?" he asked, no trace of sarcasm in his voice.

"Why wouldn't I be?" I barked, still on the defensive. I couldn't exactly tell him about my conversation with my father, even though, technically, I'd come here to do just that.

"Because you're here," he said gently, standing up and pushing my chair back for me. I took a seat. He put his hands on my shoulders. My whole body came alive. His skin was warm through my clothes. I no longer felt like a traitor, like a harlot, for wanting to be with him. My father was a monster who deserved to be punished. Christian was right. He wasn't to blame for Conrad Roth's downfall.

He sat in front of me, his glacial blue eyes twinkling with what I could swear was sheer happiness. He looked surprised, even a little giddy. "What made you change your mind?"

"Is it important?" I huffed, feeling my eyes prickling with tears again.

"Yes." He reached to fill my glass with wine. It did look like the expensive stuff. *I better not sleep with this man.* "To me, it is."

"Why?"

"Because you're not going to sleep with me as long as you think I'm wronging your father. So I want to know if the penny has dropped yet."

His words brought me back to earth. Of course Christian was only interested in me as a conquest. A shiny prize. A bonus for winning this trial, something that could be taken away from my father. I slapped my napkin open and ironed it across my lap, then grabbed a fork and twirled it over pasta. I was so hyperaware of his eyes on me, so overcome with emotions, I hadn't even touched the food on the table.

"I'm here because I needed a breather and a good meal. Nothing more." My voice was steady, but I couldn't look him in the eye.

"And I'm here because of the food," he deadpanned.

"It's good food," I pointed out, pretending to flip through the menu. I felt his gaze on me. I shut the menu, putting it down and shaking my head. "Why did you become a lawyer?" I demanded.

"Excuse me?" He raised his eyebrows.

"Out of all the professions in the world, why did you choose this one? You're bright. You're sharp. You could have done anything."

I was waiting for a joke, a change of subject, or maybe a generic response. But instead, Christian gave it some serious thought before answering. "Growing up, I've been the victim of unfair treatment. I guess a part of me always wanted to make sure it'd never happen again. If you know your rights, you know how to protect yourself. I didn't always know my rights."

I swallowed. "That's fair."

"And you?" he asked, before I could dig into what it was that had happened to him. "Why PR?"

"I like helping people, and blood makes me queasy. It was either PR or medicine."

Christian laughed. "Great choice. I can already imagine you yelling at your patients that they were being drama queens."

I laughed too. He sounded like he understood me. But . . . how could he?

The rest of the conversation flowed nicely. Even though there was a lot both of us wanted to know about one another, we stuck to a subject that couldn't garner arguments or debate—food.

He began explaining to me about each dish he'd ordered. When he was done, I pursed my lips, studying him. I'd met this man before, I decided. Maybe briefly, at a bar, one of the parties I'd gone to in college, or a charity event, but I was certain we knew each other.

"Mesmerized?" Christian's cocky grin was back on full display.

I shrugged, taking a sip of my wine. "I just think it's cute."

"What's cute?"

"How badly you want to win our bet."

Christian clinked his wineglass against mine. "One thing you should know about me, Arya—I never lose a bet."

CHAPTER TWENTY-ONE

CHRISTIAN

Present

She was here.

In my domain, in my territory, in my *claws*.

Whether it was her father who'd pushed her into my arms or the mystery surrounding me, Arya had finally taken the bait. She looked exhausted. The outline of her ribs poked through her blouse. There was something haunting about her face. But I'd take her any way I could have her. That, at least, hadn't changed.

We had a pleasant meal, although I could tell her mind was else-where. My bet was that Daddy dearest had finally owned up to his wrong deeds and she'd had to not only face the truth but swallow it whole. After I paid (I wondered if watching her write a check for all the meals I'd paid for was going to be as sweet as drowning myself inside her), I suggested we take a walk.

"I could use a walk." Arya surprised me by *not* being her usual defiant self. We strolled along Greenwich Avenue. The street was bustling with people, dogs, and life. As surreal as being with her again in New York was, I couldn't stop myself from enjoying it. Countless times I'd imagined myself as a teenager taking her places. I'd fantasized about being someone else. The son of a surgeon and a child psychologist, maybe. Taking Conrad Roth's precious daughter for ice cream. He'd have let me too.

"My father wondered if your clients would be open to a settlement." Arya wrapped her arms around herself, her cheeks flushed with the wine and the meal.

Ah. So this was what this dinner was about. A grim smile found my lips. "We weren't open to settlement pretrial, so that's a goddamn stretch if I ever saw one. Also, I'd appreciate if next time he uses his attorneys as a channel of communication."

She pursed her lips.

I nudged her shoulder with mine as we walked. "Hey. Let's not talk about that."

There was a lull, but then Arya forced herself to smile. "So tell me about your childhood. I'm still trying to figure out where I've seen you before."

This was my chance to come clean, if I'd ever had one. Since I wasn't a complete moron, I passed on the opportunity. But it was a reminder I couldn't romance this woman. I was deceiving her to the highest degree by not revealing my true identity.

"I grew up here in New York. Went to a private school when I was fourteen. My parents and I didn't really get along."

"What do your parents do?"

"My father owns a deli, and my mother managed an estate."

So far, not one lie. Although my sperm donor's shop was a continent away, and my mother had managed the Roths' estate by sweeping the floors.

"Do I know this private school?"

"You do."

"Does it have a name?"

"It does," I confirmed.

"Wow, you're really not going to tell me." But her eyes clung to my face, the distant sparkle of hope willing me to contradict her. "You're impossible."

"And you love it."

"So how did you find yourself at Harvard Law School, seeing as you and your parents aren't on speaking terms? Don't tell me you got a full ride. That's nearly impossible. Especially in your tax bracket."

She still believed I came from money. I didn't correct her assumption. This was the point when I considered how much to tell her. Only Riggs and Arsène knew my story. Ultimately, I realized it didn't really matter.

"Promise not to judge?"

"Can't promise that, Counselor. But I'm not usually the judgy type."

I stuffed my hands into my front pockets. "I had a . . . a *sponsor* of sorts."

"Phew, I was worried you were going to confess to bestiality." She pretended to wipe her brow. "What's a sponsor, exactly? Is that a code for sugar mama? Or is the correct term a cougar these days?"

"I'm not sure what the terminology for it is, but she's the one who put me through law school when I couldn't even afford the train ticket to Boston."

"Wait, she shelled out six figures for your education?" Arya sobered up. "Are you *that* good in bed?"

I let out a laugh that seeped into my bones. It was the first time I'd really laughed in decades. My body wasn't used to that anymore.

"First of all, the answer is yes, I am, in fact, that good in bed. Second, get your mind outa the gutter. Mrs. Gudinski was in her fifties when I was in high school. She was very lonely. I was a stable boy."

"Sounds like a well-produced porn movie so far."

I bumped my shoulder into hers again, and we both laughed.

"She had horses. Expensive ones. But she only came to visit them, never to ride. Her late husband was an amateur equestrian. She kept the horses to honor him but had no interest in them whatsoever. She had too much money and no one to spend it on. She needed someone to keep her company during the holidays. Someone to visit her on the weekends. You know. Someone to care."

"And that someone was you?" Arya raised a skeptical eyebrow.

I flashed her a wounded frown. "Me and my closest friends, who I roped into it. Together, we became one big, screwed-up family."

"Huh."

"Don't 'huh' me. Tell me what you think."

"You don't strike me as a caring person."

"Why's that?" I asked.

"For one thing, because all you want is to bed me. Relationship-phobe much?"

Her jealousy stirred something dangerous in the pit of my stomach. The kind of feeling you get when you realize you've just survived a near-fatal car crash.

"That's different. I don't want anything serious with you because I cannot *afford* to be with you. Dating the daughter of the person I'm suing, especially in a case like this one, is not a healthy career move."

"Do I smell leverage?" Her eyes lit up as we picked up our pace to get warm.

"No, you smell a pragmatic business decision. For you too. Imagine what it'd look like if word got out. *Our* relationship is doomed. That doesn't mean I'm against settling down when the right woman arrives."

"Way to make a woman feel special."

I laughed.

"Are you still in touch with her? With your sugar mama?" Arya hugged her midriff, protecting herself from the cold.

"Yes. What about you?" I asked.

"I don't know her, but I mean . . . I could give her a call?" She played dumb. I laughed some more. Shit. This was a lot of laughter.

"What were you like as a teenager?" I amended my question.

"Rebellious. Angsty. Bookworm."

A knowing smile tugged at my lips. I still remembered her gulping books up, at least one a day during summer breaks, like the words would fade if she didn't read them fast enough.

"Bookworm," I repeated, feigning surprise. "What's your favorite book?"

Atonement.

"*Atonement*, hands down. I stole it from my local library when I was fourteen, because it was risqué and I knew my parents would never let me purchase it. It's tragically underrated. Have you read it?"

"Can't say I have," I said, tsking. I couldn't, as a matter of principle, read the book that had caused my downfall. Because if I hadn't kissed Arya . . . if I hadn't caved in to her request . . .

Then what? You'd have stayed in the slums, with a mother who didn't love you and a girl you were pining after but who could never be yours, only to grow up to be a criminal.

Things could have gone a lot worse, I knew. If I'd stayed home and gone to a shitty school. Because even if that first kiss had gone unnoticed, the second or the third or the fourth one wouldn't have. And even if all our hypothetical kisses had gone undetected, I still couldn't have had her. I would have had to sit on the sidelines and watch as Arya fell in love with someone she could actually be with. A Will or Richard or Theodore. Who had a driver and a maid and a college adviser from age ten.

"You should," Arya said.

"Loan it to me."

She wrinkled her nose. "I don't give out my favorite hardbacks as loans. That's a rule."

"Rules are meant to be broken."

"Interesting take, from a *litigator*."

We stopped in front of Jefferson Market Library. The clock on the tower crawled to five minutes before midnight. I couldn't believe we'd spent so many hours together just walking and talking. It was like the last twenty years hadn't even happened.

Only they had.

They were there, in the inches between us, cold and lonely and filled with missed opportunities and unadulterated injustice.

"Why are you really here, Arya?" I turned toward her, my tone rough and coarse, like the scales of a sea creature. "And please, spare me the fine-dining bullshit."

She wet her lips, dropping her gaze to the ground.

"I came to tell you I'm not coming to court again. Today was my last day. I'm done punishing myself for the things he did. I can't stomach hearing what these women have been through."

"You think he did it?" I needed to hear her say that. To disown the man she'd once chosen over me. Our bodies were flush against one another. You could barely fit a needle between us now.

"Yes," she said quietly.

I reached with my thumb and index finger to tilt her chin up. Her eyelashes fluttered. They were shining like diamonds, full of tears. *Swamp eyes,* I'd called them when we were kids. But that wasn't true. They were mossy. The kind of velvety green you could stare at for hours. She held my gaze boldly.

Silver-spooned princess.

The clock hit midnight behind her shoulder, chiming once.

"The witching hour." She closed her eyes, letting two tears roll down her cheeks. "In books, strange things happen during that time."

I cupped the sides of her neck, drawing her close, breathing her in. "In reality too."

And just like that, two decades later, I made the same mistake Nicholai Ivanov had and crushed my lips against Arya Roth's, knowing the world might explode and that my demise would be worth it.

My hands were in her hair, yanking lightly, like I'd dreamed of doing all those years. My blood flooded with desire. I wanted to ravish this woman and leave nothing for the man who came after me. She opened her mouth for me eagerly, our tongues playing together, a small whimper coming from somewhere deep inside her throat. I sank my teeth into her lower lip, tugging her closer, licking her lip before diving in for a deep, feral kiss. I curled my fingers around Arya's waist, pressing her body to mine. There was not enough of her, and suddenly, I felt a little panicky. That there was only one Arya in the world. One chance at having her. I withdrew my mouth from hers, pushing her curls from her face. Her eyes were hungry. Full of things. Bad things. Good things. Arya things.

"Come home with me."

Fuck. It sounded like a command more than a request. She stiffened in my arms, descending back to earth, the fog of dopamine dissipating from her body.

She put a hand on my chest. "I'm not going to sleep with you, Christian."

"Is it the bet? Because screw the bet." I almost crushed my teeth into powder, outraged by my own desperation. I'd slept with dozens of women over the years and had always been in charge. Of the narrative, the rhetoric, the fine print, the situation.

"It's not about the bet. You're right. We can't be together, and I'm not sure it's a good idea to dive into this with you when I'm feeling so . . ."

"Vulnerable?" I offered.

"Confused," she said firmly. "I'm going through a lot. So if you're looking for more than friendship, don't contact me. I don't do forbidden."

We were forbidden when I couldn't afford the clothes on my back and you asked me to pin you against your library shelves. You liked it, then, when you wanted to destroy me.

"You'll change your mind," I said, with more confidence than I felt.

"What makes you say that?"

"We're good together. We have chemistry. We make sense. Doomed things are always sweeter, don't you know? This thing"—I pointed between us—"it's not going anywhere until we act on it. You want a friend? I'll give you a friend. But you'll want more. I guarantee it."

"Oof." She dropped her head to my shoulder, chuckling softly. "I'm too old for this."

"For what?" I pressed my hand to the small of her back, inhaling her greedily, smelling her pending departure.

"This. It was easier to hate you when I didn't know you at all."

"You always knew me," I murmured into her hair.

"You know? I think you're right. My soul . . . it feels calm when it's next to yours."

I smiled grimly.

If only she knew.

◆ ◆ ◆

The next day, I arrived at the courthouse with a mixture of irritation and relief. Arya wasn't there, which meant that for once, I could do my job without a constant semi and the hovering question of what was going through her head, but also that I didn't have the luxury of bathing in her presence. Of knowing she was only a few steps away.

Which was why, as soon as I caught up with paperwork back at the office, I gave her a call.

"How did you get my number?" She typed away on her computer on the other end.

"You gave me your business card, remember?"

"Yes. I also remember you throwing it away."

"Irrelevant. I'm a man of limitless abilities."

That was a roundabout way of saying I'd gotten my secretary to look her up in the yellow pages.

"You mean limitless bull crap."

"How about hot dogs by the New York Public Library? I have a book I need to borrow. Seven thirty okay?"

"First of all, the library closes at five. Second, no, actually." She stopped typing for a second before resuming her work. Was I the only one who was obsessing about that kiss? Apparently so. Arya sounded like she had other things on her mind. "I can't. I have somewhere to go."

"Want some company?"

Just fucking offer her your balls already. Throw in your apartment too, Christian.

If this was how I reacted to one kiss, I definitely had no business sleeping with this woman.

"I'm not sure you'd want to give me company."

"Where are you going?"

"The cemetery."

I dropped the pen I was holding, wheeling myself backward and turning to look at the calendar hanging on my wall. Shit. March 19. Arya and Aaron's birthday. I pushed my chair back to my desk, where my phone was on speaker.

"The cemetery sounds fine. Which one?" I pretended not to know.

There was a pause on the other end.

"Why would you want to go with me to the *cemetery*?"

"Isn't that what friends do? Be there for one another?"

"Is that what we are now? Friends?"

"Yes," I said, even though giving her friendship in return for what she'd done to me was crazy, even by my standards. "We're friends."

Another beat of silence. I had no idea what I was doing.

"Mount Hebron Memorial."

"Who are we visiting?"

"My brother."

207

"Do you think he'll like me?" It was a thing we'd done back then. Pretend like Aaron was still around. Argue, tease, and laugh with him.

Arya stopped typing and sighed. "I think he'd *love* you."

◆ ◆ ◆

Mount Hebron Memorial hadn't changed. The giant weeping willow was still there, hovering above Aaron's grave. I saw Arya's outline curling above her brother's tombstone like a question mark and had to stop and absorb her. Leggy and stylish in her designer pencil skirt and red-bottomed heels. Larger than life, and yet not much larger than the Arya I'd met almost twenty years ago. A firefly; small but glowing. I pushed the wrought iron gate open, a luxury I hadn't had as a trespassing kid. Arya sensed my presence and turned around, throwing me a tired smile.

"It's weird," she sighed. "That you came."

"Are you used to people not coming when they should?" I asked.

"Pretty much. Plus, I'm not your problem."

"I've never seen you as a problem. Your clothes, maybe. But never you."

"What's in the bag?" She changed the subject.

I handed it to her wordlessly. I'd stopped at the bodega down the street to see if the dude who'd fed me all those years ago was still there. He wasn't, but his son was. I asked the son to sell me all his expired stuff. After looking a little suspicious, he'd relented.

"Dinner for two. Hope you're not fussy."

"Not at all." She grabbed the plastic bag and peeked inside. "Aww. Takis. Fancy."

"There's cheese balls and Almond Joys, you know, to offer you a full, nutritious meal."

I sauntered over to settle on the same grave I used to sit on when we were kids, of Harry Frasier. I stopped when I saw there was another grave right next to him now. Of a Rita Frasier. Wife, mother, grand-mother, and doctor.

"Not alone anymore, buddy." I brushed a hand over Harry's tomb-stone before propping myself against it. When I turned to Arya, I caught her looking at me strangely. Again, I found myself wanting to get caught. For Ari to call me on my bullshit. To recognize me. Her eyes flashed with something. I wondered what she'd do next. What would come out of that pretty mouth of hers.

Nicky, how I've missed you.

Nicky, I can explain.

Nicky, Nicky, Nicky.

But she just blinked and shook her head, turning back to the grave in front of her.

"Hey, Ar. It's the other Ar. I . . . where do I even begin? Things, as you know, are a mess. Not only with Conrad. Mom is suddenly taking interest in me, probably because she's scared to be homeless in half a minute . . ." She shook her head. "It's stupid, complaining to you, when you have it so much worse. Sometimes I envy your lack of conscious-ness. Other times, it terrifies me. I still have entire conversations with you in my head. I still see you everywhere. In my mind, you grew up with me. You have an alternate life. You're married now. With a kid on the way. Aaron"—she let out a chuckle, laughing and crying at the same time—"I absolutely *loathe* your wife, Eliza. I call her Lizzy just to rile her up. She is *so* stuck up."

I bit down on my lip. Arya had been and remained a wonderfully odd girl. But for the first time, I also recognized that we weren't all that different. That both our parents had sinned greatly, even if in different ways.

"In this alternate universe, I'm looking forward to you giving me a nephew. You know I love children. Even considering having one myself. What's that? Have I met anyone myself?" She frowned, shooting me a quick look. I straightened my back, like a pupil.

"Nope. No one worth mentioning. I mean, there is this one guy, but he is off limits. He says the chemistry is stronger than us. But as you know, I flunked that subject in high school."

She talked to Aaron a few more minutes before coming to sit beside me. I opened a bag of chips and passed it between us. She munched, extending her legs and lacing them at the ankles.

"How'd he die?" I asked, because I needed to. I wasn't supposed to know.

"SIDS."

"I'm sorry."

"At least I didn't get to know him. It'd have hurt a million times over, I assume."

Depended on the person. I had yet to miss my mother.

"Do you visit him often?" I asked. We were both staring at Aaron's grave. Looking at one another seemed too . . . raw.

"More often than I should. Or so people keep telling me. A part of me is angry at him for bailing on the shit show. I need someone to be here, you know?"

"You have someone to be here," I said, with honesty and openness that should've frightened me but somehow didn't.

Suddenly, I remembered something. I passed Arya the bag of chips, stood up, found two small stones by a flower pot, and put them on Aaron's grave.

"So he'll know we came to visit." I heard the smile on Arya's face behind me and turned to look at her. "I used to do that all the time. How'd you know?" Her eyes glittered.

"Who said I'm not Jewish?" I raised my eyebrows.

"Your name. *Christian*," she laughed.

My fake name, more like.

Tread carefully now, a voice inside me warned. But I was too far gone to listen.

"Someone once told me about this tradition."

I sauntered back, taking my seat next to her, our shoulders brushing.

"Hey, Christian?"

"Yes?"

"It's my birthday today."

I know.

"Happy birthday, Arya." I kissed the crown of her head as she propped her cheek on my shoulder, looking straight ahead at the conveyor belt of businesspeople gliding along Park Avenue. "And happy birthday, Aaron, too."

CHAPTER TWENTY-TWO

A R Y A

Present

We didn't kiss again.

That, I couldn't let happen. Not if I wanted to survive Christian Miller. And already, I knew my days would be grayer, bleaker, once he was gone.

He walked me home in dignified silence. We both blew wispy condensation against the crisp air, like children.

I knew I should be terrified of opening up, giving him an exclusive glimpse into my brand of crazy. After all, newly thirty-two-year-olds weren't supposed to celebrate their birthdays at a cemetery with men they hardly knew. Especially not men like Christian—who was hell bent on destroying what remained of my dysfunctional family.

When we reached my door, Christian ran his hand over my cheek. It was warm and rough. I hadn't been with a man for over a year. Not since a Tinder date that had started with awkward sex and ended with the guy weeping on my shoulder about his ex, who wouldn't take him back. Goose bumps prickled the back of my neck. I breathed Christian in. Exhaled my inhibitions out.

"Thanks for letting me be there for you today," Christian said.

"Thanks for not running for the hills, screaming." I brushed my shoulder over his, the way he had after our dinner date. Honestly, I forgot the last time someone other than Jillian had done something so sweet for me.

"You're not as broken as you want me to think, Arya." Christian smiled, and boy, could I get used to that smile.

"Am too."

"Well, I'm worse," he offered.

"Prove it," I challenged. "Tell me what's your brand of messed up."

"Maybe. Later." But it sounded so much like *never* I didn't want to press him for more.

"Changed your mind about us yet?" His voice had a way of moving over my skin, like fingertips.

"Not in the least."

"You will."

"Don't hold your breath."

"Why not? I'm a great swimmer."

And thus, Christian kissed the tip of my nose and strolled off into the night, taking a small chunk of my heart with him.

The next day, at work, the missing piece of my heart made my chest feel empty. I wanted to see Christian again, to ask for it back. Maybe it was because he'd come to the cemetery with me. Or maybe it was our kiss the night before. Perhaps Christian was just a distraction from the real disaster encroaching into my life. My father's case was spiraling out of control. I'd given up on social media, newspapers, and news websites and declined all social invitations. I'd even gone so far as only communicating with my mother via text. Which, as it turned out, wasn't a bulletproof plan.

"Hullo." Whitley plopped on the edge of my desk, swishing her magnificent ash-blonde hair with a smile. "You have a visitor downstairs."

"I do?" I perked up instantly, ashamed of how excited I was, then cleared my throat, rearranging myself in my seat.

Whitley's smile broadened, coated with enough lip gloss to fill a bowl of slime. "Oh, honey, I think it's wonderful that you're reconnecting with her. Even if the reason for your new relationship is what happened with your father. Should I buzz her up?"

I blinked rapidly before the penny dropped. It took everything in me not to groan.

"No, I'll go down to see her, thanks."

"Arya! I'm so glad I got the address right. I thought your father mentioned something about you working on this street." My mother tugged her white leather glove from each of her fingers before removing it completely. She was clad in one of her more iconic dresses from my childhood.

"Yes, Mother. I've been working here for four years, give or take. We have biannual parties for our clients on the roof. Conrad used to come."

He used to help me clean up afterward too. My mother, however, tossed my invitations into the trash unfailingly.

She had the good sense to look embarrassed, smiling apologetically. "Arya, can we talk?"

With a head jerk toward the nearest coffee shop, I led the way. I allowed my mother to pay for our coffees, knowing she was going to make a fuss about it if I didn't. When she sat down, she produced something from her Chanel bag.

"I got you a present for your birthday."

"That's a first," I couldn't help muttering, but I opened the thing anyway. The box was lovely. Blue velvet. I thought it'd be a bracelet or a diamond choker. My mother had a soft spot for fine jewelry. But when I swiped away the fine tissue paper, I found something completely unexpected. It was a framed picture of me and Aaron when we were babies. We were both on our bellies, staring at the camera, wide eyed.

I coughed to cover my emotions. "We looked so different from one another."

My eyes were green, his dark brown. My hair was brown, his blond.

"Yes." My mother wrapped her delicate fingers over her coffee cup. "I went through IVF treatments. When I fell pregnant, it was with triplets. But your father only wanted two children, and it was a high-risk pregnancy, so the doctors sided with him. You were supposed to have another sibling."

My head flew up from my present, my eyes widening. "You never told me that."

She shrugged. "You never asked."

"What were you expecting? *Hi, Mom, what's for breakfast today? Oh, and by the way, did you ever have a selective reduction when you were pregnant with us? Yes, pancakes are fine.*" But before she could answer, I frowned. "Wait, *Conrad* didn't want any more kids?"

I had always thought it to be weird that my mother hadn't fallen pregnant again in the years after losing Aaron.

"No. I could barely get him to agree to have you two. Of course, it worked out well, as you are his pride and joy now."

Was, I was tempted to correct. Surprisingly, I didn't have any trouble believing my mother about Conrad controlling the number of kids they'd had. It was just another horrific revelation to be added to the chain of evidence mounting against him.

So I guessed we were having this conversation now.

"Forgive my bluntness, Mother, but you didn't exactly act like you were eager to raise the one child you had left." I took a sip of my coffee. Noticed my hand was shaking.

My mother put her cup down, snatching my hands across the table. "Look at me, Arya." I did. Not because I wanted to but because I had to give her the chance to explain herself after all these years. "It was a defense mechanism, okay? Your father would often threaten to take you away. In fact, whenever he and I fought, whenever I wanted to walk away, he would use that card against me. He said he'd have full custody over you, because I was such a bad parent, before I even had the chance to become a bad parent. Then I realized it wasn't going to matter. He'd have done as he wished with or without my efforts. It was a catch-22. I was conditioned not to become too close to you, because I never knew if he'd let me keep you. And he is a very persuasive and manipulative man, as I'm sure you're starting to see. I didn't want to get attached to you. Didn't want my heart to break even more after Aaron."

My chest was hurting so bad I was surprised I could still breathe. I felt like my walls were crumbling down brick by brick, and I had no way to stop it. I'd always carefully constructed my reality into a digestible picture. Dad was the saint, Mom the sinner. She was the villain in my story, not the victim, and my reality, the one thing I'd thought I had that was stable and true, no longer made sense.

"I thought you didn't love me," I said, my hands limp between her fingers.

She shook her head, her eyes filling with tears. "I wanted to hug you every day. Sometimes I physically stopped myself from reaching out and embracing you, because I knew it would make him mad. He'd say that I was trying to manipulate you. That I was making a point. I wanted us to run away together. But there was always a threat hanging over my head. I didn't want to lose you entirely."

"You did anyway."

"I did," she agreed. "But at least I got to see you every day. And then when you left for college, and after that, I tried convincing myself that I didn't care."

"Why are you telling me this now?" I pulled my hands from her grasp. "Out of the blue. What's changed?"

She shifted in her seat, smoothing her dress over her knees demurely.

"Yesterday," she started, fumbling with her pearl necklace, "I tried reaching you all day to wish you a happy birthday. You didn't answer. I wanted to go to your apartment to surprise you and realized I don't even know where you live. I found out your office address because your father had one of your business cards in his study. I called your office and asked for your address, but Jillian said you weren't there. That you had . . . a date. It struck me then how little I know about your life. About your hobbies, likes, and dislikes. The things that make your heart sing and your soul weep. I went back home, sick with shame. Your father was in one of his never-ending meetings with Louie and Terrance. I made myself a cup of tea, contemplating how I no longer had a Ruslana to do it for me, because ever since she left, I was too afraid to bring someone else into our house from fear he would sleep with her too. I took my tea to the balcony, overlooking Mount Hebron Memorial, and saw you visiting Aaron. You weren't alone."

A pensive smile played on her face. "There was a man with you. You looked . . . close. I saw the way you leaned your head against his shoulder. How you talked. And I thought . . . how I wanted to be that person for you. This rock. Someone you could count on, speak to. Someone to spend your birthday with. Then I thought back to all your birthdays over the years. At five, with nanny number eight. Or your fourteenth one, where we forgot about it until three days later, because Dad was in Geneva. I missed so much. I know that. A simple apology wouldn't do . . ." She inhaled. "But I think, maybe, seeing as our world is shattering and everything around us is collapsing, we should at least try? What do you say, Arya? Please?"

There were so many things I wanted to say. To ask. But I started with the obvious one, and it had nothing to do with me.

"Why are you letting him stay with you, still?" I frowned. "Conrad. Why not divorce him? It's a bad look. You standing by him after everything he did."

"I don't even go to court with him. He's asked plenty of times. Apparently, his lawyers think it is good optics."

When she saw I was waiting for her to elaborate, she moved her hand from her necklace to play with her earring. "Well, I suppose I'm scared of what's next. You have to understand, I spent the last thirtysomething years in a form of isolation. A prison. He managed to mess with everything in my life—even my medication. A few years ago, I found out he was in close contact with my psychiatrist and told him what to prescribe me. I cut the psychiatrist off immediately, but the damage had been done, and these days, I can't even take a Xanax without wondering if the people who prescribed it to me have ulterior motives. Whenever we went to social events, he would get deliberately chummy with my female friends—normally the ones whose company I enjoyed the most—and disappear with them for long periods of time. Making me wonder if he slept with them. He conducted very short, very efficient, *very* strategic affairs with anyone he thought could help me break free from the golden cage he'd set for me. I don't have any real friends, associates, lawyers, or family. Conrad is my only family, albeit a very bad one."

"You have me," I ground out, not exactly sure why these words were leaving my mouth.

My mother's eyes lit up. "I do?"

"Yeah. We're not close, but I'll still be there for you when you need me." Although I could see why she didn't know that, seeing as I had been ghosting her for a couple of weeks. Since news had broken about Conrad and she'd started calling me.

"Life is so short." She shook her head. "I think about all the kisses I didn't give you. All the hugs we didn't share. All the movie nights and shopping sprees and fights that made us want to throttle each other and yet love each other more. I think about all the what-ifs. The almosts. How they pile up in the empty room of my memory bank. And it kills me, Arya. It hurts so much more than what's happening with your dad."

My pulse thrummed against my inner wrists. I thought about all the moments I'd shared with Dad. Precious and small, like individually wrapped chocolates. I wouldn't exchange them for the world, even after everything that had happened. And maybe especially because of it.

And Christian. I thought about Christian too.

How much I wanted him. Craved him. Every fiber in my body knew he was going to break my heart. No easy feat, considering no man had accomplished that since Nicholai Ivanov.

"We can create new memories, maybe." A soft smile touched my lips.

"Oh." Her voice shook. "I would like that so very much."

I stumbled out of the coffee shop, fumbling for my phone. It took me a second to find his number and another two to pull myself together and call him. He answered on the first ring, his voice clipped. "Yes?"

The background noise was telling. Documents shifting; hushed voices discussing the EEOC, mischaracterization, and burden of proof. He was obviously at a meeting. Why had he picked up the phone?

"Christian?" I asked.

"Evidently."

"It's Arya."

"Is there anything I can help you with, Arya?" He didn't sound as enthusiastic as I'd thought he'd be.

Had I expected him to fall to his knees and beg to see me? Maybe not, but I hadn't thought he'd sound so . . . *unsurprised.*

"You sound busy."

There was a lull. Maybe it finally clicked that I'd called.

"What's it about, Ari?"

Ari. The nickname made my heart stutter.

"Never mind."

"I *do* mind."

"You're obviously doing something important."

"I'd rather do *someone* important," he stressed, just as I heard the soft click of a door closing. At least he hadn't said that in public. I wheezed. There was not enough fresh air in Manhattan to make me breathe properly. But Mom had said it perfectly—life was too short. If tomorrow never came, I wanted to spend today with him.

"Arya." Christian's voice was much warmer now. I realized he'd sounded terse before because he'd been among people and had a certain air to uphold. "Are you contemplating what I think you're contemplating?"

That was the trouble with good lawyers. They sniffed the truth out of you from miles away.

"Maybe."

"What's changed?"

"My perspective." I closed my eyes, swaying from heel to heel in the middle of the street, feeling completely ridiculous. "My entire life, I've avoided messy. Yet messy still found me. I'm starting to see that maybe it's time I take what I want, seeing as some consequences are inevitable."

"I'm coming over."

"You mean right now?" This gave me pause. Things were moving too fast. "It's midday. My schedule is jam-packed. I'm sure yours is too."

"I'll shift things around." The line got cut. ". . . on my way." Another cut. ". . . over. Hello? Can you hear me?"

"You're losing service," I mumbled, wandering toward the subway in a stupor. Was I really skipping work? That was a first. I hadn't even skipped a class in high school. The last time I'd taken a sick day was six years ago. I didn't do spontaneous.

The bustling life of Manhattan seeped through the line. Ambulances wailing, cars honking, people shouting. "Sorry. I was in the elevator. Just hailed a cab. I'm on my way."

"You're crazy. This could wait."

"No, it can't. Oh, and Ari?"

"Yes?"

"Your checkbook better be open, because all those meals you've stood me up on weren't cheap."

◆ ◆ ◆

When I arrived at my doorstep, Christian was already there, pacing back and forth by the front stairs. The air around him crackled with dark energy.

He turned to face me, surprising me by grabbing my hand and pressing it against his heart. "Feel it, Ari."

The look on his face said more than words ever could. There was expectation there, mixed with hope, longing, and something else. An odd fragility that hadn't been there before. It reminded me of that time, decades ago, when Nicky and I had almost gotten caught by Ruslana.

I sank my blood-red fingernails into the fabric of his shirt. "Happy to see me?"

"I'll be happier when I see *all* of you."

We took the three flights of stairs two at a time. My adrenaline was through the roof. When I opened my door, I told him I was getting a glass of water and asked if he wanted one.

"Sure?" He gave me a funny, is-this-how-we're-going-to-play-this look. I pointed toward my room and told him to make himself comfortable. When I was certain he was gone, I chugged two pints of water, then stuck my head in the freezer to try and bring my temperature down.

When I went to my room, I caught him studying my bookshelf, his back turned to me. I'd hired a carpenter years before to convert one of my bedroom walls into a library. It was extravagant and entirely unjustified, what with this apartment being a rental and all, but it made me feel more at home than any other piece of furniture I owned. Christian ran a finger along the spines of the books in a manner I found strangely erotic.

"The prized *Atonement*," he drawled, knowing I was there even though I hadn't made a sound. "First edition, hardcover."

"Don't even think about it." I pushed off the doorframe, ambling toward him. I pried the book from his hands, caressing it lovingly.

He turned to look at me, a smirk playing on his face. "Think about *what?*"

"Borrowing it."

"Why not?" he whispered. "It's just words on paper."

"What a preposterous thing to say. And death is just a long nap in a drawer." I pressed the book deeper between the two books engulfing it. "If you're so desperate to read it, get a library card."

He leaned his shoulder against my shelves, scrutinizing me for a reaction. "Why this book specifically?"

"Because."

"I'll rephrase. What event do you associate with this specific book that makes it impossible to let go of? I find it hard to believe a different copy of *Atonement*, one I could order from Amazon right now, would have the same emotional impact."

I thought of Nicky's arctic blues, twinkling as he told me he would do this for me. Defy our parents. Reenact that scene.

Of Nicky pressing me against my shelves, kissing me.

Lying beneath the pounding sun, counting the constellation of freckles on my nose and shoulders.

Nicky. Nicky. Nicky.

A sweet ache spread inside my belly.

Christian shook his head. "Never mind. Too personal. I get it."

"It's not—"

He took the glass of water I'd forgotten I was holding and placed it carefully on one of the shelves behind my head. He laced his fingers through mine and pinned my arms on either side of me, above my head, just like in *Atonement*. His fingers tightened their grip, his mouth coming down to the base of my throat, his lips brushing softly against the sensitive skin.

For a second, I actually wondered if Christian *was* Nicky. Why else would he choose to do that? But no. It couldn't be. Nicky was dead. Besides, maybe Christian had watched the movie and thought it would be hot to reenact it.

I mewed, dropping my head back and closing my eyes.

"Arya, you lovely, lying creature, you. How long I've waited to do this to you."

His mouth dragged up my neck, his white teeth grazing my chin, before he dipped his tongue into my mouth, prying my lips open. My mouth fell open in an O shape, and I writhed, my back arching, my body pressed against him, as I relished the dull ache of desire.

"Beautiful . . . sweet . . . lovely Arya." Each word was a kiss. His fingers let go of mine, and he scooped me up by the backs of my thighs, lacing my legs around his waist, our kisses deep, sweltering, filling the bottom of my belly with silky warmth. Most of my weight was supported by the bookshelves.

"How unbearably perfect you are," he murmured into my mouth. Tendrils of my hair, wild as weeds, fell over our eyes. The compliments were not said with sarcasm or contempt. They were soft whispers, curling around my neck, my wrists, like fine jewels.

There was an urgency to his movements as he devoured my mouth, plastering me against the book-laden shelves. A sense of unfinished business. A continuation of something we'd previously started. But of course, that couldn't be.

Christian's erection pressed against my center, and something inside me ignited. I rolled my ass, my legs knotted at the ankles around his waist, meeting his erection with purposeful thrusts. The state of my panties told me a long foreplay session wasn't in the cards for me.

"Christian." I raked my fingernails over his sharp jaw, my tongue dancing with his. He froze, drawing away, like I'd slapped him.

"What?" I asked, panting, as he took a full step back, leaving me to level myself on my stilettos. "What happened?"

It couldn't be anything I'd said. All I'd done was say his name. Men liked that, especially behind closed doors. And yet he stared me down as if I'd committed a great sin. *Like a betrayed lover.*

Confusion flooded me.

He closed his eyes, and when he opened them again, he looked completely different. He ate up the space between us with one swift movement, picked me up by my ass, and hurled me onto my bed. My legs flung in the air, and a loud rip pierced the silence. My pencil skirt was torn, half my ass hanging out there for him to see.

"What the . . ." I was a mixture of turned on, pissed off, and taken by surprise. "That was a brand-new Balmain!"

"Send me the bill." He propped one knee between my legs on my bed, grabbed the hem of my skirt, and ripped it all the way until it fell beneath me in one perfect square. "Better yet, let's call it even on all those dinners. I have a feeling your family won't be able to afford unexpected expenses after the legal bill you'll be slapped with."

That was low, and Christian didn't usually aim low. In fact, he'd been pretty good about not rubbing our situation in my face thus far. Which made me even more confused as to how my saying his name had changed things between us.

"What's gotten into you?" I demanded, but I quickly forgot to press him for an answer when he leaned between my legs, plastering his strong body against mine. He kissed me roughly, deliberately rubbing his five-o'clock shadow against my skin, making it bloom pink.

He used his teeth to unbutton my white dress shirt. Not with expertise and finesse. Rather, he yanked and spit them out, one by one, as more of my skin was revealed in front of him. When he saw my crème lace bra, he covered one of my breasts with his mouth completely and sucked hard. The damp heat of his mouth sent violent shivers down my spine. My fingers threaded into his hair, tugging him southward shamelessly.

"Someone's impatient," he chuckled against my navel, dipping his tongue into it before breathing cold air inside. My skin prickled with goose bumps.

"You're quite the expert, aren't you . . ." I was going to say his name again but then stopped myself. Something told me he didn't want to hear it, even though I had no idea why. Christian didn't notice my sentence was incomplete.

"This is not a conversation I'd like to conduct at this moment."

And then he was *there*. His teeth scraped the hem of my panties— unfortunately a pair of seamless, black, boyfriend-cut underwear— removing them urgently, his hands busy spreading my thighs wide. I didn't know what was sexier—watching his tan, strong hands and muscular forearms against my pale skin, or looking down at his crown of jet-black hair, knowing what was to come. Or rather *who* was to come—me, namely.

He tossed my underwear behind his shoulder, still fully clothed.

He paused to take inventory of my naked body for the first time. Like he was studying a map, calculating where to start, where to attack first.

"God, Arya."

He brushed his thumb from my clit to the base of my center, before dipping a long finger inside me. I closed my eyes and moaned.

"Soaked." I heard the pop of his mouth and opened my eyes just in time to see he was tasting the finger he'd put inside me. "Tell me what you want, Arya."

Not giving him the pleasure of hearing me beg, I sank my fingernails into his shoulders and brought him back down, his face level with my sex. He ran his tongue along my opening, and I shuddered, closing my eyes. Clearly, he wanted to have control over the situation. And clearly, he was failing.

"Fuck," he growled, his tongue lapping at me again, deeper now. He was thirsty for it. "Here I go again."

Here I go again? What did that mean?

His hands circled my hip bones, pressing me down to the mattress as he devoured me, stroking me with his tongue, occasionally stopping to suck my clit into his mouth, nibbling on it softly. He knew what he was doing. Normally, I'd find it commendable. Experience didn't always equal good performance. This time, though, my heart squeezed. Like Past Christian was supposed to know Present Christian would meet me, somehow, and had to wait it out. Which was absolutely, atrociously stupid.

There was a tiny voice in the back of my mind that told me I was doing it all wrong. This was New York, and we were in our thirties. Usually, I went through a routine. I needed to see a clean medical bill. To have the Talk. To ensure he'd come with a pack of condoms. With Christian, I breezed past the technicalities like they didn't exist.

"Condoms," I panted, feeling my first orgasm slithering its way up my skin. From my toes, up my legs, climbing higher. "Tell me you have condoms."

He shook his head, which was still buried between my thighs, just when my eyes dropped shut and my body began to quiver with my climax. I shook all over, and when I opened my eyes again, I saw him propped on his elbows, staring at me, absorbed in thought.

"I'm clean."

I don't want to get pregnant.

For a second, I imagined how that'd go. If I accidentally got pregnant with Christian's child. What would Conrad think. Beatrice too. A panicked giggle bubbled up my throat, but I managed to swallow it down.

"I'm not on the pill," I said. He began kissing his way up my abdomen, his mouth hot and damp, his breath carrying the earthy, feminine scent of me.

"I'll pull out."

"Are we in high school now?"

"What we are is in complete lust with each other. I can't wait. I'll pull out, then go downstairs and buy condoms for the next round. And there *will* be a next round."

He ascended up my body until our faces were aligned. His eyes were mesmerizing. Clear, icy blues. Calm water over gleam-tipped icebergs. My resolve collapsed, just like it always did where this man was concerned. I closed my eyes and nodded once.

Christian was inside me.

He was still wearing his suit when he entered me. He was big—bigger than average—and he closed his eyes, not moving, just relishing the moment. I stared at him in awe. Everything about what we were doing felt monumental.

He began to move inside me, flinging one of my legs over his shoulder as he stared deep into my eyes. It surprised me. The intensity of it. After all, we hadn't known each other for that long. I circled my arms around his neck while he filled me to the brim. I rolled my hips forward each time he pushed into me, meeting him in the middle. Another climax tickled inside me.

"Arya." Christian's forehead dropped to my chest as he picked up the pace. "Please tell me you're close, because I am."

"Yes." I nodded, swallowing hard. "I'm very close."

Christian groaned, pulling out of me and squeezing himself hard, staving off his climax. He tore his gaze away and looked to the floor, concentrating on a spot before pushing back into me. Already aroused and sensitive from the friction, that was all I needed to fall apart in his arms and come again. The minute he felt me clenching around him, he mumbled, "Thank you," pulled out of me, and came. Ribbons of his release coated my belly. It took me a few moments to descend down to earth and realize what we'd done. Christian rolled next to me on the bed. We both stared at the ceiling. There was the distinct feeling that we were like teenagers who'd just done something bad.

"You didn't even take your clothes off." I stared at my ceiling in a daze, wondering if he'd call tomorrow.

"No," he said in wonder, turning his face to look at me. "Let's rectify that. Shower?"

"First door to the left."

He grabbed my hand. Squeezed. "Come with me."

"I just did." I grinned.

He laughed, tugging me gently from my bed. "Here we are. One step. Then another. Not so bad, is it?"

Our mutual shower was scorching. A slow-burn make-out session. We embraced, making out under the hot water. There, I could appreciate all of him, in his entirety. His defined six-pack, the coarse dark hair on his chest, his broad shoulders. Our kisses were hot and lingering, openmouthed, and I tried to remember the last time I'd felt so happy and content. Not in this decade, I suspected.

When we got out, Christian got dressed. "I'll go downstairs to get some johnnies. Should I bring back takeout? How about Chinese?" He buttoned his shirt, perched on the side of my bed, not bothering with the tie.

"What time is it?" I checked my watch, frowning. It was eight o'clock. Jilly was supposed to be back by now. The fact that she wasn't meant she was giving us time alone. I'd texted her on my way home but hadn't thought she'd make herself quite so scarce. I looked back up at him, powering up my laptop as I settled over my pillows in my bed. No point in sitting here and pining for him while he was out and about. I could squeeze in a few emails and maybe even a contract proposal if I was lucky.

"In that case, could you fetch something from the Filipino restaurant? It's right down the street. I'll have the fried calamari and crispy pata. Oh, and their coconut boba, please. Extra tapioca balls. Here's my card." I unzipped my purse and tossed my card across the bed for him.

He stopped lacing his shoes, simply staring at me for a few moments.

I smiled tightly. "Sorry, I can be bossy. We can just DoorDash. Of course you don't have to go there."

"No, that's fine." He stood up, shaking his head. "I could use the time to answer emails." His eyes ran over my laptop. *Oops.* I should've waited until he was gone. "You really are something, you know that, Arya Roth?"

"How so?"

"You're just the most self-reliant, independent, driven—"

"Better stop before you catch feelings." I winked, cutting into his words, because they were cutting into my *skin*, and it was too much. He closed his mouth, shaking his head and walking away, leaving me, my credit card, and my extremely dangerous thoughts behind.

Forty minutes later, we were sitting cross-legged on my bed, pigging out on fried calamari, french fries, roasted meat, and assorted veggies. We shared stories about our college days and were surprised to find out our paths had nearly crossed several times during those years at parties and festivals. Christian said he hadn't been into the whole partying scene, that Arsène and Riggs were the hellions in their trio, and that he'd focused on finishing at the top of his class, because he'd known competition was going to be tight out there once he graduated. I told him I was much the same, actually. That I'd disappointed many people by being so straitlaced and not channeling the inner Paris Hilton everyone had predicted they'd see in me.

"And Jillian has always been your best friend?" Christian bit into a piece of calamari and sucked his fingers clean. I had an inkling fried food wasn't a part of his usual diet, with a body like that.

"Pretty much." I popped a piece of cucumber into my mouth. "I've always been kind of an ambivert—definitely for someone in my field—and people often mistake my assertiveness for bitchiness. I'm not in the business of cooing and playing nice. Some people appreciate it. Few, but some. She's one of them, so we keep each other close."

"Men must be intimidated." Christian popped a devilish eyebrow up.

"Not the ones worth dating."

"And yet you don't strike me as the kind of woman who goes on a lot of dates."

I shrugged. "Not everyone's worth my time." But even as I said that, I knew it was my shaky self-esteem speaking.

"Who's the one who got away?" Christian leaned on my headboard, using his chopsticks to pluck a piece of carrot from his paper plate. His shirt was unbuttoned, and there was a lazy, predatory air about him that kept me on my toes and yet made me want to bask in his attention. "There's always that one person who got away."

"Hmm." I scrunched my nose. I didn't have to give it any genuine thought, though. The answer was clear. It just sounded bad. Fortunately, I wasn't supposed to care what he thought of me. This was temporary at best and already over at worst. "Don't laugh, but this goes way back."

"High school sweetheart." He made an adorable, albeit mocking, face. "Where'd he first kiss you? Under the bleachers or against your locker?"

"Actually, before high school." I felt my cheeks pinkening, dropping my gaze to my food, moving it about with the chopsticks. "We were both fourteen. He was . . . well, he was a badass kid and my best friend. I was low-key obsessed with him. We had a little thing over the summer. His mom worked for my family. He's the one who got away for me."

When I looked back up, the expression on Christian's face made my pulse stutter. He looked like a semitrailer full of feelings had slammed into him all at once. He dropped his food on my bed—by accident—and didn't even realize as he did.

"Shit, don't worry about it. I hated those sheets anyway." I made a half attempt to scrape the oily french fries from my linen. *Lies.* These were brand-new Belgian flax from West Elm.

He was *still* looking at me weird.

I sat a little straighter, feeling my cheeks heating despite myself.

"I told you it was weird." I tucked my hair behind my ears. "I mean, it's not like I'm still pining for this teenager or something. Anyway . . ."

"No, this is interesting. So he was your boyfriend?" Christian swung his gaze back to me, all business.

I eyed him. "Um, are you sure you didn't just have a stroke? You looked . . . *off.*"

"Sorry. Thought about an email I need to write someone tomorrow. I'm completely on now." He smiled.

Nice. So he thought about work when I poured my heart out. Duly noted.

I got back to the subject at hand, feeling self-conscious. "No. We shared a kiss. That was all. But we were close."

"And why did it end?" Christian's eyes bored into mine with intensity that could light up a carnival.

"He moved away."

"He did?"

"Yes."

"Where?"

I licked my lips, feeling my nose burning with tears all of a sudden. What in the ever-loving hell was happening to me? It had been *years.* "He went to live with his father in Belarus."

"I see." He nodded tersely, taking a bite of another calamari. "Did he tell you that?"

"Um. No." I rubbed at my face, struggling to understand why I was so upset and, even more importantly, why Christian was looking at me like I'd just told him I'd murdered his dog. "My dad told me. It was all very . . ." *Abusive and insane.* "Sudden."

"Did you ever try contacting him?"

His interest in this story seemed peculiar. So many years had passed. Besides, like he'd said, we weren't in it for the long haul. Why did he care about my past?

"I did, in fact." I started picking calamari and fries from my linen and putting them back in Christian's bowl. "But then when he didn't answer, I figured I dodged a bullet. A guy who walks out of your life without even leaving you a note is not worthy of your time, thoughts, and efforts."

That was a flat-out lie. I knew exactly why Nicky hadn't contacted me—because I didn't deserve anything from him after what my own father had done to him.

"What about you?" I asked. "Any special someone over the years?"

Christian smiled, somewhat recovered from the topic, reaching over toward me to grab the bottle of water we shared and taking a sip. "None at all, in fact."

"Lucky you."

"Yeah, lucky me."

◆ ◆ ◆

Three more times, we tumbled atop each other, sheets tangled, fighting for dominance, for skin, for contact. We learned each other's shapes, likes, and dislikes. How to move like a current. We used condoms, and I made a mental note to stop by the pharmacy the next day for some Plan B. Christian was a generous lover. He seemed to know exactly what I wanted, when I wanted it, how deep, and how fast.

Finally, when we collapsed at around one in the morning, sweaty and spent, it was sort of understood—maybe even expected—that he'd stay the night. We both wanted to put off the inevitable.

"But won't you be late for court? Between going back to your apartment, getting all showered and dressed?" I asked.

Christian pointed out that any rookie lawyer knew to keep a fresh and ironed spare suit at their office, and that was that.

◆ ◆ ◆

Which was why I didn't expect to wake up the next day to an empty bed.

The side where Christian had slept was cold, the linen pressed like he'd never been there. The only evidence he had actually been here the night before was his lingering scent of expensive aftershave and decadent sex. Oh, and the pulse between my thighs, a light, persistent heartbeat, and the bite marks that covered me.

I peeked at the time on my nightstand clock. Eight thirty. Groaning, I closed my eyes and pressed my face to my pillow. When I pried my eyelids open again, I rolled over to my stomach and reached for my phone. There were four messages and seven emails. All of them from clients. There was also one missed call from my mother.

He told you it wasn't serious. Were you expecting a romantic breakfast with a side of cuddling?

For a second, I marveled at the irony. My father had insinuated I should sleep with Christian to help him, and I'd ended up sleeping with him indeed but had no plans to help the old man.

I blinked, adjusting to the light streaming from the window. Cocking my head, I noticed something peculiar about my bookshelves. An empty space that hadn't been there before. I shuffled out of my bed, still stark naked, and padded barefoot to my shelf. My hand ran over the spines, arranged in alphabetical order. My fingers stopped at the empty space. I knew what was missing. It was a book imprinted into my DNA. My most precious possession.

Atonement.

This was why he hadn't left a note or a message. Why he hadn't stuck around. He knew I'd be the one to make the first move. After all, he held something of mine hostage.

Bastard had stolen my favorite book.

233

I held myself together.

I didn't call or text him.

At the office, Jillian examined me from behind her cup of coffee, arching a knowing eyebrow and leaning against the printer while I waited for it to spew a contract for a new client.

"Long night?" She *hmm*ed.

I felt myself burning scarlet, realizing I wasn't even sure whether she had come back home or not. At least I knew I was on top of work these days, so this wasn't a dig.

"This space is a nonjudgment zone." I picked up the warm papers, motioning to the space between us while holding them.

Jilly put one hand up in surrender, taking another sip. "I'm not judging; I'm curious. And a little jealous, obviously. Is it serious?"

"Nope. The relationship's doomed from the start." I stapled the pages together, making my way to my seat. She followed me like a piranha, smelling blood.

Just because Christian and I hadn't addressed the elephant (or rather, lawsuit) in the room didn't mean I wasn't aware of it. The only thing that had changed was I no longer craved to hang his indiscretions over his head.

"Why bother, then?"

"Life's too short." I shrugged, taking a seat in front of my laptop, uncapping my Sharpie to go through the contract one more time.

"How very un-Arya of you," she laughed. "Fine. I'll revisit this again when we get back home. But Ari?"

"Yes?"

"Be careful if you see Christian. Charming as he may be, you know nothing about one of the most eligible bachelors in NYC."

CHAPTER TWENTY-THREE

CHRISTIAN

Present

I tucked the hard copy of *Atonement* under the loose floor plank beneath my bed. You'd think a brand-new building in Manhattan, with real parquet, wouldn't have slack tiles, and you would be absolutely correct. The reason it was loose was because I'd ripped it with my bare hands so I'd have somewhere to hide all the legal documents I never wanted anyone to find. A safe was highly predictable. It practically screamed to be opened. But no one was going to unglue the floor pieces under my bed.

I wondered why Arya hadn't called yet. Or better yet, barged into my office with a machete and every intent of using it on my neck.

I was going to hell, but not before making the most out of my time here on planet Earth. What I was doing to Arya was, for lack of legal terminology, a dick move of gigantic proportions.

The lie grew larger by the day, fed by time, intent, and emotions that had no business getting thrown into the mix. I'd spent my whole life cherry-picking my partners. I had the looks, the aura, the job, and the bank balance to lure anyone into my web. But with Arya, even when I had her, she didn't truly feel mine, and that was a problem.

Someone knocked on my bedroom door. Riggs's head, freshly (and wholly) shaven after another successful trip to God knew where, popped in the space between the door and the frame. "Food's here."

I waltzed through my bedroom toward the kitchen, where Arsène was unloading take-out boxes full of sashimi. Riggs sat next to Arsène on a stool.

"Back to the subject at hand, before Christian had to go back to his room to listen to his Sinéad O'Connor album while crying over Arya not calling." Arsène hit ignore on his phone when the name *Penny* flashed across it, accompanied by a picture of what appeared to be a goddamn supermodel. If I had a penny for every time he rejected a perfectly good Penny, I'd be able to buy this entire building, not just a one-bed apartment. "You have two choices here—either you cut her loose, seeing as you've had your fun, and that was the original plan, or you tell her the truth and face the consequences. Dragging this out is volatile."

"Are you crazy?" I spit out, digging through the containers. "It's too late to tell her. I'll be dropped from the case, disbarred, possibly face legal action—no, *definitely*, considering this trial is a sure goddamn win for me—not to mention I'll lose her anyway."

Arsène smirked at me like I was an adorable little puppy who'd just learned how to piss on his potty pad. "Thought you said this was not how it works. That—and this is a direct quote—you didn't get your law degree from Costco."

He had me there. But that was before Arya and I had sex. I'd thought I could keep my shit—and my dick—to myself. Watch her suffer and move on with my life.

"Thanks for the I-told-you-so. You're being real useful right now." I snapped the wooden chopsticks apart.

"Can you tell her after the trial is over?" Riggs asked, ambling toward my fridge to grab a beer. He looked buff as hell these days, but I knew unlike Arsène and me, he wasn't one for hitting the gym. Instead, he climbed mountains. Professionally. Had a bunch of companies endorsing his ass. I never understood his fascination with near-death experiences. Life had a 100 percent mortality rate. What was his rush to fall off a goddamn cliff at a 14K elevation?

I shook my head no. "The trial will be over in a few weeks. Besides, even if I tell her after it's over, she can unveil my identity afterward, which would mean all my work would have been for nothing."

I'd brushed up on the Rules of Professional Conduct. There was nothing that specifically prevented me from sticking my dick into Arya. But it didn't look good. And of course, there were those pesky catch-all rules for situations like these. A competent attorney could file a claim alleging my conduct was intended to disrupt the tribunal. And fuck, with my fact pattern, they might just win. Amanda Gispen would have my ass on a platter for ruining her case, and Conrad Roth would too. Either way I looked at it, being with Arya was simply undoable. They were right. I needed to cut her loose. But how could I, after she'd told me she'd tried to write to me? That she thought I'd moved to the other side of the world? That I was the one who'd gotten away?

I'd been so sure she was in on whatever Conrad Roth had done to me, it had never occurred to me he'd fed her a few lies to soften the blow. It twisted me inside out. The revelation she might have not known. Made me lose sleep, cases, and my goddamn mind. All this time—all this *rage*—and it wasn't even her fault.

The carefully constructed narrative of my life and my circumstances was a pile of ash at my feet. And I had no one to blame but myself, for jumping to conclusions.

As for Arya, the woman had been lied to by every man she even remotely cared about. It made me feel shitty, but not shitty enough to ruin my whole life to do right by her.

"Great. In that case, dump Arya and move on with your life," Arsène said, in the same sensible tone he might use to suggest diversifying my investment portfolio.

I tossed a piece of raw tuna into my mouth. "Fine. I don't even have to do that. All I need to do is never call her again, since she sure as hell never calls me."

Riggs smiled behind the rim of his beer bottle. "And that obviously doesn't bother you at all."

Prick.

◆ ◆ ◆

Arya didn't call the next day.

Or the one after it.

I dissected our latest interaction.

The way she'd confided about Nicky. The pain in her voice. The crinkles in her eyes.

It seemed like she genuinely cared. Then again, as established, Arya was a pretty good actress when she wanted to be.

My suspicion that she hadn't noticed the missing book had evaporated. There was no way something like that could have escaped a woman like Arya. Meanwhile, *Atonement* burned a hole through the wood of my bedroom parquet. I refused to read it. Doing so was admitting defeat, in a strange way.

I kept telling myself it was a good thing that Arya hadn't called. I could always send her the book via courier and get this shit over with. I couldn't see her again. Any more time spent with her brought her closer to the truth. And even if it didn't—what was the point? I'd wanted to get her out of my system. I had. Case closed.

The trial was going well.

My career plate was full.

So why was I still hungry?

◆ ◆ ◆

One week had passed.

I went to the gym and the Brewtherhood. She was never there. She didn't show up in court either. I was beginning to regret the temporary mercy I'd shown her by warning her off the case.

The woman wouldn't budge. Was it pride or self-preservation? Either way, it earned her more of my admiration.

There was a perfectly good chance I could have carried on like this for another month or so. I was a competitive bastard, just like her. We always made everything a game to be won. Even as kids. But one day, while I was hitting the weight section at the gym, I noticed her on one of the flat TV screens. She was a guest on a morning show.

She looked like a dream. So much so, the first few seconds, I didn't even decipher what she was saying. Just bathed in the fact I'd had her underneath me, not too long ago, writhing and begging for more.

She wore an off-shoulder dress with a fitted bodice and butterflies on it. I dropped the weights I was holding and strode to the TV so I could hear her better. The hostess, a woman whose age could be anywhere from thirty-eight to fifty-nine with a blonde bob and a lot of fake tanner, asked her about the PR crisis a certain British royal couple was facing. Arya answered all the questions thoroughly and professionally. I wondered what had inspired her to go on TV in the first place, but then when her interview was over, the hostess plugged Brand Brigade and couldn't stop gushing about it, proclaiming that she was one of their very happy clients.

Free publicity. Mystery solved.

That same day, I went to Barnes & Noble and bought a copy of *Atonement.* They only had the one with the film poster on the cover, white paper instead of crème. But that was sufficient for what I needed. I tore a page from the book, dabbed it in tea, and let it sit to dry on my office window for a few hours before tucking it into an envelope along with a small note.

> I have something of yours. If you want to see this book
> alive, follow my steps and don't try to go to the police.
> Step 1: Meet me at the Hayden Planetarium
> tonight at six thirty.
> Don't be late.
> —C

I picked up the phone on my desk, pressing the button to call my secretary.

"I need you to send something across town. *Now.*"

◆ ◆ ◆

At six twenty, I spotted Arya outside the planetarium. She stopped pacing, showered in a pool of icy blue lights reflecting from the building behind her.

In the movies, and maybe even in the books Arya was so fond of, the heroine always looked uncertain and demure, waiting for her beau to arrive. Not so with Arya Roth. The little hellion was on the phone, pacing back and forth, telling whoever was on the other end that she'd make a Birkin bag out of his skin if he didn't find her the reporter who'd leaked that juicy item about one of her clients. I stood on the sidelines, taking her in, and it finally dawned on me why I couldn't stay away—because we were frighteningly alike.

Fighters. Bloodthirsty. We'd been born into different circumstances, but our essence was the same. We were both in the business of getting down and dirty for the things we cared about. Claws out, at a second's notice.

Question was—how much did Arya still care about her father? I had no way of finding out and wasn't naive enough to ask her directly.

I resumed my brisk walk toward her. She turned on her heel, then stopped when she saw me, her pupils dilating at my appearance.

"I have to go, Neil. Keep me posted."

She tossed her phone back into her bag, launching toward me.

"Where's my book, Miller?" she barked, in full ballbuster mode.

I stopped a good few feet in front of her, enjoying her gaze on me. "That's it? No *hello, how have you been?*"

"I don't care how you've been. All I care about is that you stole my book."

"And I'll give it back to you," I replied evenly. "If you play your cards right."

"With a page missing." She pulled the page I'd sent her earlier today from her purse, waving it in my face. Trying hard not to laugh, I produced something from my own briefcase. The new copy of *Atonement* I'd purchased, which was missing the page.

"The original is safe and sound."

Arya put a hand to her chest, sagging visibly. "Good. I thought I needed to murder you. Life in prison seemed highly unappealing and yet completely necessary for the past few hours. Although I'd like to stress you are still a horrendous person for ripping *any* book, for *any* reason."

"Even if that reason was to get a reaction out of you?"

"Especially so."

"I missed you, Ms. Roth."

"Oh, put a lid on it, Miller."

We walked into the planetarium. She didn't ask why I'd had her meet me here. She didn't have to. It was clear from the moment we strode into the Nature of Color exhibition.

"You know, animals are known to use color to camouflage themselves," I noted. We walked past a stark white wall, our shadows reflecting off it in all the colors of the rainbow. Around us, kids danced to their own shadows, while their parents watched a flat-screen explaining the exhibition.

"They use it to attract mates too." Arya clutched the jacket she was holding to her chest. "Your point?"

We stopped in front of a video of a bright white flower opening up at nighttime, staring at it. "Things aren't always as they seem."

"Why do I have a feeling there's something you want to say to me, yet you never really say it?" She turned to cock her head.

Because there is.

Because I am.

Because if I'm the one who got away, how come you cannot even recognize me when I stand less than a foot away from you?

But I just smiled, handing her the second note. I'd written them in advance, which, it had to be said, was out of character for me. My main form of seduction thus far, in the rare times I went to any minimal lengths to pursue someone, was to buy them dinner. She smoothed it over in her palm, shooting me a frown.

Step 2: Introduce me to your favorite street food.

Her eyes met mine, full of sudden benevolence I doubted she was truly capable of. The princess with the Chanel purse and $500 haircut, who'd never known hunger and desperation in her life.

"Whatever happened to you and me not being able to date one another? This feels just a few kisses shy of spooning slash coadopting a French bulldog called Argus."

"First of all, I would never adopt a dog. Quote me on that. If I wanted someone to ruin my apartment, I'd get your interior designer. No offense."

"None taken. I could give a crap and a half about what you think about my apartment."

Actually, it was more like half a crap, but obviously, I didn't want to offend.

"Second, I am, above all, a gentleman. Third, the only thing remotely romantic about tonight is the fact we're both going to get laid at the end of it."

Arya shook her head, but at least she had the integrity not to contradict me. We both knew where this was headed. How tangled we were in this web of desire.

◆ ◆ ◆

And then we were on the stairs of the New York Public Library, eating waffles filled with chocolate fudge, Nutella, and cookie spread.

We probably looked perfect. The image of a textbook urban date. Two dashing thirtysomethings sharing dessert at the feet of one of the finest establishments in America. A sugarcoated lie.

"How did you not die of a heart attack by now?" I asked after three bites. I hadn't consumed anything remotely as artery clogging since I'd hit thirty and realized that in order to keep my current shape, I had to start watching what I ate.

Arya tapped her plastic fork over her lower lip, pretending to consider this. "Wishful thinking, Mr. Miller?"

"We can stop pretending we hate each other. All evidence points to the contrary."

"Never really bought into the whole diet fads. When I want to eat something—I do." She shrugged. "Maybe I'm reckless."

I snorted a chuckle. "A reckless woman would've called me a minute after she found out her book was missing. When did you realize, by the way?"

"About half a second after I opened my eyes." She licked her lips. "Give or take."

"Why *Atonement*?" I asked again. "Out of all the books in the world, you chose this. Why not Austen? Or Hemingway? Woolf, or Fitzgerald, or even Steinbeck?"

"Guilt." She pressed her lips together, squinting at the darkness in front of her. "*Atonement* is about guilt. A small act of thoughtlessness made by a child, and how it threw so many lives off the rails. I guess . . . I mean, I suppose . . ." She frowned again, two sharp lines forming between her eyebrows. "I don't know. I guess the more I grew up, the more that book grew with me. Each time I read it, I'd find another layer I could relate to."

"Does this have something to do with the one who got away?" I asked tentatively. I was treading too close to the truth. I no longer recognized myself around her.

Arya straightened her spine, jerked from a thought that shook her. "Why am I here, Christian?" She dropped her fork into her half-eaten waffle, turning to me. "You wanted to sleep with me, and you did. You left without a note, without a text, without a call—but with the one thing you expected would make me crawl back to you. What kind of game are you playing? You're hot one moment, cold another. Tender, then moody. I don't know if you are my enemy or my friend. You keep skating in and out between the territories. I cannot figure you out, and if I'm being completely honest, I'm reaching the point where the mystery outweighs the allure."

I took her waffle and carried both our take-out dishes to a nearby trash can, where I disposed of them to buy time. When I returned, I sat next to her. Her fingers were wrapped around a take-out tea.

"I'm not done with you," I confessed. "I wish I was, but I'm not."

"You go about things like a fourteen-year-old."

Because that's the age I was when you discarded me.

"In that case, how about we start over tonight? The trial will be over in a few short weeks. If we keep things under wraps, it could work. We can enjoy each other in the meantime, then go our separate ways."

Arya considered this. I kept my smile casual. She had all the power. She could say no, turn her back on me, and go her merry way. But I would never stop desiring her. I'd taken the first, the second, and the third step. I kept seeking her out.

"Fine," she said, finally. This was my cue to take out my final note. I passed it over to her.

"Another one?" Her eyebrows jumped to her hairline, but she still took it.

"Last one," I said, watching her face as she unfolded it.

Step 3: Have sex with me at a library.

This time when she looked back at me, there was no amusement in her eyes. "Are you insane?"

"It's a possibility," I admitted.

"I mean, let's start with the obvious—the library is currently closed."

Tucking my hand into my peacoat's pocket, I took out a key to one of the side doors. "Problem solved. What else?"

Arya's eyes flared. "How?"

"I know someone who knows someone who may or may not work here."

And I paid him a lot of money to make this happen, I refrained from adding.

"Well, the next reason why it's insane is because it's illegal."

"If a tree falls in a forest and no one is around to hear it, does it make a sound?"

"Yup. It's going to sound like a double-spread scandal in a tabloid." She flashed me a don't-be-cute glare. "We might get caught."

"We won't." I stood up. "Trust me. I have a two-hundred-million-dollar case and a partnership on the line. I'm not going to throw it all away for a fuck, no matter how fun and dirty."

But now that I'd said it out loud, the weight of the stupidity of this act pressed against my sternum. That made Arya perk up instantly. She shot up to her feet too. Perhaps the sheer possibility of my screwing up my career cheered her up.

"Sounds like a challenge to me."

Yeah. No perhaps about it. *Definitely.*

We walked around the building until I found the door I was look-ing for, turned the key in its hole, and pushed it open. It was pitch black inside. The warmth of the library paired with the scent of old pages, worn leather, and oak slammed into both of us. Arya's hand found mine. I squeezed her hard and led her into the study room.

"You know, I've lived in this city my whole life, and I've never visited the rare book division," I heard Arya say behind my back. I couldn't show it to her today, since we needed a key for that, too, but it was on the tip of my tongue to tell her that I'd make it happen. That I'd take her there. Only I couldn't take her there. Being seen with her in public in broad daylight would be disastrous. The kiss of death to our careers—not to mention her nearly nonexistent relationship with her family. We could only exist in the dark, two thieves of pleasure.

The study room was never ending. All the table lamps were turned off. In the dark, it looked almost like a deserted factory. Of ideas and dreams and potential. I tugged at Arya's hand to come inside, feeling fourteen again.

"Please don't tell me you hid my book somewhere in here." She glanced around the room, which was framed with shelves laden with books.

I let out a metallic laugh. "I'm not that sadistic."

"Debatable." She walked over to one of the shelves, checking out the books. I watched her. I always watched her. Her hair—the only untamed thing about her appearance—curled around her face like an angel's. I wondered if she'd taste as sweet, as sinful, as lovely, if I had her openly. If I could parade her around. Take her to company events. If her belly swelled with my offspring inside it. I wondered if my obsession with her stemmed from pure vengeance or something more. A sense of entitlement, of ownership, after everything she'd put me through.

"Christian?" she asked, and I realized that in my stupor, I hadn't noticed she was talking to me. I shook my head slightly. It always disoriented me when she called me that.

"Yes?"

"Did you listen to anything I said?" She smiled, hugging a book to her chest as she advanced toward me, a mischievous glint in her eyes.

"Not one word," I admitted. "I was preoccupied."

"With what?"

"Envisioning my hands on your ass as I take you from behind right on this table."

She sashayed to me, one hand lazily caressing the long wooden table by her side. When she reached me, she handed me a book.

"Open it randomly and read me a paragraph."

"Why?"

"Because I asked."

"That's your selling point? Because you *asked*?"

She gave me a blank stare.

I laughed. "Okay, then."

For the first time—I had this feeling she was onto me. That she knew who I was. Because fourteen-year-old Arya had known damn well that fourteen-year-old Nicholai would do anything within his power at her order. I took the book, flipping the pages, my eyes still holding hers. Very well. We were going to play it like that. I stopped at a random page, my eyes gliding over the text that stuck out to me. I read it out loud. It was about women being poisonous.

I turned the book around. *First Love* by Ivan Turgenev.

"Why did you pick this book?" I asked.

"Why did you pick this paragraph?" she quipped back, not missing a beat.

"I didn't."

"Neither did I." She smiled. "I just wanted to see if you'd play my games too."

I put the book aside, gliding toward her. She took a step back.

"I always seem to be in the market for whatever the hell you're offering."

She took another step back. Only a few feet from one of the tables. "Why is that, Christian? You don't strike me as a big romantic."

I took a step forward. "I'm not."

"Why, then?" She retreated one last time, the backs of her legs hitting the table, and stopped. I grinned, eating the space between us with one final step.

"Because, unfortunately, Ms. Roth, no one else will do."

Pinning her to the table by pressing my hands on either side of her thighs, I lowered my head to hers, my mouth pressing against her warm lips. She opened for me, tasting of powdered sugar and Nutella and peppermint tea. Of poison and destruction and inevitability. She pressed one hand against my chest, the other one circling my shoulder, her nails scraping at my hair. I groaned into our kiss, thinking she might pull me away, when her hand descended my abs, down to the button of my dress pants. My erection was impossible to manage, my cock standing to attention between us, waiting to be acknowledged.

Her hand slid down to cup it through my pants. I could no longer kiss her and concentrate at the same time, so I dropped my head to the side of her neck, covering every inch of it with lazy kisses. My body wrenched and spasmed to see what she'd do next.

Arya grabbed me by the dick—and balls—and jerked me forward, until there was no more space between us. I almost came on impact. And then she was gone, the space where her neck had been just a moment ago cold. I looked left and right, confused. I found her on her knees in front of me, undoing my button and zipper.

Okay. *Okay.*

I smoothed away her wild hair from her face. Not affectionately, I told myself, but so that I could get a better view of her lips wrapped around my dick. Said dick sprang free just as I managed to lean forward, lighting one of the lamps on the table behind her back.

Arya didn't look up at me shyly, or even seductively, the way women did a second before taking your cock in their mouths. She grabbed me, then gave my cock a thorough lick, base to tip, rolling her tongue around the crown for good measure. I let out a low hiss, looking away. It was too much. The sight of her pleasuring me.

As if reading my mind, Arya chose that moment to try and take most of me in. She grabbed the part she couldn't get to, closer to the root, in her hand and began pumping. I was willing to sign over the remainder of my life to her and everything I valued, including Arsène and Riggs, if it meant making her never stop.

"Arya." I thrust my hand into her hair, caressing her, unable to stop myself from looking at her. "This feels so good."

She didn't answer, not even with a small moan, and now I craved her words even more than I did my dick inside her mouth. Also, I was pretty sure I was going to come like a fourteen-year-old if she continued for twenty more seconds, and I wanted to spare myself from that particular form of humiliation. With that in mind, I used the collar of her dress to tug her back up to her feet, filling her mouth with my tongue in a messy, hot kiss.

"We're such a train wreck." Her breath tickled my chin, my tongue, as she roamed my body with her hands. Clutching my ass. Rolling her fingers over my back, my shoulders, my collarbone. "This is going to end badly."

I grabbed her by the waist, turned her around, and flipped up her dress. Again, while Arya was all *Sex and the City*, her underwear was definitely *Jane the Virgin*.

"Maternity undies again?" I tugged them aside, not even bothering with sliding them down. Life was too short and so forth.

"I'll have you know it's one hundred percent cotton and very good for my pH balance."

The laugh this elicited in me made my bones rattle. "Arya, you are fantastic."

"And you're not wearing a condom. Make it happen."

I dutifully put one on as she waited for me in a perfect r position, drumming her fingernails on the table.

With that, I pressed home, the side of her undies' elastics pressing against my cock.

This is how I want to die.

Watching Arya's back as she took me from behind was enough to kill me. Yet I pulled out, then in again, thrusting inside her. It was good and deep, but I managed to last longer than last time. Because I didn't have Arya's face right in front of me, reminding me *who* I was doing this with. I circled my arm around her waist and played with her clit, licking the shell of her ear. She let out little pants of pleasure that made me forget my names. Previous and current.

"I'm going to come." She sucked in a breath. I had no time to shower her with words of encouragement. She broke into shivers, tightening around me as she let out a hiss, every muscle in her body clenching against me. I pumped faster, harder, seeking my own release. I found it seconds later and stayed deep inside her, relishing every moment before it was gone.

"Well, that was certainly what the doctor ordered." Arya straightened, rearranging her panties and pushing her dress down. "Now, Christian, it's time to give me my book." She reapplied her lipstick in front of a small mirror, all business again. I threw away the condom and tucked my dick back in my pants, still sporting a semi. Maybe that was how it was always going to play out with Arya and me, until the trial was over.

"Absolutely. How about you come pick it up tomorrow night? I can't promise you waffles—I still need to get into my suits—but I can make my famous chicken breast and quinoa. Maybe even throw in a glass of wine, if you'll be nice."

I was expecting violence from her, no less. After all, I was still holding her book hostage. But instead of calling me all the things I deserved to be called—a scammer, a liar, and a fuckboy—she simply smiled.

"Know what? You can keep it for as long as we entertain each other. What's a few more weeks in the grand scheme of things? As long as we have certain rules."

"Lay 'em out for me." I smoothed my jacket, leaning against the opposite desk from her. She dropped the little mirror and lipstick back into her bag.

"Number one—no going anywhere in public together. Too risky. Number two—no meeting each other's families, friends, and colleagues, keeping everything completely separate."

"Agreed. Number three—no *L* words. Either of them," I added.

"There are two of them?"

"*Like* is a word too."

She nodded, her expression matter of fact. "And number four—if one of us meets someone else, the other will step aside without any guilt trips or trying to convince the other to change their mind. This is supposed to be temporary, after all."

I felt like I wanted to punch something, preferably the faceless asshole who was going to steal my precious moments with her. Nevertheless, I conceded. "Fair. Anything else?"

"Yes, in fact." Arya cleared her throat. "On the day the trial ends, so will our relationship. We will not have an official breakup conversation. Those are messy and entirely unnecessary. I will simply expect to see my precious hard copy of *Atonement* back in my mailbox, carefully wrapped, whole and safe."

She offered me her hand. We shook on it. That gave me at least two more weeks of Arya.

And that was all I needed.

CHAPTER TWENTY-FOUR

ARYA

Present

I met my mother three days later, at a bookshop, while purchasing a new copy of *Atonement*. She breezed in, carrying the scent of expensive hair spray from the blow-dry she'd just gotten.

Beatrice Roth air-kissed me twice on each cheek, like we were bridge-club acquaintances, and sniffed around the small bookshop like someone had forgotten an unattended bag of garbage here.

"How quaint. I didn't even know a place like this existed in this part of town. The rent must be *astronomical*."

"You know, you can donate toward their rent online. I'll send you the link. I have a direct deposit for that."

"Oh, honey. Your trust fund guilt is *adorable*." She dared ruffling my hair, like we were close or something.

Reconnecting with my mother after years of radio silence was definitely not everything Hallmark movies promised me it would be.

I walked around the narrow paths bracketed with shelves, swinging my shopping basket. I might have added three or four more books into the mix. In my defense, I worked hard for my money. On top of that, I was also getting a little restless. I'd been to Christian's apartment two days before. It was everything I'd expected it to be—modern, gorgeous, and clinically cold—and I'd tried to look for my copy of *Atonement* but couldn't find it anywhere. And it wasn't like there were many hiding places to choose from. The place was pretty much empty. I *did* spot a safe in his walk-in closet, but Christian, who was still in bed, haphazardly covered with his linen, had let out a low chuckle when he'd seen me caressing the safe's lock, staring at the numbers.

"It's not there, Ari. I would never be as predictable."

"How's Conrad doing?" I asked my mother, who trailed behind me, trying to convince myself I didn't particularly care about the answer. I did, though. I cared a lot. It was a source of shame and annoyance to me that I couldn't hate him all the way. That he was going to lose most of his fortune to legal fees and compensation.

"I don't know. He keeps to himself, and I stay in my corner of the penthouse. Frankly, I'm starting to get a bit worried about what's going to happen the day of." Mom pulled a book out of the shelf, realized it was a little dusty, and then shoved it back in, her face filled with horror and disgust.

"Why? Does he seem mentally unstable to you?" I slanted my head, studying her.

She patted her hands clean, looking at me incredulously. "What? No. I'm talking about the financial state he is going to leave me in." She shuddered at the thought. "I might have to sell the penthouse."

"Good." I slipped another book into my basket. A new one, by a debut author. I just liked the cover. It also looked like the kind of romance that would rip my heart into shreds and put the rest of me in a blender. "The penthouse was far too big for three people. Let alone just the one."

"But what about Aaron?" my mother asked, scandalized. "I live so close to the cemetery."

"He'll stay at his place, naturally." I headed for the register. I knew I was being sarcastic but couldn't help myself. The sheer self-obsession this woman was suffering from maddened me. Last time we'd met, she'd told me life was too short. Now, she was whining about the possibility of downgrading from one of the priciest places on the continent.

"Look, can I do anything to help you?" I sighed, choosing not to turn this into an argument while handing the bookshop owner, a nice lady with a gray mane, my basket.

"Yes, actually. I was thinking maybe you could talk to your dad—"

"No," I said flatly. "Sorry, but I won't do *that*."

"Why not?"

"Because he's an abusive, horrible man who doesn't deserve my help or my attention, and because he lied to me my entire life." *To name a few reasons.* The court case was also making old, bitter feelings resurface. Of how I'd forgiven him for what he'd done to Nicky, even though I shouldn't have.

I paid with a credit card, then rolled a five-dollar bill into the tip jar as the woman handed me back my books in a straw bag. Mom and I exited the shop.

"You know what your father's like. Horribly unstable."

"He also abused you emotionally for quite a while. Why would you want to ask him for any favors?" I started for the coffee shop by my house. Mom trailed next to me.

"Why, because I cannot exactly afford my own place, now can I? Even if I divorce him, which I hardly think there's a point in doing at this point, we'll have to split everything fifty-fifty. You know, his CPA tells me I am likely to be left with"—she sniffed the air dramatically—"less than two million dollars. Can you believe it?"

"I can, actually." I pushed the door to the coffee shop open. "He spent the past few decades assaulting innocent women thinking he was bulletproof. Bleeding money seems like a fitting punishment for what he did."

"*I* wasn't the one who assaulted them!" My mother banged her fist on her chest. "Why should *I* live beneath my prior means?"

"True," I agreed. "But you married a man who couldn't be trusted with his money, or his phone camera. Now, you can rent someplace nice after this is all over, or better yet, buy somewhere within your price range, which is still not a number to be laughed at, and find yourself a job."

"A job?" My mother's eyes widened. She looked like I'd just suggested she become an escort. I placed an order for both of us. Peppermint tea for her, iced Americano for me. This time, I paid.

"Yes, Mother. I didn't know the sheer act of working was quite so outrageous."

"Of course it's not," my mother huffed, convincing exactly no one in the room with her fake sincerity. "But no one is going to hire me. I have no experience to speak of. I married your father at age twenty-two, fresh out of college. The only thing on my résumé would be the summer before college. I worked at a Hooters bar. Think they'll accept me back thirty-six years later?" She arched an eyebrow.

I handed her the tea, took my coffee, and strolled back to the sunshine. Spring wrestled its way into the city, carrying cherry blossoms, sunrays, and seasonal allergies. The trial was nearing its end with every day that passed, and with it my goodbye to Christian.

"You were the head of the luncheon committee at your local country club, were you not?" I asked, skipping over a French bulldog's leash.

"Yes, but—"

"And you were the director of my school's charity board?"

"So what! That doesn't mean—"

I stopped in front of my door. I wasn't going to invite her up. Mainly because I had to get ready and meet Christian in a few hours at the pool. Indulging in this sinful affair was quickly taking over bigger chunks of my life.

"Come work for me," I uttered, without even realizing what I was saying. "You have good organizational skills, you look presentable, and you know how to convince people to put money into things. That's what you've been doing your whole life. Come work as a marketing assistant for me."

"Arya." My mother placed a hand over her heart. "You cannot be serious. I can't work a nine-to-five job at my age."

"You *can't*?" I asked. "That's a nice use of words. Because I was under the impression that you both can and should, considering the financial situation you are about to get into."

"I'm not like other people."

"Isn't that what we all think?" I wondered aloud. "That we're different? Special? Born for bigger, brighter things? Maybe, Mother, you are just like me. Just a little less well planned. And a lot more prone to surprises."

I got into my building and slammed the door in her face.

Christian was waiting for me at the indoor swimming arena of the gym, his body sprawled over the edge of the pool. He was lazily stunning, like the *Creation of Adam* painting. Each individual ridge of his six-pack was prominent, and his biceps bulged. I noticed his upper body was still dry.

He'd waited for me.

I tossed my towel over one of the benches, swaggering over to him. The pool was normally empty by the time we met. It gave us privacy. Security in the knowledge no one was going to catch us. Even if they did, what could they say? We were just two strangers, swimming in different lanes, directions, and streams of life.

"Beautiful." He looked up. For a second there, I allowed myself to fantasize that we were a real couple. Everything was normal, familiar, soaked with potential. But then I remembered. Remembered what he'd done today before coming here. Remembered this was only a charade. A distraction. A means to satisfy a very feral need. I slapped my swim cap over my head.

"Miller." I dived headfirst into the lane next to his. I resurfaced moments later, swimming to the edge of the pool, to him. "How's the trial moving?"

"Rapidly." He slid into the pool effortlessly. The water was warm, perfect, the scent of chlorine and bleach heavy around us. "We'll be making our closing statements sometime next week. You're not planning to come, are you?"

I shook my head. A part of me pretended my dad had died. In a way, he had. Because the version of him I loved so much was gone, or maybe had never been there.

Christian dipped his head into the water and emerged with water-drops clinging to his thick eyelashes. "Good."

"Are we going to compete or what?" I asked. We did a front crawl. Fifty meters. He always won. But I always tried.

Usually, that was when Christian gave me an amused look. But not today. Today, he stared at me with something that resembled guilt. But since the bastard had made it perfectly clear that he wasn't remorseful about nailing my dad's coffin to the ground, maybe it was just in my head.

"You want to compete *again*?" he asked. "When are you going to stop?"

"When I win."

"You may never win."

"Then I may never stop."

"I pity the man who marries you."

"I applaud the many women after me who'll dump you."

We ready-steady-goed. I gave it my all, fighting harder, swimming faster, than I ever had before. When I completed the lap and hit the edge of the pool, I looked back and saw that Christian was still trailing a few feet behind me.

For the first time, he'd let me win. On purpose. I didn't like that.

Don't let him pity you.

But how could he not, when he knew what was coming for me? For my family?

Suddenly, I felt very foolish. Foolish for sleeping with this man, who had gone after my father, even if he did deserve it. Foolish for giving in after I had bet Christian I wouldn't be coaxed into his bed.

Foolish because he was still a mystery, carefully wrapped in a cunning smile and a dashing suit.

When he hit the wall, he shook water from his hair. His grin dropped as soon as he saw what must have been a scowl on my face.

"What?" he asked.

"You let me win."

"No, I didn't."

"Yes, you did." We sounded like kids.

"And what if I did?" he scoffed.

"Then stop. Remember I'm your equal."

"That means I can't be good to you?"

"Good, yes." I pulled out of the pool, leaving him behind. "Deceitful? Never."

CHAPTER TWENTY-FIVE

CHRISTIAN

Present

The days felt shorter after that evening at the pool. Much shorter than their twenty-four hours. The morning after I let Arya win, Judge Lopez summoned me and Conrad's attorneys to discuss the close of evidence. In my estimation, that put us at about a week till this whole thing wrapped up. The jury, I was positive, was going to take no longer than a couple of days to come up with the verdict.

That night, Arya couldn't see me. She had dinner plans with a client, and at any rate, she explained, Jillian didn't know the full scope of our relationship. Or lack of. It shouldn't have bothered me. That Arya was keeping this from Jillian. I mean—wasn't that the whole goddamn point?

But it did niggle at me. The end was nearing. And nailing Conrad didn't feel as important as being able to enjoy his daughter.

The following evening, Arya couldn't see me. *Again.* This time due to Jillian feeling unwell.

"I think I'm going to make her chicken-noodle soup and watch *Friends* reruns with her," Arya sighed to me on the phone. I smiled and took it. What else could I do? I had no right to demand her time, her resources, her attention. We'd agreed it would be casual, and casual meant low to nonexistent expectations.

On the third day—four days before the end of the trial—Arya texted that her parents wanted to see her, and she didn't know how long they would meet for, so it was best not to make any plans together. At this point, I was sure she was avoiding me. I left court during a brief break, hailed a taxi to my apartment, banged open the loose parquet under my bed, and took out her book. I took a picture of it in my hand and sent it to her.

Christian: Enough is enough, Arya. See me tonight and no one gets hurt.

Arya: So you are not above extortion.

I'm not above anything when it comes to you.

Christian: We had a deal.

Arya: I don't remember signing any paperwork.

I waltzed back over to my front door; I needed to be in court in twenty minutes. In fact, it was time for me to personally cross-examine one of Conrad's witnesses. Now was not the time to chase skirts.

Christian: What happened?

Arya: I just don't see the point in spending every evening of the week with you when it's going to be over in a few days, anyway.

Christian: Let's talk.

I used the time it took her to answer to call an Uber. Just in case, I texted Claire to make up a good excuse in case I was going to run late. Judge Lopez was a ballbuster, even if he did like my golf moves.

Arya: What about?

The weather. What did she think?

Christian: I'll come to your place at six tonight.

Arya: No. Jillian can't see you.

Again with this bullshit. I didn't have the heart to tell her Riggs and Arsène were pretty much in the know about every orgasm we had shared between the sheets—or in my kitchen, my shower, my Jacuzzi, or her reading nook—since we'd started hooking up. I was tired of being a secret, even if I was the very asshole who had suggested it in the first place.

And for a good reason too.

Christian: I take it you don't want your book back.

Arya: I'll sue you.

Christian: I know a good lawyer.

Arya: There's a special place in hell reserved for people like you.

Christian: Heard lawyers get lava-view condos. Be nice and I just might let you room with me in the afterlife. When can I expect you?

Arya: Seven.

Christian: Don't be late.

But of course she was.

Late, that was.

Arya arrived at 7:23, not a trace of regret or embarrassment in her stony face. As I buzzed her up, I had to remind myself that she had every reason to want to cut ties with me. I was the painful reminder of everything she'd lost.

She walked in, tossing her bag onto the black leather couch, ignoring the dinner for two I'd made, which was sitting in the breakfast nook, getting cold.

"You wanted to talk?" She didn't bother toeing off her Jimmy Choos, which was suspect, since that was the first thing Arya did when she walked into my apartment after a long day.

"I made dinner." I headed over to the kitchen and grabbed two glasses of merlot. I handed her one. She hesitated before taking it. Staying long wasn't in her plans.

"You did." Her eyes traveled over my shoulder. "Sorry I was late. I had a call with a client in California. They were in no hurry to hang up."

"Not a problem. Cold steak has always been my favorite. Mind taking it to the kitchen?"

I suppose this was my version of eating humble pie. I didn't like the taste of it at all. I'd never chased a woman in my life and wasn't planning to make an exception for Arya, but I couldn't accept the idea that this was going to be over in four days. I needed more time. A few more months of an illicit affair weren't going to kill anyone. Other than, perhaps, my remaining working brain cells. I wasn't in the business of thinking straight whenever I was with this woman.

"You know what? I'd rather do this here, if you don't mind." She settled on the armrest of my black leather couch, cross-legged, holding her glass from the stem. I wanted to strangle myself for getting into this situation. All of this could have been prevented if I'd resisted the urge to meet Amanda Gispen.

Or if I'd simply passed the case along to someone who didn't have a hard-on for the Roths.

Or if I hadn't bet Arya, pushing an already defiant woman to the edge.

Or if I hadn't seduced her.

Or if she hadn't seduced *me*.

Or if I had simply told her the *truth*. That I, Nicholai Ivanov, was alive, (mostly) well, and (infuriatingly) obsessed with getting into her pencil skirt.

But I didn't think Nicholai deserved a girl like Arya, let alone the woman she'd become.

"We're leaving," I said, standing up abruptly. Arya followed me with her eyes, a little confused. It came back to me now. Teenage Arya. Small and brazen and fiercely independent. All she'd ever wanted was to be seen. And I'd put her through hell. First her father's trial, which still hadn't come to an end, then all these games. The wagers. The rules. She wanted to walk out of this with the remainder of her pride. My only chance to stop her was to give up my own vanity.

"Where to?" She leaned to put her wineglass on my coffee table.

"It's a surprise." I grabbed my jacket. It was clear to me where I was taking her. Only one place would do. I texted Traurig while we took the elevator down. Traurig had a limo and a personal driver on call twenty-four seven. These days his teenybopper daughter and her Belieber friends were the main users of this unpopular luxury, but he owed me a favor or six.

Then I remembered Traurig was on vacation in Hawaii. I texted Claire, who was working extra hard on making herself his favorite associate by moonlighting as his personal assistant whenever he was away, and asked for the limo. Claire promptly texted back that it was on its way.

Fun night planned? she added, right before I shoved my phone back into my pocket. **Can I join?**

Thank you, Miss Lesavoy.

That doesn't answer my question, she texted back. It should've, though.

Sorry. Private occasion.

"Will it take long?" Arya slipped into her own jacket, still looking like a hostage at gunpoint.

I shook my head. "I want to show you something."

When the black limo arrived, I opened the door for her.

"A bit dated, but usually works like a charm," I said, remembering Arya's promise to me two decades ago, that she would send me a limo to the premiere of her movie when she became a big movie star.

She slid inside, turned around, and gave me a wild look that said *Busted*. Had she finally connected the dots?

"What did you say?" she asked slowly.

"I said limos are dated. Why?" I gave her a meaningful stare.

Call me out. Tell me you know who I am. Break things off. I'm ready.

But Arya just bit her lower lip, looking lost in thought. "Never mind."

Darrin, Traurig's driver, caught my gaze through the rearview mirror.

"Mr. Miller." He jerked his head in greeting. "Good to see you again. Where to?"

"The usual," I instructed, flipping a button, making the privacy screen rise up between us so Arya and I could talk.

Arya didn't ask where my usual place might be. She just stared out the window, arms crossed over her chest. The air was stuffy and dense inside the limo. I could taste the impending disaster, the loss, the cataclysm.

"This doesn't have to end in four days' time," I said finally, feeling . . . what was the word for the atrocious storm brewing in my chest? *Defenseless*, maybe. It was a shitty feeling. I'd avoided it since graduating from Andrew Dexter Academy.

"And what would be the point of that?" Arya's head tilted as she took me in for the first time tonight. "We won't be able to go out in public—"

"Not necessarily," I gritted out, stopping her midsentence. "We might. At some point. In a year, maybe two. We'll need to let the media storm from the trial subside first. But there are ways. There is no law against us having a relationship."

Arya let out a wry laugh. "Oh, and then what? I'll bring you over to dinner with my parents?"

"You're not close with your parents," I pointed out.

"My father, especially—"

"He is out of the picture." I sliced through her words again, a smile beginning to tug at my lips. "You couldn't care less what he thinks. Neither could I."

This felt eerily like standing in court, only without a judge running the show. I'd almost forgotten how persuasive I could be. "Please, carry on; what other imaginary obstacles do we have to overcome?"

"Well." Arya huffed, and in that moment, she reminded me of Beatrice. Cool and dismissive. "I don't know anything about you. Not really. You've been careful to keep me in the dark."

"I'm changing that right now. We're going to my secret place." I chanced lacing my fingers through hers between us. She let me.

Her frown melted. "Sounds like the place where you hide all the bodies."

"Not at all." My thumb brushed the inside of her palm. "That'd be my *second* secret place, and I would never take you there before cutting you to pieces."

She grinned sheepishly. "How many victims have you had so far?"

"Zero," I admitted, realizing we were not talking about chopped bodies anymore. "No one's ever felt worthy of . . ." Saving. *"Killing."*

"And now?" she asked.

"And now," I said, looking deep into her eyes, "now I'm not so sure what I'm feeling."

I sat back, pleased. A few minutes later, we arrived at our destination, and I told Darrin to wait.

"Close your eyes," I asked Arya.

She laughed, shaking her head. "Please don't bother. If it's New York—I've already seen it. There'll be no element of surprise."

"Humor me, then." I smiled, getting a quick and overly optimistic glimpse of what living with this woman might entail. The sass, the stubbornness, the spine. She was going to be the death of me.

Arya screwed her mouth sideways. "All right."

She closed her eyes. When I was sure she wasn't peeking, I slid out of the limo and took her by the hand. She shifted a little as I led her the few short steps to our final destination. She could probably tell, by the background noise, that we were still in Midtown.

"Open them," I said.

Arya blinked, looking around her. I stepped beside her.

"This is my favorite place in New York City," I said. "This glass waterfall tunnel. It makes you feel like you're actually inside a waterfall. It's quiet. It's peaceful. And it's right in the middle of the Big Apple."

The water cascaded around us through the glass. Arya's face betrayed nothing. She turned to face me. "When did you start coming here?"

"As soon as I moved back from Boston to New York."

I'd only had Arsène and Riggs in my life. Arsène had rented a three-bedroom converted apartment in Midtown and let me live rent-free while I'd made a name for myself at the DA's office. I'd had no money to my name and lived off my friends' leftovers for a few months. But even at my lowest, when I couldn't even afford a gym membership, I would come here.

"You love water." Arya eyed me curiously, as if unearthing something precious, an archaeologist brushing the dust off a mummy. I wondered if she'd finally recognize me. "Christian?"

"Yes?"

"Are you hiding something from me?"

"I'm hiding your book from you," I said, not missing a beat. Not technically a lie, but not the whole truth either.

"I feel like there's more than that. You would tell me if you were . . ."

She didn't complete the sentence. Neither of us spoke for a moment. Arya was the first to take a step forward. She pressed her hand to my chest.

"I've been burned in the past. I don't know if you understand what you are offering me, but my confidence in other people—especially men—is shredded right now. My sibling, my twin, my blood, died before I could ever know him. The first boy I loved ran away, then died. The man who was supposed to protect me, my father, has lied to me my entire life. In between there were others. Men, boys, guys. It always ended on a bad note. If I let you in, you have to promise not to take advantage. To be completely honest and true, as I intend to be with you. This is the only way this could work. Because in four days' time, my world will be turned upside down, and I'll need stability. Poise."

I'd *died*? That was fucking news to me. Only not really, because I wouldn't put it past Conrad to say anything that would make his daughter stop talking about me.

Ah. But that means that she did *talk about you.*

I clasped my hand over hers, using my free hand to produce something from my pocket.

"Cross my heart and hope to die," I lied, knowing damn well I was not fulfilling my end of the bargain. That I wasn't true. I would tell her who I was. But not now. Not yet. Not like this. When I was so close to losing her. And I couldn't lose her.

Because deep down, I knew, Nicky was still there, scared of being rejected by the golden girl sitting at the piano, back ramrod straight, sneaking smiles at him when no one was looking.

I pried her hand open from my chest and pressed something into it. My apartment key. It was the closest thing she was going to get to my heart.

"I'll hold you when you fall."

She smiled, and my heart broke a little, because I knew in that moment that I was destined to lose her.

"I believe you."

CHAPTER
TWENTY-SIX

A RYA

Present

"Honey." Jillian put her hand over mine that morning at work, when I told her about Christian giving me a key to his apartment and mentioned that oh, by the way, I'd also been sleeping with him throughout my father's trial. You know, that *old thang*. "I don't know how to say this without sounding offensive and brash, so let me just be both for a second—on a scale of one to ten for crazy, when one is completely normal and ten is Christopher Walken in an award-winning movie, you're currently sitting at twelve. What were you *thinking*? The man is about to detonate your father's bank account and take an entire hedge fund company down with him." She leaned forward on my desk, reaching to check my temperature. I was grateful Whitley and Hailey weren't at the office yet. Jillian and I were early birds.

"My father had it coming." I clicked the pen in my hand rapidly, pulling away from her. "He sent dick pics to an intern and asked his former secretary if she'd blow him for a hundred grand. *And* fired Amanda for the great sin of not wanting to sleep with him. His bank account is the least of my concerns now."

"Jesus, Daddy Conrad. I did not see that one coming."

"Yeah. Neither did I."

Jillian slid off my desk with a sigh, making her way to her seat. "All I'm saying is that you had a weird feeling when you met this guy, and your instincts have yet to fail you. I'm not defending your father's actions. I've seen firsthand how you wanted to tear the skin from your own flesh when you found out about his wrongdoings. I'm just not sure starting a relationship with the man who is holding Conrad accountable is recommended. Or advisable. Or, you know, *sane*."

The truth was, I wasn't sure either. But Christian had made me feel what no other man had managed to in years, so it was worth a shot. I'd spent years refusing to get close to men.

Maybe it was time to put a little trust in someone.

I was lying atop Aaron's grave when the final verdict came down. Curled into myself like a shrimp against the cold rock, my hair splayed like the roots of the weeping willow across the tombstone. Minutes before the text arrived, I'd been wondering, idly, what Aaron would be like if he were still alive.

I knew I'd inherited my mother's personality—taciturn, indifferent, with a prudish air—but also my father's voracious hunger for life. The need to sink my teeth into the universe like it was a juicy chunk of pomegranate, crimson beads trickling down my chin.

Would Aaron have been more of a dreamer or a realist? Would he have inherited Mother's fine blonde hair or my father's dark mane? Would we have ever double-dated? Shared secret handshakes? Or bittersweet memories of scraped knees and melting ice cream and cart-wheels under sweltering summer sun . . .

Would my mother have been different? Happier? More present in my life? Would she have been able to stand up to my father?

And Nicky, would he still be here? After all, Aaron would have been the kind of protective brother who never would have let me coax Nicky into kissing me. Would Ruslana be here too?

A ping in my pocket snapped me out of my musings.

Dad: We lost. I've lost two hundred million dollars. Your boyfriend looks happy. I suppose now that it's all over, he can buy you all the pretty things your heart desires. You always were a disappointment, Arya. But I never thought you were a traitor, too.

A scream lodged inside my throat. I swallowed it down, dialing my father's number. He sent me straight to voice mail. I called him again. He deserved a piece of my mind. A third time. Then a fourth. Still nothing. I withdrew my phone from my ear, frowning.

A disappointment. A traitor.

How did my father know about me and Christian? With quivering fingers, I typed both my and Christian's names into my phone's search bar. I assumed Christian hadn't publicly declared our relationship in court, which meant whatever had been publicized about us was common knowledge. Sure enough, the first result in the search bar took me to a local news website covering Manhattan's nightlife, where a picture of Christian and me standing under the waterfall tunnel, my hand pressed against his chest, was displayed.

Rothless Betrayal: How Arya Roth Turned against Her Father . . . and Fell in Love with His Enemy.

By: Cindi Harris-Stone

It appears that pampered socialite slash PR consultant Arya Roth, 32, daughter of shamed hedge fund tycoon Conrad Roth, 66, who is currently on trial for sexual harassment, is sleeping well at night ahead of her father's impending doomsday. The beauty was seen canoodling with none other than sought-after bachelor and top litigator Christian Miller, 32, who also happens to represent her father's accusers. The pair were seen on Tuesday embracing one another in Manhattan.

Canoodling.

The word was a big, fat red sign.

The one Christian had used to describe what we *shouldn't* be doing. I hadn't heard this word in eons before he had said it, and now it was here, on the page. This, in itself, wasn't prime evidence. But coupled with the fact he definitely had a motive and interest in leaking this item, it made my blood run cold.

He'd tipped them off. He must have. The night I'd placed my trust at his feet, he'd gone ahead and stomped all over it.

Jillian's name flashed on my screen. I sent her to voice mail, calling Christian instead. I didn't know at what point, exactly, I'd gotten up and begun moving, but I had. I found my way out of the graveyard in a haze. I reached Christian's voice mail. I called again. Then again. After the sixth time—I was wandering around the streets of Park Avenue, with no direction or plan—I called his office's landline, my neck and cheeks burning with rage and humiliation. No one had ever wronged me so profoundly. So maliciously.

"Hello?" A cheerful voice invaded my ear. I recognized it belonged to Claire, the associate who was working with Christian on my father's case. Even though she was the last person I wanted to talk to, I wasn't in a position to be picky.

"Hi, Claire. I'm looking for Christian. I was wondering if you could put him through?"

In the background, I heard cheers, chatter, and the sound of a champagne bottle popping. The office was celebrating, no doubt the huge success that was Christian and Claire's case. A rush of self-loathing filled me. How could I have been so stupid?

"May I ask who's calling?" Claire purred. I could practically envision her feline smile. I stopped walking, digging my fingers into my eye sockets.

"Arya. Arya Roth."

There was a pause. I could hear Christian in the distance, laughing. People congratulated him in turns. The scream lodged in my throat rolled an inch upward, toward my mouth.

"I'm sorry, Ms. Roth." Claire's voice turned cold. "He's not available right now. May I suggest you make an appointment to speak to him? You can call his secretary. Same number, but her extension is seven-oh-three."

"Look, I—"

She hung up.

I stared at my phone. For the first time, I truly felt unhinged. I couldn't anticipate my next move or trust myself not to do something I would regret. Overflowing with rage, I yanked out the key Christian had given me for his apartment—shortly before getting in my pants *again*—and called an Uber.

Why had he given me the key, anyway? Oh, but the answer was clear—to taunt me. To make me look for my book. To watch me sweat for it. I'd always been a game to him.

Well, guess what, I was going to get the book that he'd stolen from me. Even if I had to rip his entire preppy apartment to shreds. I would not leave without it. And his only chance to pry that book out of my hands would be if I had to smack him with it on my way out.

The entire journey to Christian's house, I read through the headlines on my phone.

Dick Move: How Conrad Roth Lost Everything because of That *Pic.*

Court Orders Wall Street Tycoon to Pay 200 Mil!

Roth in Hell, Conrad!

The media was having a field day. At first, I skimmed through each article to see if my name was mentioned in any of them. Once I realized I was mentioned in virtually *all* of them, I stopped checking. Media-management expert. *Ha!* Christian had just handed me my ass in that department, and he'd done a brilliant job at portraying me as an idiot. Jillian continued calling and texting, and so did my mother, whose worst fear had come to life—she was now broke and penthouseless. After such public humiliation, I should hope also newly single.

The Uber stopped in front of Christian's place. I darted out, passing the receptionist and doorman briskly—appearing as if this were my natural habitat—and made my way up to the apartment. I unlocked the door and stepped in. His scent immediately seeped into my system, taking root. Shaved wood, fine leather, and male. Only it no longer brought me pleasure. Now, I wanted to purge it from my system.

If I were a handsome, highly intelligent sociopath, where would I hide a book?

I tried the kitchen drawers first, yanking them open one after the other, flipping their contents to the floor. Utensils flew out, spilling on the expensive parquet. I then moved to the cabinets, emptying them, too, then ripped the couch pillows from their base, unzipping the cases to see if the book was inside one of them.

Moving on to the stylish, meticulously organized pantry, I dragged my arms across the shelves. Condiments, protein powder, and spices rolled down to the floor. I flipped furniture upside down, emptied the cabinets of all the work files he kept at home, and—*fine*, this was a bonus—shattered some delicate china that didn't necessarily need to be broken. When I was completely certain the book couldn't be found in the living room, I moved to his bedroom. I started off by ripping some of his designer suits, not because I thought I'd find *Atonement* inside them but because I considered the act highly therapeutic. Afterward, I stripped his bed of the sheets, which still smelled like us, and looked in his nightstand drawers and even under the bed.

I'd swung my body back up, about to proceed to his en suite bathroom, when something compelled me to look back down. I frowned when I noticed the bump on his parquet. A slightly jagged floor tile, oddly out of place. This seemed completely out of character for Christian, who lived and breathed perfection.

Bingo.

I stretched my arm under his bed, using my fingernails to pry the tile open. My nail polish chipped, but the more I inched the tile out from its neighbors, the more I knew I was onto something.

With a snap and a clunk, followed by a ragged sigh escaping from my mouth, Christian's secret place was exposed. I patted the space under the tile, unable to peer into it from my angle. My heart dipped with disappointment when I felt a manila envelope. I removed it nonetheless, in case there was something else hiding under it. Indeed, there was. I could feel it. The delicious, firm thickness of a hardcover. I pulled it out, feeling childishly relieved, even after everything that had happened today, because I'd finally found it.

Grabbing it, I rolled away from the bed and hugged it to my chest before opening the book in the middle and giving it a hearty sniff.

Briony. Robbie. Cecilia. Paul. My good old friends.

It took me a few minutes to bring my heart rate down. After which I glanced back at the manila envelope sitting not a few feet from me, staring back at me curiously. I'd gotten what I'd come here for. That much was true. But there was still a need in me, a seed of desperation, which bloomed into vengeance, demanded to get its pound of flesh. Getting back what was legally mine wasn't enough. Christian had had leverage over me since the moment we'd met. He always dangled something over my head. My father's trial. The book. The mystery that was him. Normally, I would never betray a person in such a way. *Normally.* But nothing about my relationship with Christian was normal.

Carefully, I reached for the manila envelope, dragging it across the pristine floor toward me. I sat up, propping my back against his nightstand, and pulled the thick stack of papers inside it out.

In the Superior Court of Middlesex County
State of Massachusetts
Civil Action
In re the Name Change of: Nicholai Ruslan Ivanov
Case Number: 190482873983
PETITION TO CHANGE NAME OF ADULT
The petitioner respectfully moves this Court to change his name from Nicholai Ruslan Ivanov to Christian George Miller.

A yelp escaped my mouth. Nothing could prepare me for the pain I felt in that moment. Like someone had reached into my chest, breaking my rib cage in the process, and clawed my heart out, twisting it ruthlessly in their fist.

Christian was Nicholai.

Nicholai was Christian.

Nicky wasn't dead. He'd been here all along. Lurking in the shadows, planning his grand revenge for what my family had done to him, no doubt. The trial. The sentence. The conquest. The girl who'd turned into a woman, who'd turned into a tool.

Me.

I put together the jagged pieces. The way he'd spoken about my father . . . the hunger with which he'd fought for the case . . .

That first time I'd met him at the elevator and had that peculiar feeling. The air had been loaded with many more feelings than any two strangers could ever evoke in one another.

That strange notion in my stomach that I'd always known him, that he was somehow engraved into my skin, wasn't a false alarm. He knew who I was and had kept his identity from me.

The man I'd put my trust in had broken my heart. *Twice.*

And in the process, he'd also managed to strip my family of everything it owned, lie to the world about who he was, and out us as an item.

Middlesex, Massachusetts. Christian had changed his name while he'd attended undergrad at Harvard University, or right before. Had he planned this all along? Becoming a lawyer so he could bring my father down, and me with him? Had he sought out Amanda himself?

I was too curious to fall apart. I'd have time for that later, once I left this man's apartment. I continued rummaging through the folders in the manila envelope instead. All the paperwork for the change of name from Nicholai to Christian, his old and current passports, and the death certificate for Ruslana Ivanova.

Ruslana had died.

That was news to me. Then again, everything about this situation was. Now it all made sense. Why Christian had leaked our relationship to the press, and with perfect timing too. Right after my father's trial. He'd killed two birds—or *Roths*—with one stone. He'd just never taken one thing into consideration—that I was going to find out his secret.

I took pictures of the damning documents of the name change with my phone, making sure they were clear and in focus. Then I grabbed my book and dashed out of his apartment.

My knee-jerk reaction was to take it to my father. To show him the evidence against Christian and start working toward an appeal, now that it was clear that Christian never should have worked on the case. He knew my family too well and had a vendetta against us. I slid into a taxi and was about to utter my parents' address when I realized I didn't want to do that either.

True, Christian was an asshole of gigantic proportions, but so was my father. Ultimately, they were as bad as each other. I wanted to use the information I had against Christian to ruin him, but not necessarily in the most straightforward way, in which my father got off the hook too.

Conrad Roth definitely deserved to be stripped of his reputation, money, and social standing. He'd done horrible things to people and used his power against helpless women.

I needed to think about it, long and hard. To come up with a plan.

"Miss? Excuse me? Yoo-hoo?" The cabdriver waved his fingers in the direction of the rearview mirror. "Not that it ain't nice to sit here and watch you talking to yourself, but where to?"

I gave him my apartment address.

I was going to ruin Nicky. But in my own Ari way.

CHAPTER TWENTY-SEVEN

CHRISTIAN

Present

"Think again, Mr. Hotshot," Claire giggled breathlessly, snatching the phone from my hand. We had just walked out of the courthouse. I'd said my goodbyes to Amanda Gispen and the other plaintiffs, ignoring the journalists and photographers begging for a comment, and was about to hail a cab to Arya's office. First things first, I needed to make sure she was okay with everything that had happened. As okay as one could be considering the circumstances. Second, I needed to come clean.

She had to know who I was.

This could not be postponed any longer.

Claire, apparently, had other ideas.

"Give me my phone back." I all but bared my teeth at her, stretching my arm with my palm open in her direction. Claire bit down on her lip, glowing with pride. She'd worn a brand-new suit today to court. A double-breasted Alexander McQueen that must've cost her an arm, a leg, and her monthly rent.

"No can do, Mr. Miller." She winked, pocketing my phone. "This is an order from high up. Traurig said no distractions. He has a surprise for you."

"Give me my phone, *Claire*," I said pointedly. "I have someone to call."

"That someone can wait ten minutes. We work two blocks from here." Claire wrapped her arm around mine, tugging me forward. "Jeez, don't be a party pooper. Just make a toast with everyone, thank Traurig and Cromwell, and go your merry way. You've gotten *this* far; are you seriously not going to make it to your own partnership party?" Claire elevated a carefully plucked eyebrow. I wasn't an easily swayed man. Came with the territory of knowing the price temptation could cost you. I was about to answer her that yes, I was, in fact, going to bail on my own party, because partying wasn't nearly as important as making sure the woman I was dating was still, in fact, dating me. Just then, I felt two firm hands clapping me on either side of my back.

Shit.

"The man of the hour," drawled Cromwell, fingering his mustache like a D-grade villain.

"The belle of the ball." Traurig nudged Claire aside. "I have a Cuban cigar with your name on it and some gold lettering we need to add to the firm's name. The maintenance guy is already there, waiting for us. Hurry up."

The maintenance guy was there, waiting to put my letters up. Hunky freaking dory. Claire flashed me a look that said *Don't you dare.* She had a point. If I bailed now, I was going to look like a deranged idiot—not the best look. Plus, the outcome wasn't anything Arya hadn't been expecting. We'd been discussing this for weeks.

Ten minutes, however, somehow bled into eternity. It took the maintenance guy almost an hour to add the golden letters at the entrance to the firm, possibly because Cromwell and Traurig kept shouting at him that my last name wasn't symmetrical. After which I was dragged into one of the conference rooms, where the entire firm waited with cake, cigars, booze, and a huge present wrapped in a red satin bow.

"I'm so proud of you. I cannot even tell you how much," my PA wept. Then every single person on the floor felt the urge to congratulate me and shake my hand, one by one.

I kept telling myself that if Arya was so desperate to talk to me, she could always call my office.

When the Oscar-worthy ceremony was over—*two* freaking hours later—Traurig asked that I open my giant gift. It turned out to be new business cards with the full, new name of the firm: *Cromwell, Traurig & Miller*. Bold golden lettering over sleek black cards. I waited for euphoria to take over my senses. But all I could feel when I stared at my new business cards was: I really want to see Arya. Not this evening. Not in an hour. *Now.*

"Thank you," I said, my voice steely, circling my fingers around Claire's arm and leading her out of the conference room. I glanced at my watch again on my way to my office. It seemed like centuries since we'd left the courtroom. The fact I hadn't called Arya thus far was ill mannered at best and cunt-a-licious at worse.

When we got to my office, I closed the door behind us. My spidey sense told me there was going to be a lot of shouting in my near future.

"Give me my phone, Claire."

She winced. "So soon? We haven't even had lunch. I was thinking maybe I could buy you a drink. We have a lot to talk about, and I—"

"Phone!" I slapped my hand on the wall behind her, and she squeaked, jumping. I was not a violent person, but I was starting to lose my patience and didn't want my first move as a partner to be firing an associate who'd just helped me win a huge case. "Or you walk out of here with security at your fucking heels, Lesavoy."

With a pout, Claire produced my phone from her pocket. I glanced at it, feeling my pulse quickening against the collar of my shirt. I had over fifty missed calls from Arya. And some texts too. The minute the face recognition was on, the texts began sliding down chronologically on the screen one by one.

Arya: How could you do this to me?

Arya: You've SHATTERED my career. I can't show my face ever again. And my nonexistent relationship with my mother is over. Not to mention my father (who is dead to me, but it would have been nice to make that choice myself).

Ruined her career? Her relationships? What the hell was she on about?

Arya: What I don't understand is how you could be so heartless? How you did it on the same night you promised you wouldn't break my trust.

Arya: I'll give you that, it was a genius move. You probably had a blast laughing about it in court. Now you can go back to Claire. I know you guys were casual, but man, you deserve each other.

Claire must've seen the confusion clouding my face, because I noticed her licking her lips in my periphery, shifting from one foot to the other. "Everything okay?"

"I—" I paused, trying to understand what was happening here, until it clicked. The limo. Claire talking to Darrin. Knowing my whereabouts with Arya. The way she'd pursued me relentlessly.

Press. That was the one thing Arya and I had agreed not to involve. We didn't want to be seen or caught.

My eyes glided up from my phone. I could feel my gaze turning hard, callous, as I watched Claire's face. "What have you done?"

"I . . . I . . ." She tried to take a step back, but she was pressed against the wall, with nowhere to go. I'd never thought of myself as someone who could hurt a woman, but in that moment, I knew I could hurt Claire. Not physically, no. But I could fire her. Banish her. Make her a persona non grata in Manhattan's legal circle.

"Speak."

Claire dropped her head, shaking it as she covered her face with her hands. "I'm sorry. I just told a friend of mine who works at the *Manhattan Times*. That's it. It slipped." She cringed. But she wasn't fooling anyone, and she knew it. I took a step back, knowing full well I wasn't in control of myself. Arya must be thinking the worst of me right now.

"Leave." I breathed through my nose, digging my thumb and index finger into my eye sockets.

"To . . . my office?"

"To . . . *the fucking hellhole where you came from.*" I mimicked her tone derisively, opening my eyes again. "And don't come back. Ever."

"We just won a case."

"You lost all credibility with me the minute you leaked a story about me to a journalist."

"You can't do that!" Claire flung her arms in the air. "You can't make a decision like that without consulting Traurig and Cromwell. You've been a partner for all of five minutes."

"All right." I smiled cordially. "Let's go to Cromwell's office right now and tell him what you did. See how it's going to fare for you."

Her face whitened. What the hell had she thought? That I wasn't going to find out? Claire hugged her arms, looking down at the floor.

"What did you think?" I spit out, curious about the rationale behind this atrocity.

"I thought after the trial was over you were going to dump her. But I wasn't sure and didn't want to take any chances. And I certainly didn't think you'd care all that much. Not to mention . . ." She blew out air, her eyes glittering with unshed tears. "I simply didn't think. That's the thing. That's what happens when you're in love. Have you ever been in love, Christian?"

I was about to say no, I hadn't, and that fact had nothing to do with anything, when I realized . . . I couldn't say that for sure.

"Good luck seeing yourself out, Miss Lesavoy."

I brushed past Claire's shoulder, heading out of the office. I didn't tell a soul. My PA jumped up, asking where I was heading. She was met with no reply. My first stop was Arya's office. I buzzed the building's intercom, getting through to Whitney or Whitley or whatever her name was. The receptionist didn't answer me verbally. She did push her upper body through the window of her office and pour her lukewarm coffee atop my head before finishing the gesture by slamming her glass window shut.

Though aware that I had become public enemy number one in Arya's camp, I still thought I could salvage it. If she gave me the time to explain and I told her all about Claire, she'd understand. Arya was a highly pragmatic person with a terrific bullshit meter. She'd know I was telling the truth.

My next stop was her apartment. This time, I got a little farther than the buzzer. All the way to her apartment's door, in fact. I knocked frantically. Jillian threw the door open, leaning a hip against the frame, her face slathered in a green mask of some sort. "Yes?"

"I'm here to see Arya."

"Ambitious." She made a show of checking out her fingernails. "You know, considering the circumstances."

"Is she not here?" I narrowed my eyes. I couldn't imagine her anywhere but home on a day like this. Maybe her mother's apartment. But unlikely.

"Oh, she is here. But she can't see you."

"Why?"

"Because you're dead to her."

My teeth ground together. "I can explain."

"I'm sure you can, *Nicholai*. Feel free to do it to the door while I call the police. Which is exactly what I'm about to do if you don't evacuate the premises in the next three seconds."

With that, she slammed the door in my face.

◆ ◆ ◆

Nicholai.

Nicholai.

Nicholai.

Jillian had called me Nicholai. As I made my way home in a taxi, I tried to gauge what, exactly, I was facing. It seemed like whatever Arya knew was a lot worse than the fact that a few of our sloppy kisses had been plastered on some news websites.

It seemed like she knew the *truth*.

And the truth was unbearable, to both of us.

When I got to my apartment, there was no room for doubt. Arya had raided the place while I was gone, most likely sometime after I hadn't taken her calls and she'd realized we'd been outed by the media. The place was a dumpster fire, sans the pretty flame. The tragic part was I knew she hadn't looked for the truth. She'd looked for her *book*. Searched for it everywhere. The garbage can included. Or maybe her flipping it over had just been the final, screw-you touch. Like an exotic flower on a pretty dessert at a restaurant.

Either way, what she'd wanted was clear—to take away the piece of her that had temporarily belonged to me and make sure that I'd never have access to it again.

I headed toward my bedroom, my soul in my throat. Even before I walked in, I knew what I was going to find. The manila envelope I'd kept a secret for all those years was open, the documents scattered everywhere. I didn't have to crouch down and look for the book to know that it was gone. *Atonement* was no longer mine.

I'm sure you can, Nicholai.

Arya knew.

She'd told Jillian.

There was no reason to think Arya hadn't told her parents too. Her father's *lawyers*. But somehow, I couldn't bring myself to give much of a damn about that part. My ungraceful second fall.

All I cared about was that she'd found out and not in the way I had wanted her to.

There was no point calling her. She wasn't going to pick up. Whatever I could salvage of our relationship—of my *life*—had to wait until tomorrow.

She needed time, and I needed to respect that, even if it killed me.

I picked up the phone and called one of the very few people in the universe who knew.

"What?" Arsène barked out groggily.

"She found out," I said, still frozen to my spot at the entrance of my room. This was the time when he was going to tell me that he'd told me so, that he'd warned me.

"Shit," he surprised me by saying.

"Indeed."

"Grabbing my keys and coming. Beer?"

I rubbed my eye sockets. "Go north. Way north."

"Brandy?"

"More like a bullet."

"A bottle of A. de Fussigny and a full metal jacket coming right up."

That night, I didn't sleep. Wasn't dumb enough to even try. I ended up polishing off that cognac Arsène had brought over, then hitting the indoor gym in my building. I hopped into the shower, got dressed for work, went through the same predictable motions . . .

Only I didn't *go* to work.

The firm—the company I'd wanted to take over more than anything else in my life—had become trivial, laughably inconsequential.

A shiny toy that had kept me occupied while life happened in my periphery. Every time I tried to muster the motivation to haul ass to the place that deposited seven figures into my bank account annually, I couldn't help but feel like a hamster getting ready to hop on a wheel. The constant spinning got me nowhere. More money. More wins. More dinners I didn't like with clients I loathed.

It occurred to me that I wasn't only jaded; I was dizzy from solving other people's problems all the time. Well, now I had a problem of my own to solve. Arya knew I was Nicky and that I'd kept it a secret from her.

Even more horrifying—she knew I was Nicky and therefore that I was worthless.

I went straight to Arya's office that morning, arriving at eight o'clock sharp. An hour before opening. I'd spent enough mornings with Arya to know she was an early riser and liked to be at the office before the birds arose.

As it turned out, this was the one morning when Arya had decided to sleep in. I watched Whitley and her sidekick march through the door at nine o'clock, throwing murderous looks my way, then Jillian joining them at nine thirty. Arya was nowhere to be found until ten past ten, when I noticed her briskly turning a corner onto the side street and making her way to her office building, looking like a summer storm. An unthawable ice queen ready to conquer the world.

I stood up from the step leading to the front of her building's door. She didn't slow down when she spotted me through her sunglasses. She stopped when our bodies were flush against one another, swung her arm backward, and slapped me so hard I was pretty sure parts of my brain were splattered on the sidewalk.

"I deserved that."

"You deserve much more than that after the revenge plot you planned for me and my family, Nicky."

Nicky. I hadn't heard that name in years. Only Arya had called me that. Ruslana had tried it on her tongue a few times and found it distasteful. I missed it.

"No revenge plot." I rubbed at my cheek. I was mesmerized by her. Like I hadn't seen her dozens of times before, in compromising positions, stark naked and sucking different parts of my body. Was this what love felt like? Wanting to kiss and protect the woman you wanted to ram into from behind? How peculiar. And nauseating. And so terribly predictable of me. Falling for the one woman I could never have. Who'd ruined everything, and I, in return, had done the same to her.

And this time, I didn't even want to get even.

"Believe it or not, Amanda Gispen walked into my office one day by happenstance. Can't say I didn't live every day wanting to get back at your father for the years he put me through, but it wasn't the first thing on my agenda."

It had been the second thing, though, before she'd turned my life upside down, in true Arya fashion.

"There's no excuse for what he did that day." Arya stepped back, her face contorting in agony. "Trust me, I spent an entire year refusing to look at him. Then an entire lifetime second-guessing every decision I've made. Letting him off the hook always made me feel like I was on the wrong side of history. But he apologized for it and ended up sending you to live with your dad, like you wanted."

"Is that what he told you?" I smiled tiredly. "Before or after I allegedly dropped dead?"

Her pink lips turned down into a scowl, but she didn't answer.

"Trust me, beating the shit out of me in front of the girl I crushed on was the least of his sins. He made my mother throw me out the night I kissed you. I had to sleep on the neighbors' couch. Then he put me in Andrew Dexter Academy and told *you* I was dead."

Arya removed her sunglasses. Her eyes were shiny, full of tears. "I grieved you for years. Every day."

"I grieved you, too, and I didn't even think you were dead," I said gruffly.

"You didn't want to go?" Her voice was soft, pliant now.

I shook my head. I'd have chosen life in poverty if it meant being close to her.

"It wasn't Conrad who told me you passed away. I hired a private investigator to find you when I turned eighteen, you know." She sounded defeated. "He was the one to deliver the news."

I smiled. "Now, let me guess." I took a step forward, wanting to sniff her, to bury my hands in her hair, to kiss with both our past and our present, now that she knew who I was. "That private investigator guy, he worked for your father, didn't he?" By the look on her face, I could tell I was right. "Yeah. That's what I thought. But I'm not done telling you about the hell Conrad put me through."

"Hurry up, because I'll give you my own brand of Roth hell when you're done."

"While I was at Andrew Dexter, your father sent the headmaster to straighten me up, so to speak. Every now and again, I'd get a thrashing simply for existing. The headmaster himself wouldn't lay a finger on me, but he got other students to hit me. Conrad also ensured my mother cut off all contact with me. I only saw her once after the day she kicked me out. Not during summer and spring breaks or the holidays. I always stayed at the dorms. That's where I met Riggs and Arsène. How I created my own family."

Arya swallowed visibly. She was wrestling with competing emotions. Her desire to kill me for what I'd done to her, and her desire to maim her father for what he'd done to me. "Ruslana . . . she died?"

I nodded. "I got a theory about that too."

"Yeah?"

"When I was a junior at Andrew Dexter, I got a job as a stable boy and met Alice—my so-called cougar, as you like to call her. Suddenly, I was in close proximity to money and lived the rich life, even if by proxy.

One summer break, when I was in New York, I bumped into Ruslana. I drove around in Arsène's Bentley and wore his rich-asshole attire, head to toe. Ruslana flung herself over me and kissed me. She made a scene. I peeled her off me and told her I'd try squeezing her into my New York plans, but of course that never happened. She began writing to me after that. I never replied. She must've taken my silence as a test of her determination, because the more time had passed, the more she felt compelled to tell me everything that happened to her. I still have the letters. They were in the manila file. I don't know if you read them. She said she had a long affair with Conrad. That he had promised to leave Beatrice for her. Said when she began to doubt his intentions, his assurances, she told Conrad that she was going to tell Beatrice herself. He got rough with her, pushing her around. Apparently, it wasn't the first time he'd put a hand on her."

"That's how you knew everything about him was true." Arya pressed a hand against her chest. "Knew that Amanda and the other accusers were telling the truth."

I nodded. "Ruslana and Conrad went back and forth for a few months. Finally, he fired her and gave her hush money. A measly ten-thousand-dollar check to keep her mum. She spent it in about a week and wrote to me that she went to see him again to ask for more. That was her last letter before I got the call from the police that she was dead."

"How did she die?" Arya asked.

"The official medical cause cites a broken neck. In practice, she got thrown off the Palisades cliff. The cop who told me about her death said they suspected no foul play. That it was a classic suicide case. My mother hadn't been known as the happy-go-lucky type, and she did lose her job that same month. But it was a bunch of nonsense. Ruslana hated heights. She'd flown one time in her life, and even if she were suicidal, which she wasn't, she would have preferred any type of death over that one. Drowning, slitting her wrists, a bullet to the temple. You pick."

"You think my dad was behind it?" Arya's eyes flared.

"Short answer? Yes. Long answer? To an extent, but I'm not sure who were the key players in what happened."

"Then he should be tried for that too."

She wasn't wrong. But in Conrad's case, I knew losing everything around him—his money, his status, his kid—was punishment enough. Wandering the world a penniless reject would be more of a punishment for a man like him than sitting around with shamefaced criminals like himself in prison.

"There's no way for me to prove it, not without revealing my true identity, at any rate," I replied.

"Regardless of what's happening, I'm sorry you lost her."

"I'm not. She was a shit mother."

"And you want to tell me that after everything Conrad did to you, this move with Amanda Gispen wasn't calculated?" She knotted her arms over her chest.

"Correct." I sidestepped to let a woman with a stroller pass by, my mind immediately drifting to Arya with a baby. Dammit. The floodgate was open now, and even a sandwich reminded me of her. "I believe Conrad did something to my mother—or at least sent someone else to do it—but the way I see it, it was never my problem. The day she gave up on me, I gave up on her. I went ahead and found new friends, a new family, a woman who gave me what my mother failed to, and I'm not talking about the money here. I'm talking about courage, confidence, and the mental leg up. Someone who told me what I wanted from life was within reach."

When I moved back to my spot on the sidewalk, I made sure I was a little closer to Arya than I'd been before. Just a smidge. "No part of me wanted to return to New York. I wanted to stay in Boston. Maybe head down to DC and dirty my hands up in politics. New York has always reminded me of the Roths, of my mother turning her back on me, of that disastrous first kiss. But fate had it that Arsène is from New

York and actually likes this hellhole. Riggs is from San Francisco, but he seemed eager to never set foot in the place again. He was all too happy to move into Arsène's monstrous, rent-free condo. I didn't want to stay behind. They were the only real family I'd known, so I tagged along. Believe it or not, I worked damn hard to keep my distance from you and yours. My worst nightmare was you or Conrad walking into my life once more and screwing it up. But when the case dropped on my desk, I couldn't stop myself." I licked my lips. "We both know I yield to temptation from time to time."

"So you didn't seek revenge; it just fell into your lap."

"Yes."

Until it had become clear it had always been Arya I wanted in my lap.

"All these years I thought you were dead . . . ," Arya mumbled, still trying to piece it all together. She shook her head. "That's why I didn't recognize you. That was the only reason why I didn't think you were you. Because I'd convinced myself not to believe. Not to hope."

And I'd foolishly held it against her. Each time we'd watched one another. Assessed. Caressed. Kissed. I'd always told myself she deserved the hell I gave her, because she couldn't even recognize the boy who'd been wildly in love with her. Who'd been willing to give up the world for her and, in some ways, had.

"I spent all of yesterday trying to untangle one feeling from the other, and I still can't." Arya rubbed at her forehead.

"Let me help," I offered. I had no right asking her for anything, but especially her trust.

"That's the thing." She frowned, practical as ever. No tears or empty threats from this woman. "I don't trust you with a piece of toast anymore, let alone my life, my decisions, my feelings. I absolutely loathe you, Nicky, with every piece of my soul. All this time, all this yearning . . . I ached for you for over a decade. We were Cecilia and Robbie."

I had no idea who she was talking about, having never met a Cecilia and only one Robbie, who happened to be a tax lawyer from Staten

Island. But I wanted to throttle both these people for butting into my relationship.

Arya rubbed her cheek, getting over her own mental slap. "All the things that made you dazzling and untouchable disappeared yesterday when I saw the picture of us *canoodling* on that website."

"It wasn't me." I stepped forward yet again, daring to smooth one of her flyaways behind her ear. She swatted my hand away. That hurt more than the slap. More than that day Headmaster Plath had sent those boys to kill me. "It was Claire. Claire was the one who sent us the limo that day when I made you the promise. She tipped off the press."

"Canoodling," Arya stressed, her eyes widening. "They used that word."

I shook my head. "Coincidence. I would never do that to you, Ari. Ever."

"You're wrong." Arya stepped back, her eyes filled with tears again. I wanted them to fall. For her to break. To stop being so goddamn stubborn and better than me all the time. Because deep down, that was how I'd always felt. Unworthy of her time, smiles, and existence. "You already did. You said you wouldn't betray me." A sad smile tugged at her lips. "You lied."

"I was planning to tell you," I said.

"When?"

"I don't know." I ran my fingers through my hair, yanking at it. "After the trial? Once I was sure you fell for me? Who knows? I was worried you'd dump me because Nicky wasn't good enough."

Of course, if I told her I loved her now, she'd never believe me. My professional ass was on the line. She was one call away from ruining my career, and we both knew it. Declaring my feelings for her would feel calculated, cunning, and—above all—humiliating to her. Not to mention I didn't want to start a relationship with her thinking I was chained to her because I had something to lose. Not that I didn't. But *she* was that something. Not my job.

Arya shook her head. "Nicky was always good enough. It's Christian I don't trust."

"Then let me change that." I raised an eyebrow. "There's more I can give you. A lot more. And all you have to give me in return is one thing."

"What is that?"

"A chance."

"Why Christian?" The look in her eyes was chilling as she changed the subject. "Why Miller?"

"I changed my name legally before I attended my first semester at Harvard. I didn't want your father to find me. Knew he was going to keep an eye on me. Nicholai Ivanov didn't apply to any universities. He bought a one-way ticket to Canada and ran away. After all, as soon as we turned eighteen, all bets were off, and he knew you could look for me and that I could look for you."

Her teeth sank into her lip. She understood. After all, she *had* looked for me through her father's private investigator. And the only thing stopping me from looking for her had been the knowledge I had nothing to offer her.

"I needed to disappear. So I chose one of the most common last names in America—Miller—and Christian, which is widely one of the most popular names in the English language and also brought to mind the rebirthing, the christening of another identity. Basically, I did all I could to ensure your father never found me. The day Nicholai disappeared across the border, a John Doe was born."

She shook her head, stepping toward the entrance door. She was about to leave. I couldn't let her. Not because she could get me disbarred, or because my partnership was on the line. But because I was not ready to say goodbye. Not to her. Not at fourteen, and not at thirty-two.

"Arya, wait."

She turned around again to face me. "You know, Nicky, the first thing I did when I found out who you were was tell Jillian. It was stronger than me. My vindictiveness took over me. I needed to feel . . . *reckless*." She drew in her breath. "But I couldn't, for the life of me, tell my parents about you. Aim to where it would hurt you the most. I couldn't tell them the truth. Isn't that sad? That I hate my father almost as much as I hate you? And love you both too. I guess my love will always be dipped in hate, making every important relationship in my life bittersweet. But I want you to know I'm well aware of the control I have over you, and don't think for one second I won't use it. If you get anywhere near me, for any reason whatsoever, I am going to make sure Judge Lopez and the partners at your firm know about your connection with the Roth family. As well as the NY State Bar Association. So make sure you stay the hell away from me, because all it'd take is one call, one text, one unwarranted visit, for me to ruin your life. And believe me, *Christian*, I will ruin your life without so much as a blink."

She wasn't going to say anything.

I wasn't sure if I wanted to laugh or scream.

I didn't think the chances of Arya keeping this a secret were high. I supposed telling on me just seemed like the natural thing to do. Which was why I was more preoccupied with her forgiving me than her revealing my secret. Any other man would have taken what she'd given him and left. And maybe I had been that man two months ago. But I wasn't him today, nor would I be any day after.

"So you're saying the next time I contact you, you'll have me disbarred?" I drawled.

"At the very least."

"Very well. Thank you, Ari."

"Burn in hell, Nicky."

CHAPTER TWENTY-EIGHT

C H R I S T I A N

Present

I didn't want to fly out to Florida in the middle of the week. It had nothing to do with the mounting pile of work I had waiting for me at the office or the two puzzled partners who couldn't understand why my first move had been to fire one of their most promising associates. I knew Claire wouldn't try and pull the sexual harassment card against me, mainly because we were both ultracautious, calculated people, and she knew I'd saved all the messages she had sent me in the past in which she'd been begging me to bed her. Dragging me or the firm through court would detonate the one thing Claire valued above all else—her pride.

Plus, I *had* notified HR about it when we'd first started.

I didn't like the idea of leaving New York when things between Arya and myself were unsettled. But as Arsène and Riggs had pointed out when I'd told them about my conversation with Arya, this sort of shit was beyond their pay grade, and I needed a woman's touch to figure out where I was headed from here.

Alice Gudinski lived in a sprawling Palm Beach condo. Arsène, Riggs, and I visited her occasionally, especially during the holidays, but the past couple of years had been hectic work-wise, so I'd dropped the ball.

I'd made us a reservation for a seafood restaurant with an ocean view.

Of course, I was also ten minutes late, coming straight from the airport.

Alice waited for me on the veranda, which overlooked the sunset. She wore a kimono and was cradling a Bloody Mary the size of a champagne bucket.

"Ah, my favorite toy boy without benefits." She kissed both my cheeks, then my nose and my ear. Alice looked radiant and not a day over forty. To an outsider, it wasn't far fetched that we were a couple. A dashing toy boy whose millionaire girlfriend had bought him a little Realtor office on the beach. Only I knew she'd never take a lover after losing Henry. "You look decadent."

"You look lovely, as always." I dropped a kiss to the crown of her head before helping her to her seat and lounging opposite to her. A waitress dashed to us with a glass of sherry on cue, no doubt having gotten prior instructions from Bossy Alice.

"Shame Arsène and Riggs couldn't make it." She sipped her Bloody Mary, the orange-and-pink sunset burning the sky her backdrop.

"Riggs is currently in England, taking pictures for an article about beached whales, and Arsène quit civilization sometime after his college graduation. I'm afraid you're stuck with me."

"You're my favorite, anyway. The other two are just the side pieces." Alice took another sip, winking. "But you don't suffer from too much free time, either, which leads me to believe this is not only a social call. How can I help you?"

She saw through my bullshit from fifty yards away. It surprised me I didn't see Alice more often. And angered me too. Because during my Andrew Dexter years and then my Harvard years, I used to spend as much time with her as possible. She'd been my lifeline, providing me with direction and advice, explaining to me the ins and outs of high society. Helping me blend in with the rest of them.

"I intend to change that and make sure there will be a lot of social calls in the future for us," I informed her, waving for the waitress to come and take our order.

Alice shook her head, laughing. "Oh, silly boy. I've already placed the order for us. You really think I'm going to let some Manhattan punk tell me what the catch of the day is?"

"You've been in Palm Beach for less than two years," I pointed out.

"Nevertheless." She patted her coiffed hair. "At any rate, where were we? Oh yes. You're in trouble. Is it Traurig or Cromwell? I bet it's Cromwell, that old sod. He is suffering from some serious youth envy."

Alice's late husband was a corporate lawyer, so she knew a thing or two about firm politics.

The food arrived. More specifically—half the goddamn ocean's creatures. Alice had a healthy appetite for a woman of her physique.

"It's not about work." I speared a scallop swimming in olive oil, butter, and oregano with my fork and brought it to my mouth.

"Your investment portfolio?"

"No."

"Are you finally selling and moving to DUMBO? You could get more bang for your buck there."

I shook my head.

"Well, what is it, then?"

"Arya," I said. "Arya Roth."

◆ ◆ ◆

297

Forty minutes and five entrées later, Alice was up to speed with my Arya situation. She'd known about Arya from when I was seventeen, but not about the recent development in our story.

Alice sat back, nursing a fruity cocktail, nodding gravely.

"First of all, let me just say I can't believe it has taken you so long to find her." Her eyes glittered happily.

I scowled. Had she not heard anything I'd said? "I didn't find her. It was a coincidence."

"There is no such thing as coincidence. Only divine intervention. And it was clear from when you were seventeen that your heart belonged to that girl, along with the rest of your body. You wandered around aimlessly for long enough, but unfortunately, people—especially young people—really do need to experience things in the flesh for the thought to finally sink in."

Ignoring the fact she'd known all along something I had just found out this month, my love for Arya, I skipped to the bottom line. "What do I do?"

"Well," Alice laughed, "you *did* mess up."

"I know," I bit out, losing patience.

"Spectacularly so."

"If I wanted to hear how incredibly inept I am as a boyfriend, I could go to Arsène, Riggs, or—even better—to Arya herself. I came here because I need advice. How do I make her see nothing else matters? Just her?"

Alice smiled a closemouthed smile that told me that the answer was inside the question. She seemed to be having a jolly good time watching me squirm.

"What? *What?*" I barked.

"Repeat your words again, please, Christian."

I frowned. "How do I make her see nothing else matters?"

"Yes." She clapped her hands together excitedly. "Exactly."

"That's not an answer," I groaned. "How drunk are you, woman?"

She sucked the cherry on her swizzle stick into her mouth. "The answer is yes again."

I was about to take her back home and nurse her back into sobriety until I got my answer, when it struck me. The meaning of her suggestion. My eyebrows shot up. Alice shimmied her shoulders, excited that I finally got it.

"After all this time?" I groaned.

"After all this time."

"You sure there's no other way?"

"You just took everything this girl had. The father she adored and considered to be both her parents."

I opened my mouth to say something, but she cut me off. "Please don't tell me he deserved it. I know that. But *she* didn't, until you dragged the truth into light. Now she is forced to look at the smudged picture of her life. Because of you. Not only that, but you lied to her. Lied to her even after you slept with her. Even when she mustered the courage to ask you not to lie to her. So yes, sacrifices will have to be made, and they'll have to mean something to you. If you don't lose anything, you can't gain anything, honey."

I dropped my head forward, raising my hand with my credit card for the waitress when she brought us the check.

"Excuse me, Alice, while I catch a red-eye back to Manhattan to fire myself."

"If this is some kind of joke, I'm not getting it; please explain it to me." Traurig stared at me like I'd barged into his office wearing Julia Roberts's questionable hooker garments from *Pretty Woman*. Cromwell sat beside him, stone faced. "First you fire Claire without our consent—without even consulting us—and now you're handing us your *resignation*?"

"Ah, don't sell yourself so short, *kiddo*." I smiled, sitting on the other side of the desk, feeling perfectly okay with the fact they'd be scraping the gold letters off my door after a little under three days. "You seem to be getting everything just fine. Yes, you understood correctly. I resign. Effective immediately."

"But . . . why?" Traurig spluttered, throwing his arms in the air with open exasperation.

"The list is long, but I'll give you the bullet points: I should've been made partner three years ago; I'm overworked and undervalued; Cromwell is an asshole—no offense, mate"—I winked at a whitening Cromwell before returning my gaze to Traurig—"and you're not much better. You made me jump through hoops and enjoyed seeing me sweat for it. And for a while, I played by your rules. Until it stopped being worth it. Which happened approximately"—I glanced at my wristwatch—"three days ago."

"You're dumping your entire career into the can," Traurig warned.

"I told you the boy was trouble from the get-go," Cromwell spit out, slanting his eyes in Traurig's direction, moving his hand as if he were conjuring a spirit. "He is jumping ship and going somewhere else. Where to, kid? Tell us now." Cromwell stuck his index finger on the table between us, like I owed him something.

I yawned. When was the last time I'd dropped my manners and acted like the Hunts Point rascal that I was? Almost two decades ago, I bet. It felt good, though.

"Even if I had another job waiting, you would be the last person I'd answer to, Cromwell. You've been jerking me around since day one, and you barely even come to the office. I'd be glad to see you dirtying up your hands a little with some real work, now that I'm gone."

I stood up, starting to make my way to the door.

"We'll rehire Claire. Just so you know," Traurig said behind my back. I stopped. Turned around. Saw the shit-eating grin on his face. "Is that it?" he asked. "You had an affair with the little, cute thing, and it got out of control? Now you're cutting your losses in case she comes for you? Slaps you with a sexual harassment lawsuit of her own?"

He was so off the mark it took everything in me not to laugh.

"Miss Lesavoy got fired because she betrayed my professional and personal confidence. If you want a rat in your company, which I assume you do, since you're both rodents, I strongly encourage you to reoffer her the position."

With that, I slammed the door in their faces.

And damn, it felt good.

◆　◆　◆

I waited for Arya outside her office building that evening. Not accustomed to acting like a puppy or feeling like one, my ego took its first bruise in years.

Fine, it was more of a cut than a bruise.

Okay. My ego was completely decapitated. Served the jerk right. It'd gotten me into plenty of trouble over the years.

"Shall I remind you I'm going to get you disbarred if you don't leave me alone?" Arya complained as soon as she set foot out of the door, skipping the pleasantries. She wore a red leather pencil skirt paired with a smart white blouse and looked like heaven on earth. It was a wonder how I'd ever let her out of my bed in the first place.

I caught up with her easily as she made her way to the subway. "Disbar me," I said flatly, my shoulder brushing hers.

She made an exasperated sound, shaking her head. "Leave me alone."

"Have your parents spoken to you since the trial?" I asked.

Another sulk. "Like you care."

I put a hand on her shoulder. She stopped, turning sharply to face me, throwing my hand off, fire blazing in her eyes.

"I do." I stubbed my chest with my finger. "Care. Every single day, I try to talk to you. So don't tell me I don't care, Arya, when it's entirely possible I'm the only asshole who does in your life."

"I don't *want* you to care." Her voice broke. "That's the point. I told you I'll get you disbarred if you don't leave me alone because no part of me wants you in my life."

"No part?" I repeated.

She shook her head. "None at all."

"Liar." I took a step forward, cupping her cheeks in my hands. "I quit."

Her green eyes widened, taking over her face. "You quit?" she echoed.

"Yes." I rested my forehead against hers, breathing her in for a second. "I gave up the partnership. Told them to go screw themselves. But not before firing Claire for what she did to us. I may be a bastard orphan, but honey, so are you. I wish you weren't. I wish your parents would've been there for you the way you deserved. I'm here, though, and I'm going to try my best to be enough."

And then it just came out. Poured out of me.

"I love you, Arya Roth. I've loved you the entire time. From that first day at the cemetery, when we were kids. When everything around us was dead, and you were so alive I wanted to swallow you whole. When you put that little stone on Aaron's grave so he'd know you came to visit. I loved you that day, for your heart, and every day after that. I never stopped loving you. Even when I hated you. *Especially* when I hated you, in fact. It was agonizing, thinking you'd forgotten about me. Because Arya? There hadn't been a minute in my life when I hadn't thought about you."

There was a moment—a fraction of it, anyway—when I thought she was going to concede. Finally cave in to that thing between us. But then Arya stepped backward, readjusting the strap of her shoulder bag, her head tipped up defiantly. "I'm sorry."

"What for?"

"Being partly responsible for your decision to quit. Because it doesn't change anything."

She wasn't partly responsible. She was wholly responsible. But there was no point in pointing that out, because now that I'd quit, I knew I should've done that years ago. Regardless of her. When you do something right, you feel it in your bones.

"Yes, it does." I smiled. "It changes one fundamental thing, Arya."

"And that is?"

"Now I can chase you however much I like. Because your dad's case means jack shit to me, and you know damn well I don't give that much of a crap about getting disbarred, seeing as I just quit. It's on, Ari. I will win you."

"I'm not a prize."

I turned around and walked away. "No, you're not. You're *everything*."

CHAPTER TWENTY-NINE

ARYA

Present

While the city slid into a colorful spring, a vast black hole formed in my parents' penthouse.

No word went in and no word got out. The Roths had vanished, disappeared from the face of the earth.

My mother was the one I tried repeatedly. I felt compelled to look after her, now that I knew my father had emotionally abused her. She was unreachable via phone, email, or text messages. As for my father, I never tried to contact him again after the string of scathing text messages he'd left me the day he'd gotten convicted. His ability to cancel his emotions toward me like they were a streaming-service subscription proved that said feelings had never really been there.

Finally, after seven days of radio silence, I made my way to the Park Avenue penthouse. As I took the elevator up to the last floor, a tug of worry pulled at my stomach. I realized they might not even be there anymore. What if they'd moved? My parents owned the property, but there was no way they could keep it with the amount of money they had to pay after losing the case. I had no idea what the stipulations were. How much time they had to come up with the money. I suppose Christian could've given me answers to all these questions, but I couldn't ask him. Couldn't make any contact with him. My defenses were already spent, my mental core raw.

After stepping out of the elevator, I knocked on the door leading to my childhood home. I didn't know why, but for some reason, I did the secret knock Dad and I had used when I was a kid.

One rap, beat, five raps, beat, two raps.

There was silence from the other side. Maybe they weren't there. I could probably call one of my mother's country-club friends and ask if they'd given them a new address. I was about to turn around and leave when I heard it, coming from the other side of the wooden barrier between us.

One rap, beat, five raps, beat, two raps.

Conrad.

I froze, willing my feet to move. The traitorous things had taken root in the marble floor, refusing to cooperate. The soft click of the bolt unlocking chimed behind my back. A chill ran through my spine. The door opened.

"Ari. My sweet."

His voice was so syrupy, so placid. It transported me back to my childhood. To playing tic-tac-toe in front of a pool in Saint-Tropez. To him butchering a braiding job, making my hair look like I'd gotten electrocuted. To us laughing about it. The memories flowed like a river inside me, and I couldn't stop them, no matter how hard I tried.

Dad wrapping an arm around me, kissing my head, telling me it would be okay. That we didn't need Mom. That we made a great team all on our own.

Dad dancing to "Girls Just Want to Have Fun" with me.

Dad assuring me I could get into any college I wanted.

Dad buying a baseball bat when I turned sixteen and got pretty over-night, because "you never know."

Crumbs of happiness, littered in a lifetime of pain and longing.

"Arya, please look at me."

I spun on my heel, staring at him. There were so many things I wanted to say, but the words wilted in my throat. Finally, I managed to say the one thing that had burned in me since this nightmare had started.

"I will never forgive you."

No more being on the wrong side of history.

I'd done this to Nicky. I would not do it again.

My father dropped his head. All the anger and wrath that had burned inside him were gone now. He looked defeated. Shrunken. A shadow of his former self.

"Why did you do it?" I demanded. "Why?"

As a woman moving in corporate circles, I'd always wondered what made men feel invincible. It wasn't like greater, more powerful men than them hadn't been caught. It seemed silly to think it wouldn't happen to you. The truth had a way of catching you with your pants down. In my father's case, also literally.

"Come in?" His face twisted, begging. I shook my head no.

He let out a sigh, dropping his head to his chest.

"I felt lonely. Very lonely. I don't know how much your mother has confided in you. I noticed you two have gotten close over the past few weeks—"

"No. Don't you dare try to manipulate me. Answer my question."

"I'm not shying away from responsibility over what happened in our marriage. We both did terrible things to each other after Aaron died. But the truth of the matter is, I didn't have a wife in all the ways that mattered. So I started looking for things elsewhere.

"At first, it was just sex. Always consensual. Always with women I knew from work. I was young, good looking, and climbing the career ladder. Conducting short affairs wasn't hard. But then my needs expanded. I wanted emotional support too. And once you seek emotional support, you are expected to give it too. That's what happened with Ruslana. She wanted the fairy tale, and I wanted to have the faux feeling of going back home to someone every day. Someone who'd rub my feet and warm my bed and listen to me. You had me, and I had Ruslana."

"You told her you would leave Mom for her."

He looked up at me, smiling sadly. "I told her whatever I needed to say to keep her. And when I realized she was going to go to your mother and tell her, I lost it. I still love your mother. Always have."

You just have a weird way of showing it.

"Ruslana died very unexpectedly."

I had to be careful with what I said to him. He didn't know Christian was Nicky or that I'd seen the death certificate. No matter how I felt about Nicky's betrayal, I was never going to hand him over on a silver platter to Conrad. I wouldn't be able to live with myself.

"Yes, she did."

"Some would argue it looks like a planned accident," I poked.

My father's eyes enlarged, and his bushy eyebrows dropped in a frown. "No, no. Ruslana did that to herself. She had a lot of financial problems. I had nothing to do with her death. I swear."

"Remember when you told me she decided to quit randomly and move to Alaska? What was that all about?" I didn't let it go.

My father bristled. "Yes, okay. It's true. I knew she'd killed herself at some point, but I didn't want *you* to know. I didn't want to hurt you. I felt bad enough about what happened to her without the burden of knowing your heart would be broken too."

"And Amanda Gispen? The dick pics? All of that?"

He blew out air, closing his eyes, as if bracing himself for the worst.

"Sometime through my ongoing affair with Ruslana, we started having . . . issues. Beatrice-related issues. I wanted to make a point. That she was not the only one. That there were others. She had no right to ask all those things she asked me for. I started seeking out other women. Conducting affairs. But it wasn't as easy. I wasn't the same young man I was when you were a kid. There were other hedge fund executives, more attractive, and more willing to splurge, putting their mistresses in nice apartments, handing them their Amex cards when they sent them to the French Riviera. I wasn't one of those men. Amanda was my last mistake. But these other women . . . they all gave me mixed signals, Arya, I swear. Giggled one day and acted cold the other. I didn't know what to do with them. I got cocky. I thought if I stayed persistent, they'd cave in."

"You harassed them," I said quietly, tears running down my cheeks. I'd promised myself I wouldn't cry. But this had the anatomy of good-bye. It was final and painful and cleansing and unbearable. It cut through my bones to simply *look* at him.

"Yes," Conrad said, looking a lot like that man with the pale, sweaty expression I'd met at the Cloisters shortly before everything had unfolded. "There was a lot of pressure to be there for you. To keep your mom in check. I needed an outlet." This was the way he constructed it in his sick mind. That he had to keep my mother on a leash and be both my parents, so he had the right to abuse others. He continued, "And when you found out . . . well, it was too much. You were the one person who always looked up to me and the one woman I actually cared about. I didn't want you to witness everything I did. I pushed you away. Amanda's lawyer was a great excuse."

"He had nothing to do with this," I said hotly. I wondered if there would be a time when I wouldn't defend Nicky like my own life depended on it.

My father smiled. "Sweetheart, I know."

"Know what?" My pulse escalated, my heart hiking up to my throat.

"Who Christian is."

"I don't know what you're talking about." I straightened my spine.

"My PI, Dave, was onto him shortly after the trial had started. There was something about him. A hunger I recognized. Those damn blue eyes."

"That makes no sense," I said. "You kept asking what made him act the way he did."

Conrad shrugged. "I stopped the minute Dave came back with the information."

"But . . . but . . . if you knew, you could've . . ."

He looked away, at the floor. "And then what, Arya? Nicholai would get disqualified, disbarred, and his story would come out. The story in which I ruined his life, detailed and time-stamped. It would have looked even worse for me. He was just another victim of mine. Amanda and the rest would have gotten another lawyer, and I'd still be found guilty. All paths led to the same destination. And it had to be said"—he grinned sardonically—"I appreciated his coming full circle. He did good, that kid. If I went down, I wanted to go down in style, and he delivered. It's why I told Terrance and Louie not to file an appeal."

"You wanted to ruin his life," I repeated, dumbfounded. Even at our worst, the year following what he'd done to Nicky, I'd thought my father had anger-management problems, not that he was malicious. *"Why?"*

"Because he touched the only pure thing I had in my life," he said simply. *"You."*

"You can never tell anyone," I warned, feeling every nerve in my body on fire as I took a step toward him. "You hear me? No one. Promise me. Promise."

He stared at me intently. "You never stopped loving him, did you?"

No. Not even for a moment.

I stepped back, pulling myself together. But he knew. In that moment, he knew. He pressed his forehead to the doorframe. Behind him, I could see the apartment was only half-furnished. Someone must've taken most of the stuff out. I waited to feel the pinch in my heart, but the truth was, home had never been a place for me. It was a feeling. A feeling I'd only ever felt with my father before what had happened, and with Nicky.

"Will you ever forgive me?" His eyes were screwed shut as he spoke against the doorframe.

"No," I said simply. "You took the one person I loved more than anyone else in the world, and you ruined him for me. You need to leave the city. It's for the best."

"I am." He gave me a little nod. "Next week."

I didn't ask where to. I didn't want to know. Didn't trust myself not to contact him again.

"Goodbye, *Dad*."

"Goodbye, honey. Stay safe and take care of your mother."

"She is never going to answer me, is she?" I smashed my phone against my desk, barely containing my rage. "It's absolutely like her to go MIA after the ship has sunk. Classic Beatrice Roth for you. I wonder what she's going to do, now that she doesn't have the penthouse and the funds. She's too old to get a sugar daddy."

Jillian eyed me over the edge of her teacup, her pointed look telling me I'd forgotten to tuck my crazy in this morning. I'd been told you stopped giving a crap about what others thought about you when you turned forty. Maybe I was an early bloomer, because I just didn't care.

"Ever considered she might not want you to fix her problems this time?" Jillian suggested. "She knows that if she answered you, you'd go into damage control mode and fix it all. I mean, you always were the grown-up in that relationship."

"I didn't even *have* a relationship with her until a month and a half ago." I stood up and began shoving items into my bag. It was half past seven, and I'd made Christian wait long enough outside my building. He came to see me every day now.

"Yes, that's true, but my take is you've never had a relationship because you intimidated her and she disgusted you," Jilly explained, walking over to the kitchenette to pour herself more tea. "So my guess is she'll resurface when she is ready, and when she has a plan."

"She's never going to have a plan." I flung my bag over my shoulder. "She's been cruising through life, counting on my dad to fix all of her problems."

Jillian smiled, adding a teaspoon of sugar to the antique teacup I'd gotten her for Easter at a thrift shop. The scent of peppermint filled the air. "We'll see about that, won't we?"

"You sound like you know something I don't." I narrowed my eyes.

Jillian laughed. "I know lots of things you don't. Let me start by pointing out the most important one—it's not just your mother you are worried about. You are petrified of Christian, or Nicky, or whatever you want to call him today. You've been barricading yourself in the office every day until eight o'clock since you found out he was waiting for you each night."

"It's stalker behavior." I stomped to the door to make a point. "I'm trying to discourage it."

"You're so deeply in love with the guy I'm embarrassed for your soul. Why aren't you giving him a chance?"

How had we gotten from the subject of my mother to this? I rolled my eyes, plucking my lip gloss from my bag and reapplying it absent-mindedly. "Because I'll never trust the man again, so there's really no point."

"You keep telling yourself that, sweetie." She came to pat my arm on her way back to her desk.

I frowned. "What are you doing here, anyway? At least I've had a reason to stay late these past few days, but you didn't." I paused. "Or did you?" I grinned.

Jillian got back to her seat, grabbed a hair clip, and tossed it in my direction. "Leave now!"

I dodged the hair clip, laughing. "What's his name?"

"Out!"

I straightened back up. "Hmm. *Out.* That sounds cute and eccentric. Are his parents environmentalists? I don't know, I like Woods or Leaf more."

"I swear to God, Arya . . ." She waggled her finger at me. "By the way, you remember our meeting tomorrow, right? With the woman from Miami? Nine thirty?"

"Yes." I made a face. "I'm still not sure how we can help her. Her business idea sounds solid, but she hasn't even incorporated the company yet."

Then I was out the door, giggling my way to another encounter with Nicky.

◆ ◆ ◆

Only he wasn't there.

For the first time in a week, Nicky didn't lay siege outside my office.

Disappointment flooded me. I hated the side effects of not seeing him there. The weak knees, the way my heart dropped and my shoulders sagged. I willed myself to stand taller and maneuvered my way to the subway, plastering a deranged smile on my face. This just went to show that Nicky wasn't reliable. He'd given up on me in less than a week.

But then you did chide him and ask that he never contact you again, a voice inside me reasoned. *Numerous times, in fact. Furthermore, you were a complete bitch when he pointed out he quit his job for you.*

Logically, I knew I had no right to be mad at him for not waiting outside my office door for three hours. And *also* logically, it was true that he hadn't had to quit his job. He could have carried on with his life, safe in the knowledge I wasn't going to hand him over to the authorities. He'd chosen to repent for his deception. But maybe my issue wasn't about trusting Nicky. Maybe my issue was with trusting *myself.* After all, he was the height of everything. The desirable, ultimate, unrequited love. Had been for so many years.

Maybe I just didn't want to hand over the remainder of my heart to the man who'd stolen it nearly two decades ago and never given it back.

I spent the train journey mulling over my thoughts on the situation with Nicky. The kid he had been. The man he was today. When I arrived at my building, I saw a figure loitering at the stairway. My pulse kicked up.

He's here.

My feet moved faster. But as I drew closer, I realized that it couldn't be him. The person waiting outside was too short, too slight. My stride slowed until I came to a complete stop.

"Mom?"

The figure swiveled its head and looked up at me.

She looked exhausted, ten pounds slimmer, but still extremely put together. She patted herself clean of invisible dirt, like her mere presence in a zip code that wasn't Park Avenue dirtied her up.

"Hello, darling," she chirped brightly, her plastic smile unwavering. "Sorry I've missed your calls. I had a few things to tend to. Is this a bad time? I can come back tomorrow if you'd like."

I shook my head slowly. "No. Right now is fine. Come on up."

I kicked off my heels and threw my keys into the ugly bowl by my door upon arrival, realizing this was the first time my mother had ever been to my apartment. I flicked the coffee machine on, pulling out two cups.

"Take a seat. How've you been?" I asked, trying to keep the anger out of my voice. She'd done it again. Gone MIA on me. After a few weeks when she'd actually resembled a mother, albeit from afar and only if you squinted to really put it into focus, she'd just bailed. Again. I should've known. Should've expected it. Then why did it hurt so much?

Beatrice perched herself on the edge of my green velvet Anthropologie couch, occupying as little space as possible. "Well. Everything considered, of course."

"Coffee okay?"

"Oh, just lovely, thank you."

"Cream? Sugar?" I asked. It was wild that I didn't know such a trivial thing about my mother.

"I don't know," she said thoughtfully. "I don't usually drink coffee. Just put what you normally do in your coffee. I'm sure I'll like it."

I dumped two spoonfuls of sugar and extra cream into her cup. I had a feeling she needed the extra calories. I carried both our coffees to the living room and sat on a recliner in front of her. She took a careful sip. I found myself watching her closely. Her face relaxed after the first sip. Maybe she'd thought I'd poison her.

And if this were ten years ago, maybe I would have.

"That's actually good."

"Coffee is the nectar of the nine-to-fivers." I sat back. "So why are you here?"

My mother put her cup down on the coffee table, turning toward me fully. "There's a reason why I haven't taken any of your calls, Arya. I spoke to your friend, Jillian, about it, but I asked her not to tell you."

I almost dropped my coffee midsip. It was unlike my mother to get involved with any of my friends. In fact, I'd had no idea she was even aware of Jillian's existence. Mom licked her lips fast, her words measured and well rehearsed. "I've been doing a lot of thinking recently. I know I haven't been the best mother. Or any sort of mother at all. I take full responsibility for that. But when things with Conrad began to unravel, the last thing I wanted was to become a liability to you on top of losing everything that I had. So . . . well, I got myself a job."

My eyes nearly bulged out of their sockets. "You're going to start working for us?"

My mother shook her head, laughing. "See? That is exactly why I wanted some time to pull myself together. No. I will not be taking a position with Brand Brigade. I found a job independently. Well, more or less." She scrunched her nose. "You're looking at the new administrative and marketing assistant for my country club! Granted, a country club I can no longer afford, but the offer is great and the health insurance is quite good, or so I'm told."

A strange feeling swept over me. Like I was under warm water. Elation. Pride. And hope. So much hope.

"Mom." I reached to grab her hand, squeezing it. "That's amazing. I'm so happy for you."

Her eyes shone, and she nodded, taking another sip of her coffee. "Yes, and that's not all. I filed for divorce yesterday. It's over, Arya. I'm leaving your father, and he is moving to New Hampshire to live with his sister and her husband."

"Oh, Mom!" I flung myself over her, burying my face into her shoulder. It took me a few seconds to realize I was sitting in her lap. I was a good five pounds heavier than her at this point, but when I tried to stand up, she pulled me back down, cupping my face with both her hands. Tears streamed down my cheeks. I couldn't help it. They just kept coming. But they felt good. Cleansing.

"I'm so sorry, Arya. All this time I've ignored you. Overlooked you. Gave myself excuses. That you and he had each other. That I was just standing in your way. That is all over, now. I have a new apartment, a new job, a new life. I know it's late, but I hope it is not *too* late to be your mother."

I shook my head sharply. "No. No." I sniffed, pushing my head against her shoulder again. "Just don't do that again. The thing where you disappear for days and weeks at a time. Even if you tell me things that I don't want to hear. Even if it's to tell me to back off and not butt into your business. Parent me, Mother."

"I will, honey. I will."

CHAPTER THIRTY

A R Y A

Present

The next morning, I flicked my wrist and glanced at my watch, rearranging my skirt over my thighs for the millionth time. It was half past ten, and I was about to stand up and leave the restaurant where I was supposed to meet the potential client and Jillian.

The fact the client hadn't come was bad enough. Purely unprofessional. But what irked me was that Jillian hadn't shown up. Hadn't even answered any of my calls. Just sent me a quick text saying something had come up and that she would love to hear all about the meeting when I came to the office afterward.

We must bag this one, Ari. She's big $$$.

Well, heavy pockets or not, this Goodie woman wasn't showing up.

I was waving for the waiter to get me the check when Mrs. Goodie finally made her grand entrance. More like barged into the tiny restaurant in an explosion of colors and laughter. She was talking on her phone, waving the hostess away when she tried to ask her if she was joining a party or needed a table.

She was, for lack of a better description, human Technicolor.

". . . gotta run, honey. We should totally catch up while I'm in the city. *Totally.* Oops, here's my date for the morning." Mrs. Goodie waved at me with the tips of her fingernails, smiling brightly. "Gotta run. Yes. Tomorrow sounds good. I'll have my PA talk to yours. Can't wait to see you. *Muah!*"

She plopped on the seat in front of me, sighing as she grabbed my water glass and chugged the entire thing in one gulp. "As if I'm ever going to see that two-faced bitch again. Can you believe it? I stopped trying to figure out why people who hate me seek my company. The line between love and hate is fine indeed, but there's no need to straddle it."

I stared at her blankly.

"Oh!" She laughed, shaking her head as she flagged the waiter. I was pretty sure she blew a complete random a kiss. "I was late, wasn't I? My apologies. I forgot how bad traffic is in the city."

"No problem," I said blandly, reminding myself that I'd screwed up several deals these past few months and that I owed Jillian this account.

The waiter arrived with the check, and Mrs. Goodie scolded him. "Why, I haven't even had your pastry platter! Bring it immediately. It's the best thing this town has to offer. And coffee. Lots of coffee. Irish coffee! It's five o'clock somewhere."

"In Saint Petersburg," I supplied helpfully, figuring she'd do what she wanted to do anyway, including getting hammered first thing in the morning. I snapped my napkin over my lap, making myself comfortable.

Mrs. Goodie cocked her head sideways and smiled. "You're a brainiac," she observed.

"I don't know about that, but I like to think of myself as well read."

"No wonder he is so crazy about you," she muttered, tugging at her colorful beach dress to cool down from the journey here.

I frowned. "I'm sorry, Mrs. Goodie?"

"Please, call me Alice." She laughed, patting my hand across the table. "And it's not Goodie. It's Gudinski."

The last name rang a bell, but I couldn't put my finger on it. "What do you mean by 'he's crazy about you'? Who is?"

The earth tilted beneath me just then. I sucked in a breath. A weird combination of jealousy, fury, and gratitude filled me. The latter, I suspected, was simply because I was sitting in front of a person who was close to Nicky. Alice must've seen the war waging within me by the look on my face, because she burst out in a loud, unladylike cackle, and suddenly, I knew *exactly* what Nicky had seen in this woman.

"Oh, bless your little heart, Arya, don't be scared. I don't bite. Christian told me you might not agree to see me if you knew who I was, so Jillian and I had to give you a little nudge." She gave me a wink, peppering the gesture with a shoulder shimmy.

"And you still thought it would be a good idea?" I could kill Jillian for the way she'd schemed behind my back twice in a row this week.

Alice gave me a kind smile. "Absolutely. I was quite the stubborn woman myself when I was your age, but my late husband wore me down. I'm so glad he did, because otherwise, I wouldn't be here, dining in a fancy restaurant in New York in the middle of the morning."

"I'm sorry you lost him." I dropped my voice.

She gave her (fantastic) hair a toss. A few years ago, I would have looked at this woman and thought to myself, *I want her to be my mother.* Now, after everything Beatrice and I had been through, I only wanted someone like Alice as a friend.

"You know, it was only after I lost him that I realized how grateful I am for everything I had. It put everything in perspective. Life is uncertain, Arya. Love is not. Love is the concrete beneath your feet. It's the anchor when you're in the eye of a storm. Tossing love away because of a few complications is unheard of. This is what I came here to tell you, actually."

She reached for my hand, clasping it firmly. "When I heard about you and Nicky, I couldn't just sit by and let you two miss the chance at love again. I want you to know he loves you. He's always loved you. He hated that he loved you, but he did it anyway, because it was stronger than him. Over the years, I've watched as he fought it. As he struggled to understand why he couldn't fall in love with anyone else. Your name always came up. Every single time. He thought you scarred him. But the truth is, you just never left his mind. His heart. You know him, Arya." She spoke softly, dropping her voice. "You know better than I do what kind of person he is. He's made a few mistakes, sure, the biggest of them not telling you who he was. But he would also give up the world for a second chance with you. Please reconsider."

I opened my mouth to tell her that I'd already thought about it. That I wanted Nicky just as much as he wanted me. And Christian too. I wanted who he'd been and who he'd become. Each day spent without him felt like a terrible waste. But Alice beat me to it, standing up and taking a step back.

"No." She raised her hand to stop me. "Don't tell me. Tell him."

Suddenly, he was there. Alive and beautiful and heartbreakingly not mine. He wore jeans and a white shirt. Every nerve in my body was on alert, pushing me to jump on him in tears.

The waiter approached with the pastry platter. Alice shooed him away. "Seriously? Can't you see that they're having a *moment*? Put that on the bar; I'll take care of these puppies in a second."

I made a mental note to never, ever come back to this place again. My food was so going to get spit on.

Alice nudged Nicky in my direction before turning around and swaggering toward the bar. He took the seat in front of me. My hands shook. I couldn't believe I'd ever been mad at him for anything. This man who had been through so much because of me. *For* me. Who'd made so many sacrifices in his life while I'd lived in my ivory tower, nestled in designer everything and my own privilege.

"I get it now," he said, sounding somber and a little contemplative. Christian produced something from the leather briefcase he carried and dropped it on the table between us. A copy of *Atonement*. The spine wrinkled to death, the edges tattered from usage.

"The book," he explained. "I read it. Twice, actually. Back to back yesterday. By the time I was done, Jillian told me you'd already left work."

"I see Jillian has been doing a lot of legwork behind the scenes," I muttered.

"Well"—Christian flashed a lopsided grin—"she knew it's either her doing some legwork or you kicking me to the curb."

"Did you like it?" I swallowed. "The book, I mean."

Of course you meant the book. What else would he think you meant? Jillian's legs?

He shook his head gravely. "No."

My soul felt heavy and soggy and full of dark things.

"I fucking *loved* it. I'd watched the movie before—our library scene made Keira Knightley and James McAvoy look like amateurs, by the way—but hadn't read the book until now. It made me understand you. The book is about class, guilt, and the loss of innocence. All the things that we experienced together. That bound us. But there's one thing I don't understand." His bluest-blue eyes bore into mine, and the fine hair on the back of my neck stood on end. He parked his elbows on the table, leaning forward. "How can you not forgive me when you know Cecilia and Robbie needed to end up together? You are tampering with your own happy ending, Arya. And I won't have that. This is unacceptable. Not just for me but for you."

Tears covered my eyes. For the first time in my life, I cried publicly, and I didn't even care. I, the great Arya Roth, symbol of independence and feminism. "You fool," I groaned, pained. "You absolute, complete idiot. I've always loved you. Always been obsessed with you. I *coaxed* you into kissing me, for crying out loud." I was laughing and crying now simultaneously, always a good look. "Every step of the way, I was the one to initiate things between us. The only reason why I didn't run after you to Belarus when we were fourteen was because I was too embarrassed. I thought I was pestering you. I was mortified after what Conrad had done. Even then, I couldn't stay away. Not all the way. I kept writing and hoping and praying."

We still had that stupid table between us. I wanted to pick it up and hurl it across the room like the Hulk. Every moment not spent in his arms was a waste.

The restaurant rumbled. We both glanced at Alice, who was talking the barista's ear off at the bar, licking the spoon of the tart she was devouring.

"So. I met your sugar mama." I grinned.

"Arya." Christian made a face full of regret. "The last thing I want to talk about right now is my sugar mama. Come here. I want to show you something."

He led me out of the restaurant. We held hands. I'd never realized how right it felt. My palm in his. How perfectly we fit together. The street was bustling with the usual mix of traffic, tourists, and businesspeople. Christian tugged me into an alleyway, tucked in a corner between two buildings.

"Well, this is romantic." I eyed the industrial trash can next to us. "And private."

He laughed. "I like private. Last time I tried to kiss you out of my comfort zone, your father kicked my ass."

"No chance of that happening again." I smiled.

He held my face in his hands like I was precious. Like I was his. "No." He shook his head, his nose brushing mine with each movement. "Because I will never let anything tear us apart again. Not ever."

"I love you, Nicky."

"I love you, Cecilia." He dived down for a kiss. I swatted his chest and felt his laughter rumble beneath his hard pecs.

"Don't ever call me someone else's name when we kiss."

"Same goes to you. It's Christian now."

"I thought you didn't like me calling you Christian."

The pieces of the puzzle had clicked together. The way he'd looked at me when we'd first tumbled into bed together. When I'd called him by his new name and he'd shriveled back.

Christian shook his head. "That was before you knew."

"Knew what?"

"That I'm reborn."

That was when Christian Miller kissed me again.

And this time, I knew, no one was going to take him away from me.

EPILOGUE

CHRISTIAN

Six Months Later

"Not too shabby for an office." Riggs pokes at his lower lip, nodding to himself as he strolls along the reception area of Miller, Hatter & Co., my brand-new law firm. "Not worth the money you dropped on the interior designer, but not as soul crushing as other offices I've been to."

"Thanks for the endorsement. Your opinion means a lot. Now get the hell out." I stick my loafer between the elevator doors to ensure it doesn't leave without him and Arsène. I check my Patek Philippe again. Five past three. She should be here any minute now.

"What's the rush, Miller? Is Miss Has Your Balls in a Vise Grip coming over?" Arsène runs his hand over the sleek black marble of the reception counter.

It's about to be Mrs. Has Your Balls in a Vise Grip if I have my way.

Weeks after resigning from Cromwell & Traurig, I ran into Jason Hatter and found out he was looking for a way out of his own firm too. We quickly realized we could establish a successful partnership, combining both our portfolios. That's how Miller, Hatter & Co. was founded.

"Out," I order. "Both of you. Before I wipe the floor with your asses."

"Big deal. Your floor is cleaner than Hermione Granger's rap sheet. First." Riggs stops in front of the crème wall, checking each hanging picture in the waiting area individually, like his connection to art includes more than rolling a few curators between his bedsheets every now and then. "Tell us why you're sweating like a whore in a confession booth."

"I'm not sweating." I scowl.

"You are, actually," Arsène states before making a gagging sound. "You're going to propose, aren't you?"

Unable to deal with my friends' eighth-grade mentality any longer, I saunter toward them, grab each friend by the ear, and drag them to the elevator.

"Kinky," Riggs hisses, planting the heels of his Blundstones on the floor just to make things difficult. "Now talk dirty to the ear you're about to rip out of my head. I like it rough."

Arsène flicks my hand away but surrenders willingly, citing that he doesn't want to be here when I decorate my new carpets with semen once my girlfriend arrives. I dump them in the elevator and brush my palms clean when the chime above my head indicates they are on their way down.

Three minutes later, Arya pops out of the second elevator. She's wearing a smart business suit. Her crazy hair is in a haphazard bun. She stops in front of me, taking it all in, her eyes big and green and unnerving.

"Howdy, partner." Her smile is slow, mischievous, and uniquely hers. She reminds me of the twelve-year-old girl I couldn't look away from.

"Ms. Roth." I tuck a flyaway behind her ear, pressing a soft kiss on her nose. I step back. "What do you think about my new crib?"

"It's beautiful." She lights up, giving herself a mini tour. We've already started operating, but next week, we're opening the office. We'll have two receptionists, five paralegals, and several new associates coming in. It's going to be a lot of work, but it's going to be worth it. "As the spokeswoman for Brand Brigade, we're excited you chose to work with us."

As the spokesperson for my heart, I'm hoping you're not going to stomp on it in a second.

Arya leans against the reception desk, splaying her hands on it. "Have Cromwell and Traurig calmed down yet?"

"Not even remotely." I make my way toward her, pushing my hands into my front pockets. "They're still dragging my name through the mud all over town."

"Good." Arya smiles brightly. "I do love you a bit dirty."

I chuckle, motioning to my corner office. "Come on. I want to show you the best part of the office."

I take her hand in mine and lead her to the room that has taken the most time to design. To the interior designer's credit, all she had to work with was a few frames from a movie. No more. I push the wooden door open, and Arya gasps.

"It's not contemporary." I lower my head to her neck from behind, feathering a kiss over it while my hands find her waist. She shivers into me, inspecting the vast room, a replica of the library from the book and the movie she loves so much.

The mahogany shelves. The ladder. The books. The Persian carpet. The books. The vintage lamp. The books.

The books.

The books.

"Christian . . ." *Christian.* That's what she calls me now. Embracing the identity I've chosen for myself. Nicky isn't dead. But I'm no longer the helpless boy she knew. Now, I can protect her. And myself. I intend to do both. "This is . . . breathtaking."

"It's yours."

She turns around, looking at me curiously. "What do you mean?"

And this time, I show her.

I press her against the nearest bookshelf, and two decades later, at thirty-three, I do what fourteen-year-old Nicky couldn't. I kiss her long and hard, starting from the base of her throat, working my way up, lacing my fingers through hers. She writhes against me, mumbling my name. I can feel her unknotting against me, one thread after another. We both know no one can walk in on us. No one can stop us.

"Are we . . . are we . . . ?" Arya's pants come in short breaths as my tongue fills her mouth possessively. "Are we reenacting . . . ?"

"No." I withdraw, pressing a finger over her lips. "We're creating something new, sweetheart. Something that's ours."

With that, I tug her skirt off, then her panties, leaving her in her blouse and high heels. I drop to my knees and start by kissing the insides of her ankles, then make my way up with my lips and teeth. I stop to swirl my tongue over the side of her knee, a sensitive spot for her, and drag my teeth up her inner thigh. When I get to the insides of her thighs, I kiss them slowly, reverently, taking my time, ignoring the main event. Her fingers tug at my hair hard. She is getting desperate. That's how I want her.

"Christian." Her soft whimper hits my ears differently now. *"Nicky."*

I pause, looking up. She hasn't called me that in a hot minute. But I can see why the situation would confuse her. Last time we were like this . . .

"Yes?" I arch an eyebrow, looking up at her.

"Please," she squeaks. "Do it."

"Do what?"

She looks around us, to ensure we're alone. I inwardly smile.

"Kiss me there."

I press a soft, chaste kiss to her center, grinning.

She groans, pushing my head harder to her sex. "You're impossible."

But then my tongue invades her, pries her open, and she clenches around it. I hold her waist tightly, pleasuring her, and she is close, so close that when she comes apart, I can feel every muscle in her body yielding to the sensation.

I stand up, unbuckle myself, and press home.

Arya holds me tight, moaning. "Christian." My name is whispered breathlessly, kisses landing on my cheeks, my throat, my lips. "Christian. I love you so much."

The next thing I do very carefully. I lace my fingers through hers again, like in the movie. But unlike the movie, I add my own touch. A French-set halo engagement ring with a two-carat diamond on it. I slip it on her finger as I start to move inside her, and in her daze of passion, Arya doesn't notice. I make love to her, and she falls apart again. This time, I do too. I come deep inside her. When we both raise our heads and catch our breaths, she finally notices.

Her face changes, her expression morphing from drunk with pleasure to alert.

"Oh . . ." She straightens her fingers, stretching her arm and moving her hand here and there, letting the diamond catch the light streaming from the floor-to-ceiling window. "Is this . . . ?"

"It is," I confirm.

"We've only been together for six months." She turns to grin at me, and I have to say, for a woman who is naked from the waist down, she sure knows how to be a smarty-pants.

"Correct," I say dryly, tucking myself in, "and that's about five months too late. My bad. In my defense, I had a business to open."

She shakes her head, laughing. Then she launches herself at me in a hug, peppering my face with kisses. I catch her waist, smirking.

"Is that a yes?"

"I don't know," she murmurs to the light stubble along my jaw. "What would Cecilia say?"

"Hell yeah."

ARYA

"I still don't understand what this is for," I sigh, sitting completely blindfolded in the passenger seat of my mother's sedan. It's not exactly the Bentley she was parading around Manhattan, complete with a personal driver, prior to her divorce, but she seems oddly content with the downgrade. She ditched the expensive blowouts and designer clothes for off-shoulder flowery maxi dresses and trendy sneakers.

She even has a new boyfriend, Max, who is not only super dashing but also a geeky high school geography teacher who treats her like a goddess and has vowed to take her to try every curry in New York City. They're on their twentieth curry joint, last I checked.

"No one asked you to understand, darling. Just not to peek." Mom pats my thigh, chuckling as moms do.

"We've been driving for forever. Are we even still in Manhattan?" I'm trying to get a ballpark estimation of what I'm working with. About thirty minutes ago, she picked me up from work and told me she had a surprise to show me. It didn't faze her in the least when I told her I wanted to go bridesmaid dress shopping with Jilly. She dragged me into her car and ignored my plans.

Beatrice tsks. "Sorry. I'm under strict instructions not to give you any hints."

"Instructions from who?" I demand.

She laughs at that.

"Christian?" I try. The fabric of the blindfold itches my nose, and I twitch it back and forth.

"Darling, not everything must revolve around your hunky fiancé."

I rumble a weak response and sit back, folding my arms together. Mom talks my ear off about applying to a bunch of jobs around the Brooklyn area, now that she's moved in with Max. How she knows it's silly, but she wants to go back to school and maybe become a teacher.

I tell her it's not silly at all. How bettering our life, our circumstances, broadening our knowledge, should never be a source of shame. Before I know it, I feel my body sway as she pulls to the curb. We must've arrived at her secret destination.

"Keep the blindfold on while I make a call." She uses her brand-new Mom tone. The one that warns me not to mess with her. I secretly love this tone. It makes up for all the years I didn't have a mother. Her voice is sweet but businesslike as she talks to the person on the other end.

"Yes." Pause. "She's here." Another beat. "No, not a thing. I kept her in the dark. *Literally.* But I'm double-parked, so you better come out here."

A minute later, the passenger door opens, and I feel a pair of hands pulling me out gently. I don't need to ask who it is. I know. The calluses of his fingers. The roughness of his big palms. It's my future husband.

"Thanks, Bea, I'll take good care of her," Christian says.

"Bye, now," Mom chirps, gunning her engine as she drives away.

"This better be good, Mr. Miller," I warn as he ushers me somewhere, holding my hands. I trust him fully, but I don't like not being in the know.

Christian chuckles but doesn't answer. We make our way indoors out of the heat of the summer day through a revolving door. An avalanche of cool, air-conditioned air sweeps over my feet and hair. It gives me a sweet, achy feeling. Like I've felt it once before. My heels click over marble. My surroundings smell new. Flowery. Expensive. We're in a building. Christian calls the elevator, and I wait beside him.

"How was your day at work?" he asks. He is making chitchat while I'm still blindfolded. Unbelievable.

"Fine," I respond. "Yours?"

"Good."

"Tell me, how many people are watching me right now blindfolded, being led by a handsome, tall man in a dashing suit?"

"About . . ." He counts under his breath. "Seventeen. And I'll have you know I'm not wearing a suit but a tutu dress."

"Dashing."

"Sort of. I think it makes my knees look a little bloated."

The elevator dings, and I think I recognize the sound but I can't tell where from. We walk in. Christian holds my hand the entire time. I count the floors by the way the elevator pings each time we pass a level. We stop on the seventh floor. Christian walks out, ushering me with him, clasping my palm in both of his. Then he stops and drops my hand to enter a security number to open a door. He presses a hand against the small of my back, and we both walk in. Then he's behind me, removing my blindfold.

"Ta-da."

I blink my eyes open, adjusting to the sunlight after being blindfolded for so long, and immediately suck in a breath. No wonder I thought the noises and scents were familiar when I walked in.

I turn to face him. "No."

"Yup," he says, popping the *p*.

"Can we afford it?" I wince.

He leans forward, rubbing his nose against mine. "Absolutely. It's not your old penthouse. That, we wouldn't have been able to afford in a million years. But I wanted you to live in your childhood building. Somewhere close to Aaron. Where you can see him from your window anytime you please. I asked the building manager to call me as soon as there was a vacancy. And well . . . three weeks ago, there was."

I stride along the empty space, the sound of my heels ricocheting against the walls. Everything is bare and clean and smells of opportunity and potential. Of memories we can create here. An apartment in my Park Avenue building. Somewhere we can call our own. I'm so overwhelmed with emotions, with happiness, that it takes me a few moments to notice it. A plastic bag on the kitchen counter. The only thing inside this place.

"Hey." I walk over to it. "What is that?"

"Those are our bathing suits," Christian says behind my back, and I hear him coming toward me. "Race you to the pool for a few laps?"

His chin touches the top of my head, and all is well in the world.

"I'm going to win," I warn him, plucking out my swimsuit from the bag.

He engulfs me with his hands. "I'd like to see you try."

AUTHOR'S NOTE

BEFORE YOU GO

Thank you so much for reading *Ruthless Rival*. I'm excited to dive into the Cruel Castaways universe and introduce you to their world. As a thank-you for reading, I am offering a never-before-seen short story to my newsletter subscribers.

"Punk Love" is an angsty, funny short story, available exclusively to my subscribers.

Sign up here: http://eepurl.com/dgo6x5

All my love,

L.J. Shen

ACKNOWLEDGMENTS

This series has been in the making for a while. I've been wanting to write Christian's, Riggs's, and Arsène's stories for as long as I can remember, but it took a lot of people's support to be able to give you this book.

First and foremost, a huge thank-you goes out to my agent, Kimberly Brower, at Brower Literary, for the help, support, and direction.

Another shout-out to the amazing team at Montlake Publishing for helping this book reach its full potential, including Anh Schluep, Lindsey Faber, Riam Griswold, and Susan Stokes.

And to the amazing Caroline Teagle Johnson, for the gorgeous cover.

To my PA, Tijuana Turner, for the constant support and priceless advice, and to Vanessa Villegas, Ratula Roy, Amy Halter, Marta Bor, and Yamina Kirky. A million thank-yous for reading the book before everyone else and offering guidance and helpful pointers.

To Social Butterflies PR, and especially Jenn and Catherine—you are amazing and I love you.

To my reading group on Facebook, the Sassy Sparrows—thank you for being there for the ride. I am so incredibly grateful.

To the bloggers, Instagrammers, and TikTokers who shout out my books—I couldn't have done this without you. Not for one single day.

And to my family, my ride or die—your support means the world to me.

Thank you, thank you, thank you.

ENJOYED CHRISTIAN'S STORY? READ ON FOR L.J. SHEN'S TITLE *VICIOUS*, AVAILABLE TO PURCHASE ON AMAZON OR READ FOR FREE WITH KINDLE UNLIMITED.

In Japanese culture, the significance of the cherry blossom tree dates back hundreds of years. The cherry blossom represents the fragility and magnificence of life. It's a reminder of how beautiful life is, almost overwhelmingly so, but that it is also heartbreakingly short. As are relationships. Be wise. Let your heart lead the way. And when you find someone who's worth it—never let them go.

CHAPTER ONE

EMILIA

My grandmama once told me that love and hate are the same feelings experienced under different circumstances. The passion is the same. The pain is the same. That weird thing that bubbles in your chest? Same. I didn't believe her until I met Baron Spencer and he became my nightmare.

Then my nightmare became my reality.

I thought I'd escaped him. I was even stupid enough to think he'd forgotten I ever existed.

But when he came back, he hit harder than I ever thought possible. And just like a domino—I fell.

◆ ◆ ◆

Ten Years Ago

I'd only been inside the mansion once before, when my family first came to Todos Santos. That was two months ago. That day, I stood rooted in place on the same ironwood flooring that never creaked.

That first time, Mama had elbowed my ribs. "You know this is the toughest floor in the world?"

She failed to mention it belonged to the man with the toughest heart in the world.

I couldn't for the life of me understand why people with so much money would spend it on such a depressing house. Ten bedrooms. Thirteen bathrooms. An indoor gym and a dramatic staircase. The best amenities money could buy . . . and except for the tennis court and sixty-five-foot pool, they were all in black.

Black choked out every pleasant feeling you might possibly have as soon as you walked through the big iron-studded doors. The interior designer must've been a medieval vampire, judging from the cold, lifeless colors and the giant iron chandeliers hanging from the ceilings. Even the floor was so dark that it looked like I was hovering over an abyss, a fraction of a second from falling into nothingness.

A ten-bedroom house, three people living in it—two of them barely ever there—and the Spencers had decided to house my family in the servants' apartment near the garage. It was bigger than our clapboard rental in Richmond, Virginia, but until that moment, it had still rubbed me the wrong way.

Not anymore.

Everything about the Spencer mansion was designed to intimidate. Rich and wealthy, yet poor in so many ways. *These are not happy people,* I thought.

I stared at my shoes—the tattered white Vans I doodled colorful flowers on to hide the fact that they were knock-offs—and swallowed, feeling insignificant even before *he* had belittled me. Before I even knew *him*.

"I wonder where he is?" Mama whispered.

As we stood in the hallway, I shivered at the echo that bounced off the bare walls. She wanted to ask if we could get paid two days early because we needed to buy medicine for my younger sister, Rosie.

"I hear something coming from that room." She pointed to a door on the opposite side of the vaulted foyer. "You go knock. I'll go back to the kitchen to wait."

"*Me?* Why me?"

"Because," she said, pinning me with a stare that stabbed at my conscience, "Rosie's sick, and his parents are out of town. You're his age. He'll listen to you."

I did as I was told—not for Mama, for Rosie—without understanding the consequences. The next few minutes cost me my whole senior year and were the reason why I was ripped from my family at the age of eighteen.

Vicious thought I knew his secret.

I didn't.

He thought I'd found out what he was arguing about in that room that day.

I had no clue.

All I remember was trudging toward the threshold of another dark door, my fist hovering inches from it before I heard the deep rasp of an old man.

"You know the drill, Baron."

A man. A smoker, probably.

"My sister told me you're giving her trouble again." The man slurred his words before raising his voice and slapping his palm against a hard surface. "I've had enough of you disrespecting her."

"Fuck you." I heard the composed voice of a younger man. He sounded . . . amused? "And fuck her too. Wait, is that why you're here, Daryl? You want a piece of your sister too? The good news is that she's open for business, if you have the buck to pay."

"Look at the mouth on you, you little cunt." *Slap.* "Your mother would've been proud."

Silence, and then, "Say another word about my mother, and I'll give you a real reason to get those dental implants you were talking about with my dad." The younger man's voice dripped venom, which made me think he might not be as young as Mama thought.

"Stay away," the younger voice warned. "I can beat the shit out of you, now. As a matter of fact, I'm pretty tempted to do so. All. The fucking. Time. I'm done with your shit."

"And what the hell makes you think you have a choice?" The older man chuckled darkly.

I felt his voice in my bones, like poison eating at my skeleton.

"Haven't you heard?" the younger man gritted out. "I like to fight. I like the pain. Maybe because it makes it so much easier for me to come to terms with the fact that I'm going to kill you one day. And I will, Daryl. One day, I will kill you."

I gasped, too stunned to move. I heard a loud smack, then someone tumbling down, dragging some items with him as he fell to the floor.

I was about to run—this conversation obviously wasn't meant for me to hear—but he caught me off guard. Before I knew what was happening, the door swung open and I came face-to-face with a boy around my age. I say *a boy*, but there was nothing boyish about him.

The older man stood behind him, panting hard, hunched with his hands flat against a desk. Books were scattered around his feet, and his lip was cut and bleeding.

The room was a library. Soaring floor-to-ceiling, walnut shelves full of hardbacks lined the walls. I felt a pang in my chest because I somehow knew there wasn't any way I'd ever be allowed in there again.

"What the fuck?" the teenage boy seethed. His eyes narrowed. They felt like the sight of a rifle aimed at me.

Seventeen? Eighteen? The fact that we were about the same age somehow made everything about the situation worse. I ducked my head, my cheeks flaming with enough heat to burn down the whole house.

"Have you been listening?" His jaw twitched.

I frantically shook my head *no*, but that was a lie. I'd always been a terrible liar.

"I didn't hear a thing, I swear." I choked on my words. "My mama works here. I was looking for her." Another lie.

I'd never been a scaredy-cat. I was always the brave one. But I didn't feel so brave at that moment. After all, I wasn't supposed to be there, in his house, and I definitely wasn't supposed to be listening to their argument.

The young man took a step closer, and I took a step back. His eyes were dead, but his lips were red, full, and very much alive. *This guy is going to break my heart if I let him.* The voice came from somewhere inside my head, and the thought stunned me because it made no sense at all. I'd never fallen in love before, and I was too anxious to even register his eye color or hairstyle, let alone the notion of ever having any feelings for the guy.

"What's your name?" he demanded. He smelled delicious—a masculine spice of boy-man, sweet sweat, sour hormones, and the faint trace of clean laundry, one of my mama's many chores.

"Emilia." I cleared my throat and extended my arm. "My friends call me Millie. Y'all can too."

His expression revealed zero emotion. "You're fucking done, *Emilia*." He drawled my name, mocking my Southern accent and not even acknowledging my hand with a glance.

I withdrew it quickly, embarrassment flaming my cheeks again.

"Wrong fucking place and wrong fucking time. Next time I find you anywhere inside my house, bring a body bag because you won't be leaving alive." He thundered past me, his muscular arm brushing my shoulder.

I choked on my breath. My gaze bolted to the older man, and our eyes locked. He shook his head and grinned in a way that made me want to fold into myself and disappear. Blood dripped from his lip onto his leather boot—black like his worn MC jacket. What was he doing in a place like this, anyway? He just stared at me, making no move to clean up the blood.

I turned around and ran, feeling the bile burning in my throat, threatening to spill over.

Needless to say, Rosie had to make do without her medicine that week and my parents were paid not a minute earlier than when they were scheduled to.

That was two months ago.

Today, when I walked through the kitchen and climbed the stairs, I had no choice.

I knocked on Vicious's bedroom door. His room was on the second floor at the end of the wide curved hallway, the door facing the floating stone staircase of the cave-like mansion.

I'd never been near Vicious's room, and I wished I could keep it that way. Unfortunately, my calculus book had been stolen. Whoever broke into my locker had wiped it clean of my stuff and left garbage inside. Empty soda cans, cleaning supplies, and condom wrappers spilled out the minute I opened the locker door.

Just another not-so-clever, yet effective, way for the students at All Saints High to remind me that I was nothing but the cheap help around here. By that point, I was so used to it I barely reddened at all. When all eyes in the hallway darted to me, snickers and chuckles rising out of every throat, I tilted my chin up and marched straight to my next class.

All Saints High was a school full of spoiled, over-privileged sinners. A school where if you failed to dress or act a certain way, you didn't belong. Rosie blended in better than I did, thank the Lord. But with a Southern drawl, off-beat style, and one of the most popular guys at school—that being Vicious Spencer—hating my guts, I didn't fit in.

What made it worse was that I didn't *want* to fit in. These kids didn't impress me. They weren't kind or welcoming or even very smart. They didn't possess any of the qualities I looked for in friends.

But I needed my textbook badly if I ever wanted to escape this place.

I knocked three times on the mahogany door of Vicious's bedroom. Rolling my lower lip between my fingers, I tried to suck in as much oxygen as I could, but it did nothing to calm the throbbing pulse in my neck.

Please don't be there . . .

Please don't be an ass . . .

Please . . .

A soft noise seeped from the crack under the door, and my body tensed.

Giggling.

Vicious never giggled. Heck, he hardly ever chuckled. Even his smiles were few and far between. No. The sound was undoubtedly female.

I heard him whisper in his raspy tone something inaudible that made her moan. My ears seared, and I anxiously rubbed my hands on the yellow cut-off denim shorts covering my thighs. Out of all the scenarios I could have imagined, this was by far the worst.

Him.

With another girl.

Who I hated before I even knew her name.

It didn't make any sense, yet I felt ridiculously angry.

But he was clearly there, and I was a girl on a mission.

"Vicious?" I called out, trying to steady my voice. I straightened my spine, even though he couldn't see me. "It's Millie. Sorry to interrupt, y'all. I just wanted to borrow your calc book. Mine's lost, and I really need to get ready for that exam we have tomorrow." *God forbid you ever study for our exam yourself,* I breathed silently.

He didn't answer, but I heard a sharp intake of breath—*the girl*—and the rustle of fabric and the noise of a zipper rolling. Down, I had no doubt.

I squeezed my eyes shut and pressed my forehead against the cool wood of his door.

Bite the bullet. Swallow your pride. This wouldn't matter in a few years. Vicious and his stupid antics would be a distant memory, the snooty town of Todos Santos just a dust-covered part of my past.

My parents had jumped at the chance when Josephine Spencer offered them a job. They'd dragged us across the country to California because the health care was better and we didn't even need to pay rent. Mama was the Spencers' cook/housekeeper, and Daddy was part gardener and handyman. The previous live-in couple had quit, and it was no wonder. Pretty sure my parents weren't so keen on the job either. But opportunities like these were rare, and Josephine Spencer's mama was friends with my great-aunt, which is how they'd gotten the job.

I was planning on getting out of here soon. As soon as I got accepted to the first out-of-state college I'd applied to, to be exact. In order to do so, though, I needed a scholarship.

For a scholarship, I needed kick-ass grades.

And for kick-ass grades, I needed this textbook.

"Vicious," I ground out his stupid nickname. I knew he hated his real name, and for reasons beyond my grasp, I didn't want to upset him. "I'll grab the book and copy the formulas I need real quick. I won't borrow it long. Please." I gulped down the ball of frustration twisting in my throat. It was bad enough I'd had my stuff stolen—*again*—without having to ask Vicious for favors.

The giggling escalated. The high, screechy pitch sawed through my ears. My fingers tingled to push the door open and launch at him with my fists.

I heard his groan of pleasure and knew it had nothing to do with the girl he was with. He loved taunting me. Ever since our first encounter outside of his library two months ago, he'd been hell-bent on reminding me that I wasn't good enough.

Not good enough for his mansion.

Not good enough for his school.

Not good enough for *his town*.

Worst part? It wasn't a figure of speech. It really *was* his town. Baron Spencer Jr.—dubbed Vicious for his cold, ruthless behavior— was the heir to one of the biggest family-owned fortunes in California. The Spencers owned a pipeline company, half of downtown Todos Santos—including the mall—and three corporate office parks. Vicious had enough money to take care of the next ten generations of his family.

But I didn't.

My parents were servants. We had to work for every penny. I didn't expect him to understand. Trust-fund kids never did. But I presumed he'd at least pretend, like the rest of them.

Education mattered to me, and at that moment, I felt robbed of it.

Because rich people had stolen my books.

Because this particular rich kid wouldn't even open the door to his room so I could borrow his textbook real quick.

"Vicious!" My frustration got the better of me, and I slammed my palm flat against his door. Ignoring the throb it sent up my wrist, I continued, exasperated. "C'mon!"

I was close to turning around and walking away. Even if it meant I had to take my bike and ride all the way across town to borrow Sydney's books. Sydney was my only friend at All Saints High, and the one person I liked in class.

But then I heard Vicious chuckling, and I knew the joke was on me. "I love to see you crawl. Beg for it, baby, and I'll give it to you," he said.

Not to the girl in his room.

To me.

I lost it. Even though I knew it was wrong. That he was winning.

I thrust the door open and barged into his room, strangling the handle with my fist, my knuckles white and burning.

My eyes darted to his king-size bed, barely stopping to take in the gorgeous mural above it—four white horses galloping into the darkness— or the elegant dark furniture. His bed looked like a throne, sitting in the middle of the room, big and high and draped in soft black satin. He was perched on the edge of his mattress, a girl who was in my PE class in his lap. Her name was Georgia and her grandparents owned half the vineyards upstate in Carmel Valley. Georgia's long blonde hair veiled one of his broad shoulders and her Caribbean tan looked perfect and smooth against Vicious's pale complexion.

His dark blue eyes—so dark they were almost black—locked on mine as he continued to kiss her ravenously—his tongue making several appearances—like she was made of cotton candy. I needed to look away, but couldn't. I was trapped in his gaze, completely immobilized from the eyes down, so I arched an eyebrow, showing him that I didn't care.

Only I did. I cared a lot.

I cared so much, in fact, that I continued to stare at them shamelessly. At his hollowed cheeks as he inserted his tongue deep into her mouth, his burning, taunting glare never leaving mine, gauging me for a reaction. I felt my body buzzing in an unfamiliar way, falling under his spell. A sweet, pungent fog. It was sexual, unwelcome, yet completely inescapable. I wanted to break free, but for the life of me, I couldn't.

My grip on the door handle tightened, and I swallowed, my eyes dropping to his hand as he grabbed her waist and squeezed playfully. I squeezed my own waist through the fabric of my yellow-and-white sunflower top.

What the hell was wrong with me? Watching him kiss another girl was unbearable, but also weirdly fascinating.

I wanted to see it.

I didn't want to see it.

Either way, I couldn't *unsee* it.

Admitting defeat, I blinked, shifting my gaze to a black Raiders cap hung over the headrest of his desk chair.

"Your textbook, Vicious. I need it," I repeated. "I'm not leaving your room without it."

"Get the fuck out, Help," he said into Georgia's giggling mouth.

A thorn twisted in my heart, jealousy filling my chest. I couldn't wrap my head around this physical reaction. The pain. The shame. The *lust*. I hated Vicious. He was hard, heartless, and hateful. I'd heard his mother had died when he was nine, but he was eighteen now and had a nice stepmother who let him do whatever he wanted. Josephine seemed sweet and caring.

He had no reason to be so cruel, yet he was to everyone. Especially to me.

"Nope." Inside, rage pounded through me, but outside, I remained unaffected. *"Calc. Textbook."* I spoke slowly, treating him like the idiot he thought I was. "Just tell me where it is. I'll leave it at your door when I'm done. Easiest way to get rid of me and get back to your . . . activities."

Georgia, who was fiddling with his zipper, her white sheath dress already unzipped from behind, growled, pushing away from his chest momentarily and rolling her eyes.

She squeezed her lips into a disapproving pout. "Really? Mindy?"—My name was Millie and she knew it—"Can't you find anything better to do with your time? He's a little out of your league, don't you think?"

Vicious took a moment to examine me, a cocky smirk plastered on his face. He was so damn handsome. Unfortunately. Black hair, shiny and trimmed fashionably, buzzed at the sides and longer on top. Indigo eyes, bottomless in their depth, sparkling and hardened. By what, I didn't know. Skin so pale he looked like a stunning ghost.

As a painter, I often spent time admiring Vicious's form. The angles of his face and sharp bone structure. All smooth edges. Defined and clear-cut. He was made to be painted. A masterpiece of nature.

Georgia knew it too. I'd heard her not too long ago talking about him in the locker room after PE. Her friend had said, "Beautiful guy."

"Dude, but *ugly* personality," Georgia was quick to add. A moment of silence passed before they'd both snorted out a laugh.

"Who cares?" Georgia's friend had concluded. "I'd still do him."

The worst part was I couldn't blame them.

He was both a baller and filthy rich—a popular guy who dressed and talked the right way. A perfect All Saints hero. He drove the right kind of car—Mercedes—and possessed that mystifying aura of a true alpha. He always had the room. Even when he was completely silent.

Feigning boredom, I crossed my arms and leaned one hip on his doorframe. I stared out his window, knowing tears would appear in my eyes if I looked directly at him or Georgia.

"His *league*?" I mocked. "I'm not even playing the same game. I don't play dirty."

"You will, once I push you far enough," Vicious snapped, his tone flat and humorless. It felt like he clawed my guts out and threw them on his pristine ironwood floor.

I blinked slowly, trying to look blasé. "Textbook?" I asked for the two-hundredth time.

He must've concluded he'd tortured me enough for one day. He cocked his head sideways to a backpack sitting under his desk. The window above it overlooked the servants' apartment where I lived, allowing him a perfect view directly into my room. So far, I'd caught him staring at me twice through the window, and I always wondered why.

Why, why, why?

He hated me so much. The intensity of his glare burned my face every time he looked at me, which wasn't as often as I'd like him to. But being the sensible girl that I was, I never allowed myself to dwell on it.

I marched to the Givenchy rubber-coated backpack he took to school every day and blew out air as I flipped it open, rummaging noisily through his things. I was glad my back was to them, and I tried to block out the moans and sucking noises.

The second my hand touched the familiar white-and-blue calc book, I stilled. I stared at the cherry blossom I'd doodled on the spine. Rage tingled up my spine, coursing through my veins, making my fists clench and unclench. Blood whooshed in my ears, and my breathing quickened.

He broke into my friggin' locker.

With shaking fingers, I pulled the book out of Vicious's backpack. "You stole my textbook?" I turned to face him, every muscle in my face tense.

This was an escalation. Blunt aggression. Vicious always taunted me, but he'd never humiliated me like this before. He'd stolen my things and stuffed my locker full of condoms and used toilet paper, for Christ's sake.

Our eyes met and tangled. He pushed Georgia off his lap, like she was an eager puppy he was done playing with, and stood up. I took a step forward. We were nose to nose now.

"Why are you doing this to me?" I hissed out, searching his blank, stony face.

"Because I can," he offered with a smirk to hide all the pain in his eyes.

What's eating you, Baron Spencer?

"Because it's fun?" he added, chuckling while throwing Georgia's jacket at her. Without a glance her way, he motioned for her to leave.

She was clearly nothing more than a prop. A means to an end. He'd wanted to hurt me.

And he succeeded.

I shouldn't care about why he acted this way. It made no difference at all. The bottom line was I hated him. I hated him so much it made me sick to my stomach that I loved the way he looked, on and off the field. Hated my shallowness, my foolishness, at loving the way his square, hard jaw ticked when he fought a smile. I hated that I loved the smart, witty things that came out of his mouth when he spoke in class. Hated that he was a cynical realist while I was a hopeless idealist, and still, I loved every thought he uttered aloud. And I hated that once a week, every week, my heart did crazy things in my chest because I suspected he might be *him*.

I hated him, and it was clear that he hated me back.

I hated him, but I hated Georgia more because she was the one he'd kissed.

Knowing full well I couldn't fight him—my parents worked here—I bit my tongue and stormed toward the door. I only made it to the threshold before his callused hand wrapped around my elbow, spinning me in place and throwing my body into his steel chest. I swallowed back a whimper.

"Fight me, Help," he snarled into my face, his nostrils flaring like a wild beast. His lips were close, so close. Still swollen from kissing another girl, red against his fair skin. "For once in your life, stand your fucking ground."

I shook out of his touch, clutching my textbook to my chest like it was my shield. I rushed out of his room and didn't stop to take a breath until I reached the servants' apartment. Swinging the door open, I bolted to my room and locked the door, plopping down on the bed with a heavy sigh.

I didn't cry. He didn't deserve my tears. But I was angry, upset and yes, a little broken.

In the distance, I heard music blasting from his room, getting louder by the second as he turned the volume up to the max. It took me a few beats to recognize the song. "Stop Crying Your Eyes Out" by Oasis.

A few minutes later, I heard Georgia's red automatic Camaro—the one Vicious constantly made fun of because, *Who the fuck buys an automatic Camaro?*—gun down the tree-lined driveway of the estate. She sounded angry too.

Vicious was vicious. It was too bad that my hate for him was dipped in a thin shell of something that felt like love. But I promised myself I'd crack it, break it, and unleash pure hatred in its place before he got to me. *He,* I promised myself, *will never break me.*

ABOUT THE AUTHOR

L.J. Shen is a *Wall Street Journal, USA Today, Washington Post*, and Amazon number one bestselling author of contemporary, new adult, and romance titles. She likes to write about unapologetic alpha males and the women who bring them to their knees. Her books have been sold in twenty different countries and have appeared on some of their bestseller lists. She lives in California with her husband, son, and eccentric fashion choices, and she enjoys good wine, bad reality TV shows, and catching sunrays with her lazy cat.